"MY GOD, MATTIE! DO YOU HAVE ANY IDEA WHAT YOU'RE DOING TO ME?

"Do you know how often I have wanted to reach out and take you in my arms like this? How many times I told myself I had to leave the ranch—just ride out and not look back, while there was still time—"

"We shouldn't," she whispered. "This is so wrong. I keep telling myself that I'm married—I'm married and you're my husband's brother. It isn't right." There was anguish in her voice. "I shouldn't be feeling what I do right now. I just can't seem to help it, though."

"Mattie, Mattie, Mattie," he whispered. "I've wanted to hold you, to feel your body warm in my arms, to make love to you—"

"Morgan—stop—we can't," she gasped, but her words were stilled with his mouth hard against her lips, bruising them. He felt her tense for a moment, then gradually relax until she melted against him, returning his kisses with a fire that matched his own.

Books by Donna Grundman

A DISTANT EDEN
DAYS TO REMEMBER

DAYS TO REMEMBER

Donna Grundman

A DELL BOOK

Published by
Dell Publishing Co., Inc.
1 Dag Hammarskjold Plaza
New York, New York 10017

Dell ® TM 681510, Dell Publishing Co., Inc.

ISBN: 0-440-11680-5

Printed in the United States of America
First printing—May 1984

CHAPTER ONE

The lone rider sat on his horse at the top of the ridge looking down over the valley that spread out below him. His clothing carried the dust of miles along the trail and there was a tiredness in the slope of his shoulders. It was late evening—that time of day when the sun had slipped down over the horizon out of sight but the darkness had not yet quite taken over.

The ranch house squatting at the end of the long, narrow valley stood in silhouette, a silver shadow against the gloom. The barn and the outbuildings were a distance from the house, in peaceful quietness now. The animals that had been brought in off the range and put in the corrals were already bedded down for the night. There was a light in the bunkhouse window, blocked out once in a while by a restless figure moving back and forth inside.

Across the valley between the rider and the ranch house were a few fences, vaguely dividing the fields into a pattern of rectangles and squares that resembled a patchwork quilt from this distance.

How long had it been? Six years? Seven? A long time. He had covered a lot of territory since then. There had been no contact in all of those years—no messages passed along, no word, no letters. He had only the memory of a hardheaded old man who thought he was indestructible—a man who had settled here in the

eastern part of the state of Oregon and spent a lifetime fighting
for his land, driving himself and his sons until they both rebelled
against him. One son's anger had been overshadowed by his
fears and he spent his time seeking ways to win his father's favor
by turning the old man's anger to someone else. The other son
got on a horse one day and rode out without looking back,
chasing jobs as far north as Montana and south into the wilds of
Mexico. There had been times when he had slept on the hard,
unbending sands of the desert floor with only his horse for
company and other times when he had lain in the warm, yielding
arms of women whose eyes filled with tears when he rode on.
And now he was returning home, pulled by the same restlessness
that had caused him to leave.

A sharp splash of water cracked through the stillness, interrupting his thoughts. His horse shifted position nervously and his
hand went automatically to rest against the gun hanging from his
belt as his eyes searched the dark ribbon of water that wound its
way through the willows at the foot of the hill. After a moment
he slipped silently from his horse and moved quietly down to the
edge of the bank, where he knelt in the shadows and watched the
slim form of a swimmer cutting the water as cleanly as a sharp
knife.

His taut nerves relaxed when he saw bare flesh glowing in the
dim light. The youthful figure reached the shallows near the
shore and stood quickly, letting the water fall away in droplets of
flashing silver. He leaned forward with added interest, watching
the nude young woman toss her long chestnut hair back from her
face, letting it fall like a wet veil around her shoulders as she
stepped up onto the riverbank. She walked out onto a heavy old
moss-covered log that hung out over the water and stood poised,
ready to dive again.

A faint smile touched his lips. How well he knew that old
fallen tree and the deep pool that lay beneath it. It brought back a
flood of memories. He and his brother had spent many a hot,
muggy afternoon—when they had been lucky enough to slip
away without being caught—diving off the old tree into the cool,
clean water.

She raised her hands over her head and he saw the dark outline of her body, the perfectly formed high breasts, the slim waist, the round, firm hips and long, slender legs. He felt a quickening race through his body, leaving him unable to look away. Gracefully, she slipped into the water, hardly disturbing its surface, and he waited for her to appear again, a little distance away. Shaking the water from her eyes, she turned and started to swim with expert skill toward the bank again.

"I've heard tell of sea sprites before, but I thought they were in the ocean. Never knew of any in these parts before," he drawled into the stillness.

She gave a startled cry, her eyes searching the trees for the intruder before she slipped back into the water, standing farther out now, hidden up to her shoulders.

"Who are you?" she demanded, to cover her fright, still not able to see him in the dark shadows. "What are you doing here?"

"I might ask you the same thing," he answered. "I thought this part of the stream was on Henderson land."

"It is. I'm Mattie Henderson. Which means you are trespassing, mister, and you better get the hell out of here before someone takes a shot at you. The folks up at the house don't take kindly to trespassers prowling around at night."

He gave an amused chuckle. "You do a good job of bluffing, ma'am, but it won't work. I happen to know old Clive Henderson didn't have any daughters."

She tossed her head defiantly. "Not daughter. Wife. I'm Mrs. Henderson. Mrs. Allen Henderson. Which gives me a perfect right to be here. Now, how about you moving on, off the property, before I start screaming and wake everybody up?"

He let out a hoot, his face broken into a grin, as he stood up and moved out of the shadows into the open. "You mean ol' weak-kneed Bub actually got up enough nerve to propose to a full-blown woman like you? He not only has grown up some since I saw him last, but he's plumb loco, too. He must be, to have a wife like you and let you come down here alone at night."

"He doesn't—" she faltered, drawing her face into a frown, trying to see his features. "Who are you? You know Allen? There's nobody around here calls him 'Bub' anymore."

"Yeah—I know him. Don't rightly think he will be that pleased to see me again, though. Not too sure how any of them will welcome me, come to think of it. We didn't part all that friendly."

She took a step forward, consumed with curiosity, and then stopped, suddenly remembering where she was and her state of undress. "Hey! Are you Morgan?" When he didn't answer, she looked at him in amazement. "Son-of-a—" she gasped. "You really are, aren't you! You're Morgan. Boy—are they going to be surprised to see you!"

He was grinning in amusement now. "What do you think? Will they throw me out again when I walk in the door?" he asked.

"They may want to," she answered solemnly. "The old man is sure going to be in a temper. Lordy, I'm not sure I want to be there to see it. But he won't throw you out. They need you too bad around here right now." She looked thoughtful for a moment, chewing on her lower lip as though puzzling out a problem. "You just riding through or do you intend to stay awhile?"

"Not sure yet. Don't make plans that far ahead. Depends a little on the welcome, I suppose."

"Reckon they'd appreciate it if you were to stay," she answered slowly. It was too dark for him to see her face now, but her voice was serious, as though she were weighing her words carefully. "Things ain't been going too well lately."

"Something wrong?" he asked. He wasn't smiling anymore.

"Oh, he won't admit to any trouble right off. The old man thinks he's going to be around forever. He don't like it none if anybody says he can't do as much as he used to. But—well—it's just getting too darn much for him to handle alone. I help out all I can. Even do a man's work a lot of the time. 'Course, nothing you do ever satisfies that old man. He always expects more—"

Morgan was leaning forward, listening to her with interest. "What happened to Bub—to Allen? Don't he help out?"

"Guess you have been gone quite a while, haven't you? You don't understand. Allen is in a wheelchair." Her voice was low, the statement flat, without any emotion.

He raised his brow in surprise. "A wheelchair? What happened to him?"

She waited a long moment before answering, as though thinking over what to say and then changing her mind. "You may be comfortable, sitting up there gossiping like you're at an afternoon church social, but this water is damn cold!" she snapped. "I ain't moving around enough to keep warm. How about you turning your back and walking away so I can get out of here and get into my clothes. I got goose bumps all over me."

"Go ahead and get out. I ain't stopping you." The sarcastic humor was back in his voice.

"Talk like that ain't going to make you any more popular around here, mister, than you are already. Now get out of here. I can still yell, you know—then you can be damn sure you won't be welcome!"

"You won't, though. I'm guessing if Allen don't know that you sneak out and come down here swimming after he has gone to sleep, you ain't going to do nothing to let him find out. Am I right?"

She glared at him furiously, knowing he was laughing at her as he turned his back and walked up toward his horse.

Morgan sat on his horse in silence, looking out across the valley, his mind going over and over again what she had said. The old man—finally caught up by age. Hard to imagine that ever happening. He'd always figured that if ever a man was going to dictate to the devil, it would be the old man. He was indestructible. And Bub—no, Allen. What the hell was he doing in a wheelchair? Allen, married to a spunky, sharp-looking gal like this one, was even harder to imagine.

He heard a rustle in the grasses and turned to see the girl dressed in tight-fitting boy's jeans and a baggy flannel shirt, her wet hair pulled back and tied in a knot in the back.

"You go on and ride up to the house," she said. "I got my own way of getting back in." She paused, studying him for a long moment. "Do me a favor, will you?" she added. "Forget you saw me down here."

When he nodded, she disappeared into the darkness, leaving him alone.

CHAPTER TWO

As he rode slowly toward the house, he remembered a lot of things—things he had thought were forgotten. The memories that came rushing in around him aroused emotions he had never expected to feel again. When he left, he had told himself it was for the last time—he'd never be back. But now, deep inside, he was glad that he was here. He looked at the fences with the sagging barbed wire, the grasses turned brown from the hot eastern Oregon sun. He felt uneasy, but he knew he was glad to be back.

A light came on in one of the upstairs bedroom windows. It reminded him of the pixielike woman bathing nude in their old swimming hole, and he wondered if she'd gotten back into the house without being seen. He reached the front of the house, where the ground was worn bare from a generation of horses being ridden up to and tied there. The dirt carried new scars of tire tracks, from cars, and he turned away, wishing he hadn't seen them. Somehow he resented this change that had come while he was gone.

Slowly, a little bone-weary from the long ride, he slid from the horse and dropped the reins across the log rail as he had done so many times before and stood looking at the wooden porch, the old rocker, the two rosebushes growing near the steps. They had been planted long before he could remember, but they always reminded him of a lady with soft velvet eyes and a gentle voice—a lady who lived somewhere in the shadowy places of his boyhood.

The door opened. The old man stood in the doorway, silhouetted by a light from somewhere in the back of the house. Six feet of stubborn cussedness, the hair a little more gray, the shoulders bent, but still suggesting power and strength as he stood peering out into the darkness.

"Who's there?" His voice was a low rumble in the silence.

" 'Lo, Pa."

"There was a long pause, heavy with disbelief. "Morgan?" he asked finally. "Morgan, that you?"

"It's me."

"What the hell you doin' in these parts?"

"Just passing through."

The old man hesitated for a moment and then took a step backward, holding the door open. "Well, now that you've come this far, ain't no reason to just stand there. Come on in."

Morgan followed him up the sagging steps, across the porch, and into the house. The main room was dark, but it smelled the same—of leather, tobacco, and a trace of wood smoke from the fireplace.

"Come on back to my study. Got the light on there. Been working on some papers." The old man went first, leading the way. A lantern burned on the desk strewn with papers.

An old dog lay on the floor. He raised his head and opened one eye, sleepily regarding the intruder for a moment before putting his head back down on his paws, ignoring them.

"Christ, don't tell me Pete's still around!" Morgan said, looking down at the sleeping dog.

"Ain't worth much anymore, but he's still around, eating up more than his share of the food and claiming that rug as his." Clive reached in the top drawer of the desk and set out a bottle. He poured out two glasses and handed one across to his son. "Drink?"

Morgan took it without comment. He felt the amber liquid sear his throat, burning its way down, warming his body, loosening tight muscles. He went over and sat in the big old chair near the dog.

"How you been, Pa?"

"I'm fine. Everything else around here is going to hell, but I'm fine. How about you?" The old man was sitting on the corner of the desk, studying his son thoughtfully.

"I'm all right. Been working on different spreads—traveling around some—"

"You aimin' on staying awhile?"

"Ain't given it much thought yet. Guess I can. You got a place for me?"

The old man shrugged, noncommittal. "Your room is just like you left it. Can always use another hand, I guess. Hard to get help anymore. You just get a man broke in to where you can trust him and he gets sand in his shoes, wanting to move on. It's all this talk about a war comin' on. It makes everybody restless. Don't know what is going to happen."

"How many men you got working here now, Pa?" Morgan asked.

"Don't know about working, but there's three taking up space in the bunkhouse. Mattie handles the cookin', so don't need anybody for that anymore."

"Mattie?" Morgan hoped he sounded casual. "Who's she?"

"Guess you're behind times. Mattie is Allen's wife. He got married three—four years ago."

"Name doesn't sound familiar. Someone from around here?"

"Her pa was one of them damn fool squatters messing up the grazing land, thinking he could farm when everybody knows this land here in the high desert ain't good for nothing but running cattle. He went broke and pulled out. Mattie stayed. She was working in at Barton's store, in Bend, for a while, then she married Allen."

"Yeah? How about that. But then, I been gone awhile. Can't expect things to stay the same. Guess ol' Bub has grown up some since I saw him last."

"Changed some, too. Won't let anyone call him 'Bub' anymore." The old man paused, studying his glass. "He went back to school after you left—got himself a degree. Thought he was too good for working on the ranch, where he was needed. He had a lot of big, fancy ideas for a while and opened his own law office there in Bend. Ain't worth a damn now.''

"He always did like school. Hated it when you made him stay home and do chores. What happened? What's the matter with him now?" Morgan asked, his eyes half closed, waiting for the reply.

"You'll find out soon enough, I reckon. What about you? You been listening to all this talk about war? Not thinking of enlisting, are you? That why you came back by here?"

Before he could answer, a noise behind them caused them both to turn. Allen sat in a wheelchair, blocking the doorway.

"Thought I heard voices. Anything wrong?" His eyes traveled from one man to the other, resting on the newcomer. "Well—I'll be damned. Morgan." He wheeled his chair into the room. "To what occasion do we owe this? You just passing through or you looking for someplace to stay?"

Morgan heard the way his words slurred together when he talked, saw the flush on his face. There was an insolent challenge in his brother's eyes.

"Depends. Don't ever stay no place where I don't earn my keep," he drawled.

The old man's face darkened in a scowl as he strode across the room, out into the hallway. "Mattie!" If his body had lost some of its fire, his voice hadn't lost any of its timber. It still echoed through the rooms when he yelled. "Mattie—come on down here! We got some company!" He went back over to his desk, picked up the bottle still sitting there, and leaned over to fill Morgan's glass again, as well as his own.

"Ain't passing it around?" Allen asked sarcastically.

"Reckon you've already had more'n your share," the old man answered.

Allen shrugged indifferently. "Don't matter. Rotgut anyway." And he smiled in amusement when he saw the old man bristle.

"Can't everybody afford the fancy label that you drink," the old man retorted. "Pure waste of good money, the way you toss it down."

Morgan felt the antagonism laying heavy in the air between them.

"You want me?" Mattie walked slowly into the room, looking from one man to the other. She was wearing the same pair of tight-fitting boy's jeans but she had changed from the baggy flannel shirt to a white blouse covered with a loose-knit sweater. Her hair was in a tight braid and wrapped around her head, making her face look too thin, her eyes too large. She darted a quick glance toward Morgan and then looked away. "Thought you would be in bed by now, Allen."

"Bet you did," he sneered. "Asleep, so I wouldn't hear you slipping back down the stairs. Which one of the hands were you meeting out in the barn tonight, Mattie?"

Morgan watched her draw her breath in sharply and bite her lower lip to keep from answering. She just stood there, her hands tucked in the pockets of her jeans. He wondered what had happened to the spunk she had showed earlier.

"Look here, Morgan," Allen was saying. "Ain't she something? Bet you didn't think ol' Allen would get a looker like this." He reached out and grabbed her roughly by the arm, pulling her over beside him. "You was always the one with the girls tagging along behind you, having your pick of the town. 'Course, she was just a squatter's brat. Imagine that!" He gave a coarse laugh. "A Henderson marrying a squatter's daughter. Everyone in these here parts thought the old man would blow up over something like that instead of taking her in like he did. But, you see, he found out how hard she can work, and the old man always did like another hand that didn't cost too much. She's all woman, Morgan, and just in case you been noticing, remember that she is taken."

Morgan watched a slight tinge of color touch Mattie's cheeks as she looked away.

"Don't start nothing tonight, Allen," the old man warned, his voice firm. "Mattie, Morgan's room been kept aired? He's going to stay a few days."

The girl shrugged. "It'll do. I better go up and lay out some more blankets, though. It's starting to get cold at night now."

Morgan stood up and stretched. "Reckon I'll go on upstairs

now, too. Been a long day—covered a lot of miles." He started to follow her from the room and then turned back. "We'll talk some more in the morning, Pa."

"Morgan?"

"Yeah, Pa?"

"Glad you're back."

Morgan nodded and went on out of the room.

Her jeans pulled tight across her well-rounded behind as he followed her up the stairs and he smiled to himself in admiration. He liked what he saw. Behind them, he heard the sounds of the wheelchair rolling out into the hallway and he knew Allen was sitting at the landing, watching them.

"Mattie!" She paused at the sound of Allen's voice but didn't turn around. "My brother and I never was too good at sharing our things. Don't know about him anymore, but I ain't changed much."

Morgan saw her back stiffen, the sharp tilt to her head. Without turning, she answered, "I'll be back down in a minute, Allen, and help you get ready for bed. I won't be long."

She stopped in front of the door to his old bedroom. "Your stuff is all in there, just like you left it. The old man wouldn't let nobody move any of it." She turned to take a blanket out of the closet behind her.

"How come you let Allen talk to you like that?" he asked quietly.

She shrugged, making an effort to appear indifferent. "You mustn't pay any attention to Allen. Having to live in a wheelchair ain't so easy. He drinks some, to help the pain. You don't want to listen because he don't really mean what he says. He gets kind of irritable sometimes. Guess I would, too, if I had to stay down, that way. Most folks would."

"He ain't changed that much. Only difference is, he never used to be so out in the open with it."

She spun around, anger snapping in her eyes. "You got no call to talk like that! You better learn how to get along with folks if you plan on sticking around here for very long. Allen was going to be a lawyer, with a practice right there in Bend. He got his schooling, and he has a certificate framed and hanging on the wall. He's real smart. He knows about the law, and how to talk and to dress. He had a lot of plans. He does some work now, but nothing like what he was going to do. Besides, it wasn't his fault. The accident, I mean.''

''Nothing ever is his fault,'' Morgan drawled. ''Always been that way.'' Then his face broke up into a grin. ''Of course, there were plenty of times I wasn't too innocent, come to think of it. I felt the taste of the old man's belt lots of times, thanks to Bub, but there were a lot of other times when I got it because I earned it, without any help from anyone else. I always seemed to be the one getting into one scrape after another.''

''Well, I just hope you both have grown up some since then,'' she answered sharply. ''Seems as though we already have enough troubles round here without you coming back and creating more. I got to be getting back downstairs. Allen is waiting.'' She turned and brushed by where he stood blocking the doorway, leaving him to go into the room alone.

Morgan found the lamp on the table and scratched a match against the roughness of his pant leg. Most places had electricity by now, but he guessed they hadn't strung power lines out from Bend to the ranches yet. The light flared up, casting shadows on the walls, across the narrow bed where he had slept as a boy, and it played across the fishing pole and gear standing in the corner. Nothing had changed—here in his room at least—just like she said.

Morgan dropped his shirt across the back of the old chair and stood at the window, silhouetted against the night, stretching his aching muscles. His bare torso turned to copper in the flickering yellow light from the lamp.

What the hell am I doing here? he asked himself. If I stick around for a while, all I am going to get out of it is a whole lot of back-breaking work without much thanks for it.

He lit a cigarette and lay back on the bed, his hands behind his head, studying the ceiling. He let his thoughts drift.

The old man, showing signs of age catching up with him but still hard as nails, still fighting to hold on to his own.

What about Allen? Sounds like he's still blaming the rest of the world for all his troubles. Wonder how he got in that damned wheelchair? Nobody seemed to want to talk too much about it.

Mattie. This house sure needed a woman in it. He drifted off to sleep thinking about her slim figure cutting through the water of the old swimming hole, the way she held her small chin in the air and the way her eyes flashed when she talked. He thought about her round, firm hips ahead of him on the stairway and the proud way she held her head. Mattie.

No denying it, he was glad to be home—even if it was just for a little while, even if it might mean trouble.

CHAPTER THREE

It was the last part of August, pushing toward September, and even though it was still warm during the day down in the valleys, high up on the peaks of the mountains there was a dusting of new snow. Leaves were starting to turn yellow and the grasses were a dull, lifeless brown.

Morgan rode along the trail leading up the slope, away from the house. He had gotten up early and ridden out alone because he wanted to look over the ranch, get his bearings again, see what needed to be done, and check the herd. He wanted to think, and the only way a man could do any real serious thinking was to get off alone, in the open.

The trail followed the edge of the trees for a while, then disappeared into a grove of willows, where it wound back and forth across a stream bed that was nearly dry now, up and over loose rocks that made the going slow and awkward, finally breaking out on a ridge where the path was smooth and worn. He was a long way from the house now. A touch of the reins and his horse stopped while he sat and looked out around him as he smoked a cigarette.

The Cascade Mountains were sharp and clear along the horizon. The Three Sisters were white with fresh snow against the blue sky. The pine trees were dropping their cones, and an occasional squirrel could be seen racing across the ground, stopping to scold Morgan for intruding. It was a country he was familiar with—a country where he had grown up.

There were dust clouds off in the distance. He could hear a cow bellowing in the early morning air, and as he watched he could make out a lone rider circling the herd to the left, slowly working them down from the higher range, bringing them in closer to the ranch. As he watched, a couple of steers broke loose, headed for the open sagebrush and another rider he hadn't seen before cut away, chasing after them, turning them back, the sounds of his cursing riding on the winds.

Morgan smiled to himself as he watched, his hat pulled low to shield his eyes from the sun. Good looking bunch of beef, he thought. All can't be bad around here if the old man had a herd like that to pick and choose from for the fall market.

Morgan watched as they bunched up near the water hole, the two riders circling, watchful, cussing and yelling at the stubborn, bullheaded animals. The cows were looking for their young and were restless until they had them at their sides again. The dust was beginning to settle a little. This was his life, what he loved. Working with cattle, the horses, knowing the openness of the range. It was a good life. But how much longer would it last? The war seemed only a remote echo out here, unable to touch them with its threats—but he knew better. How much longer did he have, until the call of the war posters and his conscience told him he had to leave his horse and gear at the ranch and catch the stage from Bend into Portland to enlist? That's where he had been headed several days ago when, without knowing why, he had taken the other fork in the road and wound up at the old home place. He flicked the reins and rode slowly on down the side of the bluff toward the grassy bench where the cattle were milling.

One of the riders had spotted him and rode a little ways out toward him, watching him approach.

"You want something, stranger?" he called out.

Morgan shrugged. "Just watching. Good-looking herd you got there."

"They'll do," was the laconic answer. "You better keep your

eyes open. We got a couple of bad ones in that bunch.'' The rider was a tall, lean fellow with a face bronzed by the summer sun. He was watching Morgan with interest. He had the quiet eyes and strong features of a man used to living in the open. ''You been hired on by the old man?''

''You might say that. Name's Morgan. Morgan Henderson.''

The rider was close now. He pulled off a glove and held out his hand. ''Howdy. Name's Monty.'' He studied the other man. ''Henderson. Morgan Henderson? Hey, you the old man's son? The one that's been gone for a while?''

Morgan nodded. ''Can you use some help getting the herd settled?''

''Wouldn't mind.'' The two of them turned to ride back to where the other rider was waiting. ''Glad to see you here. Old man Henderson can use your help. Don't tell him I said so, though,'' he added with a grin. ''Ol' bastard still thinks he can do the work of two men. Come to think of it, he damn near can.''

Morgan grinned. ''He was the best in his day. Could work any man I ever knew right into the ground.''

''Hey, Wes!'' Monty sang out, and the other rider came toward them. ''Wes, this is old man Henderson's other son, Morgan. Says he'll give us a hand gettin' the herd settled.'' He turned back to Morgan. ''This close to home we only need one man to watch them, once they're bunched up, so we'll take shifts. Wes drew first shift, so when we get done I'll ride back in with you.''

Wes's face was split with a broad grin as he held out his hand. ''Hey, Morgan, glad to see you! You remember me, don't you? By God, you ought to!''

Morgan held out a hand. ''How could I forget an old ornery woman chaser like you? Surprised to see you still around these parts. Sure figured some jealous husband would have done you in by now.''

''Naw. Too old and too wise to get caught anymore. We did have some times together, didn't we?'' Wes chuckled. ''Good to have you back. Since Allen got all busted up in that wreck he ain't much help around here. 'Course, he never was too much good at ranching anyway. Had his mind set on being a lawyer.

Who knows? He might've made it if he could've left the booze alone.''

Monty rode off, headed toward a stray, and the two men sat quietly watching the herd.

"What accident, Wes?" Morgan asked. "What happened to Allen?''

Wes rubbed his chin thoughtfully. "Thought you already knew or I wouldn't have mentioned it.''

"None of the folks at the house seem too anxious to talk about it. Maybe you better tell me.''

"Might as well, long's I've opened my big mouth already. You'll hear about it sooner or later, and might as well be from me. Some of the versions are a little colored, but I know Mattie pretty well, and I don't put much stock in some things I hear.''

"So—she was mixed up in it too, huh?''

"Yeah. 'Fraid so. They'd already been married a year or so by then. Allen had been in town that day. He had a small office set up in Bend for his lawyer work, but he wasn't spending as much time in it, tending to business, as he should've. Allen likes to 'socialize,' you might say. They had the car by then, and Mattie learned to drive, but since Allen already had the car in town, she took the buggy and went in after supplies she needed. Allen hadn't come home the night before, but she didn't think too much of it because sometimes when he was working late he slept in the back of the office, to save having to drive all the way back and forth. Anyway, he'd been throwing a real good one, and when she found him, he wasn't in any shape to drive that car home alone.

"So Mattie put the horse and buggy up at the stables and a couple of boys helped her load him into the car and she started out to drive him home. From what I gather, they must of had a hell of a row on the way. That Mattie can be a real spitfire when she gets her back up. Don't know just what happened after that. She might've been driving too fast, or Allen could've grabbed for the wheel and she wasn't watching or expecting it—could've been they blew a tire, maybe. Anyway, she lost control of the car and they went off the road and tipped over just 'fore they crossed the small bridge over the creek. Was a real mess. Damn near totaled the car.

"Somehow Mattie got out and made her way back to the house on foot, her hair all tangled up and full of briers, her face scratched and her arm bleeding, and she was crying and screaming that Allen was dead—that she had killed him. Couple of us fellows rode on out there right away and we found him. He had a nasty bump on the head and he messed up his back some, though I doubt he felt it much. He was still pretty full of whiskey. He weren't dead, but just between you and me, Mattie would have been a lot better off if he was." He paused and then went on. "Sorry, Morgan. Guess that wasn't the thing to say, him being your brother and all. Don't really wish nobody dead—I was just thinking of Mattie."

"Yeah—I know." Morgan nodded. "It's all right. What happened next?"

"The doc did what he could for him, and when Allen mended enough to travel, the old man paid to have him taken to Portland to that big new hospital there, where he got a lot of special treatments of some kind. He was there quite a while and it must have cost the old man a bundle, though he ain't never said nothing about that part of it. Allen came back home riding in that fancy wheelchair he's got. The doctors said they couldn't do no more for him. They don't know why he can't walk—at least with the help of canes. Guess it's something wrong in his back that keeps him from using his legs. He blames Mattie for making him a cripple. That little lady has got a lot of fire in her, but I guess she blames herself too, 'cause she just sets back and takes whatever he hands out, like it's her duty now."

"How'd he happen to marry her in the first place?" Morgan's voice was thoughtful, his mind busy with what had been said.

"You blind or something?" Wes asked. "You should be asking that question the other way around—why she married him. Any man that got her kind of drew the prize, to my way of thinking. Guess, tho', she didn't have a lot of choice. Her pa was a squatter, trying to dirt farm right in the middle of ranch country. There was just her and him, and when the cattlemen put the pressure on him, he pulled out one night and forgot to take her with him. She worked in town for a while, and I guess with so much bad luck she was kind of impressed with Allen and his schooling. He can be damn convincing when he's after something. You ought to know that."

Morgan sat thinking it over before he spoke, trying to put the pieces together. "What did the old man think of all of it? The wedding, I mean."

"Tickled as hell. He's too stubborn to ever admit it, but he's real fond of that little gal. She's the only one on the whole ranch that'll stand up to him and I guess he likes that. When the two of them clash—*Whoooee!*—the rest of us just sort of get out of the way and take cover. She does more than her share of the work around here. Yep—she's quite a gal. Too good for Allen, far as I'm concerned."

"What does the old man think about the accident? He blame her?"

Wes shifted positions uncomfortably. He wasn't used to long conversations like this. "Like you said—the folks at the house don't talk about it much."

Monty rode back up to join them. "Everything looks quiet now. You think you can handle them alone, Wes?"

Wes shrugged. "You headed back in toward the house?"

"Reckon so. Ain't been in for an evening off for over a month now." A grin cracked his lean features. "Sure got a sight of catching up to do."

"Well, don't try to do it all in one night, ya hear? Want you able to ride out here in the morning. Tomorrow's my turn."

"Want me to stay out here with you for a while, Wes?" Morgan asked.

"No need. Besides, knowin' the old man, he's probably chomping at the bit, wondering where you're at, with a bunch of work lined up and waiting."

Morgan nodded. "See you tomorrow, then." The two men turned their horses and started to ride away.

"Hey, Morgan," Wes called. When the other man looked back, he added, "Glad to see you back!"

"Thanks." Morgan smiled to himself. He was glad to be

back. It felt good to be working on the home range again. For a while, anyway.

It was almost five o'clock and Mattie had the evening meal spread out on the long dining room table when they came riding in. A couple of fellows were already washing up at the bench where she had set out a big pan of water and some towels. Another man was just heading in from the barn.

"Looks like we timed that just right!" Monty beamed in appreciation. "Sure been lookin' forward to one of her meals again. Had just about all of my own cooking that I can take."

The table was heaped with food—enough for twice as many men as were beginning to gather around it, filling plates. Platters of fried chicken, one at each end of the table, corn on the cob stacked one on top of each other like cord wood, boiled potatoes waiting for the butter churned only that morning.

Mattie looked warm, coming in out of the kitchen, carrying another large pot of coffee. She was dressed in the usual jeans and plaid shirt, but her sleeves were rolled up above the elbow and wisps of hair curled around her face where it had escaped from the tight knot in back.

Morgan met her in the doorway, and without comment he took the heavy pot from her hands. He saw the startled look in her eyes and then the faint touch of color brush her cheeks as their hands met.

"I can carry it," she started to object, and then released her hold on the handle, lowering her eyes in confusion. "I'll go get the pies from the oven."

"Mattie does all the kitchen work by herself?" Morgan asked when he pulled out a chair and sat down next to his father, near the head of the table.

"She don't complain none."

"Why? 'Cause she thinks it's expected of her or because she wants to do it?" For some reason he was irritated.

"Now hold on there, boy," the old man said, bristling. "You know how it is on a working ranch. Everyone has to do their share. Nobody ever said it was easy."

Morgan looked down the length of the table. The men he had

met briefly around the ranch this morning and Monty, already helping himself to the chicken, were there. His eyes rested on the empty chair at the end of the table. "Where's Allen?"

"He went into town this morning. Had some business to take care of." The old man reached for the hot rolls. "He's beginning to spend more time at his office. That's good. It's good for him to be wanting to work again. To keep busy. Don't need legs to handle a desk job. Might stop him from brooding."

"He able to handle the buggy by himself?" Morgan asked.

The old man nodded. "As long as someone helps him get the chair in and out. That's why we keep the buggy around. Mattie drives the car if she has to go somewhere, though she doesn't like it much." He poured the thick, creamy gravy over the biscuits on his plate. "The doctors thought he might be able to walk some, with the help of a cane, before now. Don't seem to be happening though." Morgan caught a hint of discouragement in the old man's voice.

Morgan reached for the potatoes, suddenly feeling the pangs of hunger, remembering how early he had got up this morning and how long it had been since breakfast.

"Morgan?"

"Yeah, Pa?"

"We got enough troubles around here as it is. Don't go looking for trouble where there ain't none. Leave well enough alone."

Morgan shrugged and went on with the business of eating, without answering.

It was late—long after the supper hour had passed. Monty had left to go into town for the evening. The other men had gone to the bunkhouse, worn out after a long day of working with the cattle, getting them ready for the fall market that was coming up before long. Monty had invited Morgan to ride into town with him, but he had turned the offer down.

Morgan was restless, prowling around the empty house, listening to the echoes. The front room looked pretty much as it had always looked in the past fifteen years or so—the last bunch of newspapers on a low table, the old sofa, the same old worn chairs, the fireplace with the dead ashes—no need much for a fire these days. Wouldn't be long, though, before the wind came howling across the range and the snow started falling.

He poured a drink from the bottle standing on the side table, grimacing as he felt the fire of it sliding down his throat. He went on out into the hallway. He could see a light under the door to the old man's study and he could imagine him sitting in there, the gray head bent over the desk, working on his books. The house was too quiet. He wondered where Mattie was. He played with the idea of going down to the creek and then shrugged it away, but the image of her slender, nude body swimming alone in the cool, clear water kept tugging away at him.

He went on out onto the porch, letting the door slam behind him. The old rocking chair was still there, just like the day he had left. He remembered how they used to sit out there on the steps at the end of the day in the heat of the summer, trying to catch any stray breeze that might come their way before going upstairs to their stuffy rooms. His eye scanned the horizon. There were some ugly storm clouds building up over against the mountains. There would probably be an electrical storm off in the distance tonight. He absently watched a swirl of dust at the end of the lane and made out the shape of a horse and buggy in the fading light. Allen must be coming home from town.

As he stood there in the shadows, Mattie came from around the back of the house and stood watching the buggy approach. Her hair was dry, he noted. She hadn't been swimming after all.

Morgan watched as Mattie went out to help lift the wheelchair down from the buggy and hold it steady as Allen swung himself down.

"Where you been, Allen?" she asked. "The old man has been looking for you for several hours."

"Well, now that you have given me such a warm, loving welcome, how about helping me get this contraption up the steps so I can get into the house," he said, slurring. "It is touching that you took time out to notice that I was gone."

"Did you see Judge Crawford while you were in town?"

"What you trying to say, Mattie? Was I working or socializing?" he snapped. "Is that what you want to know?"

"No. That isn't what I meant. You said when you left that you had to see the judge to get the papers signed that you were working on. I just wanted to know if it went well for you. I'm just glad to see you working again, Allen."

"You don't pay any attention to what happens at my office," he snapped. "It doesn't concern you. What do you know about it anyway? You—you who never learned anything more than how to work on a ranch."

"You've been drinking, Allen. Let's don't fight. Not tonight."

"You got nothing to say about whether I had a drink in town or not, either. My God, a man has got to talk with other people once in a while—got to talk about something else besides cattle and bills and weather. I've got to be with people who don't smell of the barn. Look at you, Mattie. What is there about you to coax a man to spend more hours at home? Running around in those outgrown boy's jeans you found in the closet and men's shirts. You look more like a runaway kid than a woman."

Morgan saw a small spark of anger flash as she raised her chin when she answered. "Maybe if all I had to do was sit around in the parlor and flirt with men, I might have time to dress in fancy clothes and fix my hair up in those silly curls. Stuff like that wouldn't last long over the cookstove or doing the cleaning for you menfolks."

"Yeah, that's right, Mattie. And that is what you are best suited for. You just go on doing your work like you are supposed to, and being here when I get home, ready to take care of me like a good wife. After all, if I weren't stuck in this confounded wheelchair I wouldn't need what little bit of entertainment I can get in town, would I? And we both know who put me here. We both know who took away my legs, don't we? It takes a drink once in a while to try to forget—to try to ease the pain. But there is no forgetting, is there, Mattie?"

Allen was settled in the wheelchair now. One of the men had come out of the bunkhouse and was taking the buggy back toward the barn. Morgan stood looking at his brother's rumpled clothing, his tie pulled loose from the knot, the way he carelessly slouched in the chair, and made his own deductions as to where and how Allen had spent most of his day. He stepped forward, out of the shadows.

"Give you a hand, Mattie?" They both looked up at the sound of his voice.

"Well, if it isn't big brother, still hanging around." Allen leaned back in his chair and grinned at the other man. "Decided to stick around for a while, did you? Somehow I kind of thought you might have ridden on out of here by the time I got home."

Mattie picked up two long, heavy boards that were lying beside the steps and fixed them in place to make a ramp, so she could pull the chair on up to the front door. Allen slouched back and waved his hand carelessly. "Sure, you can help. Why not? Mattie does a good job taking care of me all by herself, but you can give her a hand. How does it feel to be well and able to walk around on two legs, pushing me around in a chair? Not much competition for you, am I, this way? Does it make you feel like a big man, Morgan, to offer to help?"

"Not looking for any arguments, Bub—just offering to give you a hand getting into the house," Morgan answered quietly.

"Why the hell did you have to come back, anyway, Morgan?" Allen asked. "Things were just starting to get bearable around here—hardly ever heard your name mentioned; you were just about forgotten—until you had to come riding back in. What is it you want around here? I kept asking myself that all day, wondering why you're staying. You thinking that if you work your ass off the old man is going to forget what you did and leave this spread to you someday? You thinking that he's got money stashed away that he isn't talking about?" They had the wheelchair up on the porch now, and Morgan stood holding the door open so Mattie could push him inside. Allen leaned forward, still intent on his insolent jabs. "Or is it seeing Mattie here that made you decide to stick around for a while? She's something, all right, isn't she? But forget it, big brother. Take a look at her. Go ahead, take a good look. All woman she is. But look is all you better ever do. She knows where her place is. I married her—just a broken-down squatter's daughter. Brought her here and gave her some respectability. I gave her the Henderson name, some money— better than she ever had it before in her life, and she isn't one to let all of this get away from her. No, sir! Mattie's grateful to me for what I've done for her.''

Morgan saw her back stiffen and watched the way the hurt clouded her eyes as she avoided looking at either of them. They were in the house now, and Mattie pushed the chair down the hallway toward the bedroom door.

Allen stopped the chair just inside the doorway and turned to look back at Morgan. ''Just in case you've been wondering why this is my bedroom and Mattie sleeps in the one up at the head of the stairs—I get mighty restless at night and like to sit up and read. I like my privacy, where I can work on my papers if I want to—on days when I'm not feeling well enough to go into town. But don't let it fool you. Like I said, she's all woman, and she knows her duties as a wife, in the bedroom. In case you're curious, Morgan, I'm not all that much crippled,'' he added with a twisted grin.

Morgan turned sharply on his heel and went back toward the light that was still on in the study, wanting to be away from them. He had wanted to reach out and take Allen by the shirt collar and shake him. He had wanted to punch him for the way he slurred his insults at Mattie. His knuckles ached with wanting to lash out in anger. What the hell was the matter with him? It wasn't any of his business. After all, it was between a man and his wife. Worse yet, his own kin. It was his brother and his wife. Maybe he should just ride out of here again and forget the whole bunch of them, while he still had a chance. Staying here was going to be nothing but a whole lot of hard work and a bunch of trouble. Maybe he would—in a couple of days. It would be the smart thing to do.

''Morgan? That you?''

''Yeah, Pa.'' He pushed the door open and went inside.

''Was that Allen I heard coming home?''

Morgan nodded. ''Mattie's helping him get ready for bed.''

''From the noise, I reckon he's been drinking again.''

''Some. Not bad. He's okay.''

Morgan walked across the room and sat down, reaching over to scratch the old dog on the head before he settled back in the chair. The old man had a big ledger open on the desk in front of him and he went back to the figures entered in round, block handwriting. It was a while before either of them spoke.

It was the old man who broke the silence first. "You get a chance to look around some today?"

Morgan nodded. "That was a good-looking bunch of beef Wes and Monty brought in from the high range."

"Many calves with them?"

"Better 'n average. Feed must have been good this year. They all looked prime. You got more?"

"There's a bunch up at Willow Spring that's got to be brought in yet."

The old man laid the pen down, reaching into the desk drawer for the bottle he had stashed there. He poured a drink for himself and handed one across to Morgan. "It's going to be rough this fall." He studied the liquid in the firelight before he raised the glass to his lips. Morgan saw the way the lamp brought out the gray in his heavy mass of hair, saw the lines in his face that hadn't been there before, the fatigue around the eyes. "It's all that business about the war going on in Europe. Everyone figures we're going to be in it any time now. It's got everybody on edge. Sending meat prices up—higher than they been in a long time, but so is everything else. Men are leaving—can't get good help." He looked across at his son. "What's on your mind, Morgan? You been thinking of enlisting?"

There. It was out in the open between them. "Been thinking some about it."

"If you ain't in a big hurry, there's room for you here for a while. I'm going to need someone to ramrod the fall drive into the market. Thought maybe I wouldn't go this year. Too many things here at home need taking care of for me to go."

Morgan thought awhile before he answered. The smart thing to do was to get that stage out of Bend and keep moving. He knew it. It wasn't going to be anything but more trouble if he stayed. He looked across at the tired slump of the older man's shoulders. "Yeah, Pa. If you need me. I'll stick around just until the fall work is done," he answered.

The old man nodded. He picked up his pen and went back to the figures in the book. Morgan watched him for a few moments, a smile tugging at his mouth. Same as always. The old man hadn't changed. Too proud to ask for help and too stubborn to say thanks when he got it. Well, he'd stay on just until he got the cattle into the market for the old man. Wouldn't matter if he stayed that long. He could keep clear of Allen. He'd be too damned busy to get mixed up in anything anyway.

CHAPTER FOUR

Mattie stood at the back door, her hand raised to shield her eyes against the warm afternoon sun, looking out across the yard, beyond the corrals, at nothing in particular. She was restless and wanted to be outside. It would be several hours before the men came in for the evening meal. The chickens were already stewing and the potatoes were peeled, sitting in cold water until it was time to start them cooking. At least she had some help now. She could hear Betty in the kitchen behind her, moving around, cleaning up, washing the baking pans. Betty had been here several days. It would be good to have help with the fall roundup coming and all of the men taking their meals at the house.

Mattie glanced back over her shoulder into the kitchen. Everything was caught up. She had a little time to herself now before they had to start getting the food ready to put on the table. There was enough time maybe to walk down to the creek and see if there were any wild berries left. She might be able to pick enough to put in a pie in the morning. She always liked to do her baking early, before the kitchen got hot. On a sudden impulse, she said a quick word to Betty and slipped out the door.

Mattie followed the path across the field, seeking the stillness of the willows near the water's edge. Fall was here, and winter was moving in fast, but there were still a few scattered days like

today when the sun came out warm and inviting, making her
want to sneak away and be out-of-doors anytime she got the
chance.

As she walked, she thought about the ranch and the way things
were. Morgan had been back a week, taking his place beside the
old man, working as hard as any man on the ranch. Harder,
maybe. Except for the old man. Nobody put in more hours than
he did. But she could see the way it was helping him, having
Morgan here. He didn't look so tired at night now. He didn't
always look so worried. He wouldn't say anything, of course, but
she could tell.

She let her mind wander around on its own as she walked.
Morgan. Tall, lean, hard. Couldn't call him good-looking—Allen
was a lot better looking. But there was something about him—
something so masculine, so virile. Bet the old man looked just
like him when he was young and in his prime. She knew it was
Morgan who had made the old man hire Betty, the part-Indian
girl, to help with the work. He was like that, seeing that she had
too much to do, but not wanting anyone to think he cared enough
to notice. She wondered how long he would stay. She'd heard
stories about how he had just ridden off one day after he and the
old man had tangled over something. No one had heard from him all
those years. Well, easy enough to see how it had happened. The
old man had one hell of a temper, and folks said Morgan was just
like him when it came to stubbornness.

Allen wasn't like that, she told herself. Allen had always liked
books better than he had ranching, wanting to go to school and
study law. He had never been able to talk the old man into letting
him do it, though—not until after Morgan had left. She guessed
the old man had figured he might lose both boys if he didn't let
Allen do what he wanted. He sure had been wrong there, but he
hadn't known it. Allen wouldn't have left. He might have wanted
to, but he didn't have the fight in him to stand up to the old man.

She kicked up little dust swirls as she walked and thought
about the days when Allen had been courting her. He sure had
been good-looking, wearing those dark suits and white shirts,
talking with all of those big, fancy words. She remembered how
impressed she'd been, hardly able to believe that he would really

single her out. Seemed more likely he'd take to the banker's daughter, even if she was sort of overweight and giggled too much.

Mattie's face grew somber at the memory of those days. There had been some scary times after her pa had packed up and left. She had been damned lucky to get that job in town at the dry goods store. She had had more money on that first payday than she had ever seen at one time before in her whole life. She and her pa had farmed ever since she could remember, on one place after another, never able to make enough to make the payments, so they moved on. He had been so sure they were going to make it this time, when they had come out west, following the railroad. "Land, free for the taking," he had said. He just hadn't counted on the ranchers getting so mean because he wanted to fence in what they considered open grazing land. "Oregon's different," he'd told her. Maybe it was, in the western part of the state, where she'd heard they had large farms and it stayed green all year round. Folks didn't seem to feel that way here in eastern Oregon, where it got dry in the summertime and the creeks almost disappeared. It took more land to feed the stock.

"You're going to have to make it on your own now, girl," her pa had said. "I can't take care of you no more." She thought he was just feeling low and sorry for himself, as he did sometimes, but when she woke up in the morning he was gone. That's when she had moved into town and got a room on credit at the boardinghouse until she could get her first paycheck at the dry goods store. Lord knows what she would have done if they hadn't been needing somebody so bad about that time. Didn't matter how hard the work was. She was used to helping her pa, and anything they gave her to do at the store was easier than working in the fields.

But she had still been scared, just knowing she was alone. Then Allen had asked her to go to supper with him. It hadn't been as though he were the first man to ever pay attention to her, of course. There had been others. But she stayed away from them, not wanting anything to do with any of them. She might be dumb in a lot of ways, not knowing how to dress or talk properly or use fancy words as some of the others did, but she knew all about taking care of herself. And dating those whiskey-drinking cowhands that collected in Bend for a good time on Saturday night wasn't the way to do it.

Allen had been different. He had finished his schooling and opened a law office in town. Of course, he had been drinking a lot even then, but she had just never noticed. There sure had been a lot of gossip when they got married. Folks hadn't believed he ever would go through with it, said he was just leading her on. Some had said he only did it to spite the old man. Her lips turned up in a half-smile when she thought of the first time she had met Clive Henderson. She had heard about his cussedness but knew that, even so, most of the folks around those parts looked up to him with respect. Had to say this for him—once he had known she was going to marry Allen, he had stood up for her just as if she were one of his own. He had been more of a father to her than her own pa ever had, even though he did expect her to do her fair share of the work around the place. He didn't know how to show affection, though. Anything like that embarrassed him. But he had been good to her in his own way, and she was fond of him.

Things might have turned out all right for all of them if it hadn't been for the accident. There were so many "ifs" in her life. If Allen hadn't started drinking so much. If she hadn't had a temper equal to the old man's or had known how to control it better than he did. If she hadn't had that big fight with Allen on the way home that day and been yelling so hard she wasn't watching the road as closely as she should have been. It didn't matter that Allen had reached out and grabbed for the wheel as he had, wanting her to turn back and take him back to town. She had known how drunk he was and should have been paying attention. If they just hadn't run off the road right there where there was such a deep bank before they came onto the bridge. Oh, well, she really didn't have things so bad. Lots of women put up with a lot worse. Besides, she liked the old man—he made her proud that she was a Henderson. She just wished that they all could get along better.

And now Morgan was back. She wondered how long it would be before the old rivalry started up again between the two brothers.

Morgan didn't act like he cared much one way or the other, but she knew Allen wasn't too glad to see him back. Somehow she sensed that Allen felt threatened, but she couldn't figure out why.

Mattie reached the scrub brush that bordered the winding creek. The berry bushes grew the thickest here and she took off her straw hat, dropping the plump red fruit into it as she picked. The sun beat down on her and she could hear a bee nearby, its buzzing the only sound in the warm stillness. She was so absorbed with her thoughts and with picking the berries that she didn't hear the horse approach or see the rider dismount and walk toward her.

"Thought it was some rancher's kid out collecting berries until I got closer," Morgan drawled. "If you was just barefoot and tied your hair into pigtails, you could still pass for one, dressing the way you do."

Mattie spun around, startled that anyone could come up behind her without her hearing. Morgan stood there, his angular frame relaxed and easy, an amused grin on his face. His clothes were dusty and she saw the sweat marks where his shirt pulled tight across his hard muscles. It gave her an odd, prickly feeling seeing him standing there, so close.

"You must have been snitching some—you got berry juice on your face."

"What are you doing down here?" she snapped, angry because he always seemed to put her on the defensive. "Thought you were supposed to be working. The old man isn't going to like it none if he sees you."

He stood looking down at her in the hot afternoon sun. There was a look in his dark eyes as they traveled across her face and down the length of her figure that left her uncertain and a little frightened.

"Got warm and thirsty. Came down here to get a drink of cold water and cool off." With a shrug, he walked past her and knelt at the edge of the stream. Unable to look away, she watched the muscles rippling across his shoulders as he cupped his hands, splashing water over his face and taking a long, cool drink before he stood up again. When he moved, it was with the sinewy ease of a mountain cat. He was lean and hard, his features chiseled by the years spent out on the open range, but when he turned to look at her again, she saw that his eyes seemed to hold some secret thought that amused him.

"Does this mean we're going to have berry cobler for breakfast?" He was close, standing in the pathway in front of her, looking down at the hatful of berries. She hadn't realized how tall he was. His presence was overpowering, and she couldn't seem to control the racing of her pulses that pounded in her ears, blotting out the other sounds of the afternoon.

She tossed her head defiantly. "Maybe. I got to be going. Let me by."

"Why? Betty's there, isn't she? What's the hurry all of a sudden?"

"Maybe I just don't like your company," she retorted. "Maybe I just came down here to be alone. Anyway, I got enough berries. I got to be going." He saw the uneasy wariness in her eyes.

"What's the matter, Mattie? Are you scared to be alone down here with me?" He was grinning that easy smile again and she felt uncomfortable, as though he might be laughing at her. "What are you afraid of?"

"I reckon you got some bad, mistaken ideas about me," she answered, her brows tugged into a frown. "I heard all those stories about when you used to live here—the way all the girls in the country used to throw themselves at you. You're thinking maybe I would do the same thing. You might as well forget it, Morgan. I don't want anything to do with you."

"I wasn't planning on you throwing yourself at me, Mattie," he answered quietly. "I just thought we could start being friends. You're my sister—almost. It doesn't seem right, you always snapping at me the way you do."

"Ain't too much in your attitude that's brotherly," she quipped tartly. "I know what you're thinking. You think I'm all hard up—married to a cripple and not getting properly satisfied, ready to fall into the arms of the first man that makes me an offer. Well, you're dead wrong, Morgan."

He reached up and pushed his hat back on his head and let out a long, low whistle. "You sure do talk plain enough when you get your dander up! When you got something on your mind, you just spit it out, don't you? You're a little mixed up, though, Mattie. That isn't what I think of you at all.''

"No?'' She looked at him with a new curiosity. "Then what do you think? You been here awhile. You see what's going on. What do you think about all of us, anyway?''

He let his eyes travel down the length of her, lingering for a moment on the way the shirt pulled tight across her firm, round breasts, then back to meet the eyes that were snapping with angry fires as she watched him. "I'm thinking that you probably would be one hell of a fine woman, if you was given the chance, Mattie. Might even look like one, if you was to wear dresses once in a while, like you ought to. Too bad Allen doesn't realize what he's got and try a little harder to make you happy.''

She lifted her head and he saw the stubborn tilt of her chin. "Don't you worry none about Allen. We understand each other.'' She tried not to look at his tall, lean body, the hard lines of his face with the little laugh crinkles near his eyes, or see the way his hair curled damply with the water from the creek. "I got to get back to the house. Maybe you got time to stand around doing nothing, but the rest of us got work to do.''

"You're right, Mattie. Work's waiting.'' He bent quickly and without warning brought his mouth down hard against her lips before he turned to stride back toward his horse, leaving Mattie staring wide-eyed after him, completely unaware that she had dropped the straw hat full of berries on the ground.

She took off for the house, walking fast on the dusty path, seething with anger at herself for the truant emotions that were tearing around inside of her. She didn't want to remember the way her pulses had raced when he stood so close or when his lips had touched hers so briefly. By the time she reached the house, her temper was short and she felt hot, dusty, and irritable.

"Where you been?'' Betty asked pleasantly when Mattie came into the kitchen. "I put the potatoes on. The chicken is done. Do you want dumplings in the broth?''

"Might as well.'' She walked across to the wash stand and began splashing water on her warm face. "I went looking for berries. We needed something for the pies in the morning.''

"Didn't you find any? I thought there still was some late ones down by the creek."

Mattie looked down at her hands. Damn! She had dropped the hat during her encounter with Morgan and forgot all about it. Now what was she going to do? Sure couldn't go back now, looking for it. Betty was watching her with a curious look on her face. Damn that man! "I decided to make a boiled raisin cake instead. We ain't had one for a while," she answered, trying to sound offhand.

It was getting late. The two women worked busily now. There wasn't time for thinking during the next hour or two. One thing about a bunch of men on a ranch—they sure ate a lot! They weren't too fussy about how fancy it was served, just so long as there was plenty of it.

Morgan came in late, going right to his place at the table where the men were already eating. His hair was still wet from washing up outside before coming in. The old man was there already, sitting at the head of the table as he always did. The talk turned right away to the stock they were working with, and Mattie was too busy to pay any attention to the conversation. She and Betty always ate later, after the men had cleared out and they had the kitchen to themselves.

It wasn't until they had started the cleaning up that she saw her straw hat sitting on the bench against the wall, filled clear up with red, ripe berries. She stared at it, feeling the color burning on her face. Damn him!

Allen sent word back to the ranch that he was going to stay in town. He was working on some case papers that would take him longer than he had thought. Mattie shrugged it off, thinking it was just as well. After a day like today, she could use one evening of quiet. Might even find time to do a little reading. She did that sometimes, taking down some of the old books the old man had up on the shelf—books that must have belonged to someone else, because they were stories about folks who lived different from anyone she had ever heard of. The women wore long, beautiful gowns, and the men were in fancy clothes. There were stories of romance and mystery—things folks around there never had time for. Those were the evenings she liked best of all—nights when the weather was chilly and Allen went to his room early or stayed in town. She liked to slip into the old man's study and curl up in that big chair by the fire with the dog lying at her feet. She'd read while the old man worked on his figures in the ledger. Sometimes she'd bring in some hot coffee and some leftover cake, or once in a while she'd pop some corn. The old man never seemed to mind her being there. 'Course, he never invited her in, either. But that was his way. If he hadn't wanted her there, he'd have said so. Probably wouldn't be many evenings like that anymore—not with Morgan back.

There was mending to do. Maybe she had better tend to it instead of wasting time reading. That's one thing about this place, she thought. A person never lacked for something to do. She had her chickens and the garden, and there was the cooking, the cleaning, the scrubbing, and once in a while she rode out with the old man, loving the freedom, the openness of the country. He always acted as if he enjoyed having her ride with him. He didn't seem to mind that she wore pants most of the time instead of dresses. Sure made getting around a lot easier. She had found them in Morgan's room—left over from when he was a boy—and she figured he couldn't wear them anymore, even if he did come back someday.

Seemed like it took longer than usual to get the kitchen cleaned up tonight. First one thing and then another. When she went to the door to check on the wood pile to see if kindling had been split for morning, she heard a horse riding out, headed down the lane. Morgan, headed toward town. Well, that figured. For all his reputation as a hell raiser, he hadn't been in that big of a hurry to go in with the boys in the evening when the chores were done. He seemed kind of a loner. She watched the small cloud of fading dust thoughtfully. Wonder who he was going to see. Wasn't any of her business, but she wondered.

Betty was already in her room off the kitchen. Mattie closed the back door and blew out the lantern. She went through the darkened front room, headed for the steps up toward her bedroom. The old house was quiet with everybody gone. She'd never noticed it before. Guess she would read after all.

"Mattie? That you?" She turned back at the sound of the old man's voice coming from his study.

She pushed the door open. "You want me?"

"Come on in. Don't just stand there in the doorway like that." He was looking at her kind of funny, like maybe he was really seeing her for the first time in a long while. "We been so busy lately, all of us, that you and me ain't had time for talking, have we?"

"I been here." She didn't want to tell him that every time she had come to the door in the evening Morgan had already been there, sitting in her chair by the fire.

"What's the matter, girl? You tired tonight?"

"Nothing's the matter. Why?" She went on into the room and sat down. She wondered what the old man was leading up to. He hardly glanced up usually when she came in here to sit and read. He never asked questions like that unless he had something on his mind.

"Havin' Betty working here been a help to you?" he asked.

"Yes. Thank you. There's a lot needs doing this time of year, what with the canning and all, getting ready for winter. I wasn't complaining, though." She was watching him now, waiting.

He nodded. "Gives you a little free time once in a while. That's good. A woman needs some time to herself—long's it don't interfere with what else is going on."

"I'm still doing my share. I ain't stopping nobody else from doing theirs, either. What are you gettin' at, old man?" She leaned back in the chair, reaching down to scratch the old dog's head, wishing he would hurry up and get to the point so she could start reading.

He sat playing with a pen, studying it, thinking over what he was going to say. It was a long time before he answered. "I was riding up around the rim on the south side of the house this afternoon. Just happened to look down across the creek. Saw you leaving that clump of willows, kind of in a hurry. I was surprised to see you there that time of day. Made me look a little closer. I seen Morgan's horse standing there. He came out of that same bunch of willows soon after you did."

Mattie sat bolt upright in the chair, angry fires flashing from her eyes. "What are you trying to say, Clive?"

She never called him Clive unless she was mad. He knew all of the danger signals by now, and she was near the boiling point. "Now, girl, all I'm trying to say is that I don't want no trouble aound here. We got enough on our hands just trying to get this damn place back to paying for itself after Allen's hospital and doctor bills. Sometimes I wonder how we're going to do it. Those two boys of mine never could get along, without having a woman standing between them causing more trouble."

She started to get up out of the chair but he held up his hand. He had to be careful—didn't know when he'd seen her looking so all-fired mad. "Whoa now, Mattie—don't go flying off the handle until I've said my piece. I know life ain't been easy for you around here, what with Allen in that damned invalid chair and drinking the way he does. A woman likes to get a little attention once in a while. Something to make her feel special, and wanted. A woman gets lonesome—"

Mattie was mad. "What the hell do you know about women?" she flared. "Except when it's mealtime and your dinner ain't ready, maybe? Where the hell do you get off preaching about what a woman feels inside, or wants, or thinks?"

" 'Cause I was married to one once, that's how I know!" he shouted back. He had started to get up out of his chair, but he sat back down, lowering his voice, trying to stay calm, when he spoke again. "You think I forgot, just because I don't talk about it? You think I can't remember back to when I was married, remember what it was like to have a woman beside me, loving me, believing in me?"

Mattie sat back down suddenly, her eyes wide open. She had never heard the old man talk about his wife before. Something in his face stopped her from answering. Something all soft that she had never seen there before.

"She had soft gray eyes and shiny long hair. When she took the pins out at night, it reached down below her waist." He was silent for a long moment, memories clouding his vision. "You find it hard to believe that I ever loved a woman like that? You think that no woman could ever love me enough to want to live out here with me? We didn't have much of a town nearby when we first got here. It was a two-day trip there and back to get to where we could buy supplies. We lived in a lean-to while we was building this here house, and she never complained. Let me tell you something, girl—we was happy on this here place. She loved me—she believed in me, knew I could build this ranch from nothing. Ain't never seen another woman that could take her place.''

Mattie wasn't ready to give in quite that easy. ''You loved her so much you let her work herself to death out here at the edge of nowhere, stuck out here with no other womanfolk around, having her babies with no one to help—''

''Now see here, Mattie—that's not fair. It was her dream, too. She worked side by side with me because she wanted to. She was so soft and gentle, but she had fire, too. I remember the time I came around the house and found her planting those roses at the front doorstep. Lost my temper when I seen it and I yelled pretty loud I guess. 'Can't eat roses!' I remember shouting at her. 'We need a garden, woman! Potatoes and carrots and turnips! Why the hell you wasting your time planting roses?' She just straightened up and put her hands on her hips and looked me right in the eye and she answered, 'Because I need them, Clive. I need some flowers.' Oh, she had a lot of fight when she wanted something. I remember what happened when I tried to send her back home to stay with her folks before Morgan was born. I never even mentioned it when Allen was on the way.''

Mattie sank back in the chair but she still didn't answer. She didn't know what to say.

''There's times you remind me an awful lot of her.'' Mattie looked up, startled. That was the closest he had ever come to paying her a compliment. ''You been good for Allen. He needs someone like you. Someone strong. You remember that, and watch your step, girl. Neither one of those boys have much sense. It'll be up to you. Don't go letting any trouble happen between the boys because of you.''

Mattie got up out of the chair and headed for the door. ''Don't intend to.'' Her head was held high, her chin firm. Her eyes were dark with anger. ''Looks to me like you got better things to do with your time than go around spying on folks, seeing things that ain't there, like some gossipy old woman.'' She left the room, pulling the door shut behind her, leaving the air heavy with hostility. Clive leaned back in the chair and his shoulders slumped forward, showing his weariness. He'd handled it all wrong, he guessed. He hadn't meant to make her so damned mad!

CHAPTER FIVE

Mattie stood in front of the mirror hanging over the chest of drawers in her room and critically inspected the reflection staring back at her in the early morning light. Her brows were knitted in a frown as she studied what she saw.

"Sure isn't going to be as easy to get around this way," she muttered to herself. But somehow it just didn't seem right to go on wearing Morgan's outgrown jeans and those comfortable flannel shirts anymore—especially with him back now and making cracks about her looking like some rancher's kid instead of a grown-up woman.

She smoothed the crisp blue-and-white-checked gingham down across her hips and picked up the apron hanging across the back of a chair. "Blamed full skirts keep getting in the way when I hurry, and I'm going to have to keep an apron tied on over them to keep from getting dirty." She gave a big sigh. "Oh, well—guess it won't hurt me none. Besides, it looks kind of nice. Funny how a change of clothes and pinning your hair up can make a person look so different—feel so different inside."

She glanced quickly at the clock sitting on the table, took time to tuck one more pin in place to hold her hair in a roll, and hurried toward the stairway. She had fooled around so long getting dressed this morning she was going to be late getting breakfast on, and then there would be trouble! The men were putting in long hours now and they needed to be fed before they left the house—not just something put together in a hurry, but a hot meal that would stay with them while they worked.

Betty was already in the kitchen. The teakettle was steaming when Mattie came in. She could feel the heat seeping out from the big old wood cookstove and smell the fresh aroma of a new pot of coffee coming to a boil.

"Good morning!" Betty greeted her with a smile. "Are you going into town today or something? You look real nice in that dress."

Mattie hesitated for just a moment, and then shrugged casually. "Ain't nothing special. Just gingham, fit for ranch work. Guess a woman my age ought to wear dresses more. Ain't proper to be running around looking like a half-grown kid."

Betty grinned, her soft brown eyes sparkling teasingly. "Especially when the menfolks around here are noticing more how you look once in a while." Her good-natured remark was rewarded with such a black look that she turned hastily away and began dumping the flour into the crockery bowl to start the hot cake batter going.

It wasn't until later in the day, after the men had all left for the corrals and Allen had driven down the lane, headed toward town, that Betty brought up the subject of the basket social at the schoolhouse.

"Sure wish you could go. Is there any chance that Allen might take you, Mattie? We could all go together—just make a real party of it. Those gatherings are always a lot of fun. It's about the only chance we really get to visit with the other women."

Mattie shook her head. "He doesn't like going to places like that. It is just too hard for him to be able to get around, always having to depend on other folks to help with that wheelchair. He doesn't like being in a chair and watching the others walking around, dancing."

"Do you suppose you could go anyway? We could go together. You just never seem to get out anywhere, round other folks—to visit."

"No. It wouldn't be right. It would just remind him of—of the things he can't do no more." She gave a sigh. "I could never have a good time, dancing and visiting, knowing how Allen feels. Oh, Betty, I do so wish he would get well. I wish he would be able to walk again. It's been two years since it happened. Been over a year since the doctors sent him home, saying there wasn't anything else they could do for him. They seemed to think if he exercised—if he practiced trying to make the muscles in his legs work—someday he might be able to walk. Not like before, of course, but maybe with a cane." She shook her head sadly. "It just doesn't seem to be happening, though. It hurts too much when he tries. I know all of you think he drinks too much, but he says the pain is so bad—he drinks for the pain because he just hurts all of the time."

"How did the accident happen, Mattie? I mean, what *really* happened?"

"Doesn't matter how it happened. It just did. I was driving the car, and I should have been watching closer than I was. It was my fault. If Allen had been driving—"

"If Allen had been sober, you mean," Betty answered sharply. "Wes thinks—"

"What Wes or anybody else thinks doesn't matter!" Mattie snapped. "It happened, and standing here gossiping about it isn't going to make it any different. It is just something I have to live with—and pay for, for being careless. It doesn't concern anyone else." She paused a moment, then spoke in a determinedly cheerful tone. "What about the basket social? Are you planning on going?"

A slight touch of color brushed the other woman's cheeks. "I'm not sure yet. There's been some talk about it, back and forth. I thought I would go ahead and fix a box supper, just in case."

Mattie smiled. "I have the perfect box for you to use. It's one that Clive's boots came in. Some pretty wrapping on the outside, a ribbon—" She looked across at Betty with curiosity. "Who do you want to bid for it?" She was teasing now. "If we knew who might be doing the bidding, we could put in his favorite dessert—"

"How do I know who will bid on it? If anyone bids at all, it will probably be old Doc Thompson or some other old bachelor who doesn't get much home cooking,'' Betty answered, turning away but not before Mattie had time to see the blush.

Nothing more was said. Allen spent the evening in town. Betty left in the wagon with several of the men from the bunkhouse who were headed in to town, assuring Mattie that she would have no problem getting home after the schoolhouse social. She could always ask one of the families from another ranch to drop her off on their way home. That is, if one of the men wouldn't be bringing the wagon back to the ranch about the time the social was over. Morgan was out at the line camp and wouldn't be back in until morning.

Feeling restless, Mattie popped some corn and went into Clive's study to read. For once, Clive closed the ledgers early and took the chair on the other side of the fire. Then it was just the two of them in the big old house, reading and listening to the echoes from the empty rooms.

CHAPTER SIX

It was Monday morning. Morgan felt a little guilty, bouncing along on the rough road, listening to the uneven pounding of the pistons in the engine, watching for potholes, hoping to hell that he could get clear into town and back again before the fool car decided to quit and leave him stranded. There was too much work needing to be done for him to take time out to go into town. It didn't seem right leaving Wes with so much to do while he headed in to the hardware for parts and then went across to the bank. They were things that needed doing but he still felt guilty.

Wes was a good man. There was no reason for him to worry about anything when Wes was there. Especially when the old man was there, too, pushing everyone all of the time, doing more than his share of the work and still sitting tall and straight in the saddle, not looking tired at the end of the day like the others.

Thoughts of the old man twisted his mouth into a grin. Now there was a man to look up to. His hair had turned gray, his shoulders were a little bent, but he was made of steel. When Morgan had been younger, he hadn't seen his father quite the way he did now. He'd fought against the constant authority, against the way the old man thought everyone ought to work eight days out of every week. Morgan had been young then, wanting to spend more time in town with the men, trying to swagger a little to cover up a busting headache from too much drinking the night before, trying to copy the hell-raising hands, not fully realizing what the old man was trying to build. He had always worked hard enough. Nobody could say Morgan ever backed away from work. But when day was done, he had a lot of things he wanted to do. When he was a kid, it had been adventure enough to sneak off to the swimming hole and spend an hour or two skinny-dipping, or maybe even fishing. Later, he had learned how to smoke Bull Durham, practicing rolling the papers without spilling any of the tobacco when he thought nobody was looking, until he could do it as casually as the other men.

Was had been with him the first night he drank too much in town and got so damned sick. It was Wes who had ducked his head in the water trough, holding him down while he kicked and swung his fists, trying to get air, and then made him bend over under the pump and wash up in the ice-cold water so they could go home and face the old man. It was Wes who had laughed so hard at him when he had to work all the next day without getting any sleep. Every time his butt had started to drag, the old man had given him more to do.

Then there had been girls. Once or twice he and Wes had been chasing after the same one, winding up in a fist fight while the girl waltzed off and married someone else. He used to think the old man was pretty rough on him in those days. Funny how much smarter the old man looked to him now. He hoped that someday he would wind up being half the man Clive Henderson was.

Clive had come out here as a young man, settling on his homestead, fighting every inch of the way to build what he had into a working ranch. A damned good ranch it was, too—one a man could be proud of. He had done it all without too much help. His wife had died while still a young woman, leaving him with two small boys to raise. Morgan had never thought before about how rough it must have been on the old man, trying to do the work and raise them, too.

Allen had always hated ranching—hated the hard work. He had always looked for an easy way to get things done without letting himself in for any more trouble than necessary, finding ways to keep from getting caught when something went wrong.

Morgan smiled to himself as he remembered how he had never been able to avoid trouble the way Allen had. Even then, he'd been filled with the same stubborn pride as the old man, which got him into a lot of trouble until he had been knocked on his backside often enough to make him look at things a whole lot different. To prove that he was a man in his own right, he had ridden off one day without looking back.

And now here he was, back at the old home place, helping the old man out of a bad spot when there was too much to do and too few to do it, before he left again, this time to enlist in the army.

There had been a lot of changes while he had been gone. Allen had been in that car wreck, and was drawing heavily on the ranch to pay for his medical bills, leaving Clive and Mattie feeling responsible for him—Clive going into debt to see that he got whatever new doctoring could be had for him, Mattie consumed by guilt every time she looked at him sitting in that wheelchair.

Mattie. Funny—no matter what he was thinking about, he seemed to always wind up with her on his mind. For all of Allen's complaining about the rough deal life always gave him, he sure had had one stroke of luck when he got Mattie. Too bad he wouldn't open up his eyes and see just what a hell of a woman he had. Or maybe he did realize. Maybe this was his way of holding her, afraid he couldn't do it any other way.

With a woman like Mattie at his side, a man could do just about anything he set his mind to. There weren't too many like her. His mother must have been a lot like Mattie—full of fire, loving the land out here in the West, ready to fight for what was hers and yet so soft and gentle and full of love that a man just naturally wanted to reach out and hold her in his arms.

He had wondered a time or two why the old man had never married again. A ranch like theirs needed a woman. Now, seeing Mattie, living in the same house with her, getting to know her, he began to understand a lot of things about Clive. After having a woman like Mattie to love, it would be hard to ever take another wife.

Coming back to the ranch had been a mistake—staying on had been even worse. Mattie was the woman he had been searching for all these years—the woman who until now had been just an image living in the back of his mind as the one he wanted when he settled down. And now that he had found her, she belonged to someone else. She was his brother's wife.

The car was beginning to heat up, threatening to boil over, bringing his attention back from his wanderings. It was the same car that had been in the wreck. It had been hammered back into shape with some baling wire and a few new nuts and bolts here and there to hold it together. It took constant tinkering to keep it running. Damned thing was a trial to the patience, all right. Kicked like a mule when you turned the crank to start it and was temperamental as a woman to run, but it was faster than a horse and handier, especially when you had to bring supplies or parts back from town.

He parked in front of the bank and turned off the ignition. He had made it this far—if the car sat awhile and cooled off, he might make it clear back home. He reached into the back for his sheepskin jacket and headed up the sidewalk. He glanced toward the sun. If everything went well, there was time to get done what had to be taken care of and he could still make it back in time to help with evening chores.

The small town was sleepy-eyed this time of day, especially on a Monday. Most of the ranchers were pushing to get caught up before the winter rains set in. He finished up at the bank sooner than he expected and cut across the street in the middle of the block, walking toward the row of small buildings where Allen had his office. Might as well stop in for a minute or two.

Morgan stood on the boardwalk, looking in through the plate-glass window. A big oak desk was scattered with papers. An empty chair was pushed back and turned a little toward the back of the room, as though whoever had sat there last had gotten up and gone toward the door standing ajar, leading to another room. Maybe Allen was back there, working where it was quieter, away from the street noises. He went inside, shutting the outside door behind him.

When no one came out, he started toward the back. He could hear slow steps pacing back and forth, so Allen must be back there with someone else—a client, most likely. The door was ajar, so it must be all right to go on in. What he saw caused him to push his hat back on his head and let out a soft whistle of surprise.

Allen was in the center of the room, slowly walking back and forth across the floor with only the help of a cane.

"How long's this been goin' on, Bub?"

Allen turned with a start to see his brother lounging against the doorjamb watching him through half-closed eyes that were cold and hard, full of angry speculation.

"What the hell do you mean, sneaking in here like this?" Allen flared in defensive anger. "You're supposed to be out at the ranch. You taken to spying on me or something?"

"If you don't want folks walking in on you unexpected, you ought to see that the door is latched," Morgan drawled. "You're getting careless." The lines of his face were tight, showing the disgust he was feeling inside.

Allen dropped into the wheelchair, letting the cane fall to the floor, making an unnecessary clatter in the heavy air that lay between them in the room. His face was flushed, his eyes wary, as he watched the other man, wondering how far the accusations were going to go.

"Doctors said I had to keep trying to move my legs," he began, trying to make the explanation sound casual. The old, competitive hatreds that dated back to their childhood burned just below the surface, but he tried to mask them with a half-hearted grin. "Doctors said I had to keep trying, even with all the pain it causes. Doesn't matter how much it hurts. I'm supposed to exercise the muscles." He let the grin fade into lines of resignation. "They said someday I might be able to walk again—or walk with the use of a cane, maybe—if I just kept working at it. That's what I was doing, Morgan. Just working at the exercises. Seeing if I could take a step or two with that cane."

"That's mighty interesting." Morgan nodded thoughtfully. "You been practicing like this for long? Seems to me you was making it across the floor there a mite too easy for it to be a first try."

"None of your damned business how long I been working at it! I don't need you watching over me, finding fault all the time. You're so damned sure of yourself, coming back here after all this time, making me look bad to the old man 'cause you can walk and ride, letting him think he can depend on you for help.'' Allen's voice was low, his lips curling in the hate that was consuming him. "What you watching me like that for? You insinuating that I've been able to walk for a while without telling anybody?"

"Didn't exactly mean that, Bub." Morgan shrugged carelessly. "I was just watching you walk and thinking to myself about how pleased Mattie is going to be to find out her husband can walk a little." He rubbed his chin thoughtfully. "You been pretty rough on her, making her feel guilty all the time, waiting on you hand and foot—worried all the time. It's a cheap, shoddy trick to use, Bub, to hold a woman."

"That's it! It's Mattie. That's what you're after!" Allen's eyes lit up as he spit out the words. "You think I don't see the way you been looking at her? You think maybe you got a chance with her?" He leaned back in the chair, watching Morgan closely. "Well, let me tell you about Mattie. She ain't the kind of woman you been used to. Once she gets married, she stays that way. Mattie belongs to me, Morgan. She's mine. I aim to keep her."

Morgan kept his voice low, trying to control his temper. "Mattie's a fine woman, Bub. Gentle and loving, with a lot to offer a man. Maybe if you started treating her that way, you wouldn't have to worry so much about how to hold on to her. Come to think of it, I imagine the old man will be real happy to hear your good news, too. Maybe if he hears that you can walk a little without that chair, he can quit worrying himself so much about the bills. That's right, Bub. It's been rough on them, and those two are going to be mightly pleased to hear your news. You planning on telling them real soon?"

"I'll tell them when I get damned good and ready! And stop calling me 'Bub.'" He was sullen now, not wanting to meet his brother's eyes.

Morgan nodded. "Sure. Whatever you say. You handle it the way you want to. Only—don't take too long. I sure do hate to see them worrying themselves so much about you, you having a secret like this hidden away that could make both of their lives a lot easier."

"Are you threatening me?" Allen's face was dark with the fury he was trying to contain.

"Wouldn't exactly call it that. I'm just looking forward to seeing their faces when you come back to the ranch tonight. After supper, when things get quiet, you could make a big try at getting out of your chair all by yourself and let them see you take a step or two without any help. A step or two would do it. We don't want them thinking it is too easy for you, do we? Yep! Going to relieve their minds a whole lot." He stood there smiling quietly as though thinking ahead to the happy scene at home, but all of the time he was watching the defeated look on Allen's face.

The son of a bitch, Morgan thought to himself as he saw Allen reach for a bottle and a glass sitting on the desk. He turned and walked out of the office, not bothering to close the door after him.

Morgan glanced up toward the sun—it was starting to slip low in the sky. On an impulse he changed his direction, going on down the street toward the bar at the end of the block. No use being in such a hurry to get back home. In fact, if the truth be known, he'd like to get out of going back to the ranch at all this evening.

The whole episode in Allen's office had left him with a bad taste in his mouth. He wondered how Allen would do it—making them think this was the first time he had tried to stand up. Maybe he would take a few halting steps—basking in the happy words of praise for his efforts, but making Mattie feel the pain he was going through while he was doing it. Yes, even while he was watching her smile, he would make sure she felt the pain, too, as real as though it were her own. Morgan's hands clenched unconsciously at the thought. No. This was one evening he didn't want to be at the ranch house watching what was going on. He didn't trust himself.

He went through the doorway of the bar, squinting into the gloom after being out in the sunlight. Familiar sounds and smells that hadn't changed over the years drifted out and met him. He'd been coming here since he was tall enough to lean his elbows on the bar and exchange banter with the other ranchers. The place held a lot of memories.

"Morgan! Been wondering when you'd get around to looking up your old friends. Heard you were back in town." A woman's husky voice greeted him from across the room. Minnie. She was still here after all.

The hard lines around his eyes softened as he relaxed into an easy grin. He felt better already. Minnie was just the sort of person he needed right now—to have a friendly visit, laugh a little, get his mind off all of the things that had been bothering him. He squinted a little as his eyes adjusted to the dim light, and he saw her standing behind the bar watching him. Well over two hundred pounds and then some, probably. Her hair was dyed to hide the gray and her face looked like a road map, it was so full of wrinkles, but her eyes were dancing with humor. Minnie had been around these parts forever. She had gone through four husbands and was looking for the fifth, some folks said. She knew everyone by his first name and she knew where all the skeletons were buried. No one he knew loved living as much as Minnie. Nothing seemed to ever get her down. She could put her hands on her ample hips and toss her head back in laughter right in the face of a disaster. There wasn't anything so bad that she couldn't twist it around a little until it looked amusing.

"Come on over here where I can get a good look at you," Minnie insisted. "The first one is on the house. Glad to see you again, Morgan. I been waiting. Knew you would be in sooner or later."

He grinned across the bar at her. "Now, you know I couldn't stay away forever, remembering that you were right here in this town, waiting for me. You always been my favorite girl friend."

She inspected him carefully as she set the cold beer down in front of him. "You're looking good. Always was kind of lean, but you look . . . solid. You remind me of Clive, back when I first knew him. He was about the age you are now." She let her eyes linger affectionately across his broad shoulders. "How is Clive? Haven't seen him for a while. He all right?"

Morgan nodded. "Same as ever. How you been, Minnie? Taking good care of yourself?"

She shrugged carelessly. "I'm getting by. Going broke trying to keep this place open. Don't know why I stick around these parts. Maybe someday I'll just chuck it all and head toward a big city. Always wondered what San Francisco was like.''

Morgan grinned to himself as he listened to her talk. She probably had half the money in the whole county tucked away in a stocking somewhere—all the time she complained about going broke, keeping the place open. She wouldn't leave until they put her in the ground, because this was her home, these were her people.

She poured herself a beer and came around the end of the bar to sit on a stool beside him. For the next half hour she rambled on, bringing him up to date on the happenings that had gone on while he was away, bringing back to mind names of people and places he had thought were forgotten. He felt himself unwinding, relaxing, chuckling at the tales she spun.

"What about Wes?"

Morgan looked up, puzzled by her remark. "What about Wes?" he countered.

"You think he is serious about that li'l girl you got working out at your place now helping Mattie?"

"Don't know what you're talking about," he answered slowly. "We got a new woman working out there, right enough. Her name's Betty. She helps Mattie with the cooking. But what's she got to do with Wes? Don't think he's even noticed her."

Minnie threw up her hands in disgust. "You men are all alike. Can't see nothing when it's right in front of your nose. I knew right off that something was in the wind when he didn't show up here with the boys on Saturday night. At first I figured that maybe he was riding line or something. Wes ain't one to miss a little Saturday night hell raising unless he's got work to do. Then I heard he was over at the schoolhouse that night—at a basket social.''

Morgan looked up, his mouth twisted in a disbelieving grin. "You're wrong this time, Minnie. Not Wes. A basket social? You're not talking about Wes. He ain't been near a schoolhouse since about the fifth grade."

She nodded her head, looking wise. "They had a fund raising going for some new school books. He was there, right enough. Heard he bid a gawd-awful price for a basket of food that he could have eaten at home for nothing. I knew right off that that old bandy-legged cow puncher was going to get himself caught if he didn't watch out.''

Morgan stared at her in disbelief. "Wes—at a basket social?"

Minnie nodded solemnly. "That's right."

"I can see why he wouldn't come back and tell anybody a thing like that. Sure you ain't wrong?''

"You know damned good and well I ain't wrong. You know me better than that. You would probably have noticed yourself, if you weren't wearing blinders. How about it, Morgan? Something else been taking your attention so you don't see what's going on around you?''

He shook his head, laughing at her. "Now you're fishing. Any gossip you got about me is up the wrong trail, unless you heard I been working my ass off, baby-sitting those damned cows. The old man is making up for lost time. We been putting in some long hours.''

"I know. It's good you're back. Clive has had a lot of trouble. He needs you.''

Morgan rubbed his chin, his eyes twinkling. "Wes—at a basket social. I'll be damned.''

Minnie tossed her head defiantly. "Well, what's so wrong in that? It would be a good thing for Clive if she does manage to tie Wes down. I hear she's a real nice li'l woman. They could both go on working there and Clive wouldn't have to worry about Wes getting restless and moving on. Good help is damned hard to get lately. It's all this news in the papers about the fighting going on over there in Europe. The President says he's going to keep us out of it—but the young bucks are looking for excitement, standing in line at the recruiting office, wanting to be in on it.''

Morgan nodded, a shadow falling across his face. "Might be hard to stay out of it, no matter what the President says.''

"Let them fight their own gawd-damned wars," Minnie said, bristling. "We got nothing to do with it. We got enough troubles right here at home to take care of without mixing in something that doesn't concern us. Why should our boys get killed fighting their battles for them anyway?''

"Maybe joining in will keep the war across the water, away

from our own country,'' he answered seriously. ''If England and France can't handle it without some help, we could be the next ones to be attacked.''

She studied him thoughtfully, her brows drawn into a frown. ''You sound like a man who's been thinking this thing over a little. You planning on enlisting?''

''Been giving some thought on it.''

''What's Clive think about it?''

''We haven't talked too much about it. I told him I would stay until the fall work is done—stay until things get caught up again. Then—'' He shrugged his shoulders. ''There ain't too much holding me back.''

''Nothing holding you back, or something making you think it's wiser if you move on?''

Morgan unwound his long legs and stood up, laughing down at her. He was ready to move on. The conversation was getting too personal, touching on areas he didn't want to think about. ''I've sat here swapping tales with you for so long, supper will be all over before I can get back home. Think I'll get a bite to eat down at the hotel before I head out. Take care of yourself, Minnie.''

When he passed by Allen's offices, he saw that the lights were all turned off. He cut across the street and went into the hotel dining room.

When he got back to the ranch that night, most of the lights in the house were already out and the bunkhouse was dark. He stood on the porch for a long time smoking a cigarette, looking into the stillness before he flipped the butt onto the dirt and went up the stairway to his room, feeling alone and lonely for the first time in years.

CHAPTER SEVEN

It was late September, almost the first of October, and already the early snows were deep on the higher ridges. The air carried a snap to it, smelling of the heavy winter rains that would be moving in at the lower elevations of the desert any time now.

Five weeks so far—five weeks of hard, back-breaking work, long hours, with Morgan coming in at night too bone-weary to be haunted by a saucy pixie face, a slim, boyish figure, and yet she was always there in the back of his mind. The stock had been brought in from summer pastures, branded, separated, counted, marketed, and the rest of the cattle were settled in for the winter closer to the ranch buildings. With help so hard to get, every man did the work of two at times. Morgan had eaten dust and dirt until he felt the rough dryness scratching at his throat—but it had been worth it. The market had been high, with lots of ready bidders. Clive was looking forward already to spring with a new enthusiasm—talking about buying several new bulls to improve the breed.

It had been good, the two of them working together, father and son, building a new closeness based on mutual respect.

Morgan sprawled comfortably in the large chair in the study, feeling the warmth of the fire from the grate, holding a glass of bourbon in his hand, letting the bite of the liquor unravel his tired muscles. He and Clive had been going over the tallies, discussing the bulls to be bought, planning how they would haul them out to the ranch—looking ahead. He heard a noise in the hallway and looked up in time to see Mattie turning away from the door.

"Did you want something, Mattie?" Clive called out after her.

"No. Nothing. Just wondered if you wanted some more coffee before I let the fire in the kitchen stove go out." She had wanted to go in, sit down in the chair in the corner, and pick up a book, not talking to them but being a part of the planning anyway, feeling like she belonged.

"Damn him!" she swore under her breath. "Damn him all to hell!" Why did Morgan make her feel like this—on the defensive, thinking things she had no business to think about. Before he came, she wouldn't have thought anything at all about walking into the study, picking up a book, sitting down and getting comfortable, not bothering Clive when he was working but enjoying the closeness anyway. It was something in Morgan's eyes, the way he looked at her sometimes, making it hard for her to look away. She was too aware of him to relax when he was in the same room. She had stood in the doorway watching the two men for a few minutes before they had known she was there. She had seen the way his shirt pulled tight across his shoulders when he leaned forward to hand Clive some papers, saw the fluid way he moved, the tanned, leathery look to his face from being out-of-doors so much, the lines of his lean, hard body, the strong arms. For a crazy moment she had wondered what it would be like to have those arms reach out toward her—touch her—to roughly pull her close against him, to hold her close enough to feel the warmth of his body against her own, to make love to her.

That's why she had turned away, angry with herself, when they had looked up and seen her standing in the doorway. She shoved her hands in her pockets and went across the hallway to Allen's bedroom, shutting the door firmly behind her. He was sitting in a chair with a book open in front of him, but he wasn't reading. There was a half-empty bottle sitting on the desk at his elbow. She started picking up clothes, straightening things, filled with a restlessness she couldn't explain.

"You been practicing walking any more this evening?" she

asked. "If you want to try it again, maybe I can help." This is where she belonged, in the room with Allen, not curled comfortably in the study with Clive and Morgan, she told herself critically. Especially not with Morgan.

"You can help by not pushing so damned hard," he grumbled. "I'm tired. I ache all over. I was just sitting here thinking, trying to relax some while I work on some problems that have been bothering me."

"I'm not meaning to push, Allen. It's just that with you being able to stand alone, taking a few more steps each day—it just seems like maybe if you keep at it, things might finally turn out the way you wanted."

"I'm doing the best I can, Mattie. What's the matter? You getting tired of having a cripple for a husband?"

She turned away, wishing he wouldn't always feel so sorry for himself. It made her want to reach out and push him out of his self-pity. She turned away because she was ashamed of herself for her impatience.

"You used to tell me how you were going to be the best lawyer in this whole area and I believed in you," she answered quietly. "Now it's beginning to look like maybe you can go ahead with those plans. I know how hard it has been for you, having to depend on the wheelchair to get around. But now you are able to stand—to walk a little. If you keep trying, it will get even better. There's a chance to plan ahead again. You can do it, Allen. I know you can."

"Don't mess with those papers on the desk, Mattie. How many times do I have to tell you to leave everything alone?" he snapped. "You stick to cleaning the rest of the room. What's on the desk is personal—it's business papers and doesn't concern you." He turned and picked up the bottle, pouring out another drink.

Mattie turned away, going over to the window to look out into the evening light settling over the valley. "I didn't disturb anything. I just thought things needed a little straightening, that's all." She looked back at him across the room. "I know you must be tired, Allen, and your back must be hurting you pretty bad after the walking around you have been doing today, but do you really need that drink? You've already had a whole lot."

"Don't start lecturing again, Mattie. I need it for the pain. It's the only way I'm able to sleep at night. You don't know nothing about pain. You don't know nothing about what it's like, having everyone pushing you to keep trying, wanting you to take one more step, even when every move is so much agony. No, Mattie, you don't know—you were just the one driving the car, not the one who got hurt." He smiled inwardly as he saw her wince.

"I'm not meaning to push you. I just think that it would be good for you to start taking an interest in things again. Work's good for folks, Allen. Life just seems to be a whole lot more worth living when you are interested in something—when you wake up in the morning with your head all full of plans, looking ahead, wanting to get the day started."

"I've got plans," he answered sulkily. "I've got plans you wouldn't even guess at. That's what I was sitting here thinking about when you came in."

"What do you mean?"

"It isn't going to be too easy following through on them, not having any more understanding from my family than I do, but I got some big plans going. Everyone around here has cow shit on their boots—they can't think any further ahead than the fall market for those damned bawling steers. I've got a wife without any decent background—doesn't know how to act and dress like a lady. But you wait and see, Mattie. I'll make it on my own. I got friends—friends in the right places, where it counts. I was talking with a couple of men just last week. They drove all the way down from Portland just to see me. I never told you that, did I? I've been giving a lot of serious thought to what they had to say."

Mattie was curious now, wondering what he was leading up to. "What are you talking about, Allen? What men from Portland? Why would they drive clear down here to see you?"

He poured another drink and leaned back in the chair, grinning smugly at her. "Politics. I've been thinking really seriously about running for public office. Just might go into politics, Mattie."

"But what about your law practice in town? I thought you were proud of having your office there and being a good lawyer, knowing all the folks around here and having them all come in to see you when they needed some help. I thought that was what you wanted."

He drew his handsome brows together into a frown. "You think I intend to spend the rest of my life right here in Bend, not ever getting anyplace, doing the same thing year after year, having folks stalling until fall to pay their bills, if I manage to collect them at all?"

Allen took a drink, tossing down the amber liquid and waiting to savor the taste before he continued. "Money, Mattie. Money is the secret to everything. Takes money to get along in this world. Takes money to have folks look at you with respect. You've got to have money to get anyplace, Mattie, and I can't do it by staying in this town forever."

He raised himself stiffly from the chair, walking with slow, awkward steps across the room toward the bed, leaning heavily on the cane. "Can't do it by just working day to day, either. Got to gamble a little, take a chance now and then. Got to know the right people—the ones who are in the power circle—and be there when they are looking for the right man to fill an office."

"I don't understand what you're talking about, Allen. What kind of politics you planning on going into? Who are the men you're talking about?"

"Businessmen from Portland. Men interested in construction, land development, building roads." Allen sat down heavily on the side of the bed. "They're the right kind of people to know, Mattie. The kind of people who can help me get to where I want to wind up. In public office. Mr. District Attorney. How does that sound? Pour another drink for me and come on over and sit on the bed beside me. Let's talk about it."

Mattie was at the window again, peering into the darkness, her hands plunged deep in the pockets of her apron. She should be feeling happy. She should be glad he was thinking ahead again, making plans, wanting to do things on his own. She couldn't understand the uneasy wariness that gripped her as she listened to him talk. Something bothered her, but she couldn't put her finger on it.

"You known these men long?" she asked finally.

"Long enough. Anyone who can talk about something else besides the cost of feed and breeding ability of a bull knows who they are. Come here."

"What do you want?" She looked across to where he sat on the side of the bed.

"You know what I want, damn it. I want you, Mattie. Let's go to bed."

"I still got some things to do yet in the kitchen. You go on and get into bed. I'll be back later." Mattie felt suddenly tired, empty, sexless.

Allen had taken off his shirt. He stood up to unsnap the fly to his trousers. "Never used to be too busy—or too tired," he answered, watching her closely. "What's the matter with you lately? Someone else been taking up your time while I've been working my ass off, figuring out a way to get ahead for us?" He reached out and took a firm hold on her wrist, pulling her down close to him on the side of the bed, bending his head to kiss her roughly on the mouth. His anger flared when she turned her head away, his fingers biting into the flesh of her arm.

"You're mine, Mattie. You're my wife. You belong to me. I found you among all that junk at the dry goods store and I brought you home. I made a Henderson of you. You were nothing before that. You forgotten already?"

"Stop it," she cried out, trying to pull away. "You're hurting my arm."

"Am I? Nothing like you are going to be hurt if you start playing around. You got eyes for Morgan? Is that what's the matter?"

"Allen, don't. You've been drinking all evening. You don't mean what you're saying."

"Drinking? Sure, I been drinking A man has to, to put up with the crap that goes on around here. I'll be so damned glad to get away from this ranch—to start living like real folks—get rid of the smell of the barn—"

He pulled her close again, his hands moving against the but-

tons on her shirtwaist, pulling the checked gingham away to
expose the soft skin of her bare shoulders. "How about it,
Mattie? You like the idea of being the wife of the next district
attorney? You think I can't do it?" he murmured as his mouth
sought the hollows of her throat and his hand traced the line of
her thigh.

"You probably can, if you set your mind to it," she answered.
"It's just how you go about it that worries me."

"Then stop worrying. I'm smart enough to keep out of trouble.
Old Allen is going right to the top, baby, and I'll take you with
me. I'll buy you good clothes—maybe some furs. I'll give you a
big house to live in—"

He was pushing her backward into the softness of the quilts,
his hand finding and tenderly caressing her breasts as he talked.
"Mattie?" His voice turned soft and pleading. "Mattie, don't let
me down. I need you. I need you," he murmured into the dark
mass of her hair where it fell loose around her shoulders. "I got
to know you are there, Mattie, believing in me, or I can't do it. I
can't do anything without you. It was because of you that I tried
to walk again. If you weren't here, believing in me, I couldn't
have done it," he whispered as his hand sought the warmth of
her inner thigh and his lips moved down to gently tease the small
pink nipples. "Promise me, Mattie. Promise me you will help
me—don't turn against me. Help me, Mattie. I need you."

Mattie thought back to when Allen was courting her, to how
impressed she had been with his handsome, dark good looks, his
fine way of speaking, the way he dressed—always in suits and
white shirts, while most of the men she knew wore flannel shirts
and rugged jeans. She had been willing enough then to promise
to love him, to stand by him. What was it that caused her to draw
away inside at his touch? What made her feel empty—and lonely—
when he pushed his body demandingly against hers, expecting
her to respond? What made her so restless, wanting something—
but what? What was the matter with her?

"Mattie?" He lifted his face to look into her eyes. "Mattie?
Will you help me? It will be a hell of a future for us—it's what I
want. I can do it if you are at my side, believing in me. I need
you, Mattie. I can't do it without you."

She tried to look away, but couldn't shut out the pleading in his dark eyes. With a sigh, she reached out and brushed his hair back, drawing his face to her breast and comforting him as she would a child. "It's all right, Allen. I'll be here, whenever you need me. I'll do my best. Just be careful. I worry. I know you can do anything you really set your mind to, but be careful." She forced herself to relax as she felt his weight pressing her down against the mattress.

"It's just you and me, baby," he whispered. "We don't need anybody else. None of them. Just you and me. Love me. Love me, Mattie. Prove to me you don't need anybody else."

Mattie slipped out of the checkered gingham, letting it fall in a heap on the floor beside his trousers. He held out his arms to her as she slipped beneath the covers to lay beside him.

A new confidence crept back into his voice as he murmured, "You're mine, Mattie. We belong together. I'm going to be the next district attorney, and I'm taking you with me—all the way, baby. Just you and me. We don't need anybody else."

Mattie forced herself to respond to his demands as his hands skillfully sought and found the secret places he knew would kindle the fires that smoldered deep within her body. When he finally fell asleep, his arm carelessly across her, holding her, she lay sleepless, staring into the darkness of the room.

CHAPTER EIGHT

The cold winds of October were blowing down from the mountains, making the men burrow deeper into their sheepskin coats. Morgan and Clive had been out most of the day, riding the fence lines, checking on the winter quarters for the stock, speculating on how much water there was going to be next spring. It had rained steady for days, letting up only for a few hours once in a while, long enough to let the sun make a weak attempt to bore through the heavy clouds.

"Wouldn't be surprised to see snow down here any day now," Clive drawled, glancing up at the sky. "You can smell it in the air. Going to be an early winter."

"Well, I think we're ready for it," Morgan answered, pulling his collar up a little closer around his neck. "The stock is in good shape. We shouldn't have too much trouble. No more than usual, anyway."

Clive pulled his horse up on the edge of a ridge and sat looking down across the valley. "What do you think about that forty over there across the creek?"

Morgan reined up beside him, wondering what the old man was leading up to. "What about it?"

"Wes wants to buy it. He came in and talked to me about it yesterday. Says he has been looking for a small spread—a place where he can build a house, maybe run a few head of cattle—"

Morgan thoughtfully lit a cigarette. "Wes planning on quitting?"

"No. Don't think that is what he has in mind. He doesn't have the money to buy up enough stock to make a living, anyway. Says he's getting tired of living in the bunkhouse—wants a place of his own—thinking about settling down. He figures that forty would be about right. Close enough, where he can work here and spend his free time putting his place in shape. Wants to have a house built on it by spring."

Suddenly Morgan remembered what Minnie had said the last time he was in town—about Wes going to the basket social at the schoolhouse. He grinned across at Clive. "You think Betty might have something to do with him getting this urge to have a house of his own?"

"Kind of thought something like that was in the wind. He could do a lot worse. She's a good woman. You got any objection?"

"To what? Wes getting himself roped and branded or you selling the forty to him?"

"Splitting off that forty and letting him have it. Not too anxious to let any of this land go." Clive was studying the valley that sprawled below them.

"Betty is a damned good cook. She's been a big help to Mattie and, besides that, they seem to be good friends. If Wes decided to settle on that forty, it would almost be like having them still living right on the place, and yet they'd feel like they had their own home—something that belonged to them. Hell, Pa, you got a couple thousand acres—you won't miss that little forty. Why don't you give it to them for a wedding present? Wes has been around here so long he's like part of the family anyway. He's probably earned it, couple times over."

"That's sort of what I had in mind. Wanted to talk it over with you first, before I did anything about it."

"You said anything to Allen?"

"Nope." Clive glanced up toward the sky. The rain had stopped. "He's got his mind too full of all this business about going into politics right now to have much time for talking about ranch affairs. What you think about these new friends of his?"

Morgan shrugged. "Can't say. Don't know much about them. You met any of them?"

"No. Allen hasn't brought them out to the ranch. Guess maybe we don't measure up—not enough window dressing to suit him. Just hope to hell he knows what he's doing."

"If he's got his mind set on this, maybe it'll be a good thing in the long run. He never would be worth a damn as a rancher. Think we both know that. As much law as he has studied, he ought to know enough about right and wrong to stay out of trouble."

As they sat their horses on the ridge looking down over the valley, their attention was caught by a car coming up the lane toward the house. Clive shifted in the saddle. "Looks like we got company. Never seen that car around here before. Maybe we better ride on in."

"Now that we got the work done, looks like it is going to clear off some," Morgan answered, looking up toward the dark clouds with small patches of sunlight sifting through. "Sun might even come out." He turned his horse, following the older man along the trail.

As the two men rode around the corner of the ranch house, they could see the car parked in front. Wes and several of the men were looking it over with lively interest.

Allen was standing back, resting against his cane, talking to the others with animated gestures. Mattie had come out of the house and was standing back out of the way, listening to them talk.

"Where'd that car come from?" Clive asked as he rode up to join the group.

"Brought it out from town," Allen answered, with a touch of defiance in his voice. "Just took it on trial. Wanted to see how it ran. It's one of those Model T's that Ford makes. Everybody's talking about them."

"We got a car already." Clive stepped down out of the saddle. "Don't need another one."

"Sure—we got a car." Allen bristled irritably. "It's beginning to rust up where the dents were pounded out. Never can be sure when you start out that you'll make it to where you're going and back again without it breaking down. It boils over every time you try to make it up a hill. Come on—take a look. It sure as hell isn't a Packard or a Pierce Arrow like some of my friends are driving, but it doesn't cost as much, either.''

"Looks to me like a person could get damned near drowned if it started to rain," Clive commented drily.

"Hell, Pa, it's a convertible. I put the top down so the fellows could see inside. Wait a minute—I'll put her back up again.'' One of the men stepped up to help and the black canvas top snapped into place. "Look how much room there is. Two can sit in front, real comfortable, and it isn't too crowded for three in back.''

Wes had been walking around it, looking at the tires. "Start 'er up, Allen. Let's hear it running. Want me to crank it for you?''

"Hell, this baby don't need cranking. She's got an electric starter. No, sir—don't have to worry about maybe breaking your wrist when the crank kicks back at you. Here—back up out of my way. Let me in. I'll show you what I mean.''

He twisted a lever, turned the starter several times, adjusted the spark, and the moter turned over and caught. Morgan's horse reared up and backed away, rolling its eyes in fright until Morgan gentled it with a touch of his hand.

"Listen to that!'' Allen said triumphantly, his dark eyes shining. "Purrs like a kitten. Four cylinders. Not going to win any races, but won't cost too much to run, either.''

"It very hard to learn to drive?'' one of the men asked. They had collected near the front fender. Someone had lifted the hood and they were studying the engine with avid interest.

"Nothing to it. Hell, even Mattie could drive it and not get into any trouble.'' He opened the door, drawing their attention to the floorboards near his feet.. "See these three pedals? You push one in to change gears. The second one is the brake and this other one is the reverse.''

"How do you think it will be at climbing hills?'' a doubtful voice asked from the group of men. "We got a lot of them in this backcountry.''

"It'll take the hills better than any other car in town,'' Allen boasted. "If the grade is too steep to take it going forward, you just turn around and put it in reverse and back up the hill. It's got a lot of power in reverse. It works the same way if you get to going down a hill too fast and afraid you can't stop it with the brakes. You push in the reverse pedal, too. Gives you all kinds of extra braking that way."

"Well, I'll be damned," Wes said in admiration. "What they going to come up with next!"

Allen grinned across at him, feeling good about the attention the car was getting. "Of course, if you use the reverse to help stop the car, you got to remember to get your foot off the pedal when you get slowed down—otherwise, it will start going backwards and lead to all kinds of unexpected surprises."

Clive was rubbing his chin thoughtfully. "How much they asking for it?"

Allen grew serious, giving his full attention to the older man. "The price is the best thing about it. Only eight hundred and fifty. It's the cheapest and best-running car on the market."

"I can see you got your mind pretty well made up already," Clive drawled slowly. "How you intend on paying for it?"

"I told them at the bank that you would go ahead and pay for it now—and I'll pay you back. Won't take long. I'll have the money for you before spring."

Morgan watched the angry color touch Clive's cheeks as his eyes narrowed and grew hard. "Don't you think we should have talked it over some before you made any promises like that?"

The other men drew away, pretending sudden interest in the other side of the car.

"What the hell do you mean?" Allen snapped. "The market was higher this year than it has been in a long time—probably going up even higher, with the war talk. I haven't seen the figures, but I know damn well you came out all right this fall. I ain't asking you to buy the gawd-damned car—I'll have the money before spring. Once I get in office, I'll have the money."

"You that sure of winning?"

Allen stood tense, his weight heavy on the cane. "I'm that sure."

"Must be mighty powerful friends that you have." Clive

turned away, leading his horse toward the corral, his back stiff, with anger showing in his stride.

Morgan had been watching Mattie the whole time. She hadn't said a thing, staying back away from the others. When Clive left, she turned and went toward the house. Allen didn't seem to notice that she had been there or seen her leave. The other men suddenly remembered chores left undone and they, too, moved off in the direction of the barn, leaving Allen alone with the car.

Morgan found Mattie later, sitting alone in the kitchen with a cup of coffee in front of her on the table.

"What are you doing out here all by yourself?" he chided. "Thought you might be wanting Allen to take you for a ride in your new car."

She gave him a quick, sharp look. His smile was friendly enough, but she read the sarcasm in his words. "I'll go riding in it soon enough," she retorted. "I know what you're thinking. That Clive will wind up paying for the car. You think Allen is wrong, telling the bank the ranch will stand good for the bill. Well, Allen is going to be the next district attorney if he says he is—and he can't go on traveling around the country in a buggy. Especially now that he's beginning to get some use of his legs again and he can drive. It isn't right. He needs a car—one that he doesn't have to crank, one that he can depend on."

Morgan took a mug off the shelf and poured himself some coffee from the big pot sitting on the back of the stove. "Well, Mattie, I wish him luck. Having a woman like you believe so strong in him should make a man able to do just about anything he sets his mind to. I hope he makes it. For your sake, I hope he makes it."

She watched the easy way he moved across the room, hardly making a sound even though he was a big man, built tall and lean, with powerful shoulders. She could feel the nearness of him even with the distance of the room between them. When he pulled out a chair and sat down across from her, she had a strong desire to reach out, to lay her hand on his, to touch him. She saw the crooked smile he gave her as he talked, and she fought back the impulse to smile back at him. The thought of trailing her fingers along the hard muscles of his shoulders made her pulses race a little faster.

"Don't you worry yourself none about me, Morgan Henderson," she flared, on the defensive again, trying to cover up her thoughts. "We don't need no luck. Allen will do it all on his own. If he makes up his mind to do it, he will. Allen's real smart."

"I hope he's smart enough to stay out of trouble. If not, I hope he doesn't let any of it touch you. I don't want you hurt, Mattie," he answered softly.

"Never you mind," she snapped. "I can take care of myself." She set her cup down on the sideboard and walked from the room, her chin in the air.

Morgan studied the tiny bubbles floating in his cup. Don't know why we always strike sparks that way—every time we try to talk, he thought to himself. All I got to do is walk near her and she backs off, raising her fur and hissing like a tiny kitten that thinks it's in danger.

Another thing he couldn't figure out was why it bothered him so damn much. He'd known a lot of women in his time. None of them ever caused him to lose any sleep. Yet here was this small bundle of female independence snapping at him all the time, and all he wanted to do was to reach out and grab her, protect her, keep anything from ever hurting her. He wanted to hold her in his arms and kiss her until she quit spitting fire and turned into a warm, loving woman. It didn't make sense. He should just want to stay out of her way, to ignore her, but he couldn't get her out of his mind.

His thoughts drifted back through time to a lady who lived in the memories of his childhood. He wondered if that was how it was for the old man when his mother was alive.

CHAPTER NINE

The fresh, sweet smell of bread dough flavored the air when Mattie walked into the kitchen. Betty was standing at the table punching the huge white mass down, rolling it, kneading it, tiny puffs of flour dusting her apron as she worked.

"Thought I'd set aside some of the dough for Bismarks, if that's all right with you," Betty said without looking up. "They don't take as long as doughnuts to make 'cause I won't have to spend all that time cutting circles and punching out the holes. I can just roll the dough out and cut it into oblongs. We've got some blackberry jam that I can fill them with, and then I'll roll them in white sugar right after I fry them."

"Sounds like a real good idea to me," Mattie answered. "The men will like it. They never turn down any kind of sweets. You'll have them in here sitting at the table before you can finish ringing the dinner bell if they smell Bismarks in the air." She went across the room, took a mug from the shelf, and poured some coffee. "I heard Wes say the other night how he favored Bismarks with blackberry jam filling. That couldn't be what made you think of it, could it?" She smiled when she saw Betty turn away to hide a blush. "You got a list made out? I'll finish this cup of coffee and then I should be leaving. I want to allow myself plenty of time to drive into town and still make it back well before evening. If I should have any kind of car trouble, I don't want it to happen after dark."

"You ain't planning on going into town alone, are you?" They turned to see Clive leaning against the doorway. He was a big, powerfully built man, and in his sheepskin coat his bulk almost filled the entrance.

"Well, I was—unless you'd like to go with me," Mattie answered. "Allen left the Model T here when he took the stage to Portland. He said I could use it while he's gone. That other old car isn't dependable at all anymore. Besides, I always have to ask someone to crank it for me."

"I don't like the idea of you going alone," Clive said, frowning. "Not in the winter like this."

"It doesn't seem too bad outside right now. Besides, I'm leaving right away, so I can be back before dark."

Clive walked over and stood looking out the window. "Still don't like it. There is an ugly line of clouds hanging low over the mountains. It's the first of December. They will move in fast this time of year. No, Mattie. Don't want you going alone. Morgan ain't busy. I'm going to send him with you to do the driving. I'll go get the car out of the barn and get it started for you. Let it run a little and get warmed up. You come on out as soon as you're ready."

Her protest fell on emptiness as he left the room, headed toward the barn.

Betty was dividing the dough into lumps, shaping them for loaves. "How long's Allen going to be gone this time?"

"Another four or five days. They're having a meeting or something in Portland. A whole group of them is going to be there, I guess, from what he said." Mattie was fastening her large motoring hat in place, anchoring it with long, sharp hatpins. She glanced out of the window and saw Morgan sitting in the car, Clive standing beside him, talking. Seeing them there like that, she couldn't help but think again how much alike the two men were—tall, strongly built, their chiseled faces showing their pride and their stubbornness. "Guess I better hurry up. Looks like they're waiting for me."

The trip into town was quiet for the most part. Mattie sat up on the high front seat, her back straight, her coat collar pulled up against the cold. She tried to ignore Morgan most of the time, except to steal a sideways glance at him once in a while when she thought he wasn't looking. Just having him so close made little truant waves of excitement race through her veins and she would look quickly away. She didn't want to talk. Just seemed as though every time she and Morgan got into a conversation they wound up snapping at each other. She didn't know why. Guess it was the way he looked at her sometimes, his eyes sort of saying soft and gentle things even if he was only talking about the weather. Like just now, when he had asked her if she was warm enough and she had answered back, real sharp, that her coat was heavy and she was fine, while all the time she was wondering what it would be like to slip across the seat closer to him and kind of lean against his shoulder out of the wind. He had grinned back at her, and the way his eyes crinkled around the edges she felt he must know what she was thinking. She turned away and fastened her gaze on the line of mountains with their snowy tops as though admiring the scenery.

It was kind of like a holiday today, getting away like this on a shopping trip without any need to hurry right back, knowing there wasn't a lot of work waiting for her. With Allen being gone, she had time to relax a little, just be herself, without always wondering what he was going to find fault with next. With Allen being a lawyer, she always felt a little on the defensive, wanting him to approve of her but never quite sure if she measured up. Especially when he kept reminding her that she was only a squatter's daughter. Morgan kept her on the defensive, too, but in a different way. It was the way he looked at her, as though liking what he saw a little *too* much.

Morgan parked in front of the bank building and Mattie collected her gloves, her purse, and her umbrella, ready to take off on her errands. She stepped out onto the running board and Morgan handed her down to the ground, lifting her as though she weighed no more than a feather.

"How long you figure on taking, Mattie?" he asked. "We could meet somewhere—maybe have lunch at the hotel dining room."

"I know what I'd like to do," she answered with hesitation. "You'll probably think it is real silly, though." He stood waiting, so she took a chance and continued. "I'd like to go to Davidson's Ice Cream Parlor and have a big chocolate sundae with lots of salted peanuts scattered around on top." She waited for him to refuse or make fun of her, almost wishing she hadn't suggested it.

"That might be fun." He surprised her with his answer. "Make it seem like a special day. We'll see if we can't get them to heat the chocolate syrup a little and have the nuts extra salty."

Mattie took off up the street, humming a little to herself as she walked. Days like this were few and far between. She intended to make the most of it—might even buy a sack of peanuts in the shell from the barrel at the general store to take home to Clive. She knew how much he liked them. And maybe, if she could find it, some soft, pretty flannel for Betty, so she could start making some nightdresses for her trousseau. Wes hadn't gotten up the nerve to propose yet, but everybody knew he was going to—especially after Clive turned over the deed to that forty acres west of the ranch house to him. Guess he wanted to get the house started first, to show her that he had a home to take her to.

Morgan was lounging outside the food store, talking to some of the men, when he saw her coming up the walk, her arms loaded with packages. He came across to meet her, taking the bundles out of her hands. "Let me put these in the car, Mattie, before we go find that ice cream sundae. Looks like you got more than you can carry." His eyes crinkled in amusement as he looked down at her. "You must have about bought out the stores, didn't you?"

"Guess I got carried away. We still have to go back to the general store and pick up the flour and stuff. They got them set to one side for us."

"We'll stop on the way out of town." Morgan didn't seem the least bit embarrassed going into the ice cream parlor and sitting on one of the white iron chairs with the black leather seats—even though his legs were a little long for such small quarters. A grin tugged at the corners of his mouth as he watched her chattering away about all of the things she had found without having to order them from the catalog, but she couldn't seem to stop talking. She lowered her lashes, not wanting him to see how much she was enjoying herself.

She felt a tingle of excitement at his touch when Morgan stood and placed his hand at her elbow, ready to go back to the car for the trip home, and yet she hated to leave, to let the day come to an end.

The road from town followed along the edge of the mountains for a ways before turning and heading east across the high desert toward the ranch land. There had been a lot of snow at the higher elevations and the Three Sisters stood out sharp and clear against the darkening sky. Mount Jefferson, a little to the north, looked harsh and forbidding with its jagged peaks reaching toward the sky. Lower down, the heavily forested ridges were such a deep green they were almost black against the white background. If she turned a little, Mattie could see Cinder Butte, farther to the south, that funny round mass of volcanic ash, looking like an ice cream cone standing upside down, its sides as smooth and round and steep. Folks said there had been a big volcano erupt in this country a thousand years or so ago that left Cinder Butte and all of the hundreds of acres of lava flow cooled and twisted into mysterious caves that filled with ice and stayed cold all year round, even when it was boiling hot outside in the summertime. A lot of folks went to the ice caves during the summer to get ice for their kitchens.

To Mattie's left, in sharp contrast to the mountains, lay the miles and miles of sagebrush-covered high desert, where the ranchers homesteaded and ran their cattle. It was toward this country that Morgan turned the car, driving along the dirt roads filled with ruts that had been carved out during the winter rains.

Mattie grew quiet, her thoughts tumbling around ahead of her as she braced herself against the jolting of the car. She thought about Allen and the men from Portland.

Well, one thing about politics—it had given Allen reason enough to keep exercising until he could get around really well with just a cane. There must have been times, though, when his back hurt something awful, because he kept drinking, using the liquor to cover up the pain. At least, that's what he said when she tried to talk him out of having another drink because he was already slurring his words and his temper was so bad.

Mattie pulled her coat collar up around her face. The wind was getting colder. You could smell the heavy dampness in the air. It had been fun in town today. She had enjoyed herself more than she had in quite a while. She stole a glance at Morgan, but he was looking straight ahead, watching the road, not paying any attention to her. She wondered what he was thinking about. She let her eyes stray to his hands, noticing how strong they looked holding on to the steering wheel, and guiltily she hurried her thoughts back to Allen.

"Allen be home by the end of the week?" Morgan's voice sounded harsh after the long silence.

"That's what his plans were when he left," she answered. "I'm glad he went to Portland. It's been good for him, getting away, getting interested in something again. I'm glad he's starting to look ahead." She felt safe now, having the conversation on Allen, away from the emotions Morgan could stir up in her by just looking at her the way he did, his eyes gentle and yet smiling a little as though he might be amused at something no one else knew about.

"You think Allen is serious about running for district attorney?" he asked, glancing sideways at her.

"He's serious, all right. He'll do it, too. You wait and see," she answered firmly. "Allen is real smart. Smarter than most folks."

"Think he'll get elected?"

"If he sets his mind to it, he will. Besides, he says there isn't too much doubt about it. Those men that he went to Portland to see—guess they usually get what they want. Guess they want Allen for the district attorney over here." Her voice trailed off and there was a shadow of a frown across her face as she talked.

"You don't seem too happy about it, Mattie. Something about it that's bothering you?"

"No. Nothing, really. I just get to worrying sometimes. Just hoping Allen don't get himself into some kind of trouble. I don't understand people like these new friends of his, I guess. Never been around folks like that before. That's another thing that has me worried." She paused, as though deep in thought. "You see, moving around the way we did when I was growing up, I never had a chance for much schooling. I can read real well—I always loved books—and I think I'm as smart as the average woman when it comes to learning, but I just never took the time to study. It didn't seem all that important—not until now."

He felt her uncertain hesitation. "It's become important to you now?"

"Oh, yes!" She turned to him, her small face serious, a touch of anguish in her eyes. "Don't you see? Allen needs a wife who won't embarrass him. He needs a wife who knows all the right things to do and will make him proud. I have to learn how to talk the right way. I got to stop cussing when I get mad. I got to learn how to walk. You know what I mean? Not just put one foot ahead of the other to get someplace. I got to learn how to walk like a lady. I was watching some of them in town today. You ever look at them?" At his grin she broke out into laughter. "Yes, I guess you have. That was kind of a silly thing to ask you, wasn't it? Well, anyway, I am going to learn. Got my mind all made up. I'm going to learn how to talk, how to walk, how to act around folks from a big city like Portland."

"Mattie—there is nothing wrong with you. You got to quit thinking that way. You're a fine woman, just the way you are. I'm not sure I want to see you change any at all." The laughter was gone from his eyes. "You want to do all of this for Allen? You think it will help him—is that why?"

She gave a big sigh. "Yes. And for myself too, Morgan. Maybe I want to do it most of all for myself I don't want people to look at me and think I'm nothing but a squatter's daughter, without any education or proper upbringing. I want to be able to hold my head up and know that I'm just as good as the rest of them."

He took his attention from the road for a moment, letting his eyes linger on her face, trailing down across her small figure sitting so straight and tense beside him. "Did you ever consider that you might have a few things going for you that other women don't have? It isn't just knowing how to walk and how to use fancy words that makes a man turn his head and take a second look.''

She answered quickly, angry that with just a glance he could make the color rush to her cheeks and her breath catch in her throat. "There you go again, Morgan. Teasing—not taking me serious. Don't know why I even tried to tell you what I was thinking about.''

A few spatters of rain hit the windshield, making patterns on the glass. Morgan looked over toward the mountains, at the high clouds piling up, the black rolling motion of the thunderheads, felt the way the temperature had dropped while they were talking. ''Could start raining hard at any time now. Afraid that storm is going to hit before we can make it clear home.''

Bursts of wind were breaking the clumps of sage loose, tumbling them along the ground until they caught against a fence row. The sky turned dark and ugly, and the rain started coming down in sheets, driven by the wind. The small streams were rising fast and left their banks to race across the dirt road, causing new ruts and washouts. Lightning cracked across the sky, followed seconds later by the rolling boom of thunder.

Morgan could see that Mattie was nervous, the way she sat so stiff on the seat beside him, peering out through the windshield into the rivulets of water on the glass. She wasn't doing any talking now, just sitting there, tense and quiet, but it was the way she kept twisting her handkerchief that let him know how frightened she was.

They were both getting wet. The wind was driving the rain in around the corners of the hood where the canvas didn't fit tight against the body of the car, letting it drip down on them. He had lit the headlamps, but they weren't much good in a storm like this.

"Miserable damned weather!" he cursed under his breath, trying to dodge a large chuckhole.

When the tire blew, he wasn't certain if it was a tire or the crash of thunder until he felt the steering wheel pull from his grasp and the car slide toward the ditch. Mattie screamed out in terror, covering her face with her hands.

"It's all right, Mattie. It's all right. We just blew a tire. No harm done." He tried to keep his voice calm.

She took her hands from her face. When she spoke, her voice was shaky. "I thought we were going to tip over." He saw how pale she was, how large and dark her eyes were. "What are we going to do now?"

"Can't change the tire until the storm blows over," he answered quietly. "Can't stay here, either. This thing leaks like a sieve. I've got to get you in somewhere to dry out until it lets up. There's a cabin just back by the tree line. We used to use it sometimes when we were out riding fence. Isn't too far to walk. Not more than a couple hundred yards. Can you make it?"

She lifted her chin defiantly. "I can if you can."

"Then let's make a run for it."

The wind caught them with its full force as soon as they stepped away from the shelter of the car. The rain was coming down in sheets, soaking their clothing, making it hard to see where they were going. Morgan bent to hold her close to him, giving her what protection he could with his body as they made their way across the field of wet, muddy grasses. The lightning flashes lit up the sky and then left everything in darkness as the thunder pounded behind it, leaving the smell of sulfur in the air. Morgan was walking fast now, almost running, his strong arms almost carrying her as she hurried along beside him, struggling to keep up.

The cabin loomed up suddenly in front of them, outlined by the jagged shard of lightning that found its way to the ground, splitting a large pine as though it were kindling. Morgan shoved the door open, pushing her inside. After the violence of the storm outside, the dark interior seemed hushed in quiet. She brushed the wet, clinging hair away from her face and tried to shake the water from her clothing as she looked around, trying to see in the darkness.

"Stand still, Mattie, while I strike a match and see if I can find a lamp. The old homesteader who built this place ain't been around in a long time, but there should be a kerosene lantern somewhere." Morgan already was moving about the room. The match flared, showing his outline as he looked for the lamp. In another moment or two a lantern sent its warm glow out, softening the darkness with a flickering yellow light.

"We're in luck. Whoever used this place last left a stack of dry wood inside out of the wet." He was kneeling by the small stone fireplace, arranging the kindling, adding small pieces of wood, coaxing the flickering flame to start eating away at the curling bark. He took off his sheepskin coat, dropping it in a corner.

Mattie stood near the door where he had left her, watching his strong, broad shoulders, the narrow line of his hips, the almost catlike grace in the way he moved, then bent over to add larger pieces of wood to the growing flames. Her teeth were chattering now, and she was shivering, from the cold and from something else—something she couldn't explain.

Morgan stood up and turned toward her, grinning in amusement. "You look like a drowned kitten—like you went swimming in the creek without taking your clothes off first."

Mattie's face flushed, remembering how they had first met. She'd been at the creek, swimming nude in the silvery evening light, thinking no one was around to see her, but he had been watching from the patch of willows.

He drew her over close to the fire and she felt the warmth reaching out to her. He took her coat from her shoulders and spread it out over the back of a wooden chair so that it could start drying. "Sit down, Mattie. Let me get your shoes. Can't do much about the mud on them, but we can get them dry, at least." His voice was gentle as he knelt in front of her loosening the fastenings, drawing her shoes off her slim cold feet.

Her hands were trembling and she couldn't make them stop. She watched him, without speaking, as he set her shoes near the fire.

Morgan brought several old, well-worn blankets off the narrow cot in the corner and spread them on the floor near the open hearth. "Here, Mattie, sit down beside me. Let me rub your hair dry for you. You're going to take a chill." She had lost the pins and her hair hung like a veil around her shoulders. Silently, she slipped from the chair and sat beside him on the blankets, watching the flames climb higher, dancing, licking away at the wood, feeling the touch of his hands against her hair.

"Your hair is like silk, Mattie," he said softly into the dark stillness of the small cabin. "It shines in the firelight like long silken threads."

She felt the gentle touch of his fingers trailing through the long strands where it hung loose about her shoulders.

His words were barely audible now. Only a whisper. "Beautiful hair. Beautiful Mattie. So lovely and desirable. And very special. All this talk this afternoon about wanting to change yourself, wanting to be like someone else—don't do it, Mattie. Don't ever change. Always be like you are right now."

His hands were touching her as he talked, leaving a trail of fire on her skin as he caressed the line of her throat and moved down to her shoulders. She felt his arms enfold her and she couldn't resist when he pulled her close against him.

"You're trembling, Mattie. What is it?" he murmured.

She put up her hand to push him away and felt the bareness of his hard chest, the hairs that curled there against his open shirt. His arms were strong and firm, but he held her with a gentleness, as though her slim body were very precious to him. She looked up at him with wide dark eyes filled with fearful wonder, and then, as though not able to resist, instead of pushing him away, she let her fingertips trace the chiseled lines of his face, softened by the firelight, and let them linger to touch his lips.

"My God, Mattie." His voice was husky, choked with emotion. "Do you have any idea what you're doing to me? Do you know how often I have wanted to reach out and take you in my arms—wanted to hold you like this? How many times I told myself I had to leave the ranch—just ride out and not look back—while there was still time. Only I couldn't do it—I couldn't face not seeing you again—" His eyes were smoky with desire as he looked down at her.

"We shouldn't," she whispered. "This is so wrong. I shouldn't be feeling the way I do."

"Feeling how, Mattie? How do you feel? Tell me. I want to know." His lips were warm against the hollow of her throat, making her pulses race.

"Don't rightly know—I never felt like this before." The words were caught in a little sob as she swayed against him. Her eyes were like naked mirrors exposing her soul, leaving her feelings out in the open for him to see, letting him know of the turmoil going on inside. "I keep telling myself that I am married—I'm married and you are my husband's brother. It isn't right." There was anguish in her voice. "I shouldn't be feeling what I do right now. I just can't seem to help it, though."

"Mattie, Mattie, Mattie," he whispered, as though just saying her name gave him pleasure. "I've wanted to hold you like this for so long, wanted to feel your body warm in my arms, wanted to make love to you—" He pulled her closer against him until she could feel the pounding of his heart blending with the sound of her own.

"Morgan—stop—we can't—" she gasped, but her words were stilled with his mouth hard against her lips, bruising them. He felt her tense for a moment, then gradually relax, until she melted against him, returning his kisses with a fire that matched his own.

Breathlessly, she drew back a little, her eyes searching his face, watching the shadows from the firelight flickering across his skin, turning it to a coppery tan, outlining his rugged features against the darkness of the room. "I've never felt like this before," she whispered, frightened by the emotions that were carrying her away, destroying her reason. "I never knew it could be like this—sort of wonderful and yet hurting real bad, all at the same time."

"It's always been there, hasn't it?" he murmured. "From the first time I saw you, it's always been there between us—even when we didn't want to admit it, even when we were snapping at each other, trying to cover up how we felt."

The roll of thunder booming across the valley almost blotted out his words. Lightning flashed, burning the air around them. They clung together, not hearing the storm, aware only of the fires that were raging uncontrolled between them.

"Morgan, hold me, love me," she cried out, tears glistening on her pale cheeks.

"I've always loved you, Mattie. I've loved you even before

we met. You are the woman I've been searching for. There will
never be anyone else.'' He drew her closer against him as he
gently eased her back against the blankets.

She clung to him with a new urgency as her body came alive
to the touch of his fingers removing her clothing slowly, one
piece at a time, exploring in wonder each new secret her body
revealed to him.

Her fingers found the buttons of his shirt, and when he shrugged
his way free of it, her fingers hungrily traced the lines of his
shoulders and her lips trailed little kisses down across the hardness of his chest.

He discarded the rest of his clothing and they lay with their
bodies entwined on the blanket in front of the fire, touching,
tasting, exploring, murmuring phrases of love as they probed into
the depths of the new and consuming emotions they were discover-
ing together.

The flames in the fireplace bit into a large, dry chunk of wood,
sending sparks shooting high into the chimney, but it burned
unnoticed by the lovers, who were at that moment reaching new
heights of uncontrollable passions that drew them together as
one.

Inside the tiny cabin, the need for each other so long denied,
once unleashed, was as wild as the savage storm raging down
from the mountains and across the desert.

He felt her stir slightly where she lay at his side, her tousled
hair brushing against his face. ''Morgan?'' she whispered. ''Listen.
It's so still outside. The storm is over.''

He reached for her, needing to feel her body soft and warm in
his arms. He needed to know that what they had shared was real
and not a dream. For a moment she clung to him, wanting to
linger in the circle of his embrace, but knowing that once they
left the shelter of the cabin the wonder of his lovemaking would
have to end. It must be forgotten.

''Morgan, I love you so much.'' Her words were choked with
hurt as she reached out, needing to touch him one more time.

His arms were like steel bands, holding her close against him, as his mouth sought hers with a new fierceness, not able to let her go.

"No!" she cried out at last, managing to find the courage to push him away. "The storm is over. We have to leave."

"Not yet," he answered, trying to pull her back into his arms.

"We have to. Someone's going to see the car out on the road. They'll worry about us, wondering what happened. They'll start looking for us, wondering where we are." With a newfound determination, she slipped out of his reach, hurrying into her clothing, dry now but stiff and uncomfortable, with traces of mud.

Morgan began to dress, his mouth pressed into a hard, angry line. "What are we going to do now, Mattie? Nothing will ever be the same. We can't go on pretending."

"We don't have much choice, do we?" She tossed her head defiantly. "We met too late. I'm not free. I don't have the right to love you."

"How are you going to be able to deny what happened between us?" There was angry hurt in his eyes.

For a moment she almost relented, wanting with all of her heart to run back into the circle of his arms. "I love you, Morgan," she answered softly. "Guess I love you more than I have ever loved anyone or anything before in my life." Tears threatened the corners of her eyes, but she held her head high as she looked at him. "It won't ever happen again. I won't let it. It's all wrong, don't you see?"

"You can go back to Allen—after what we have just shared?"

"Yes. I have to. Damn it! You just don't understand, do you? What right do we have to carelessly destroy other lives because we couldn't control our emotions? It isn't just us—just you and me. What about Clive? Do you know what this would do to him? What about Allen? He loves me. He needs me."

"I need you too, Mattie."

"Not as much as Allen needs me. You're strong—Allen isn't. Allen spent over a year in a wheelchair—he is still crippled. I did it to him. I put him there."

"The hell you did! His drunkenness put him there!" Morgan was growing enraged, dark lights snapping in his eyes.

"Stop it. You don't understand. You won't even try." Mattie was becoming angry now, too, fighting to keep her reason while her heart wanted to give in and run back into his arms. "Besides, our love wouldn't last very long if we took our happiness by destroying other lives. That's what we would do, Morgan. We would destroy both of them and wind up hating each other for it."

Taking a quick breath, she tipped her head in new resolution and opened the door to the cabin. Not daring to look back, she set out with firm, determined steps across the fields to where the car was parked at the edge of the road.

It was a grim-faced, unsmiling Morgan who changed the tire, pumped air into the spare with the hand pump, silently cursing the mud, the rain, and life in general. He raised the hood, wiping off the wet cables and wires with a greasy rag. He didn't speak to her. His features were hard, angry, his eyes distant.

Needing to keep busy, Mattie checked the parcels stowed on the back seat. The bags were already limp and tearing apart from the heavy rains that had dripped moisture into the car. She settled herself up on the front seat, her head high, her back stiff, for the silent, tension-filled trip the rest of the way back to the ranch. She kept her eyes on the road ahead of them, not trusting herself to glance in his direction. The lighthearted joy of the shopping excursion was forgotten as she fought back the memories of the warmth of his arms, the thrill of his body claiming hers, the wonder of the forbidden love they had stolen during the storm.

CHAPTER TEN

"What? Did you say something?" Mattie glanced up from where she sat near the window, darning a hole in the toe of Clive's wool stocking. Betty was watching her, a puzzled look in her dark eyes.

"Sure I said something. I've been talking to you for the last ten minutes and you haven't heard a word." Betty dusted the flour from her hands onto the corner of her apron and reached up to push a stray wisp of hair back in place. "Is something wrong, honey? Is there anything I can do to help?"

"No." Mattie shook her head. "Nothing's wrong. Just daydreaming, I guess."

"You've been like that for a week, with your mind off somewhere else. Are you worrying about Allen?"

"No reason to worry about Allen," Mattie answered sharply. "He said the trip to Portland went real well. Guess things are turning out for him just like he wants." She inspected another stocking and slipped the opaque glass egg inside the foot, in preparation to mend another hole.

"I wondered if you and Morgan have been scrapping. You're always on edge when he's around, which isn't too often lately. Seems like he's been avoiding the house most of the time during the day and he's been going into town every night. He never used to spend so many nights in town."

"What Morgan does is his own business," Mattie snapped. "It's no concern of mine." She laid the stocking down and looked across at the other woman. "I'm sorry, Betty. What were you saying?"

Betty shrugged. "I was just going to ask if it would be all right if I was gone for a few hours this afternoon. Wes invited me to ride over to his new place with him and see how they're coming on the house."

Mattie sighed. "Honestly, I don't know what's the matter with me. I didn't mean to snap like that. Of course you can go. I hear they got the foundation done and are working on the walls and the roof now. It doesn't take long, when they all work together on it that way. I'd offer to go along with you so I could see it too, but I reckon I wouldn't be all that welcome, would I?"

"Of course you would be welcome—but I guess I'd like it better if you waited and went over with me some other time. If you really want to go today, it would be all right—I don't think Wes would mind—"

Mattie laughed at Betty's confusion. "I was only teasing. You go ahead. No need to hurry. There's not much to do this time of day."

Wes had the buggy waiting out in the yard for Betty, and they rode together down the lane to the road leading over to the forty acres where he had begun to build his house.

"Look," he pointed out as they turned up the drive. "I put up a mailbox this morning. Don't have a name on it yet, but I kind of like the looks of it standing there. Looks like someone lives here already, doesn't it?"

The house was shaping up. The walls were in place, the roof was on, and tar paper had been put down to keep out the rain until the shingles could be nailed down. Even the windows were already in, still wearing the stickers from the glass company.

"It's beautiful, Wes," Betty cried out, her dark eyes shining. "I had no idea it was so near done. It's a lovely little house!"

"Well, can't exactly call it that, I don't think. It hasn't been painted yet or nothing." Wes was embarrassed but proud over the way she was talking. "Come on. I'll help you down so we can go inside."

He stopped at the doorway. "You got to watch your footing here, Betty. I don't have the porch done yet. Wanted to get the rest of it done first, so everything wouldn't get so wet inside. Figured I could add the porch on later."

"Wouldn't need a big porch," she answered, looking around carefully. "Just large enough for a rocking chair—or two, maybe. Could even plant a few flowers along the edge there in the springtime." She turned and let her eyes wander out across the yard. "There's an awful nice place for a garden. It would get lots of sun, and still be close enough to the house to be easy to care for."

He pushed the door open, taking her arm, leading her inside. Their voices echoed in the emptiness of the rooms. "This here's the sitting room. Thought maybe later, when I get caught up, I could build a fireplace, but right at first I guess I'll have to depend on a big wood heating stove."

She stood looking around at the bare wood walls, still without paint or plaster. "It's beautiful, Wes. The room is so large— could be made real comfortable. A braided rug for the floor, some bright chintz for curtains and slipcovers on the furniture—"

"Well, here, come on back to the kitchen. 'Course, don't look too much different than the sitting room right now. I didn't go ahead and put in the cupboards and stuff. I thought maybe you would help me figure out where they should go. A woman knows about those things more than a man does."

Betty walked thoughtfully around the room, opened the back door, looked out, and then shut it again. "Two windows! Always nice to cook in a kitchen with lots of light."

"You like it then?" He waited nervously for her answer.

"It's a lovely house, Wes. Any woman would be proud to live here," she said softly.

"Gawd damn it, Betty! I never had trouble with words around women before! You just ask Morgan. Nobody ever accused me of being bashful in my whole life. Not until I met you. When you smile at me the way you're doing right now, my tongue gets all twisted up in a knot and my brain acts like it's addled."

She moved closer to him. "What is it you're trying to say, Wes?"

He turned away. "Reckon it wouldn't do no good, if I could say it. What would a young, pretty woman like you want with a ragged old cowhand like me anyway?"

She was standing real close now, looking up at him, love spilling out of her eyes. "You won't ever know if you don't ask, will you? Ask me, Wes."

"You mean you really would?" His face lit up like the sun coming out after a rain shower.

"I been trying to say yes, honey, but you got to ask me, first. You got to say it, Wes. I want a real proposal—all properlike."

He opened up his arms to her. His voice was gruff with embarrassment. "Betty, I been building this house for you. With every board I nailed in place, I was thinking what it would be like living here with you, having you here all of the time, knowing that you was mine."

There were tears of happiness glistening in her eyes. "Guess that's about the nicest proposal a girl ever had. I would be proud to be your wife, Wes."

He was looking down at her, bewildered. "I really heard right, didn't I? It's going to be you and me? You and me, Betty?"

"You and me, Wes." She didn't tell him about all the sewing she had been doing—the rows of tiny stitches on the pillowcases, the sheets, the towels. "Show me the rest of the house. Where are the bedrooms?"

He shook his head. "Come on. I got to get you back outside. Someone might be riding by and know we was in here with the doors all shut. Don't want nobody to get the wrong idea!"

She realized he was blushing and she laughed softly as she followed him back outside to the buggy. She rested her head happily against his shoulder as he turned the buggy down the lane toward the road. "I just wish everybody was as happy as we are right now," she sighed wistfully.

"Who you talking about, honey?"

"Oh, I don't know. Everybody. Nobody in particular. Things aren't right over at the big house. There's more going on there than meets the eye."

"Allen's not in trouble again, is he?"

"Who knows what Allen is up to?" she answered with a shrug. "He's so wrapped up in all that talk about being the next district attorney that he don't pay any attention to anything else. And Mattie is worrying over something. Don't know just what, but she sure isn't herself lately. And Morgan. You can usually always count on him being in a good mood if no one else is, but all he does is bolt his supper and take off for town, like he doesn't want to stay around the house any more than he has to."

Wes was quiet for a moment. "There's some things that a person can't do nothing about, Betty," he said finally. "When you go trying to figure things out and doing something about it, it's not called being helpful; it's plain old meddling." He put his arm around her, pulling her close against him. "It's best to let them try to work it out for themselves. Right now I feel as drunk as a hoot owl and I ain't had a nip. Let's us talk about ourselves. I got to know how you want the house finished up. The boys are going to help me, and I want to get it done before spring."

The war news was getting more serious all the time, Mattie thought anxiously. When the *Lusitania* had been sunk about a year ago, everyone had been up in arms, and that was all you heard folks talking about for a while. It was an English ship but it had sailed from the United States with almost nineteen hundred people on board—nearly two hundred of them Americans. It was a big ship—the biggest passenger ship in the world. The papers said it was like a palace inside, with everyone having a good time, not thinking about war, but it had been sunk off the coast of Ireland by a German submarine. Without any warning, it was hit with a torpedo, and within ten minutes the ocean liner went under, taking over twelve hundred men, women, and children with it. A lot of folks thought the United States ought to declare war right then and there.

Allen had looked at the whole thing a little differently. Of course, he had just gotten out of the hospital after the accident, and there wasn't much he could do about it anyway. He had had plenty to say, though. "President Wilson is right. We got no business going to war. They're always fighting about something

over there. Why should we step in and get in the middle of
something that doesn't concern us? If those Frenchies turn coward and want to surrender, let them do it. Leave them alone. Let
them fight their own battles.''

There must have been a lot of other people who felt like Allen,
because in the last election Woodrow Wilson had been reelected
for another term. The papers said he had gotten a promise from
the German government that they wouldn't sink any more passenger ships without giving a warning first. Folks had begun to relax
a little. After all, the East Coast was a long way away from the
West—and Europe, Germany and France, were even farther—
almost on the other side of the world. There were other things a
lot closer at hand to worry over.

But now the newspapers that Allen brought out from town were
carrying more serious headlines about the war—telling of passenger ships being fired on by German submarines, Allied ships
being sunk without warning. Men were enlisting without waiting
to be called. Mattie saw how Morgan kept reading the headlines,
his face closed and dark. She wondered how long it would be
before he thought he ought to sign up, too.

The possibility of the United States declaring war was all the
men could talk about whenever you went in town. Mattie might
have been even more concerned, but she had another problem to
worry over. She had checked the calendar hanging on the wall in
her room and then gone back, counting off the days carefully,
double-checking, hoping she had made a mistake. Her monthly
period was overdue. She was pregnant—she was sure of it—and
she knew exactly when it had happened.

They were in Allen's bedroom—the one downstairs that he
still used as a bedroom and a place to work on his papers at home
in privacy, even though the stairway was no problem for him
anymore. It had been some time since Mattie had pushed him in
the wheelchair. Though his limp was noticeable, especially when
he was tired, he walked most of the time with just one cane.

"You're not listening, Mattie."

She turned from where she had been standing at the window,
looking out into the night. "I'm sorry. What did you say?"

"I was trying to tell you about the plans for the campaign, but you're not listening. What you got on your mind that's so damned important you can't hear what I'm saying?"

"Allen—I think I'm pregnant." She hadn't meant to tell him—not yet—but the words just tumbled out.

He took the news better than she had figured he might. In fact, he didn't question her at all. He just seemed real pleased. "It's the best thing that could happen right now!" he told her with real enthusiasm. "By the time the elections are held for the district attorney, I'll have a wife *and* a kid. A real family man! Just what the voters want!"

Mattie looked across the room at him. "I was afraid it might complicate things right now."

"You just better hope the kid looks like you, Mattie," he said with a grin. "Don't want no redheaded boy with freckles, looking like one of the ranch hands."

"That's a rotten thing to say!" she snapped back angrily.

"You told anybody else yet?" he asked.

"No. Isn't quite time enough to go around broadcasting it to everybody. Wouldn't be proper. I thought I would wait a little."

"Well, just see that the old man knows right away, huh? Goin' to tickle the hell out of him." He leaned back in the chair, a smug smile on his face. "Yep. The old man is going to be real proud about your bit of news, Mattie. Might just change a lot of things around here."

"Change things? How?"

"For Christ's sake, Mattie, use your head. Morgan has always been number one son. This might change all of that. I'm going to be the next district attorney. I'm married—I'm a family man—I'm going to have a son. Morgan hasn't shown any signs of getting married or settling down. Looks like that will just about move me up into number one place with the old man. My son will be next in line. Hey, Mattie—maybe we ought to name him Clive. What do you think?"

"I think we ought to wait until we see if it's a boy. A little girl named Clive would be kind of unusual."

Allen took a lot of pleasure in boasting to Morgan about Mattie's news. He went out of his way to find him, to be the one to tell him. Maybe Mattie was reluctant to talk about it yet, thinking things like babies were a private matter until they were more obvious, but he wanted Morgan to know.

"Being a family man is important nowadays. Shows you're settled, reliable—gives you more respect in the community. The old man can rest easier knowing Mattie's carrying an heir to the Henderson ranch. It's like I told you, Morgan, when you first got here. Mattie's a mighty fine woman—but she's taken. She belongs to me. Won't do you no good hanging around, speculating on your chances with her."

Morgan wanted to reach out, to smash the sarcastic smirk on Allen's face. Instead, he offered his congratulations and turned away, going out toward the corrals. His thoughts went back to that day when he and Mattie had been caught in the unexpected storm. He was filled with doubts—a lot of doubts and unanswered questions. He remembered the things they had said there in the cabin to each other—the way she had come into his arms, her eyes full of the wonder of the love they had found together. He wondered if in her guilt over what had happened she had gone home to Allen's bed more determined than ever to make the marriage work. He wanted to go to her, talk to her, ask her questions, reach out and hold her—God, how he wanted to hold her! Somehow, in his heart, he felt the child was his, and he wanted to take her in his arms and make her admit the truth. And if he did—what then? Watch her crumble with hurt and shame? What about the others who were involved? The others, who would also feel the hurt? Instead, he put on his hat and coat and headed toward town.

Morgan did a lot of thinking and a lot of heavy drinking that evening, but the liquor had little effect on him. By the time he started out for home, he had reached a decision.

The light was still on in the study when he came in the door. The rest of the house was quiet, but he knew the old man was still up. He went across the hallway and pushed the door open.

"Okay if I come in?"

Clive glanced up and nodded when he saw Morgan standing in the doorway. He was sitting in the big old chair near the fire, a book open on his lap. He studied the serious look on Morgan's face but made no comment other than to wave his hand toward the chair on the other side of the fire.

"Been doing a lot of thinking, Pa. President Wilson may be doing all he can, trying to keep the country out of war, but I think everyone knows it's just a matter of time now before we are in it. He isn't going to have much choice, the way the Germans are firing on our ships."

"You trying to tell me you're leaving—going to enlist?"

"That's about the size of it, I guess."

It was awhile before Clive answered, staring thoughtfully into the fire as though the right words were hard to find. "Hate to see you go—but a man has got to do what he thinks is right."

Morgan nodded. "Thanks, Pa. I had hoped you would understand. We got things in pretty good shape around here. Wes is a damned good man to have as foreman. Now that he's getting married, you can be pretty sure he'll be staying around."

"When you planning on leaving?"

"In the morning."

The old man's brows raised in startled surprise. "Got to be that soon?"

"Long as I got my mind made up, there's no reason in hanging around."

Clive stood up and held out his hand. "Take care of yourself, son. We want you back home again when all of this is over." His eyes were moist and his voice was husky with emotion.

"Thanks, Pa. For not asking a lot of questions. Thanks for not saying too much. For understanding."

The old man nodded without answering, but when he was alone again, his mind began to worry away at thoughts that left him shaken. He remembered little things, things that he had seen or heard—things that didn't seem important until they were all added up together. Like the way the sparks seemed to jump back and forth whenever Mattie and Morgan were in the same room—the way Morgan's eyes followed her when he thought she wasn't looking. He remembered the day he had insisted that Morgan drive Mattie into town—the day they had been caught in that storm and were so late getting home. Mattie had been like a thundercloud after that, short-tempered and distant, while Mor-

gan took to going into town every night, staying out of her way
as much as possible. They were trying to fight it, he guessed, but
when two people were drawn to each other like those two were,
it was a mighty hard battle. What a pair those two would have
made! It just made his blood run hot thinking about it.

But Morgan had gotten there too late. She was Allen's wife.
Allen was a damned fool, going off and leaving her as much as
he did. Now Mattie was pregnant—and Morgan had decided to
enlist, going off to war. Well, at that, maybe it was the best
thing. If he stayed around much longer there would be really big
trouble, because Morgan wasn't the kind of man to sneak around
about anything. Yes, there'd be real trouble, right enough. The
old man leaned back in his chair with a sigh, his shoulders
slumping tiredly.

Morgan went past Allen's closed bedroom door and on up the
darkened stairway to his lonely room at the end of the hall. I'm
doing the right thing, he thought to himself. They need men bad
right now. Single men, without families to take care of. I have to
go. I couldn't live with myself if I didn't.

He glanced toward Mattie's door before he went into his room.
I can't go on living so close to Mattie, he thought, and not let my
feelings come out into the open where they would make things
rougher for her than they are already. She's Allen's wife, and
she's determined to make the marriage work. That's the kind of
woman she is. And now there's a baby to consider. He lit a
cigarette and stood at the window, staring out into the night. The
thought of leaving her was tearing him up inside, but he couldn't
stay. He couldn't listen to Allen's sarcasm and slurred insults
directed toward Mattie without forgetting himself and bringing
the issue out into the open. Maybe if he wasn't there, life would
get better for her.

Mattie stood in the hallway the next morning, watching him as
he came down the stairs carrying his pack over his shoulder. Her
face was a stormcloud, her eyes dark, full of anger.

"So, it's true. You really are leaving, aren't you? You're
running out again. Well, go ahead and go. Nobody around here
gives a damn anyway."

Morgan set his pack down on the floor. When he spoke, his voice was soft, carefully hiding any emotion. "I only told the old man that I would stay until after the fall work was done. You know that. I wound up staying on through the winter, and here it is, damn near spring. I can't stay any longer, Mattie. We both know why. It would only make matters worse." She looked so pretty standing there with narrow shafts of early morning sunlight coming in through the window and tangling themselves in her hair. He wanted to reach out and catch her in his arms and kiss all of the anger out of her stormy eyes.

"What's going to happen if your father gets sick or something? What if he needs you to help him?" she asked. "You're going to be God only knows where, clear across an ocean."

"Be honest, Mattie. That old man is going to be calling the shots around here and running things just like always for a lot of years yet. I helped him out when he needed it, but I can pack my saddlebags and come and go as I damn well please. There is nothing to tie me here—or is there?" His voice was gentle, his eyes wanting to say more than his words were telling. If she only knew how it was killing him to leave her. But there was no way to let her know without saying things they both knew couldn't be said. "Besides, Allen is here. He's able to walk with that cane of his, and that will make a difference. He's all fired up on that political campaign of his, but he's here. Maybe things will work out for the two of you—for everybody."

The very nearness of him was almost more than she could bear. She wanted to run to him, to cry out that if he was leaving to take her with him. She wanted to tell him that she had been wrong about staying with Allen—she didn't want to go on living without his love. Instead, she tossed her head, throwing her angry words at him. "That's right! Allen is here!" Her voice echoed in the stillness of the hallway, slicing into him, wanting to hurt him as bad as she was hurting inside. "We all thought you were tough. Made of the same fiber as the old man. But we were wrong, weren't we? Everybody always said Allen was weak, Allen couldn't stand up to the old man. Allen ain't the man his brother is. Well, looks like folks were all wrong, weren't they? You are a coward, Morgan Henderson," she hissed. "You hear me? You're a coward. Soon as life don't turn out the way you think it ought to, you just pack up your bags and ride out, thinking it's easier to just clear out instead of facing things. Well, Allen stayed last time you took off and he's staying now. Allen is here when he's needed. Allen doesn't run away."

"No. He doesn't run away. You're right, Mattie. He just hides. In a bottle." His voice was deadly low and Mattie could feel the hard anger lying just under the surface. She knew she had hurt him and she wanted to cry out that she was sorry, she hadn't meant the hateful things she'd said. It was only because she loved him so much. She couldn't stand to see him leave, and she couldn't beg him to stay. She reached out and lashed at him, needing to fight back somehow.

He caught her wrist, his fingers biting into her flesh, pulling her roughly against him. She stared up at him while he studied her face, as though committing every line and feature to memory. "I'm leaving my horse, my gear, all of my things here," he said, his voice low. "Wes is waiting outside. He's taking me in to where I can make connections for the stage to Portland." He bent his head and her heart beat wildly as she raised her face for his kiss. His hard mouth bruised her lips, and she clung to him in her desperation.

His voice was husky now, the words catching in his throat. "Take care, Mattie. Take care of yourself—and the baby." He let her go and turned quickly away.

"Morgan—don't go. Don't leave. I need you—I love you . . ." But he never heard her anguished plea because the words never reached her lips as she watched him go out the door and close it softly behind him.

CHAPTER ELEVEN

A week later, Morgan left from Portland along with about fifty other men on a train bound for the eastern part of the country. The newspapers from Portland carried the story on the front page, along with several large pictures of the group gathered at the station. Allen brought the newspapers out from town with him when he brought the mail, tossing them carelessly on the table in the hall.

Later, when she was alone, Mattie spread the papers out in front of her, reading the articles and studying the pictures, trying to find the one face she sought in the crowd. Some were like Morgan, with the hard, leathered look of the rancher who had lived his life in the open. There were several who seemed hardly old enough to shave, a boisterous swagger to their walk. Some wore sheepskin coats and wide-brimmed hats. Others wore dark suits, white shirts, and a look of the city. It was a collection of the best and the worst the West had to offer, answering their country's need for volunteers.

Most of the men were headed to a basic training camp for the infantry. Two others had the same destination as Morgan. They were going to the newly formed Aero Division of the army. Mattie found his name in the article that listed all of the men leaving that day, but she wasn't able to pick his face out from the group in the pictures. She studied the clippings for a long moment and then cut them from the paper to file away in Clive's study.

They didn't hear from Morgan for several months, though Mattie anxiously watched for the mail and saw the dark, distant look on Clive's face when no letters arrived.

Betty glanced up from where she was putting the crimped edges on several apple pies that were destined for the evening dinner table. "Sounds like a car coming up the lane. Were you expecting Allen home early?"

Mattie put the white shirt she had just finished ironing across the back of a chair and carried the heavy flatiron over to the stove for reheating. "Yes. He's making a speech tonight in Bend. He said he would be home early because he wanted to change his clothing and rest a bit." She paused at the window and watched Allen step from the car and walk toward the house. One hand was hooked in the neckline of his jacket tossed carelessly over his shoulder. The other hand held the cane. The wind lightly ruffled his hair and she saw the confident way he carried himself. Allen seemed to thrive on the long hours and tension, the building excitement of campaigning.

"Are you going with him?"

Mattie put her hands at the small of her back and stretched her tired muscles. She had been standing at the ironing board most of the morning, and she was feeling the strain of it. Her thickening waist was putting an added burden on her slim back and she tired easily. "Not tonight. I don't think I could face a long evening on those hard wooden chairs. Not tonight. Not on ironing day."

"Good. I'm glad you're staying home," Betty retorted sharply. "You really shouldn't travel these rough roads with him as much as you're doing. You're pushing yourself too much, Mattie. It isn't good for you—isn't good for the baby."

Mattie brushed back a stray wisp of hair from a face that was too thin, too pale, and smiled across at the other woman. "You worry too much about me. I'm fine. Honest. Besides, it's important to Allen that I'm there with him. It gives him confidence, he says. Some politicians pass out cigars and kiss babies to win the popular vote. Allen says that he prefers to have his wife with him. A wife who is obviously in the family way gives a steadying image to a candidate," she added, letting her hands rest momentarily on the bulge below her waistline. "And I am getting pretty obvious, aren't I?" She felt movement, so slight that it could hardly be recognized as more than a twinge of a muscle, and smiled warmly. "There's no need to worry, Betty. We both are fine."

"Mattie! I'm home!" Allen's voice carried out to them from the hallway.

Mattie picked up the shirt and hurried out to where Allen was already going toward his bedroom. "Will you be home long enough for supper or will you be eating in town?"

"I'm having dinner with Jeffries and Williams. We have to go over some material before the meeting." He went across to the desk and poured a drink from a bottle sitting there. Mattie saw the way he gulped the amber liquid as though it was something he badly needed. "By the way, I may be in Burns for the next few days, Mattie. Are my clothes ready, so you can pack for me?"

"Oh, Allen!" Disappointment showed plainly on her face. "You won't be gone Saturday, will you? Saturday is the twentieth of June. You know that's the day of the wedding."

He began spreading papers out across the desk as he loosened his tie and pulled out the chair. "What do you think is more important?" A frown darkened his face. "The elections won't wait for me to be done socializing. I'm working round the clock now and you know it. I'll try to make it, but if I can't, I can't. I think the Hendersons have done enough already for Wes, without being obligated to attend his wedding. How many hired hands get forty acres for a wedding present? I still can't believe it. The old man is so damned proud of this ranch and so tightfisted when it comes to money, and yet he split off that forty and signed it over to Wes. I tried to tell him it was a fool thing to do, but he wouldn't listen."

"Wes isn't exactly just a 'hired hand,' " Mattie answered tartly. "He has been here for a long time. He's worked hard. The old man feels as though he's almost part of the family. He depends on him. He likes him."

"And he has been paid well for whatever work he did, without giving him that forty as a bonus." Allen picked up the glass, taking a quick drink and waiting for the bite of the alcohol to release the tension in his tight nerves.

Mattie began laying out the suit Allen would be wearing that evening. "How much longer do you think you can keep up this pace? You haven't taken any time off to just relax for weeks. Can't you forget the trip to Burns and spend a few days at the ranch relaxing this weekend?"

"Not until the elections are over," he snapped. "I just need a drink or two to unwind my nerves and I'll be fine. A drink or two and some quiet. The meeting this evening is important."

Mattie shrugged her shoulders in resignation. "Was there any mail?"

"I left it on the table in the hall, along with the newspapers. Just lay out my clothes, will you? And then leave me alone so I can go over these briefs."

He was sitting at the desk, the paperwork in front of him, a drink at his elbow, so engrossed in what he was reading that he hardly noticed when she left the room.

Mattie flipped through the envelopes. Most of them were letters for Clive. Nothing for her. On the bottom of the stack were two picture postcards. Without turning them over, she knew they were from Morgan. One was a picture of Chicago; the other was of the skyline of New York.

Her hands were trembling as she studied the bold, firm writing. There were only a few lines on each card. They'd been written several weeks apart. "Dear Dad. I am well," it said on the card from Chicago. "I've finished the training. I have my wings." Damn him for hating to write letters. She tried to picture him sitting at a table, the empty paper in front of him, striving to put his thoughts into words—his impatience, his frustrations. The air training must have been strenuous, even frightening at times. The Aero Division to the Army was new, experimental. There weren't enough planes, enough pilots. The casualties were high even before they completed their training, long before they were sent into combat. She knew. She had read every editorial, every news item, every story she could find. She didn't want to read it in a newspaper or magazine. She wanted to hear about it from him.

The message on the back of the New York skyline card was equally short. He was leaving for England. Mattie felt a coldness close in around her and her hand went unconsciously to rest against her swollen abdomen. England. He was so far away. Worlds away from the ranch, from her.

She laid the cards and letters where Clive would find them and went on into the sitting room, carrying the newspapers with her. She sat on the sofa and scanned the headlines, the ironing temporarily forgotten.

There was a picture on the front page of a troop ship ready to leave New York harbor. The decks were lined with men in uniform, watching the tall buildings slip away into the fog as the brass bands played "Over There" while a hysterical crowd of onlookers shouted cheers and waved handkerchiefs. The war news filled the front page, with news of the local political rivalry during the campaign pushed into the background, on page two.

"Dear God," she prayed silently. "Let his ship reach England safely. Don't let anything happen to him."

Wes and Betty were married at eleven o'clock in the morning on Saturday at the small church at the crossroads on the outside of town. Monty stood up with Wes as his best man. There had been some early rain showers that cleansed the air, making everything smell sweet and pure. The sun came out then, sending warm, colorful rays streaming through the colored glass of the church windows, touching the bride and groom with sunlight as they stood before the altar.

Wes looked embarrassed and uncomfortable in a new suit purchased just for the wedding. Betty smiled shyly, her face glowing with happiness, as an uncle from Warm Springs took her hand from his arm and placed it in Wes's hand. She was lovely in a swirl of white batiste, her blue-black hair like jet against the white of the gown.

Because of her advanced pregnancy, Mattie stayed in the background, sitting beside Clive during the ceremony. Tears threatened the corners of her eyes as she watched the proud look on Wes's face as he kissed his new bride and saw the love for him radiating from Betty.

After the wedding, there was a huge reception at the ranch.
Folks came from miles around, eager to join in the celebrating.
The women brought hot dishes, cakes, and pies. The men brought
bottles, tucked out of sight in the wagons, lest their wives object.
The yard was crowded with wagons, the teams unhitched and
tied in the shade, and a few cars.

The house and the barn spilled over with ranchers, women
anxious to visit, children of all ages playing noisy games, and
cowhands ready to join in the fun.

A group of musicians warmed up the fiddles on a platform of
hay bales. Everyone danced, including the children. As the evening wore on, the smaller ones were put to sleep on coats along
the sidelines, while grandmothers knitted and watched over them.

Allen didn't make it back in time for the wedding ceremony,
but he was there for the barn dance that followed. From time to
time she caught a glimpse of him talking with different groups of
men, a drink in his hand, a smile on his face. She saw the way
the young women watched him, flirting as they talked, and the
way he responded, enjoying the attention. He's the best-looking
man here, she thought to herself. Even with the cane—it makes
him look dashing. It's no wonder the women admire him.

Mattie tapped her toes restlessly to the music. She hated sitting
on the sidelines, away from all of the fun, but her figure was too
bundlesome now for it to be proper for her to consider a slow
waltz. As she watched, she saw Clive circle the floor with a
young matron in his arms, laughing at something she had said.
She watched his tall figure, his wide shoulders, the thick, wavy
iron-gray hair, and she smiled with pride. He carried himself
with such dignity, and there was something so strong, so virile,
almost baronial about him.

"Mattie?"

She looked up to see Allen standing beside her. "Yes?"

"Aren't you getting tired? Shouldn't you go inside and lay
down? It's been a long day for you."

"But the guests—" she protested.

"They'll understand." He took her hand and gently helped her
to her feet. "I'll walk in with you. I want to be sure you're all
right."

"Of course I'm all right," she snapped impatiently, not wanting to leave the merrymaking but knowing it was the right thing to do. She turned for one last look around the barn. Betty was dancing with a ranch hand from over near Sisters, her face flushed and laughing. Much later, when they could finally slip away, Wes would take her to the house he had built on the forty down the road, but for now all of the men were claiming their right to kiss the bride and dance with her. Wes was getting a little unsteady on his feet as toast after toast was drunk by the merrymakers.

With a reluctant sigh, she turned and let Allen guide her toward the door, away from the noise and the fun.

When Allen closed the door to her bedroom, the cool darkness reached out to her and she realized finally that she was very tired.

"We haven't had a chance to talk since you got back this afternoon. How did the meetings go in Burns?" she asked as she started to unbutton her dress.

"It's in the bag, Mattie. The election is as good as won." He smiled across at her confidently. "Baby, we got it made." He watched as she slipped the flannel gown down over her head and reached for the hairbrush. "Mattie, I want to tell you how much it means to me, the way you've supported me through all of this." His voice was low, filled with seriousness. "I couldn't have done it without you there behind me, believing in me. You don't know how much I need you."

Mattie slipped between the cool sheets, propping a pillow behind her head. "Then you have what you've been trying so hard to win, don't you? You will be the next district attorney?"

"Can't lose. But that isn't where it will end, Mattie. That's only the first step. It's just a beginning. Attorney general. I want to be the next attorney general for the state. I can do it, if I know you are with me. And from there—who knows?"

Mattie lay back against the pillows in the darkness after Allen had left to go back to the barn. The window was open to the evening breeze and she could hear the sound of the fiddles, laughter, once in a while a shout. The child moved within her womb and she laid her hands across her middle, drawing warmth and comfort from the impatient signs of life.

In three more months the child would be born and Allen would be congratulated. She alone would know the true parentage of the babe, and it was a secret she intended to keep. Sometimes all honesty could do was hurt. Clive Henderson, a proud and honorable man, would feel the shame if she were to tell. Allen, for all of his swaggering and boisterousness, was not strong enough to handle the truth. And Morgan. If he knew the child was his, he would stop at nothing to claim it openly, to carry her and the baby away with him to someplace new. And how she wanted to go! Her very soul cried out to be with the man she loved.

A tear slipped from her eyes and fell on the pillow in the darkness. What good was a happiness that could only be won by destroying others? Clive would grow cold and hard and look at her with hate in his eyes. Allen had a whole career ahead of him. He wasn't strong and he needed her. He depended on her. If she left him, she would ruin his career. She had nearly destroyed his life once—with the accident. She couldn't do it again.

And Morgan. Was his love for her strong enough to survive all that he would lose by winning her? No. She couldn't take the chance. The secret would remain hers alone, and she would protect those she loved. She would be a good wife to Allen. She would try hard to make their marriage sound, and maybe, in time, she would find a way to stop the longing just the sound of Morgan's name could bring.

As she drifted off to sleep, her last thought was of Morgan, and the day of the storm.

The summer and the early fall that followed were eventful, and Clive sat in the study one evening late in September trying to put it all down on paper in a letter to Morgan. He hated to write letters almost as much as his son did, but there were things Morgan would want to know.

Mattie had had a boy last night—a fine, healthy seven-pound boy with a lusty set of lungs that could be heard in the next county when he wanted attention. He was a real Henderson, sturdy and handsome. Mattie had named the baby Clive. Pride showed plainly between the lines, as the old man wrote. Allen was the new district attorney. That group of friends of his was in office.

The spring crop of calves was better than expected. The market prices were high and going up because the Americans were now in the war. Wes and Betty were married, living in the house that Wes had built on that forty he had given them for a wedding present.

He had stopped at the bar the last time he was in Bend and seen Minnie. She was fine. She had a postcard from Morgan tacked up on the wall.

It wasn't until March that an answer from England came back to Clive's letter. Morgan said there were constant rumors that they were to be sent to France before long. He was flying DeHavilands. The D.H.4. England wasn't much like the country around the ranch. It was cold and damp most of the time. He sent a photograph of himself in his uniform and a picture of his squadron—the 50th Aero Squadron.

Mattie bought a small picture frame in town. It was an oval of highly polished rosewood with a curved glass. She was standing in the study, fitting the picture into place when the men walked in and found her.

"Thought you might like to have it for your desk," she explained. "I put the one of Morgan's squadron on the wall. He'll probably want it someday, when all of this is over." She stood looking down at the stranger in uniform. It was Morgan, but he looked so unfamiliar. Tall, thinner than she remembered in the straight-fitting jacket, the wide belt, the wings over his breast pocket, the pants tucked inside the calf-high boots. "He looks so different—so serious."

"War is serious business, Mattie," Clive answered softly. "It isn't all victory speeches and brass bands playing 'Johnny, Get Your Gun.' Those men are risking their lives."

"Risking their lives, all right," Allen snorted. "The fly-boys are the glory seekers. Dressing up like doormen at a fancy hotel, risking their damned necks to fly a muslin kite and thinking that makes them heroes. They parade around in silk scarves, carrying swagger sticks, and the girls go crazy. What about the men on the ground, wading ass deep in mud, doing the real fighting? They're the real soldiers—the heroes.''

"Allen!" Mattie wanted to stop him from saying more. Why did he always have to lash out this way, saying such hurting things, whenever Morgan's name was mentioned.

The old man's face grew cold, his eyes hard. "How come you're home like this in the middle of the day, Allen? Thought you had so much to do in town.''

"Had some briefs I had to work on here at the house. By the way, now is as good a time as any. I want to talk to you about the remodeling on this old house. I thought it was going to get started before now.''

"We will. Soon as I can spare the men.''

Allen raised his eyebrows in surprise. "You're not expecting those cowhands to do the work, are you? For Christ's sake, what do they know about carpentry? You want the place to look halfway decent when it gets done, don't you?''

"Just what exactly do you have in mind?" Clive asked, his voice skeptical.

"We've got to start with the bunkhouse first. Once we get a kitchen built on so they can do the cooking out there, we can start doing something to the house. Damned place ain't fit to invite any friends out here the way it is.''

"The place has been all right so far,'' Clive answered coldly. "Ain't never been ashamed of it in front of my neighbors.''

"Look—'' Allen faltered. "I know a couple of men—damned good carpenters, both of them. I kind of owe them a favor or two, and they're out of work. I told them to come out here in the morning. They might as well get started on it.''

"Just what remodeling you got in mind?" Clive's voice had a razor-sharp edge. "As long as I'm paying the bills, I'm the one who says who goes to work and who doesn't here on the ranch.''

"Now, don't start getting your back up already,'' Allen answered softly. "Just the bunkhouse at first. The ranch is growing. The men need more space. They need a cook—a place to eat—so we can have the dining room for just the family. We can invite people out here without the table being filled with the ranch hands.'' He looked over at Mattie, appealing to her for help, but she turned away. "We need more room in the house, too. An extra bedroom or two. Young Clive is almost six months old. He needs a room of his own. The family is getting bigger." He gave the old man a triumphant look. "Evidently Mattie hasn't told you yet that she thinks she's pregnant again. She's carrying another kid."

He watched the look of surprise on the old man's face, feeling satisfied that he had won. If the remodeling was for Mattie's sake, Clive wouldn't carry the argument any further. One way or another, Allen wanted the house fixed up. He had a reputation to keep up, an image to build. He needed a place to invite his friends. It paid to look prosperous.

CHAPTER TWELVE

Mattie took a last critical look in the mirror, wanting everything to be just right. She was wearing a soft blue wool dress with white lace at the collar and around the cuffs. She had seen the dress in the dry goods store a while ago, but she hadn't wanted to spend the money on it right then. Besides, she would have had to use the money intended for supplies to do it, and it didn't seem right to use that money for something so frivolous. But she hadn't been able to forget the dress and in a reckless moment she'd bought it on her last trip into town. She'd even bought the blue wool shawl to go with it, loving the soft feel of it when she draped it across her shoulders. It was the finest dress she had ever owned and she felt really proud of the way it looked as she stood in front of the mirror.

It was the first time in quite a while that Mattie had worn a pretty dress-up dress—a dress that fit right, following the curves of her slender body, with a belt at the waistline. With one pregnancy following the other so close, there hadn't been much chance for pretty dresses. Maternity clothes all looked the same. God, how she hated those dresses—all cut with a frill of some kind at the neckline to distract attention from the middle, where there was always a drawstring around the waist. Everybody could tell what kind of a dress it was but they looked the other way, pretending not to notice, and then acting surprised, as though babies just "happened."

There had been times when she had resented the life that continued to grow within her, pushing her out of proportion, slowing her steps, making her ill in the mornings, demanding her attention, taking over her body, leaving her without any identity of her own beyond the role she played at the ranch. It had nothing to do with wanting children and loving them. She was a good mother. But she still wanted to be herself.

Then, when the boys were both here and her body was again her own, there were a whole new batch of problems she had to learn to cope with. They were healthy children and they energetically cried out their demands for her attention, wanting to be fed, to be played with, and their cries turned to gurgles of delight when she stopped whatever she was doing and swooped them up in the air in some silly game that ended with kisses on their plump, rosy cheeks.

One of the biggest problems came in trying to keep them quiet when Allen was home. He insisted he couldn't concentrate on his papers with their noise, their sticky fingers leaving prints on his pants leg, their demands coming ahead of his while he waited until they were fed, changed, put to bed. He couldn't stand it when he reached in the closet for a fresh shirt and it wasn't there, but there was always a stack of diapers getting boiled in a kettle on the stove and being hung out on the line. Just seemed like she was running all the time and couldn't get caught up.

Then, too, there was the remodeling being done on the house. Of course, it was a whole lot nicer now that it was almost done, but it just seemed like every place she turned for the past year, there were carpenters underfoot.

It was no wonder she hadn't taken the time to primp a little, to spend extra time on her hair, to buy a new dress. She had felt lucky to just have the energy to get through the day and keep up with all of the things waiting to get done. She kept neat and clean, of course, but there just wasn't time left over for putting her hair up in curls or wearing bows and ribbons.

Today was going to be different because she had made up her mind to make it that way. She knew she probably should have done it sooner. It was time she looked more like a lady. It was her fault Allen got so upset with her sometimes, telling her she wasn't anything but a squatter's daughter and wouldn't ever change.

Well, she would show him she could change if she set her mind to it. She could talk about something else besides babies and cooking and cattle. She had been watching her language really closely and hardly ever swore anymore. And today she was going to try extra hard. Today she was going to dress up like a lady and she was going to town. She was going to stop in and see Allen at his law office. She smiled to herself in pleasure at the thought. Allen was going to be so surprised!

Morgan used to tease her about her hair—said she looked like a little girl playing at grownup when she wore it down her back and tied with a ribbon. Well, she'd been working on her hair, too. She'd seen in the newspapers the way some of the women in the big cities were getting their hair cut real short now, but she hadn't wanted to go that far. She couldn't quite bring herself to cut it off, but she studied a picture of a woman whose hair was pulled back and twisted into an elegant figure eight. It took quite a while, but she finally got it looped just right and pinned into place. The effect was flattering, giving her a touch of reserved dignity.

Betty was taking care of the boys for her today. Now that the bunkhouse had a kitchen built on, and there was a camp cook who did everything except the baking, Betty had more time. Jonathan was sleeping in his crib, one thumb contentedly in his tiny rosebud mouth. She had named him Jonathan, after her own father, even though she hadn't seen him since that night he disappeared, leaving her behind. Young Clive was downstairs, where Betty could keep an eye on him while he played with a stack of jar rings and pie tins. Now that he was beginning to learn to walk, he was a handful to keep track of and needed constant attention.

Mattie waited until she knew that Clive and the other men had left the house. She didn't want them to see her when she went out to get into the car. She felt so self-conscious with her new appearance. She didn't want any of them to tease her. On the drive into town, she kept the windows rolled up even though it was warm. She didn't want the wind messing up all of the careful fixing she had done.

As she walked down the board sidewalk, she caught her reflection in one of the store windows and she couldn't help but straighten up a little and tuck in her tummy, feeling good inside about the way she looked. Allen was sure going to be surprised!

Now that Allen was talking about running for attorney general, maybe even going to the capital in Salem to live, she had to try harder. She wasn't too happy about the idea of moving to Salem. She didn't want to live in a city. She didn't want to leave Clive all alone here, without any family. She didn't want to leave the ranch. But what had to be done had to be done. If Allen was so all-fired determined to be the attorney general and live in a city, then she was going to have to learn city ways. Might take a while, but she could do it.

The door to the back room of Allen's office was standing ajar and she could hear voices. At least he was in. He used the front office where she was standing as sort of a waiting room. The back room was where he did most of his work, away from the noise of the street. She adjusted her shawl around her shoulders and gave her hair a reassuring pat. She wanted to look just right, wanted Allen to look surprised when he first saw her, and then smile at her the way he used to do when he was courting. Maybe he would ask her to go to lunch with him. They hadn't done that in years—it would be a special occasion.

She paused at the door, her hand on the knob. She could hear the voices inside. She heard a woman's voice. Must be a woman client, needing help with some papers. Maybe it was one of the women from a neighboring ranch, someone she knew. She raised her hand and tapped lightly on the door, half wishing she hadn't come right now, hoping she wasn't interrupting, hoping he would be pleased to see her.

She heard him call out for her to enter. Too late now to turn back. She had to go in.

Allen was sitting at his desk and there were papers spread out all over in front of him. Across from the desk sat one of the fanciest-dressed ladies Mattie had ever seen. She couldn't be from around these parts anywhere. She didn't look as though she came from the West—even a Western city. You could see immediately that she had never done any work out-of-doors because her skin was white as milk and just as creamy.

Mattie couldn't help staring at the woman's dress. She had never seen anything like it, even in pictures from the catalog. It was sort of dark green, and it shimmered and clung in all of the right places even though it didn't have a belt at the waistline at all. It was shorter than the dresses women in Bend wore. The woman sat with her long, slender legs crossed at the knee and Mattie could see silk stockings and shoes with high spike heels and long pointed toes. She didn't wear a shawl. Instead she wore a fur stole carelessly across her shoulders and had a silly little hat trimmed in the same fur perched at an angle over her bobbed hair.

Suddenly Mattie wished she weren't standing there, but was down the street somewhere doing her shopping. The dress she had been so proud of felt uncomfortable and too tight. The new shoes were beginning to pinch. Her hair was fixed so old-fashioned. Everything was wrong.

Allen stood up and came around the desk to meet her. "Mattie. This is a surprise! What are you doing in town? I didn't know you were coming in today." He looked surprised all right, but not in the way she had intended.

"I—we needed some things from the store." She lifted her chin and straightened her back defiantly. "I left the boys with Betty. I thought we could have lunch together, if you weren't too busy."

He was looking at her dress. Lord, please don't let him say anything—not now, not in front of this other woman.

"Mattie—I'm sorry. I already have plans for lunch. It's business. Irene—Miss Bancroft—is in town from Chicago to settle an estate. She's inherited the old Bancroft Hotel. You knew old Bancroft died. She's his only heir."

Yes, Mattie knew about Bancroft dying and leaving the hotel to someone from the East. Allen had mentioned it a few nights ago, saying the heir wanted nothing to do with the hotel, and Allen was handling the paperwork so it could be sold. He hadn't mentioned that the heir was a woman. An attractive, expensively dressed woman, who was obviously bored with the small Western town and what it had to offer.

"I'm sorry, but I had already asked Miss Bancroft to lunch," Allen went on. "At the hotel dining room, of course, so we can look over their books while we're eating."

Mattie turned away, trying to hide the disappointment in her eyes. "It's fine, Allen. It doesn't matter. It was just a fool idea anyway." The other woman was openly watching her, a look of curious amusement on her face. "I don't really have the time myself. Got a lot of things I need to do. You just get on with your work, Allen, I'll see you tonight when you get home." She paused in the doorway. "Nice to meet you, Miss Bancroft. I hope you enjoy your stay in our town."

"Thank you. It seems very tiny after Chicago, but I shall try." Her eyes went back to Allen when she spoke, smiling at him. "Yes. I'll try to find something to amuse myself with while I'm here."

Mattie hurried through the shopping, anxious to be on the road toward home. The fun of the afternoon trip into town was gone. To hide her disappointment, she scolded herself soundly. What did she expect? All of Allen's clients couldn't be men with dust on their boots from the ranches. Women needed to see lawyers once in a while, too—even pretty women who wore expensive clothes and looked like something out of a New York magazine.

By the time the car was bouncing along the deeply rutted dirt road toward the ranch, she had gotten back her sense of humor and was able to laugh at herself and the whole incident. No wonder that woman had smiled at her like that. She must have looked pretty silly, trying to look like something she wasn't. Folks ought to be themselves. Anyway, she didn't care. It *was* a pretty dress. She was proud of it. Her mind ran on ahead of the car, to the ranch and the two small boys, knowing how their faces would light up and their small hands would reach out toward her when she walked into the room. She pictured Wes's one-sided grin when he waved to her as she drove into the yard, Betty's smile of relief when she saw that she was back, because she could use the help with the dinner. When it came right down to it, she felt sorry for that Irene Bancroft and her fancy clothes and city ways. It must be terrible to not have folks needing you, happy to see you walk in, to be bored because you had nothing to do. Still— No—she wasn't going to think about that woman anymore.

As soon as she got home Mattie changed into the checked gingham. She glanced up at the mirror and took the pins from her hair, letting it cascade down her back. Hastily, she brushed it out and twisted it into the familiar knot and reached for her apron. Jonathan was crying. She scooped him up from his crib, smiling at the way his sobs quickly turned to gurgles as he snuggled against her breast, and headed toward the kitchen.

There had been a stack of mail for Clive when she stopped at the post office. She laid the letters, the newspapers, and several magazines on his desk where he could find them. That evening, after the dinner dishes were all washed and put away, she went into his study. The babies were in bed and the house was quiet. Betty and Wes had left for their house down the lane. Allen hadn't come home yet.

"Wasn't there a letter from Morgan in today's mail?" she asked, knowing full well that she had recognized his handwriting on one of the envelopes.

The old man closed the book in front of him and nodded. "He's in France. In Paris when he wrote."

Mattie went across and curled up in the chair near the fire. France. Paris. She turned the words over in her mind. "You ever been to France, Clive?"

He shook his head as he handed the letter across to her.

"I heard the men talking when I was in town the other day. Ben Williams's son was leaving to enlist. The men were teasing him about the gay mademoiselles of Paris. Do you suppose Morgan is having himself a good time in Paris?"

He gave her a long, thoughtful look before he answered. "Maybe you better read this magazine that came in today's mail. It has quite a story, with a lot of pictures, about the war in France. It'll answer a lot of your questions."

Mattie scanned through the pages and then went back to study the pictures carefully. The sound of the fire crackling on the hearth faded away and the walls of the study melted as she tried to see beyond the printed page to what it was really like where Morgan was right now. She had imagined Paris as a gay, careless city, but the pictures showed dirty, narrow streets, buildings needing paint, broken windows covered with boards. She could almost smell the stench of defeat that hung in the air and was written on the faces of the people in the villages surrounding the town. There was a picture of women wearing black and weeping helplessly as they watched their men leaving for the battle lines. There was a picture of wounded men returning with an empty coat sleeve or pant leg. The article told about the cafés where the men on leave drank and partied, trying to make every minute of their leave give them something to remember when they moved back up to the front lines. It told of children begging in the streets, orphaned and homeless. It told of young mademoiselles haunting the cafés, laughing and drinking with the soldiers, willing to sell their bodies for food, for chocolate, for silk stockings. It told of muddy roads, rain, young French boys and old, middle-aged men called into service, and a French people who had been ready to admit defeat and quit when the Allies moved in and took up the fight.

She picked up Morgan's letter. It was brief, as usual, saying that he was in France, with the 50th Aero Squadron, flying D.H.4's. He had been to Paris for three days. He was well.

The kitchen window was open, letting in a cool breeze and ruffling the white curtains. The fire had to be kept burning in the stove because it was ironing day and the flatirons needed to be heated. The kitchen table was lined with neat stacks of completed laundry. Betty was busily folding towels while Mattie stood at the ironing board. Beside her was a basket of starched, sprinkled, and rolled shirts, waiting for her.

Clive came in from outdoors and stood in the doorway watching the two women. "You real busy, Mattie, or can you stop what you're doing for a while?"

Mattie moistened the tip of her finger and tested the heat of the iron. "Just about through with this stack of shirts," she answered. "What do you need?"

"I'm going to ride up toward Willow Spring and check on the stock. Thought maybe you might ride along with me, for the company."

"Well, I don't know—"Mattie hesitated as she looked down at the basket of sprinkled laundry waiting to be pressed.

"Of course you can!" Betty interrupted. "Both boys are down for a nap and everything is caught up. The fresh air will do you good. Here. Give me that iron. I can do his shirts just as well as you can."

It didn't take too much encouragement. The breeze coming through the window had been tantalizing her, making her yearn for the open outdoors. She ran from the room to exchange her dress for a pair of riding pants while Clive went out to saddle the horses.

The day was warm and clear, the air carrying the smell of desert flowers with a hint of sage. Mattie sat up on Black Diamond, her back straight, her hair loose against her shoulders, a smile playing on her lips as she rode alongside Clive on the trail away from the ranch buildings. She loved the openness, the beauty of the desert, with the high Cascade Mountain Range to the west. It had been a long time since she had ridden with Clive. She had used to ride with him a lot before Allen's accident, before Morgan came back, when Clive sometimes asked her to help or she just rode out with him to check on the stock because she liked to do it.

Clive pulled his horse up at the edge of the ridge, dropping the reins loosely around the horn of the saddle, and sat looking down across the valley. Mattie stopped beside him, letting her horse nibble on the wide-bladed desert grasses as her gaze followed his off toward the horizon.

"Things are starting to look real good, aren't they?" Clive said at last. "The stock is in prime shape, prices are up—"

"The remodeling shows up nice from here," she answered quietly. "It looks nice, doesn't it, Clive? The whole valley spread out there in front of us—the house, the barns, the stock grazing in the distance, things still green before summer. It looks like a picture."

"You like it here, don't you?" He smiled across at her. She

was sitting so straight in the saddle, at ease on the big black, the wind ruffling through her hair, her eyes glowing proudly at the view spread out below them.

"Guess I always will feel this way about the ranch." She nodded. "First time in my life I really felt as though I had a home—a real home, a place where I belong. I just wish I could stay here forever." He heard the wistfulness in her voice.

"Any reason why you can't?" he asked.

Mattie shrugged. "Forever is a long time, Clive. Things change—people change. I guess it's what people call 'progress'— getting ahead. Nothing stays the same, no matter how much we want it to. You got to move ahead, keep up . . ."

"You're talking about Allen—his wanting to be the state's attorney general, maybe having to move to Salem. Mattie . . ."

"No. Don't," she interrupted him. "Don't say anything. I don't want to talk about it today. I just want to ride out here in the sunshine with you, see everything looking so good, with spring showing up all over. For just a little while I want to pretend nothing will ever change. I only want to think about the good things, forget about the worries. You and I just don't seem to have much time to spend together anymore, do we? Not like we used to. Remember how we used to sit by the fire in the evenings and read? I miss it, Clive."

"Wondered if you still ever thought about coming into the study, bringing the coffeepot and some cake, maybe making popcorn. I know those two younguns take a lot of your time. Especially now, when they're still so small. I've been looking forward to when they're old enough for me to start teaching them to ride. Got a lot of plans for those two boys."

She smiled affectionately across at him. "It won't be long, the way they're growing. And then you're going to complain to me because they're always under your feet, wanting to follow you everywhere."

They sat in silence for a while, each enjoying his own thoughts. A few clouds, soft, fleecy puffs of cotton, floated overhead, covering the sun for just a moment and then drifting on so that its warmth reached down to them. The stream hadn't started drying up yet for the summer, and they could hear its song as it raced across the rocks. A lazy spiral of smoke rose up from the house. A bird circled overhead.

He likes this, Mattie thought. Sitting up here on the high ridge, looking down on all that he has worked so hard to build, feeling satisfied with himself. He's quite a man. Hard as nails on the outside, caring on the inside, and proud. A proud man, always taking care of what's his. He makes me proud that I'm a Henderson, that I'm a part of his family. It makes me want to always do what is right, so I won't ever hurt him.

"Mattie." His quiet voice broke into her reverie. "There's been times when I guess I should have done more than I did. Other times, folks called me a meddling old fool. Right now, I'm wishing I could do something about the things that are troubling you—things that aren't going right. There are things I want to do, but they're not in my control anymore."

She turned to look at him, a question in her eyes, but she didn't speak.

"It's Allen. He's a little big to take the belt to anymore. Been tempted to use a whip—that's what he needs."

Mattie didn't answer, not sure what he was leading up to. Not sure she wanted to listen. Today was too pleasant. There were things she didn't want to think about, things she didn't want to talk about.

"You know, Mattie, Allen tends to get carried away with an idea when he gets one. He doesn't weigh things out too well or look at things from other people's angles. Take these friends of his—the men he's mixed up with lately. Can't say I care very much for them. Guess I always believed that the only way a man gets anything that's really his is to work for it. Never could understand how some men would rather make deals on paper— trying to outsmart each other—getting rich overnight on someone else's losses."

Mattie sat watching something off beyond the horizon, letting him talk.

"Have you seen her yet?" Mattie was startled by his question. She didn't ask who he meant. Somehow, in the closeness they were sharing right now, she knew that he guessed who was in the back of her mind. Somehow he knew about Allen's new client. He knew about Irene Bancroft.

"Yes. I met her one day in town—quite by accident. She was in his office, and they were going over the papers from the Bancroft estate. She's just a client, asking his help with the papers, Allen said."

"Do you think that is all it is?"

It was hard for Mattie to answer. She didn't want to say things that she wouldn't admit, even to herself, when she had worried over the number of evenings Allen stayed in town. "Miss Bancroft is from out of town, Clive. Allen is her attorney. He feels it his responsibility to spend some time with her." She turned and looked across at him, searching for the right words. "She's a very attractive woman, Clive. 'Pretty' isn't quite the word for it. She's very confident—sure of herself, of how she looks, of how she talks. She's not like women around here. She's from a big city, and she knows how to dress, how to use all the right words in all the right places. She's also very rich. I can see why folks would want to gossip."

He nodded. "I been hearing some talk about her. Her and Allen. From all that I can tell, her fine ways and her money don't amount to all that much, really. They don't make her a lady. She seems to be just as willing to climb into the hay with him as any two-dollar-a-night tart in town. So what makes her seem special enough for you to worry about?"

Mattie grinned across at him, her eyes lighting up with new humor. "Don't really know, now. Listening to you talk about her, it sounds different than the way I was thinking. Maybe what's so special is how she goes about it. Or maybe it's 'cause I understand Allen so well. You know how impatient he is with this small town, with the people, how he's always looking up to the ones who come from the city, wanting to be like them. And, Clive, she's 'Big City'."

"Allen has always been like that—jealous about hanging on to his own things and still reaching out, wanting what he can't have, thinking it might be better. Having a lot of money and wearing fancy clothes, trying to impress folks with a family name or background—this doesn't make a person better than anyone else. What is real about a person is what's down inside. I wouldn't waste too much time worrying about her, if I was you. When her business is done, she will pack up and go back to where she came from—and folks will find something new to gossip about. They always do.''

Mattie flicked the reins, impatient now. ''Thought we were going to ride up to Willow Springs.'' Her horse was dancing and she slackened the reins, letting him run. Clive had no choice but to follow her on the trail—to watch the way her hair streamed back when she rode, sitting up straight in the saddle, holding her face up into the wind.

Allen's a fool! he thought to himself. A gawddamned fool. Having a woman like Mattie and wasting his time following after a tart done up in a fancy wrapper, waving her money around. Takes a red-blooded man like Morgan to deserve a woman like Mattie. Those two belonged together. What a pair they would have made! But Morgan had come back to the ranch too late, and Clive had done what he could to interfere, to keep them apart. He had thought it was the right thing to do—maybe he had been wrong.

CHAPTER THIRTEEN

Morgan flexed his fingers, trying to relax. The strain of the last two days was beginning to show around his eyes and in the hard, unsmiling lines of his face. His nerves were drawn taut as fiddle strings and the tightness tugged at his insides as he listened to the talk of the men standing with him, studying the large map spread out in from of them.

In the background he could hear the sounds of the engines being revved up. The ground crews of mechanics were working against impossible odds to make the repairs. He let his eyes stray from the map and looked at the faces of the men near him, seeing the tiredness and feeling the tension. They were cold, wet, tired, and yet they wouldn't give up.

For the past two days they had been flirting with death, flying missions across the Argonne Forest in an attempt to locate a battalion of men pinned down by the enemy somewhere in the heavily forested area of the ravine. It had been two days of returning with oil lines leaking, engines misfiring and punctured with bullet holes, fabric riddled, and framework splintered. The night gave them little sleep because when they closed their eyes they remembered the five men who were missing from the group. Two planes with pilots and observers hadn't come back. A third plane had made it back, but the pilot was so badly wounded that it was uncertain whether he would live long enough to make the journey in the Red Cross ambulance to the hospital located well behind the lines.

On October 2, four days ago, the men of the First Battalion, 308th Infantry, 27th Division, supported by the Second Battalion, had began an advance through the Argonne Forest on the American left flank, making an attempt to penetrate the Argonne Forest and reach the far slope of the Charlevaux Valley, where they were to dig in and establish a stronghold. It was part of what had been intended to be a massive Allied offensive—and it had failed.

Morning light proved that Major Charles Whittlesey and his 550 men were the only Allied troops in the sector who had reached their objective during the night. He and his men were now surrounded by the enemy, cut off from their supporting forces. Their only hope of contact with Division Headquarters was by means of carrier pigeons. They sent out urgent requests for artillery support and supplies so they could hold out until the lines were reestablished, but they were never sure whether or not the carrier pigeons would get through.

A war correspondent picked up on it, sending the story back to his New York editor, who in turn released the story in screaming headlines across the nation, calling the two divisions the "lost battalion," building it into a human-interest story that attracted the attention of the world. The actual truth to the story was somewhat different. The battalion wasn't "lost." It was, in fact, the only battalion that had reached its approximate destination and it was exactly where it should be. The problem lay in the fact that the men were cut off from the rest of their forces, pinned down without enough ammunition or supplies to protect themselves, and the whole damned thing was turning into a bloody massacre. There was nothing they could do but stay hidden, wait, and pray that their location could be pinpointed and help would arrive. The only way their exact location could be pinpointed, however, was to find out where the enemy was hidden. So the Allies would try to make the Germans give their location away by drawing their fire, and then look for the battalion in the area where there was no firing.

On October 4th, the 50th Aero Squadron, Morgan's squadron, was brought in from Remicourt. It was the men of the 50th Aero Squadron who flew the D.H.4's, dubbed "flying coffins" by the other squadrons. The D.H.4 was larger than most of the other planes. It was a biplane with two open cockpits—one in front for the pilot and one for an observer. There was a Lewis machine gun mounted on a swivel just behind the rear cockpit.

For two days now, Morgan and the others had flown over the area, trying to find the location of the battalion so they could drop supplies. Artillery fire from the higher ridges made the flights dangerous and took its toll of men and planes, and yet the men kept trying.

Morgan brought his attention back to the group bending over the map.

"You men know the seriousness of the situation," the officer in command was saying. "There is no need to keep talking about it. The battalion can't hold out much longer. By this time they have no food, no water, no ammunition. God only knows how many of them are wounded—or dead."

Lieutenant Rassmussen spoke up. "On the last flight we flew at five hundred feet, sir. We still weren't able to see them. We can't get any lower without flying right into the artillery fire. I'm not a coward, but it's like committing suicide."

The commanding officer nodded. None of these men were cowards. They had proved it over and over again. But another try had to be made. "I won't send anyone out. It is strictly volunteer, men. I'm asking you what we should do."

Lieutenant Harold Goettler and Erwin Bleckley stepped forward. "We will make one more try—this time at two hundred feet. If that doesn't work, nothing will. We're volunteering, sir."

Morgan glanced across at his observer, Lieutenant Bailey. Bailey nodded, so slightly it was hardly perceptible. "We'll double the odds," Morgan spoke up. "Maybe one can draw the fire and the other can get through. Bailey and I are going, too."

Morgan snapped the strap on his helmet and adjusted his goggles now as he sat in the airplane, listening to the steady beat of the engine. The controls responded to his touch when he did the rundown, doing a final check. It was late afternoon, almost evening. There was a heavy cloud cover with the promise of rain. Water stood in large puddles on the muddy ground. For just a moment he allowed himself to think of the hot desert sun of eastern Oregon—the open expanse of range land, the old man, and Mattie, the only woman he would ever love. He eased the throttle forward, giving the engine full power, and they began to roll across the hard ground, gaining speed.

They were in the air now. There was no room in his mind for anything except his mission—no room for tiredness, no room for fear—only a steel determination that kept his reflexes sharp, his mind alert. His fingers tightened on the controls, feeling the instant response of the D.H.4 to his touch.

He made a sharp bank to the left and came in low. He caught a glimpse of Goettler and Bleckley in the other plane, a two-seater biplane with the "Dutch Girl," the insignia of the 50th Aero Squadron, showing plainly on its side. They skimmed the tops of the trees for the length of the ravine. The Germans opened up with everything they had. The artillery fire was close—too damned close. Morgan knew his plane had been hit a number of times. He tried not to think of the other planes he had seen go down, leaving only a trail of black smoke to mark their path, followed by a yellow flash of fire.

At the end of the ravine, he pushed the throttle forward, fighting for altitude so he could make a turn for another pass. He saw Bleckley in the other plane, already nosing down to sweep into the ravine.

Morgan felt his airplane shudder, like a bird wounded in flight, as it took another direct hit. He turned back in time to see Bailey slump forward in the cockpit. He heard the misfire of the engine, saw the framework splinter, the canvas tear, the pieces of fabric waving in the airstream like a banner. He fought the controls, willing them to respond by sheer force of determination. The engine was throwing oil—he felt it on his face and saw it on his clothing. When he reached up to rub it away from his eyes so that he could see, he found streaks of red mixed with the oil.

At first he thought he had been hit in the face—he stared at the growing patches of blood mixed with oil and realized that it was running down his arm from somewhere on his shoulder. He wondered why there was no feeling—no flashes of agonizing pain, nothing to tell him that a fragment of a shell must have torn away at his flesh—nothing but a growing patch of red soaking through the sleeve of his jacket.

He felt nothing, just a hopeless anger that dimmed his sight. As his vision blurred, he saw Mattie's face smiling at him with love spilling from her eyes, as she had smiled that afternoon in the cabin. It was as though she were in the cockpit with him, near enough to touch.

"Mattie!" He cried out her name, but the winds tore the words away from him. He fought to stay conscious and work the controls of the plane as it went into a stall and fluttered toward the ground like a wounded bird.

The impact of the crash left Morgan stunned and disoriented. A deep instinct for survival took over, driving him on to free himself from the safety belt, work his way out of the damaged cockpit, and painfully stand on the ground leaning against the torn side of the aircraft. His next concern was for his observer, Lieutenant Bailey, but it took only a brief look to see there was nothing he could do to help the man. The shells had found their targets with accuracy, taking away his life and part of his face with their shattering force. Smoke was curling up from around the engine. Any moment it could burst into flame. He had to get away from the crumpled framework of wood and canvas before the fire consumed the airplane, taking him with it.

A new urgency drove him now. He had to hurry—get away before the German patrol came searching for the wreckage, get away before he was found and taken prisoner.

A line of trees lay several hundred feet in front of him. His vision blurred as he tried to focus on their shadowy forms. His only chance of escape lay in reaching their shelter, where he could hide before the patrol arrived. He concentrated on putting one foot ahead of the other, trying to ignore the pain in his shoulder that was starting to hammer away at his dulled senses, making each jarring step a new hell of agony.

It was starting to rain. He had to hurry. He felt the cool dampness of the rain against his face. "Hurry, Mattie," he muttered. "If we reach the trees we'll get out of the storm." No. That wasn't right. Mattie wasn't here. The noise he remembered wasn't the sound of a tire blowing. It was the sound of a crash. His plane had crashed. He had to reach the trees. The rain would help to blot out any tracks that he might leave. His every thought was centered on walking, one step at a time, with deliberate concentration on keeping moving until he reached the shelter of the forest.

It seemed darker now. He brushed his hands across his eyes. Was his vision fading or was it the shade from the trees overhead filtering out what light escaped from the stormclouds overhead? He felt the wet brush clinging to his clothing, wet leaves against his face, and he knew he must have reached the protection of the forest. He could hear the dripping of water from the branches hitting on the carpet of the forest floor.

His foot caught against a root. He stumbled, falling to one knee. Had to keep going. He got up and braced himself against a tree trunk, allowing himself to rest for only a minute before he started out again. He still wasn't far enough away. Had to keep going. He had to reach the cabin and get Mattie out of the thunderstorm. No. That wasn't right. He was tired. It was harder to think now. Strange and distorted thoughts kept running back and forth through his mind, confusing him.

He stumbled and fell again. This time he lay still. This time the undergrowth was heavy, sheltering, and the spongy moss under him felt comforting. It was too much of an effort to get back to his feet. He moved a little, trying to shift some of the weight from his shoulder, tried to ease the pain that burned like a fire.

He heard voices in the distance, words he couldn't understand. The few phrases of German he had picked up were no help to him now. The voices grew louder, closer, blending with the noise of a truck. He tried to lift his head, wanting to get back on his feet, but a heavy weight seemed to be holding him down, making it impossible for him to move. The voices moved farther away, fading into the distance. He shut his eyes.

He should start a fire. The cabin was cold. Mattie needed to dry out her clothing. He reached for her and pulled her into his arms, feeling the warmth of her love as she melted against him. Mattie. A soft, black stillness wrapped itself around him, taking away the pain, letting him float into an oblivion where there was no need to hurry, no danger, no searing agony in his shoulder.

Morgan's first sensation, as awareness gradually returned, was of being cold. His clothing felt damp and uncomfortable. He had no idea how long he had lain there on the wet ground. He listened to the sounds around him. The rain had stopped. There was only an occasional drip of water here and there falling from a leaf overhead. Otherwise, everything was still.

He tried to move. His muscles were cramped and his wounds pulled against his clothing, causing the shoulder to throb. He tried to sit up, moving cautiously at first, trying out his arms, easing his legs into a sitting position, until at last he was on his feet, leaning against a tree for support.

He tried to remember what had happened, where he was, and how he had gotten there. It took a moment or two to get his bearings, to try to remember which direction he had come from, and to decide which direction he must take now. Then the urgent need to keep moving returned and he knew he must keep going, working his way back to safety.

It was nighttime. The sky had cleared and there was a smattering of stars overhead, showing through the trees. The moon was only a pale sliver against the inky sky. He had no idea how far he had walked before he lost consciousness, but he knew it wasn't far enough. He had to get farther away from the wreckage. The next hours were a blur of walking, stumbling; he was kept alert by the searing pain eating away at his shoulder.

Morgan reached the edge of the forest and he stopped, not wanting to leave its protective cover. Ahead of him lay a tiny valley bathed in the silence of the early morning hours. A small farm cottage squatted near the weather-worn barn in the center of the clearing. Everything was quiet, removed from any sign of the battles being fought on the other side of the ridge. He heard a dog bark sharply in the distance and then it was quiet again.

Carefully, he judged the distance to the barn, weighing it against his remaining strength. A barn could mean hay, a place to hide—shelter until he could rest enough to travel farther. It could also mean discovery, being handed over to the Germans. He stood still, watching closely for any sign of movement in the house. He felt the blackness threaten him again and knew his body was weak from the loss of blood. The tiredness was returning, and his vision was distorted. Again he measured the distance across the opening. He would have to take the chance. Somehow he had to make it across the clearing as far as the barn. He was too weak to travel on any farther.

A small, shallow creek flowed between him and the hay loft he had his attention fastened on. The creek, with its sounds of water splashing against the stones, brought back a wave of memories—of another creek, one with a swimming hole, a young woman bathing nude in the moonlight. Mattie.

He waded across the stream and kept walking, each step taking him closer to the barn. The dog barked again, the sound shrill in the stillness. Someone came to the door of the cottage. There was a flicker of light, someone calling out to the dog. The light disappeared and everything was quiet again.

Morgan leaned heavily against the door of the barn, exhausted from the trek across the grassy meadow. His numb fingers found the latch and he pulled the door open, careful not to make any noise. The familiar smells of the hay, sounds of a cow shifting positions in a stanchion, warm, comforting sounds and smells reached out to him as he slipped inside and waited until his eyes became accustomed to the darkness.

He saw the shadowy form of a ladder leaning against a wall, leading up to the overhead hayloft. He gathered together all of his remaining strength for the climb. Up one step. Two steps. He would rest now—tomorrow he would find the battalion. He had to . . . He sunk down into the soft, warm hay. He felt Mattie's arms cradle his body against her, felt her cool touch on his face, heard her soft voice whisper to him that he was safe. He closed his eyes and slept.

CHAPTER FOURTEEN

Allen came into the house carrying the latest editions of the
Portland newspapers he had picked up on his way out of town. In
his hand was a telegram. He looked around the rooms, but no
one was there. Mattie must be upstairs with the boys. The others
must be outside somewhere. He dropped the newspapers carelessly down on the table and went on outside. He had to find the
old man, had to give him the telegram from the war department.

Mattie looked up from where she was folding stacks of diapers
and putting them in the chest of drawers in an upstairs bedroom.
She thought she heard a car. Allen. Why would he be coming
home in the middle of the day? She glanced over to where the
two small boys were sleeping, taking their afternoon naps under
heavy protest. Confident that they hadn't heard the noise and
were sleeping peacefully, she slipped quietly out of the door and
went downstairs to see what had brought Allen home so early.

She went into the sitting room, but it was empty. He must
have gone on outside. Her eyes fell on the newspapers and she
went over to pick them up, to straighten them. Toward the
bottom of the front page, the paper on top of the pile carried the
story in a harsh black headline—OREGON FLYING ACE
MISSING IN ACTION.

Mattie dropped into a chair with the paper spread out across her lap. Her hands were cold as ice, her body numb as she stared at the story below the headlines, unable to believe what she was reading. It was a fantasy—a nightmare—and soon she would wake up and know it wasn't true. The paper in her hand was nothing more than a piece of white newsprint with rows and rows of little black inky marks. It didn't mean anything. It was impossible that anything so impersonal could deliver a message so shattering.

Newspapers were cranked out by the thousands by some big, noisy machine. They were bundled up and dropped off the backs of trucks to be hawked on street corners by cold, noisy little boys she had seen when she'd gone to town. They were bought by men who were in too much of a hurry to stop and read that devastating bulletin. This wasn't the way to announce that Morgan was missing in action. It wasn't so. It couldn't be true.

She wanted to crumple up the paper, tear it into shreds. She wanted to cry out, "Not true! Not true!" It was only a rumor to sell their newspapers. That's what it was—a rumor. She put her head down and sobbed helplessly, her tears shaking her whole body. "It's not true—it can't be true!"

This is how the men found her when they returned to the house.

"My God! It must be in the newspapers already!" Allen swore angrily. "I never thought to look. I brought the telegram home as soon as it arrived. I picked up the newspapers as I left town. Didn't stop to read them."

Clive crossed the room with long strides and stood behind her, putting his hands protectively on her shoulders, drawing her against him. She lifted her tear-stained face and looked up at him. "There was a telegram? What did it say?"

Allen held out the piece of yellow paper. "Not too much. Missing in action. That's about all they can say. Another pilot saw him go down. He went down behind the enemy lines, so they had no way to reach him—no way to know if he escaped the crash, if he was captured, if he— Hell, Mattie—missing in action can mean anything. Maybe he walked away from the wreck and managed to keep from getting caught."

Clive patted Mattie's shoulder and walked away from them with misted eyes, going into his study and shutting the door firmly behind him.

CHAPTER FIFTEEN

Mattie stood in the kitchen taking the last of the pies out of the oven while Betty watched, smiling in admiration. "One thing about it, Mattie—you do turn out the best piecrust of anyone in the county. I hate to admit it, but you got me beat. Those friends of Allen's who are coming to dinner tonight are in for a real treat."

"They expect it," Mattie answered with an indifferent shrug. "Something about coming out into the country—city folks expect steaks, hearty foods, home-baked breads, and desserts hot from the oven."

"Does it bother you much, having those men here?" Betty asked. "It would make me kind of uneasy."

"No. Not anymore. I just finally made up my mind that I'm as good as any of them. Maybe a whole lot better than some. No one is ever going to make me feel awkward and stupid again by flashing their diamonds and looking down their nose at me. I just don't care enough to get upset."

"Well, it's about time you started feeling that way—sure of yourself, I mean. Lord knows, you are a lot better looking, and when you dress up and fix your hair, she can't hold a candle to you."

Mattie looked up with a frown. "We were talking about the

men that are coming to dinner this evening, not another woman."

Betty grinned good-naturedly at the reprimand. "Yeah. Sure. Anyway, Wes was in town yesterday and he saw that woman leaving on the stage, along with two big steamer trunks and four suitcases. Guess she got tired of life in our small Western town and is headed back to the great big city of Chicago, where things are more exciting. Maybe she found out that having a lot of money doesn't buy everything you want."

"Betty, you gossip too much!" Mattie snapped. "Wes is getting just as bad. 'That woman,' as you call her, is Miss Bancroft, and she was in town on business. Allen was in charge of settling the estate for her. You know that."

"And having a good-looking lawyer willing to make the stay more interesting doesn't hurt any, either. I mean, if you like that sort of thing." She turned away, knowing she was treading on dangerous ground. "The dining room looks just like one of those pictures out of the *Ladies' Home Journal*. Allen ought to be real proud of you. Are you sure you don't want me to stay and help serve?"

Mattie shook her head. "You've done enough for one day. You must be tired. Why don't you go home whenever Wes is ready. I'm going upstairs to bathe and start dressing. The boys have been fed. I'll put them to bed just before time for the guests to arrive. Allen said they'd be here about seven."

Betty gave a deep sigh as she sat up on the buggy seat beside her husband. Wes gave her a sharp sideways glance.

"What was that all about?"

"Oh, nothing. Just thinking how lucky I am. Going home with a man like you. All I have to worry about is whether you're comfortable—that everything is the way you like for it to be. Doesn't matter what anyone else thinks. Don't know how Mattie does it."

"You mean the company they're having tonight?"

Betty nodded. "That big house is fixed up real nice but Allen's always finding fault, worrying about what people will think. Mattie is such a pretty little thing, but the life just seems to have gone out of her lately. Oh, I know, she's been spending a lot of time fussing over her dresses and spending time with her looks. She reads a lot, too—always studying the pictures in them women's magazines. And she keeps up on all of the news in the papers until she can talk as intelligently as any of the men about all sorts of things—not just ranching. But it's the war news that she goes to first, every time the papers get here. And she's so quiet most of the time. She's changed a lot, don't you think?''

"Suppose. Only on the surface, though. Underneath she's the same old Mattie—full of spunk and fire. She's just got a lot on her mind, that's all. They had any news on Morgan?''

Betty shook her head. "Nothing. That's what I mean. Mattie's hurting something awful inside, Wes. She thinks it doesn't show, but I know her too well. She can't hide things like that from me. She's worried sick about him, not knowing what has happened. She's been drawn to Morgan since the first day she met him. Must be terrible, loving a man like Morgan and being married to Allen.''

"Betty, now, you shouldn't be talking like that,'' Wes drawled. "It's none of our business. Just wish I knew what kind of trouble Morgan is in, though. Wish we would hear something, one way or the other. It's the not knowing that's so bad.''

"It's pretty hard on all of them. I hate to see what it's doing to the old man. He won't talk about it much, but you can see it in his face. It's tearing him up inside not knowing if Morgan is dead or alive.''

"Well, as long as he is still listed as 'missing,' there's a chance. If anyone can make it, Morgan can. He's pretty damned tough. A hard man to put down. Makes it bad, though, not knowing.''

"All that worry, and now Allen is talking about moving to Salem to live. He figures pretty strong on being the next attorney general for the state. If that happens, he will have to be over there most of the time. Mattie doesn't want to move to Salem, but there isn't much she can do about it. She hates to go off and leave the old man alone, without any family—especially now.''

"When you figure they'll be moving?''

"When and if he's elected. I think that is what the dinner tonight was all about.'' She reached out and laid a hand on her husband's arm. "Shouldn't let it bother me the way it does. But they're just like our own family—we been so close. What upsets Mattie makes me feel bad, too. When they leave, I guess it will be up to you and me to sort of fill in for them—look out for Clive and try to keep him from thinking he's all alone."

CHAPTER SIXTEEN

Mattie's first view of the house in Salem caused her to catch her breath in surprise. Allen had been talking enthusiastically about it ever since he had decided to make an offer for it, but somehow it was not quite what she had expected. She knew he always leaned toward extravagant, showy places, but she had thought he might pick something that was at least a little more personal, more friendly for their own home. She had to smile to herself at her choice of words to describe the house she was looking at. Friendly? A house is a house—just a structure of nails and boards and paint. How can a house be friendly or unfriendly? It takes the people living there to turn it into a home, to give it character, to give it life.

"Do you think we need something this big?" she asked hesitantly, knowing he was waiting for her opinion. "I mean, it just seems so—large," she ended helplessly, not knowing how to describe her feelings.

"Doesn't look much like the old ranch house, does it?" Allen grinned proudly. "This house has respectability—it has status. Anybody driving by and looking in knows that whoever lives here is somebody important." He had stopped the car in the drive, letting her get a full view of the house and the lawns before he drove on up to the door.

A high laurel hedge gave privacy to the wide expanse of freshly cut green grass. Here and there were well-tended beds of rhododendron bushes, their leaves glistening a dark, shiny green in the sunlight. A holly tree was to the left of the drive, standing nearly twenty feet tall, pinpointed with dark red berries. Everything looked so neat and orderly, with an air of established respectability.

The house was three stories high, with double doors opening out onto a wide porch that circled the front and traveled on around to follow down one side. The white paint was fresh and clean-looking against the background of green trees. A portico extended out across the driveway to protect passengers alighting from cars against the rains so prevalent here on this side of the Cascade Mountains.

"Well, what do you think, Mattie?" Allen wanted to know. "A damned impressive-looking place, don't you agree?" He drove on up the drive, stopping under the portico. "Wait until you see the inside." His eyes were glowing with pride, his voice filled with enthusiasm as he talked. "This is just the kind of house I always wanted to live in. I bought it from the original owner. He was one of the first settlers in the Willamette Valley. One of the first anyway that stayed and did something with their lives. He made his money in merchandising. He started out with a small general store, bringing his inventory into Portland by ship and then transferring it to wagons for the rest of the trip down here to Salem. He was a shrewd businessman and he kept growing until he owned a large department store here in Salem and one in Portland, and he's still expanding. That's why he finally decided to sell. Wants to move to Portland to be closer to the hub of where things are happening. Too bad Portland isn't the capital. We're too far south here—too far away from the center of transportation."

The boys were beginning to stir in the back seat of the car, where they had been put down for their naps. Young Clive sat up and rubbed his eyes sleepily. Jonathan rolled over onto his stomach and tucked his thumb in his mouth, watching the shadows of the trees against the car window, his cheeks warm and flushed from where he had been lying against the wool blanket.

The door opened and a middle-aged woman appeared dressed in a neat, tailored gray dress with crisp white collar and cuffs. A stiff smile was on her lips as she came forward to meet them.

Mattie looked at Allen with a puzzled question in her eyes and he grinned a little sheepishly. "Mrs. Burton. The housekeeper. I told you I had everything ready for you, didn't I?"

"But—a housekeeper, Allen?"

There was no time for an answer. Mrs. Burton was already taking the sleepy-eyed Jonathan in her arms and reaching for young Clive's hand. "Let me help with the little ones, Mrs. Henderson. The poor things must be worn out from the long trip. Cook has some hot chocolate waiting for them in the kitchen."

"Cook?" Mattie asked in alarm, but Allen was already holding the door for her, waiting to lead her inside, to show her the rooms of their new home.

All of the rooms were large, designed for entertaining. Several of the rooms had fireplaces, including the library. Mattie followed him quietly, listening to him talk, heard the pride in his voice as he pointed out the different features to her, but to herself she thought, This house was built by someone who wanted a background for his possessions rather than warmth and comfort. I wonder if I'll ever get over the feeling that I'm only visiting— that I don't really belong here.

Allen led her up the wide stairway toward the second floor, where the bedrooms were. A large, heavily carpeted, velvet-draped room that she would share with Allen, with doors leading off to a separate dressing room for each of them. Across the hall were the bedrooms for the boys, with an adjoining bed-sitting room for their nurse.

It was here that Mattie finally balked, putting her outraged thoughts into words. "I'll take care of my own sons. For heaven's sake, what else is there for me to do? You hired a live-in housekeeper without asking me. And it seems we must have a cook somewhere, who is feeding my sons hot chocolate right now, but I wasn't invited to inspect the kitchen, so I'm not sure. What am I supposed to do with my time, Allen? Besides, I don't want another woman taking care of my babies. They're too small to be shuffled around like this."

Allen took her arm and drew her into the privacy of their bedroom. "Now, Mattie, let's don't quarrel our first day here—especially not where the servants are going to hear. How the hell do you think it's going to sound? We're going to be in the public eye a lot more now that I am the attorney general. Folks are going to gossip. You're going to have to remember that."

Anger flashed in Mattie's eyes as she answered him. "Servants be damned! Whatever made you think we needed servants anyway? I'm perfectly capable of taking care of my own house, my own children—doing my own cooking. Whatever made you think we needed a big barn of a house like this in the first place? The old man will go right through the roof when he sees all of this—and knows how much it must be costing!"

"The old man isn't paying for it!" Allen retorted sharply. "I don't give a damn if he approves of the way we're living or not. I told you I was going to get rid of the odor of cow shit on my boots and, by God, that's what I'm doing. I'm on my way, Mattie." His voice lowered. "And I'm taking you with me, baby. Be reasonable. Give me a chance. You believed in me when I ran for district attorney, didn't you? That was small potatoes, honey. You didn't think I was going to be content to stay there, did you? I've made it to attorney general now, and we're going to start moving up in the world—going to start living like we *are* somebody. Appearances mean a lot. We've got to keep up appearances." A small grin tugged at the corners of his mouth. "Who knows, Mattie? Maybe someday I'll even make it to the governor's chair."

Mattie's eyes opened wide, her face bewildered. Her anger was momentarily forgotten as the new worry took over. "But this, all of this, must cost a fortune, Allen! We don't have that kind of money. If you don't go to the old man for help, where is the money going to come from?"

He reached out and drew her into his arms, caressing her body as he held her close against him. "You let me worry about the money and where it will come from. That isn't any of your business. I know what I'm doing. All you got to do is keep running things smoothly here at the house. I'm going to depend on you a lot, Mattie. We'll be doing a lot of entertaining—going

out—meeting people—having them here at our home. I need you
beside me, helping me—loving me. I need to know that you
believe in me." He bent his head, brushing her lips with his
own. "You're just tired, baby. It's been a long day for you. The
packing, the long drive, the worry over the kids on the trip—
everything. Let's get washed up and go down to dinner.
Everything's going to look different to you in the morning."

Mattie drew away. "Yes. I suppose you are right. I should be
getting busy, shouldn't I? There must be a thousand things to do.
Dinner to get ready—" And then she stopped. "I suppose that is
all taken care of, too."

Allen laughed in delight. "See, Mattie? You're tired, wanting
to bathe and have a quiet evening? You can, honey, you can. All
you have to do is give a few orders to the housekeeper and you
can sit back and relax and do just what you want to do. You
don't have to keep pushing yourself the way you've been doing.
You're going to have a chance to enjoy life a little for a change.
It's going to be a good life, Mattie. I promise."

Mattie stood in the middle of the bathroom, slowly letting her
clothing fall piece by piece to the floor as she unfastened the
hooks and let them slip from her fingers. She stretched her tired
body and turned to survey herself in the full-length mirror. She
raised her arms and let her fingers trail through her hair, loosening it until it fell around her shoulders in a thick, rich mahogany
cloud. Having the two babies so close together hadn't harmed her
figure. She still was as slim and supple as ever. Her breasts were
fuller, but still high and firm. The curved line of her thigh led
from a tiny waist to gently rounded hips and slender legs. There
was a difference, though, she thought, as she studied the young
woman staring back at her from the mirror. A new maturity. And
something else that hadn't been there before. The corners of her
mouth crinkled in amusement. I'll bet Morgan wouldn't mistake
me for a neighbor's kid now, she thought. Even with me dressed
in jeans and a baggy shirt, he would know better.

Morgan. At the thought of his name a dark shadow crossed her
face. Where was he tonight? Was he safe? Was he wounded? If
only they would hear something! Her dreams had been plagued
with thoughts of him wounded, needing help, crying out her

name in the night, causing her to stir restlessly in her sleep and wake, to lie staring into the darkness, her heart aching with pain.

Perfumes from the bath oils floated upward invitingly from the white enamel tub. She tested the water with a toe and then slipped into its depths, relaxing as she let its magic work its wonders on her tired body. So. This is what it was going to be like to be Mrs. Allen Henderson, wife of the prominent young politician, wife of the new attorney general. Maybe he was right. Maybe she could learn how to enjoy the position and all that it stood for. Maybe she could learn how to stop worrying all of the time about the things he was doing—things she couldn't understand—his friends that she couldn't seem to like, no matter how hard she tried. She would just let Allen take care of the business end of their lives and she would concentrate only on the role she must learn to play as his wife. Goodness knows, she was going to have a lot more time to spend with the boys, and that was something to look forward to. She stretched out her toes, playfully chasing the soapy mounds of bubbles floating on the surface of the water, and sighed. More time for luxurious baths in tubs that were filled with water from a tap. Hot water by turning a faucet. At least for tonight she would relax and let tomorrow take care of itself. Tonight everything was like a dream—an unreal dream, like when she had lost herself in the pages of a book, curled up near the fire in the old man's study.

Idly, she wondered if Betty had finished with the day's work and gone home with Wes. The ranch house that they had remodeled and expanded must be even more empty and lonely for the old man tonight with them gone. A wave of something like homesickness washed over her, but she shrugged it away. She wasn't going to think of anything further ahead than what was happening to her right now.

Allen was waiting for her when she came out of the dressing room wrapped in a soft, velvet robe, her hair in moist curls from the steam of the bath.

"It's good to have you with me, Mattie," he murmured, pulling her close into his arms. "Here, in our own house, where there is no one around—just us. We can do what we damn well please without having to think of anyone else but ourselves. It's our home, Mattie. You and me. We don't need anybody else. I want us to be together all of the time—I don't want you staying at the ranch, me seeing you only when I can get away to go over there. I want you here, at my side, where folks can see what a lovely wife I have—a wife who loves me and believes in me."

He was loosening the ties of her robe, his hands slipping inside to explore the lines of her body, his eyes clouded with desire as he bent toward her. "I need you, Mattie. I've always needed you." His lips were caressing her tenderly as he softly whispered his words of love. "I need to know that whenever I come home you are waiting here for me and everything is right between us."

Mattie turned in his arms. "I need to check on the boys before bedtime, Allen. Let me go."

"Not tonight. Please, Mattie—don't leave me."

"They have never gone to sleep without me tucking them in before," she protested. "Everything will be so new to them—the new beds, the new room. They won't know what to think. They will be frightened if I'm not there."

"The housekeeper is taking care of them. They're probably sound asleep and you'd just wake them up if you went into their room now. Tomorrow their nurse will be here, but Mrs. Burton will watch them tonight. Don't leave me, Mattie. Not now. God, how I want you."

With a new urgency he scooped her up in his arms and carried her over to the wide bed waiting for them. She reached out her arms, drawing his head to her breast, holding him close to her, soothing him, comforting him with her own words of endearment, pushing her own worries and doubts into the background. He lay beside her and she felt the weight of him as he moved to press her down against the cool sheets, felt the hard urgency as he lifted himself to claim her body, felt his mouth hard and demanding against her own.

Later, she listened to his even breathing as he lay on the pillows beside her, relaxed in sleep. She lay awake, watching the shadows on the wall, letting her thoughts ramble. Allen always seemed so insecure. He needed constant reassurance, needed people around him, titles, possessions, words and objects to prove that he was successful, that he measured up to what he thought was expected of him. He needed her. Even when he was playing his games with other women, he needed her. Even though he tried to keep her from finding out, she knew somehow about his affairs. But that was his way. He loved her, wanted her, needed to know that she belonged to him alone, and yet he needed to prove to himself that other women found him desirable, too. They didn't mean anything to him—but he needed to know that they found him attractive.

She stirred a little, turning on her side away from him, and sighed softly in the darkness, remembering the feel of Morgan's arms around her, the strength and security they offered to her, not demanding from her, but giving, offering her a love she could not accept, even though her very soul cried out to go to him, because she was Allen's wife and he loved her and he needed her so much.

She drifted off into a troubled sleep, wondering where Morgan was, wondering if he was safe, if he was well, or if he was lying in some uncaring place, wounded and needing care. She never allowed herself to consider the possibility that he might not be alive. She felt in her heart that if he had died in the crash, somehow she would know without being told.

CHAPTER SEVENTEEN

Mattie spent her days restlessly roaming through the large house, trying to do things to make it feel like it was her home. Exchanging a vase here and there, moving a picture, bringing in fresh-cut flowers. Other times she wandered out across the lawn with the boys, sitting under a tree watching them play in the grass until the nurse came to claim them, scolding because it was past the time for their naps. The nurse kept the boys on a rigid schedule, insisting that meals, naps, playtimes must all be at the same time each day, determined in her belief that healthy, well-adjusted children should be tended by the clock. Mattie rebeled against fitting her time with them into a routine and often showed up at the nursery at odd hours, picking the small, wriggling bodies up and holding them close to her in a tight hug that made them laugh in delight.

Mattie's first trip out into the kitchen left her feeling as though she had trespassed into forbidden territory. The cook eyed her suspiciously as she toured the spotless room, inspecting cupboards and the stove, checking the supplies.

"Is something wrong, Mrs. Henderson?"

"No. Everything is fine. So clean and orderly." Mattie awkwardly tried to sound casual and friendly.

"Is there something I can help you find?" The cook's voice had a wary edge.

"No. I just wanted to see what sort of things we kept on hand—what we might be needing—"

"I always turn my list into the housekeeper every Wednesday." The answer was crisp, leaving no room for discussion. "The housekeeper gives her approval and I do my shopping early Thursday morning, when the produce comes into the market and is the freshest. Is there any complaint about what I've been doing?"

"Of course not." Mattie smiled, trying to close the gap between them. "The meals have been excellent. You are a very good cook, Mrs. Hansen. I have meant to say so sooner."

"I do my best," the cook said, sniffing. "If you're planning some special entertainment, you just let Mrs. Burton know. If there is some complaint about the prices—" The woman was still on the defensive. "I've always been known as a shrewd shopper. The war has driven the cost of things right up out of reason. There are so many things you can't find at all anymore, no matter how much you're willing to pay."

Mattie moved over toward where the teakettle was singing on the back of the stove. "I have no complaints at all, Mrs. Hansen. I just wanted to . . . I thought perhaps a cup of coffee—"

The other woman took the teakettle from her. "Of course. You didn't need to come out here for it, ma'am. If you had just told the housekeeper, she would let me know." She frowned her disapproval as though Mattie had made a social blunder. "I'll have it ready in a few moments and the housekeeper will bring it to you. Will you be in the sitting room, ma'am?"

"Yes. Thank you." Mattie turned and fled, feeling as though she had committed a horrible error for even thinking the cook might share a cup of coffee with her at the small table near the window. With a rush of homesickness, she remembered the times she and Betty had sat at the kitchen table with a cup of coffee and laughed away the problems of the day.

Mrs. Burton, the housekeeper, was more friendly and sympathetic, somehow guessing Mattie's loneliness. Though she never crossed the boundaries of her station, it showed in her gentle

smile, the manner in which she suggested small things to make
Mattie's day a little smoother, go a little faster. It was from Mrs.
Burton that she learned the best places to shop for dresses, the
beauty salons with the reputation for the latest styles, until she
knew her way around town well enough to seek these places out
on her own. It was Mrs. Burton who moved like a quiet shadow
around the house, keeping everything in order without making
Mattie feel she had no part in the planning.

Allen was motivated by a new burst of enthusiasm, his energies held at a constant high pitch, fueled by a martini whenever
he felt himself beginning to tire. Where he used to drink to relax
and soothe his frustrated nerves he now relied on the alcohol to
refuel his energy whenever he felt himself beginning to tire. He
seemed to thrive on late hours, little sleep, tension, and excitement.
Regardless of the hour he retired, he was sometimes awake and
impatient to leave for his office, even before Mattie was dressed.
She often ate a light breakfast, sitting alone at the breakfast room
table, browsing through the morning papers, searching the casualty lists, reading the latest war news before she planned the day
that stretched out in front of her.

There were the invitations to afternoon bridge, luncheons,
clubs, but the hours she enjoyed the most were the ones she spent
in volunteer work with the Red Cross, rolling bandages and
knitting socks and scarves, packing huge boxes to be sent over-
seas to the soldiers. In the back of her mind, she always wondered if one of them might reach Morgan.

The months dragged by for Mattie in the house in Salem.
Young Clive turned three, and he was in constant trouble for his
adventurous escapades, drawing sharp reprimands from a stern-
faced nurse. Jonathan, close behind at two, was quieter, more
content to play with his toys or to sit beside the nurse as she read
from the nursery rhymes. Of the two boys, however, it was
Jonathan who had the quicker temper. He demanded her attention,
wanting to be held, while young Clive ran away laughing, daring
her to catch him, turning it into a game that left them both
flushed and giggling as she would sink down onto the carpet
beside him, ignoring the nurse's frown of disapproval.

Mattie found dinners hard to plan because often Allen called at

the last minute, his voice apologetic as he explained some business meeting that would keep him away. Or there were the
evenings he spent at home, closeted in the library with other
men, talking long into the night after she had gone up the stairs
to their bedroom.

Mattie missed the busy, demanding life of the ranch, but each
time she asked Allen when they would be going back for a visit,
he found some way to put her off, saying, "Later, Mattie.
Christ, I can't leave right now!" She filled her hours and her
days planning dinners to entertain Allen's friends and their wives,
spent lazy afternoons on her hair, shopping for new dresses,
studying the fashion magazines, telling herself she was content.

Allen opened charge accounts for her at the better department
stores and encouraged her to buy new clothing, to follow the
latest fashions. When she tried to discuss costs with him, he
turned away. "Right now it's more important that you look the
part, Mattie," he explained. "Let me do the worrying about
where the money is going to come from."

CHAPTER EIGHTEEN

Mattie sat at the table in the breakfast room, slowly sipping an iced glass of orange juice and absently nibbling on a slice of toast as she intently scanned the morning papers. She still wore the soft floral lounging robe that she often wore until it was time to dress for whatever appointment was on her schedule. Her hair was still loose about her face and she hadn't bothered with any makeup.

Allen wasn't up yet. It had been close to the early hours of morning when she had heard his stumbling steps in the hallway. She had kept her eyes closed, feigning sleep, turning her head on the pillow, away from the strong smell of cigarettes and alcohol.

The newspapers were spread out in front of her, the society page and the business section laid aside until she finished with the war news. She carefully read the casualty lists that were published each day and then studied the detailed maps showing where each battle line had changed. This had become routine for her, searching the papers for the war news at the beginning of every day—searching for some word, some sign, something to prove that "missing in action" did not mean a battle casualty.

"The telephone, Mrs. Henderson. It's for you—"

Mattie glanced up to see the housekeeper standing in the doorway.

"Thank you. I'll be right there." She carried the paper with her, still reading as she walked slowly toward the phone in the hallway.

"Mattie—Mattie, that you?" She heard Clive's voice above the static on the line. For a moment her heart caught in her throat. Clive was calling. It had to be important. He hated to use the telephone.

"Yes? Yes, this is Mattie. Clive, what is it?"

"We got another telegram from the war department, Mattie."

She felt the cold, icy fingers of alarm racing through her veins and her legs turned weak. She reached out to take hold of the back of a chair for support. "No! It isn't—" She found it difficult to talk, the words caught in her throat.

"It's all right, Mattie!" Clive's voice boomed across the wire, full of strength, reaching out to her, reassuring her. "Can you hear me, Mattie?" he shouted. "We just got the telegram. Morgan's alive—he's safe! By God, Mattie, he made it!"

The newspaper slipped unnoticed from her numb fingers and fell to the floor as she sat down hard on the chair, unable to speak. "Mattie! You there? Can you hear me all right?"

"Yes. I can hear you, Clive," she answered finally. "Where is he? What do they say?"

"Not too much. Just that he was found and he's safe and has been sent to a hospital somewhere in England."

"A hospital? Oh, my God. Is he hurt? Clive, why is he in a hospital?" She waited impatiently for his answer, her imagination running wild.

"Doesn't say. Reckon we'll be getting a letter from Morgan himself before long. Damn it, Mattie, why does it have to take so long for mail to get here?"

Mattie was crying softly now. Tears of relief spilling from her eyes and trailing down her face. Tears of joy, making it hard for her to talk. "I don't know, Clive. Does it say which hospital?"

"Got the address right here. Listen, Mattie, it's too damned hard to hear. Too much static. I'll mail the telegram on over to you so you can read it for yourself. Just wanted you to know right away."

"Thanks, Clive—oh, thank you for calling. Clive?" But the line went dead.

Allen came down the stairs, knotting his tie in place as he walked.

"Mattie? Hey, you're crying! What the hell's the matter? Was that the phone I heard? What's going on?"

She tipped her face up, smiling happily at him through her tears. "Yes, Allen. It was Clive. He must have used a phone from in town somewhere. There was so much noise in the background, it was hard to hear. He called to tell us they just got a telegram from the war department." She jumped up from the chair and ran toward him. "Morgan is safe, Allen. He's alive. He is back in a hospital in England. In a hospital, but he's alive. He made it, Allen!"

"Well, I'll be damned! That's good news! Bet the old man sounded pretty happy, huh?"

She nodded, wiping her tears on the back of her hand. "Haven't heard him with so much vitality in his voice in months. He was laughing and shouting at me. Allen, he's been so worried all this time."

He looked down at her, saw the way her face was radiant with happiness, like a bright ray of sunlight breaking through the clouds after a long storm. It had been a long time since her eyes had danced this way, so vibrant, so alive, and he turned away, angry with what he saw.

"Did they say why he's in a hospital?" he asked as he walked toward the breakfast room.

She shook her head. "Guess we'll have to wait to find out the details. But he is alive—and he will be coming home again. At least I think so. I mean, he's back in England. Surely that means they'll be sending him home, right, Allen?"

He shrugged his shoulders at her impatient question. "I don't know. It depends on what is the matter with him, I suppose. Could be he's just there to let them check him over before they send him back to the front again." He reached over for the papers she had left scattered on the table. "Just hope for the old man's sake that this damned war gets ended before they decide what to do with him. He's fool enough to let them patch him up

so he can head right back out into it again. Isn't breakfast ready?
I'm running late this morning.''

For Mattie the day suddenly had meaning. She chattered along
endlessly as Allen ate, though usually she was quiet this early in
the morning, letting him read the papers without interruption. He
glanced up at her from time to time, frowning across the table at
her, but she just couldn't seem to stop talking.

Mattie walked to the door with him and then turned and ran
with lighthearted steps up to the nursery, where the two little
boys were just finishing their hot bowls of oatmeal.

"Did you want something, Mrs. Henderson?" The nurse looked
up in alarm as Mattie burst in the door, humming under her
breath. "The boys haven't finished their breakfast." Her face
showed clearly her disapproval at having the meal disrupted.

"No. Nothing is wrong. I just wanted to see Clive—to see the
boys for a little while. I wanted to be with them."

Young Clive slipped from his chair and ran over to her side.
"Are you crying, Mama?" he asked, his small face anxious.
"Your eyes are all red."

"No, darling. Not really. They are tears of happiness." She
wrapped her arms around his small body, holding him close as
she rested her face against his hair. "Grownups are so silly
sometimes, Clive. Sometimes they can't cry when they are very
sad and hurt inside, and then something wonderful happens and
they start to cry."

He wriggled loose from her hold and looked up at her, his
brows drawn together in a puzzled frown. "But *why* are you
crying, Mama?" he insisted. "Do you hurt someplace?"

"Not anymore, son. Not anymore," she answered him with a
smile.

He was leaning his elbows against her knee, his small chin
cupped in his hands, watching her face. "What happened, Mama?
What made you want to cry?"

Jonathan sat at the table, not wanting to leave his breakfast.
Little droplets of milk clung to his chin as he divided his attention between watching his mother through large, solemn brown
eyes and spooning up his cereal.

Mattie's voice was soft, trying to find the right words so they would understand. "Your grandfather called us this morning. You see, Grandfather had two sons—just like I do. One of his sons is your father, and the other son is Daddy's brother, your Uncle Morgan. Your Uncle Morgan went away to war and he has been gone a long, long time. He was hurt in the war, and for a long time we didn't know where he was. But, this morning, your grandfather called on the telephone and said they had heard from your Uncle Morgan. He's safe. They know where he is—and he'll be coming home."

Young Clive twisted up his face as he thought over what she had said. "Will he be coming here?"

"No. He'll be going home to the ranch, darling. That is his home. He lives on the ranch with your grandfather. It's very good news and that is why we are all so happy." She stood up, gently pushing Clive toward the table. "Now—you must finish your breakfast like a good boy."

"Can we go to the ranch and see him?" Clive persisted.

"Maybe. One of these days," she nodded. "One of these days when your father is able to take the time, we'll go back to the ranch for a visit."

Jonathan pounded on the edge of the table with his spoon. "Me too, Mama! Me, too!"

"Yes." Mattie smiled down on her youngest. "You too, darling. You too."

Young Clive settled himself down on his chair and looked across at his brother with an air of superiority. "You're too little, Johnny. My Uncle Morgan is coming back to the ranch and he's going to teach me to ride a horse. When I grow up, I'm going to live on a ranch," he announced importantly. He looked over at his mother. "When I live on the ranch with Grandpa and Uncle Morgan, you can come visit me, Mama."

Jonathan beat on the table again with his spoon, splashing his cereal. "Me too! Me too!" he cried, large tears forming in his eyes.

"Neither of you will grow up big enough to learn to ride a horse if you don't eat your breakfast," she scolded, trying to look stern. Mattie pretended not to notice the nurse's growing concern over the interruption of their schedule. "I have an idea.

If you finish your breakfast, we could go to the park—the one down by the river. Would you like that?''

"I always take them for an outing on the lawn in the afternoon," the nurse interrupted. "There are too many other children in the park. It's public, you know."

"I know. And it sounds like wonderful fun. Today I am going to cancel all of my appointments and spend the whole time with my sons. Why don't you take the afternoon off, Miss Bryant? We won't need you. You must have some shopping or something you want to do."

The nurse looked uncertain. "What if Mr. Henderson calls? What will he think?"

Mattie laughed merrily, feeling very young, very alive. "Tell him I finally asserted my rights as a mother. Tell him I kidnapped them. We ran away to the park. If he wants us, he will find us at the swings or sliding down the slides—or maybe we might even go wading."

"Wading? In the river?" The nurse's brows climbed up to near her hairline. "Really, Mrs. Henderson! I don't see how I can permit it!''

She gave an impish wink at the two wide-eyed boys. "Then I guess we'll have to go without your permission. Hurry up, fellows! I bet I can beat you getting dressed."

Mattie slipped quickly from the room. She had a sudden wild desire to be out-of-doors, away from other people, away from this house. She wanted to be alone with her sons. She wanted to walk in the park and feel the sun and wind against her skin. And she didn't give a damn what people thought or said.

CHAPTER NINETEEN

Several weeks later, a letter came from Betty. Mattie found it with the afternoon mail, lying on the table in the hallway. Clive wasn't well and Betty was worried about him. The doctor said it was influenza. She didn't want to worry them any, but it would be real nice if they could come for a visit. Clive knew she was writing and said to tell them there was nothing wrong with him but a cold—he'd be up and around in a day or two.

That night Mattie found it hard to sleep, even though she was tired. Each time she turned out the light and closed her eyes after looking at the clock, her mind raced around with worry. Worry over Clive, wondering just how sick he was, and anger. Anger with Allen because she hadn't been able to reach him all evening. The last time she had looked at the clock, it was two thirty.

She must have slept a little, drifting in and out of restless dreams, when she heard his footsteps in the upstairs hallway— heard him fumble with the doorknob to their bedroom, heard him stumbling into unfamiliar objects in his path, and heard his curse as he groped for the light switch.

Warm, soft light flooded the room. "What the hell?" She knew he saw the suitcases. "Mattie?"

She pushed the covers back and sat up in bed, watching him, without answering.

"What you got these damned suitcases sitting out for?"

"I'm going back to the ranch in the morning. I plan on leaving as soon as it is light enough to travel."

He sank down into the padded velvet chair and lit a cigarette, letting it dangle carelessly from his lips as he loosened his tie, struggled with his shoelaces. "Didn't know you were planning a trip. When did you decide this?"

"This afternoon."

"Short notice, isn't it? You can't go away now. You ought to know that. You should have waited and talked it over with me before you did all that packing. We've got that dinner coming up for Judge Williams. How's it going to look if you aren't here?"

"We got a letter from Betty this afternoon. She thinks I ought to be there. Clive isn't well, Allen. She's worried about him."

"Oh, for Christ's sake! Is that what's the matter with you? You unpack those suitcases the first thing in the morning. If you're worried about him, use the telephone. What do you think those damned phones are for, anyway? I had one put in over there, and now I can't get anyone to use it, unless they're listening to the gossip on the party line. It's a bunch of damned foolishness, but if it will make you feel better, go ahead and call him up. You'll probably get an earful for your trouble. You think he's going to want you running over there every time Betty writes that he has the sniffles—like maybe you think he's getting too old to take care of himself anymore?"

"No, Allen. Clive never asks for help—not from anyone. Betty said he knew she was writing to me. That's why I'm worried. He needs me and I'm going. There's no use trying to talk me out of it."

He was angry now, snubbing his cigarette out in the tray with short, vengeful stabs. "What am I supposed to do about that dinner? Too late to call it off. Why don't you think about me? What I need? Things like this are important—can't be pushed aside because you decide to take a little trip over to the ranch! Judge Williams is the key to that highway work we want done over along the coastline. This dinner is important. God damn it, Mattie, I want you here to handle the details."

"You're going to have to take care of things yourself this

time, Allen. Or get one of your—friends—to act as hostess. I really don't care. I won't be here. Clive needs me and I'm going."

"What about the boys?"

"I'll be taking them with me. You don't object, do you?"

"Why the hell should I? How you planning on getting there?"

"Driving. That's one of the benefits of living like we do, isn't it? A large, comfortable car for me to use when I want it? It will be easier on the boys to travel by car. I can make it in four, maybe five hours. The weather is good now, so I won't have any trouble. The car is dependable."

Allen stood up and began to unbutton his shirt. "It's no good, Mattie. Your place is here, with me, when I need you. Maybe we can go over later, take a little vacation—when things let up at the office."

Mattie shook her head. "But he needs someone and he has no one but me. Betty said she had written to Morgan at the last address we had, hoping she could get word to him. Having him home on leave would do Clive more good than anyone and all of the medicine they could give him. Clive don't say much but he has been worrying an awful lot about Morgan."

Allen looked up, bristling at her remark. "Now why in the hell would Betty take it upon herself to do something like that? Morgan is off playing soldier boy. You think the army gives their men leave to come home just whenever they want to? Thought he was still in England, anyway."

"They were going to transport him home and we've never heard any different. We still don't know why he was in the hospital over there. Betty thought she ought to try, at least."

He turned away, going over to the closet to hang up his jacket. "I'm not going with you. I can't leave right now," he said over his shoulder.

"I didn't think that you would." There was a touch of sarcasm in her voice. "Allen, your father doesn't take to his bed for any length of time unless there is something wrong—seriously wrong. You know that as well as I do." She slid out of bed and found her slippers with her toes. "It's almost morning. I might as well stay up. The earlier we get started, the better. I'll call you from there and let you know how he is.'' She went out of the door leading toward her dressing room.

Allen knew better than to say any more. Mattie may have smoothed out a lot of the rough edges and learned how to control her temper some, but she still was as stubborn as ever. Guess that part of her would never change. When she raised her chin and tilted her head in that manner, there was nothing going to talk her out of doing what she had her mind set on. Damned inconvenient for him right now. Mattie should have thought of that.

Betty heard the car when it turned off the highway and headed up the lane toward the house. She was standing on the porch waiting for them. She caught young Clive in her arms as he tumbled excitedly out of the car, setting him down on his sturdy, short legs, and then reached for Jonathan.

"Can't believe how much these young ones grew since we seen them last," she exclaimed. "Let me help with the things, Mattie. Leave the suitcases. Wes will get them later. I got a fresh pot of coffee on, and your rooms are aired and ready. I knew you would come, just as soon as you got the letter."

"How is he?" Mattie asked, her eyes clouded with concern.

Betty shook her head. "I'm real worried. It's the influenza that's been going around. Lots of folks have had it, but he just don't seem to be able to shake it off. I don't know—maybe I shouldn't have written and asked you to come over here like I did, but I was real worried. I just felt that if he had his folks around him it would make a difference. He's been awful lonely."

"You haven't heard any more from Morgan?"

"No. There haven't been any more letters. Just that one. It's got Clive upset, thinking there is something really wrong. That's why I wrote to him. Thought maybe if he knew—" She shrugged. "Don't know what he could do about it, though. England is a long ways away from here. But if he was headed back this way anyway, maybe somehow he could hurry it up a little."

They were in the house now, putting away coats. "I finally got him to move downstairs to the big bedroom. It's a lot closer to the kitchen and saves a lot of steps. Me and Wes have been staying over here nights since he took sick. I just couldn't bring myself to leave him.''

Mattie put Jonathan down for a nap and sent young Clive off with Wes to inspect the new calves while she washed the road dust away and freshened up before going in to see the old man.

The room was darkened, the air carrying the sickroom smells of camphor and disinfectant. Mattie caught her breath in alarm at her first glimpse of Clive. His face, usually ruddy with an outdoor tan, was almost as pale as the white pillowcases he lay against as he slept. He looked so frail, so defenseless, lying there. She wanted to cry out with the injustice of it.

He turned his head and opened his eyes at the sound of her footsteps.

''That you, Mattie?'' There was a scratchy hoarseness in his voice.

''It's me, Clive. I'm here. Everything is all right now. I'm here to take care of you.'' The words caught in her throat. It was frightening to see the power behind the Henderson clan so white and drawn and helpless. ''Can't have you in bed when there is work to do, now can we?''

''Just a damned cold. Nothing serious,'' he answered weakly. ''You shouldn't have come all the way over here. I'll be out of this bed in a day or two. Just tired. So damned tired, Mattie.''

She reached out and smoothed the covers. ''I needed an excuse to come over here anyway,'' she said softly. ''Don't fret. I was lonesome to see you. You shut your eyes and rest, Clive. Everything is all right now. I'll go out and see what I can do to help Betty. We'll fix you some hot broth—something to make you feel better. I'll be back in in a little while. You rest, so we can talk.''

''The boys with you?'' he wanted to know.

She nodded. ''I'll bring them in so you can see them after you've finished your nap. Jonathan is taking his nap now, too. I'll bring them both in a little later.''

He shut his eyes. ''All right. Just tired, Mattie. Tired. I'll be up after while.''

Mattie found Betty waiting for her in the kitchen. ''Have you had a doctor out here yet?''

"Several times. I didn't write to you at first, because he seemed to get better for a while."

Mattie tied an apron on over her dress. "You look tired too, Betty. I'm here now. Why don't you and Wes go to your own home tonight. You will probably rest better, being back in your own bed. I'll stay with him. I can rest tomorrow, during the day, while you're here."

That evening Mattie took the two small boys into Clive's room, setting them on the side of the bed where he could see them, and for a little while he seemed to enjoy listening to them chatter. But she could see the effort it took for him to talk, so she led them off to their own beds, explaining to Clive that it had been a long trip and the boys needed their rest.

When the doctor was there the next day, he had little to say to encourage her. "He's a sick man, Mattie. I'm doing all I can. If it goes into pneumonia, we're going to have a real battle on our hands."

"But he has always been so strong!" she protested. "I don't know of him ever being sick before."

The doctor just shook his head. "Watch him closely. If you think he is worse, call me. I'll come out anytime you need me. His fever is up today. Don't like it much. Give him cool sponge baths—use rubbing alcohol—get him to drink as much water as you can. Betty hasn't been able to get him to eat. Maybe you can get him to take hot soups, beef broths, that will be strengthening for him."

Mattie stayed at Clive's side, tirelessly caring for him, getting what rest she could by sleeping in a large chair in his room where she could hear him if he called out to her. She withstood his bad temper when he raged over not being able to be up and about, and she was gentle with him when the fever blurred his senses and he called out to her, thinking she was Carrie, his dead wife.

There were times, too, when he clung to her hand and asked when Morgan would get there. He needed to see Morgan. She would gently wipe his brow and tell him, "Any day now, Clive. Any day now. We heard from him. Did I tell you? He is on his way right now. All you have to do is rest, so you'll feel better when he gets here. There will be so much to talk about. You need to rest.''

The way he relaxed after she told him this, she knew it wasn't wrong to lie a little. Maybe it might even be true. She had sent a telegram and maybe it had reached him.

The doctor drew Mattie aside, his face showing his worry. "You been able to get hold of Morgan?" he asked.

She shook her head. "We don't know for sure where he is. Why? He's worse, isn't he?" She knew the answer without the doctor confirming it. "He's been sleeping most of the time. He just seems too tired to open his eyes—"

The doctor nodded and reached out his arm, trying to comfort her. "I'm sorry, Mattie. Just wished I could do more, say something to give you a little hope. You better get hold of Allen. He ought to be here. I don't know how much longer the old man can hold out. It's his heart. His heart is tired. This fight has just been too much for him."

"How much longer do you think he has?" The very question caught in her throat, not wanting an answer, because as long as Clive was alive there was still hope that he would be able to pull through.

"How can I say? A few hours? A few days? If we can keep him going longer than that, he might make it. But if he should pull through, he will never be able to lead the active life he is used to."

She lifted her chin. "He'll make it! He's too stubborn to give in. Clive has always been a fighter! I'll help him, and he'll make it."

The doctor smiled sadly at her. "I hope so, honey. You go call Allen now. I'm going out to the kitchen and see if Betty can get me some coffee and a bite to eat. I'm going to stick around for a while. Got no other patients needing me this afternoon. Might as well just have some of Betty's good cooking and a visit with Wes."

She knew why he was staying. She went into the study to the telephone. She needed to call Allen. She needed to talk to him.

It took several calls before she located him, and then she had to wait for someone to call him to the phone. "You better come right away, Allen. The doctor says there isn't much time left. He's been asking for you. I—I think he knows.''

"Christ, I can't leave right now, Mattie. You had me called out of a meeting. Listen. You take care of everything. I'll leave first thing in the morning.''

"It might not be soon enough, Allen.''

"What difference will a few hours make? I promise. I'll leave first thing in the morning. I'll drive right straight through. I should be there by noon.'' There was a long pause at the other end of the line. "Mattie? What's the matter, honey? You all right? You sound tired.''

"Tired? I don't know. I never stopped to think about it.''

"You been pushing yourself too hard. You shouldn't do that. You heard from Morgan?''

"No. We sent a telegram. Don't know if it reached him or not. He could be in transit somewhere, where they can't find him.''

"Yeah. That's probably it. Honey, you get some rest. You hear me? You sound like you need it. I'll be there early, tomorrow.''

The line went dead. Wordlessly, she hung up the phone and sank back into the chair.

Sure. Get some rest. Clive, you just got to put off dying, because you can't do it right now. Allen is all tied up in a meeting right now and can't get away, and we haven't been able to reach Morgan because he's off playing soldier, and I'm tired. I need to get some rest. Tears glistened in her eyes and she wiped them away with the back of her hand before she stood up and went silently into the darkened bedroom.

"Mattie?'' The voice was weak, but clear.

She went quickly to the side of the bed and took the thin hand in both of hers. "Yeah, Clive? I'm right here. You want something?''

"Just wanted you here beside me. That's all.''

"I'm here, old man. I'm not going anywhere. I'll be right here beside you if you want me. You just rest now.''

"Mattie—there's something I never got around to telling you. Feel bad about it. I want to do it now, while there is still time.''

"Hush. Don't talk now. You're supposed to be resting. You can tell me later."

"No. Waited too long already. Always meant to tell you. Just like my own daughter, you been. I'm right fond of you, Mattie. Stay here with me."

Tears choked her until she could hardly answer. "I knew you felt that way. Guess I always knew it. You didn't have to tell me. But thanks, Clive. Thanks for saying it. Now close your eyes and rest. I'll be right here. I might even lay my head down on the coverlet beside you, where I can hold on to your hand and we can both take a rest."

He was content. He sighed and shut his eyes and slept. Less than an hour later the doctor came in and found them both apparently asleep. He picked up the old man's wrist, feeling for a pulse—but there wasn't any.

CHAPTER TWENTY

The funeral service was held in Bend. Allen was there, looking very handsome and well groomed as always in a black suit and tie. Mattie was a quiet, dark shadow at his side. Her two sons were with her, watching wide-eyed and solemn. They were too young to understand what was going on, but somehow they knew it wasn't the time to poke each other or make any noise.

To Mattie the services were but a muffled blur. It seemed as though she were off in the distance somewhere, looking down and watching the other people, not finding any of it real or believable. None of this could be happening. Not to them. Not to Clive. Clive was indestructible. He had been around forever—solid, dependable, always there when he was needed, holding the rest of them together. He couldn't leave now. He was needed now more than ever. They were wrong. All of them were wrong. Clive would wake up pretty soon and make all of these people go away and leave them alone.

Vaguely, she heard Allen explain several times to different people how Clive's death had come as such an unexpected shock to all of them. She heard him say how he had left his office as soon as he heard that the old man had taken a turn for the worse, driving straight through without stopping, but he hadn't been able to get there in time. Who would have thought that a cold could turn into something more serious so quickly, taking them all by surprise. She listened as he talked about his plans for the ranch, the improvements and the changes he would make, and she turned away with a heavy heart. Clive wasn't even in the ground yet and already Allen was making changes.

Mattie felt ill. There were too many people collected here for the size of the chapel. The heavy smell of flowers was overpowering. There were banks of flowers—large, elaborate floral arrangements with cards bearing names she recognized as the men Allen dealt with in that political world of his—gaudy next to the smaller, more conservative sprays from Clive's friends. A handful of the men had even come here from Portland and Salem to attend the funeral services, conspicuous among the ranchers and their families, and Mattie resented their presence.

Standing quietly, lost in memories that kept flooding in around her, Mattie gradually became aware of someone watching her. She glanced up to see Morgan standing alone across the room. As their eyes met, Mattie felt her heart beat faster and a small cry of joy escaped from her lips. He was here! He was safe! Morgan was home at last. He must have received the telegram. If only he could have been a little sooner. Her eyes feasted hungrily on his tall, wide shoulders, the harsh lines of his face, the dark shadows near his eyes. He was dressed in his military uniform, carrying his cap under his arm, his jacket and pants pressed with creases as sharp as a knife edge. He was standing alone, a little away from the others, and as their eyes met, an electrical current passed between them as real as though he had reached out across the room and physically touched her. She watched as his gaze finally left her face and traveled down to rest on young Clive. He studied the little boy for a few moments and she saw a look of pride erase the last of his doubts and soften the hurt in his eyes. Somehow he knew. She wanted to turn and run to him, to throw herself into the arms she knew would welcome her, to kiss him until the hard lines of his mouth softened to reveal the gentleness she knew was hidden there.

It was the touch of Allen's hand on her arm that brought her back to the reality around them, and with reluctance she brought her gaze away from the tall figure across the room. Though she tried to concentrate on the conversations around her, her heart and her thoughts were filled with the tall, rugged man in uniform who could cause her very soul to sing with only a glance.

After the funeral, they all collected at the ranch. Allen, Mattie, the two boys, Wes, Betty, Morgan, local ranchers who had known Clive Henderson for many years and wanted to pay their respects, and others who hardly knew Clive but came because of Allen. The women from the other ranches had brought hot dishes, as was the custom, and were busily setting up a buffet, putting out food, pouring coffee.

The dining room table was lined with an assortment of home-made pies, cakes with swirls of chocolate icing, a large roast of beef for slicing, crispy on the outside and pale pink and juicy on the inside. Someone had baked a ham, and there were relishes and pickles, jams, and fresh home-baked bread and mounds of yellow butter churned early that morning.

While the women saw to the food, the men gradually broke up into smaller groups around the large living room discussing the war, the beef market, the elections. From time to time Mattie caught a glimpse of Morgan quietly talking with some of the other ranchers, shaking hands, receiving their welcome-home wishes along with their condolences, managing to be a part of the gathering and yet remain withdrawn at the same time.

Allen opened up the liquor cabinet and glasses were filled and passed around. The women were tending to the smaller children or gossiping in the kitchen as they washed up the dishes, while their menfolk pursued their heated discussions of war and politics over their bourbon. Allen was at his best now, moving easily among the men, talking with confidence, holding a glass in his hand, his dark features handsome and polished as he took over the role of the host.

As the evening shadows began to darken across the valley, the women gathered up their young and the ranchers began to take their leave, needing to be home in time for chores, until the only ones left in the living room were the men from the city who came to pay their respects as well as to discuss business with Allen.

Mattie's head was beginning to ache—a dull ache that numbed her senses, leaving her unable to follow the conversations going on around her. She felt an overpowering tiredness that had nothing to do with lack of sleep. She felt stifled by the heavy air around her, closing in, suffocating her. She slipped quietly from the room and went upstairs to look in on the boys. Betty had put them to bed earlier and they were already asleep, relaxed, innocent-looking. Jonathan's dark curls were damp across his forehead, and he lay curled partly uncovered, his thumb in his mouth. Young Clive had tossed one arm out across the pillow. As young as he was, she could see in him the firm, strong features of the old man beginning to form. Mattie watched them for a moment and then turned and left, pulling the door shut quietly behind her with a sigh.

Mattie paused in the hallway outside Clive's study. The light was out, the room silent. Voices drifted out to her from the sitting room, and her small frame shivered slightly at the thought of going back in there right now and trying to smile and pick up on the conversations. She needed desperately to be alone for a while, away from the other people, so she turned toward the front door, seeking the cool, night stillness of the porch.

Outside the air was fresh and clean, carrying a hint of rain. Mattie moved to the quiet protection of the shadows at the far end of the porch, where the only sound breaking the silence was the call of a night bird off in the distance. Did he even have to carry on his campaign at his own father's funeral? she sighed tiredly as she leaned her head against the post, looking out toward the mountains in the darkness. She tried not to think of Clive as she had seen him last, dressed in his best suit, resting on a satin pillow, surrounded by the banks of expensive, ornate floral sprays. He would have hated it, she thought. He never liked showy displays, particularly when he might not have even recognized some of the names on the cards. He had been such a dynamic man, but a private man, too—not given to a demonstrative show of feelings. He felt deeply, but he wasn't one to put it into words. You just sort of knew how much he cared by the things he did.

"You all right, Mattie?"

She turned at the sound of his voice. Morgan stepped out of

the deep shadows where he had been quietly smoking a cigarette and watching her.

"Yes," she nodded. "I just couldn't take any more of the noise in there. I wanted to be alone for a while. I'm all right now," she answered softly.

"I got your telegram. I came as soon as I could. I tried, Mattie. I just couldn't get here any sooner." His voice was low, edged with the hurt he was feeling.

Her eyes were hungrily searching his face, seeing lines that hadn't been there before. "I know," she whispered. "I kept telling him you were on the way. He wanted so much to see you. We didn't know where you were, if you were able to travel. We didn't know if the telegram would even reach you or not. I told him we had heard from you and you were coming. It made him feel better, thinking you were safe and headed home. He tried to wait, Morgan. He just couldn't hold out any longer."

"You were with him?"

She nodded. "Morgan, just before he—the end—he took my hand and he told me I was just like a real daughter to him, that he was fond of me." The words caught in her throat in a little sob. "He never said anything like that to me before. Guess I always knew he felt that way, but he just never said it before."

Morgan saw the way her back stiffened, the way she fought to keep her lips from quivering. Unable to stand it any longer, he held out his arms to her and she fled into their shelter. At his touch, the flood of tears that she had been holding back for so long was released. Morgan let her cry, knowing it would heal her. He held her gently in his arms, resting his face against her hair as he felt her heart beating against his chest.

Her sobs gradually lessened as the tears washed away all of the worry, the fear, the pain that had been building up inside of her since that day he had left to enlist and she had hurled the defiant words at him, telling him to go ahead and leave.

Though she still rested in his arms, she turned a little so that she could look up into his face, her eyes lovingly touching every familiar line. "I can hardly believe that you are really here," she murmured. "It's been so long. Oh, Morgan, I worried so—the days, the weeks that I have prayed for your safety. I watched the papers, the mails. Then, when that telegram came, I wanted to die, too, if anything happened to you."

He felt the tremor run through her body and he drew her closer against him, feeling the old familiar stirring within him at her nearness. "It's all right, Mattie," he whispered. "It's over."

"I knew you were alive," she said as she reached up to touch his face with her hand, as though to reassure herself that he was really here and it wasn't a dream. "I never gave up hope. It seemed like an eternity before we finally got word that you had found your way back—that you were in a hospital in England." She touched his face, his hair, ran her fingers down across the rough wool of his uniform, raising her arms to encircle his neck.

His arms tightened around her, holding her warm body close against him. "It doesn't matter anymore, Mattie. It is all over. I'm back." He ran his hands along the lines of her body that he remembered so well, unable to believe that at last he was holding her in his arms again. "I had to come back, Mattie," he whispered. "I couldn't stay away. I kept thinking about those few hours when we forgot the barriers that are keeping us apart and we made love there in the cabin with the storm raging outside. The memory of it made me keep fighting to stay alive because I knew I had to come back." He bent his head and their lips met, stopping time. For a few short moments, as they clung together, there was only the two of them, and nothing else mattered. Nothing mattered but the love they had for each other.

Mattie pushed abruptly away from Morgan when they heard the front door open and someone step outside. Allen stood there, a fresh drink in his hand, watching them. If he had seen them kissing, he didn't let it show. His suit coat was off and he had the cuffs of his white shirt rolled up one turn. He looked relaxed, in command of what was going on inside the living room behind him. Morgan couldn't help but notice how self-confident Allen seemed now. There was a certain smugness in the one-sided grin as he spoke.

"Well, Morgan, been looking all over for you. Then I realized that you would probably be off in a corner somewhere by yourself, not fitting in too well with the businessmen inside. Most of the ranchers have gone home. Welcome back."

"Thanks, Allen. How's things going?"

"Just fine, Morgan. Just fine. Couldn't be better. Hasn't Mattie filled you in on what we're doing? We're going places, moving up in the world. What about you? Surprised to see you here. Thought you were still in England. Didn't figure you'd be coming home this soon from the sound of things. How'd you manage to get leave?"

"I'm being discharged. It's just a matter of paperwork now."

"Oh, yeah? Interesting. War isn't over yet. You got hurt over there or something, didn't you?" He waved his hand carelessly. "We can talk about that later. Like to hear about it, though. Never hurts to have a war hero in the family. You were in France, weren't you? You meet any of those wild little French mademoiselles I been hearing about?" Allen winked broadly at him. "Understand they are really something, eh, Morgan?" His face grew serious then and he studied his brother for a moment. "You made any plans?"

Morgan shrugged, struggling to hold his temper. "Not yet."

"That's good! Good. Just might have something for you. Been pretty busy over in Salem. Mattie and I live over there now, you know. The boys are even talking some about maybe running me for governor. 'Course, that's a couple of years away, but never hurts to be looking ahead. How about that, Morgan? Me, the next governor! With the old man gone, I'm going to need someone here on this place to keep it going for me. General foreman or something like that. Know what I mean? Don't worry, Morgan. We'll find a spot for you someplace. Look me up later when we got more time to talk about it." He didn't seem to notice the way Morgan stiffened, the way his hands clenched. "Mattie, you better come back inside with me. We have guests. Your place is inside. With me."

Mattie started to follow and then she paused to turn back for a moment. "Your room is the same as always, Morgan. Except for putting in the electricity and adding a better bed—things like that—I left it like it was. It's still your room—your home."

He nodded quietly, his face grim. "Thanks. Good night, Mattie."

* * *

The next morning Allen was restless, pacing the floor, finding fault with little things he would hardly have noticed at any other time. Mattie tried to keep the small boys out from underfoot, but the confusion and disorder left them fussy, clinging to her skirts and wanting her full attention.

"Why the hell didn't you bring their nurse along, if you didn't want to leave the boys at home?" Allen complained angrily.

"Because this is a private thing," she snapped back sharply. "I didn't want her here." And then she tried to soothe over her outburst by adding, "I just wanted some time with the boys, without schedules and rules laid down by outsiders. I wanted Clive to see them again."

Morgan left the house early that morning, before anyone else was up. Only Wes had seen him saddle up a horse and disappear over the ridge, headed out toward the summer pasture in the foothills, wanting to be alone. Wes didn't say anything, figuring that Morgan was saying his own private good-byes to the old man. Or maybe he was just wanting to be away from the group collected at the house until he could get himself unwound, trying to find his way back from the war years to the slower-paced remoteness of the ranch.

Allen spent a lot of time on the phone, closeted in the old man's study with the door shut, coming out once in a while to go to the liquor cabinet to refill his glass and to grumble because the lawyer who had drawn up Clive's will had not appeared.

"There is so damned much to do," he complained. "It's a hell of a time for me to be away from Salem right now. Why can't that old attorney get his ass out here so we can get the formality of reading the will over with? Does he think all I got to do is sit around waiting on him?" He kept walking to the window looking out toward the main road. "Don't know why the old man went behind our backs, insisting on going to that old fool anyway, when he had a damn good attorney right in the family. I need to be on my way back to Salem. I can't sit around twiddling my thumbs. There is only one way for this ranch to be taken care of anyway. Everyone knows that. Reading the will is just a formality to go through so that old duffer can collect his wages."

But the reading of the will turned out to be more than a formality.

"To my sons, Allen and Morgan, I bequeath the sum of one dollar each. . . ."

Allen leaned forward on his chair, unbelieving, his mouth gaping open, but too stunned to utter a protest. The older attorney looked at him over the top of his glasses and then went on reading.

> To my grandsons, Clive and Jonathan, I leave the balance of my estate, whatever it might be, hoping that I am around long enough to be able to teach them the value of a dollar better than their father ever learned.

> In the event that I have to leave this earth before I am willing, the ranch is to be kept in trust, the profits reinvested in stock and improvements until the boys reach legal age. To be sure this is done, I am appointing Mattie Henderson as trustee, hoping that she will have the good sense to ask Morgan for his help. With Morgan's knowledge of ranching and Mattie's natural knack for thriftiness, maybe I won't rest too uneasy, knowing the future of the ranch will be protected until the boys are old enough to take over. For these services and to cover their expenses, they each are to receive a salary of—

"What kind of bullshit is this!" Allen exploded, not able to keep still any longer. "Let me see that paper!" His face was red with anger, the veins standing out on his forehead. "It isn't legal! No will like this would hold water in any court!"

"It's legal, Allen," the old lawyer answered calmly as he removed his glasses from his nose. "Clive Henderson went to a lot of trouble to see that it was, knowing what your reaction would be."

Allen turned on Mattie, who was sitting in stunned silence. "You did this! You came over here when he was sick, and you got him to change his will. Not of sound mind. That's it. He wasn't of sound mind, running a fever. He was sick when he wrote it!"

The older man shook his head, snapping his briefcase closed. "This will has been in my safe for over a year, Allen. Signed, witnessed, legal as all hell. Clive Henderson was a strong man who knew how to fight for what he wanted. We may not understand it, but I'm sure he had his reasons for doing what he did."

Mattie turned away from the blinding anger in Allen's face to look across to where Morgan sat lounging back in his chair watching the exchange of words with a slow grin of amusement on his face. He nodded toward her. "Well, I was sure right about one thing. The old man is determined to go on calling the shots around here, even from wherever he is right now. He don't give up easy."

"Wipe that asinine smirk off your face and get serious!" Allen snapped. "Don't you understand what happened? We've both been written off—one fucking damned dollar apiece! And after all we've done around here!"

"Maybe that's all he figured we were worth," Morgan answered quietly. "The old man planned on being around for at least another twenty years. He must have been having trouble with his heart for a while, but he never let any of us know about it. He got worried. He wanted to be sure the ranch would go on operating just like it would if he were still here to do it himself. That's why he put Mattie in charge, making her the trustee. She's the only one with guts enough to stand up to the rest of us—the only one he felt he could really count on to do exactly like he wanted things done. The old man always was smarter than either of us ever give him credit for being."

Allen put his suitcase in the back of a shiny new car and left for Salem the next day. Instead of resenting him for leaving without offering to help put things back in order, Mattie only felt relief. His anger, his accusations against the old man, his bitterness had been almost too much for any of them to take. There was so much to do after the long days of Clive's illness when everything else had almost been left at a standstill. She felt it would be easier on all of them with Allen gone. She had to go through the old man's personal things. She couldn't expect Betty to do a chore like that. Besides, she wanted to be alone, to have time to think. The past days of worry, tension, of losing Clive and seeing Morgan home safely had all taken their toll, leaving her exhausted.

It was evening. The house was quiet. Mattie sat in a chair near the fire in the study. The lantern was gone. In its place was an electric lamp. A telephone stood on the edge of the desk. The same old furniture was still here. Wasn't no way the old man was going to let her or anyone else change this room. It was his. She looked up at the shelves lined with books along one wall. The big ledger where he kept his figures lay open on the desk. The room echoed with the sounds of memories all around her. If she shut her eyes she could almost see his gray head bent to work on his papers in the evening light as he kept track of the stock, the breeding records, the bills coming in, did the payroll. She could smell the popcorn she used to fix for them to eat while she sat there in the quiet with him and read from the books that had belonged to another woman a generation ago. Why hadn't she done it more often in the last few years instead of spending so much time worrying over Allen's career, entertaining his friends, having babies, being too busy to think about an old man alone in this big old house? All of them had left him, and he must have been so lonely. Morgan off God only knew where, getting himself shot up, she and Allen moving away to Salem, bringing the boys back only once, not thinking that Clive might have wanted to have them around more, to watch them grow.

Everything had changed so. Look at herself. From Morgan's outgrown jeans and baggy flannel shirts to beauty salon hairstyles and silk dresses. Couldn't sit around reading and eating buttered popcorn in front of the fire in a dress like she was wearing. She had grown thoughtless, inconsiderate of other people, thinking her own problems were all that mattered. And yet—the old man must have still believed in her. Why? she wondered. She hadn't given him much reason.

"Am I intruding, Mattie?" She looked up to see Morgan's large frame in the doorway. He had discarded the uniform and was wearing a pair of rough pants, a plaid shirt, and there was dust on his boots as though he had been out riding. He was carrying his sheepskin coat across his arm.

"No. It's all right. Come on in."

"Don't want to bother if you'd rather be alone. You looked like you were studying pretty hard about something."

She gave a deep sigh. "No. I think I need company. I'm not liking my thoughts too well right now."

He came on into the room, his boots leaving dusty prints on the floor as he went across to sit in the other chair on the far side of the fire. Both of them avoided the chair that Clive had always used.

"You've been out riding alone, haven't you?" she said. "Is it so hard, Morgan, to come back home again? Trying to forget the war? Trying to find your way back to us?"

"There's no way to go back, Mattie," he answered quietly. "The hard part is learning how to put the past in the place where it belongs, because we can't just wipe it out. We have to try to put everything in its proper place and keep on going ahead." They sat in silence for a minute or two, and then he asked, "What were you thinking so hard on, when I came in and interrupted? What's bothering you, Mattie?"

"I don't know. Nothing. Everything. I've been sitting here thinking over the last few years, wishing I could do it again—do it better—at least where Clive was concerned. I'm feeling a little frightened, too. I guess I didn't realize how much I depended on him to always be here. He was always so . . . : solid. No matter what else happened to the rest of us, how things changed, how we changed, we could always come back here and feel safe. Do you know what I mean? He was the only thing in this crazy, mixed-up world that seemed to stay the same. He stayed sane and dependable. I was sitting here thinking about everything—and I wonder what is going to happen to us without him." She gave a lonely little sigh as she talked. "I feel lost, and I guess I'm frightened, too. I'm scared—like the day I woke up and found my own pa gone, knowing I was all alone, not knowing what was going to happen next."

Morgan saw how pale she was, how vulnerable she looked in the soft light. He didn't know what to say to comfort her. He wanted to go across and lift her in his arms and love away all of the hurt and the doubt until she was able to laugh again—until she was the old Mattie, full of fire and fight and laughter.

"Morgan, I don't know where to go from here. I don't know what is expected of me." Her eyes were smudged with tired shadows. "There's Allen—angry and resentful, expecting me to come to Salem right away, somehow blaming me for the way the will was drawn. And there's the boys, not understanding what's going on and needing me more than ever to keep reassuring them that everything is all right. Here at the ranch there's so much work to be done. Wes and the hands are keeping busy, taking care of things the best they can, but they need someone to step into Clive's place and make the decisions. The whole damned world is falling apart all around us. What is happening to all of us? What am I supposed to do? Everyone expects so much of me and I don't know where to turn next. What's going to happen to *us*, Morgan? To you and me?"

He wanted to reach out, to touch her, to kiss the tears from her eyes, to say to hell with the ranch, to hell with Allen, to hell with everything that was keeping them apart. He wanted to leave and take her with him. He wanted to take young Clive by the hand and tell the world that he was his father. It didn't matter what others thought. He knew in his heart that the boy was his. But he couldn't. The old man had seen to that. The old man left the ranch to the two small boys and made Mattie trustee of the estate. Mattie couldn't leave. She had to stay to protect the inheritance for her sons. And he couldn't leave. He couldn't leave Mattie. The old man was playing games with their lives and he knew it.

"You will stay here—at the ranch—won't you, Morgan?" She was watching him closely now, waiting for his answer. "Like Clive wanted? I can't do it without your help. My God, I'm only one person. I can't be in Salem and be here at the same time."

"What about Allen? Won't he resent my being here? Think I'm intruding? Isn't it going to cause more trouble if you turn to me for help instead of going to him?"

She shook her head. "He's too angry right now over the will. I can't even talk to him about the ranch. He won't listen. He counted pretty heavy on it all being his. I don't think it ever occurred to him that it wouldn't automatically go to him if anything happened to the old man."

"But he never liked it here."

She lowered her lashes and shook her head. "No. He hated it. He hated everything about the ranch. He couldn't wait to move away. He envied the men from the city—the way they dressed, the way they talked, the way they lived. He still does."

"Then why, Mattie?"

"I don't know. The prestige of owning a ranch like this, maybe. Clive worked hard all of his life, and it is one of the best ranches in this part of the state." He saw the flicker of pride in her eyes when she spoke of the ranch. "Maybe because it is a valuable piece of property. Maybe it's because he just didn't want anyone else to have it. I don't know what his plans were— but there is no way he can touch it now. Not even any of the income from it." She gave a tired sigh. "No. I'm afraid I can't expect any help from Allen."

"Even though it belongs to his sons?" Morgan studied her thoughtfully as he talked. "Isn't he thinking of their future? What it will mean to them?"

"I don't know what he's thinking. I just know that Allen is too upset right now to even talk about it. How could the old man do this to me?" The more she thought about it, the more angry she got. "I just don't understand what he was thinking about. How could he possibly expect me to oversee something as big and demanding as this ranch, when he knew I had to live in Salem with Allen?"

She got up from the chair and began to roam about the room restlessly, pausing in front of the desk, looking down at Clive's ledger open in front of her.

"I love this place. I worked as hard as I could when I was here, because I felt as though I belonged, as though this was my home," she said quietly. "I even rode out with Clive, when he was checking on stock. I did what I could, but that is a lot different than sitting in his chair, giving orders. Even with Wes being the foreman and Betty running the house, it's a full-time job. I can't be here all of the time. He knew I had to leave. We talked about it. He knew I had to move to Salem." She glanced up at him, angry sparks beginning to flash in her eyes. "I just don't understand the old man at all! Damn it, how could he do this to me?"

Morgan sat staring thoughtfully into the fire and it was a long time before he answered. "I been doing a lot of thinking too, Mattie. That will was a big surprise to all of us, I guess. The old man was too damned smart to do something without giving it a lot of thought first. He knew what he was doing and I've been trying to understand what he meant by writing the will the way he did. I think I've got it figured out. He knew he couldn't leave the ranch to Allen and me. We've never been able to get along well enough together—we see things differently. It wouldn't have worked and he knew it. If he left it to Allen and cut me out, it would have been buried in debt within six months. Or sold. The old man worked too damned hard to build this ranch and he wasn't about to let that happen. If he left it to me—maybe I wouldn't come home from the war. Maybe I wouldn't want to settle down and stay here. He was trying to figure out a way to get what he wanted." Morgan glanced up at her, holding her attention. "So he left it to *our* sons." At her gasp, he held up his hand, stopping her words. "He made you trustee, knowing you would fight tooth and nail to carry out his wishes, even if you didn't understand them. He knew all too well that it was more than you could handle if you weren't here all of the time—if you lived in Salem—so you would need help. He knew that I wouldn't be able to walk away if you really needed me. He knew damned good and well how I felt about you. He must have guessed that I felt young Clive was my son. He knew I would stay and help."

She turned from the desk, looking intently at him across the room. "And will you stay?" she asked. "Will you be here to take care of the ranch when I need you?"

He rose from the chair and went over to stand in front of her. He tipped her face gently with his fingertips until he could look into her eyes. "The old man knew me pretty well, I guess. I can't stop loving you, Mattie, though I've tried. There've been times when I just wanted to toss you over my shoulder and ride away with you—but I knew your guilt would never let you be happy and I could never do anything to hurt you. I knew I should stay away, but I had to come back. I had to see you again. I think the old man knew. He understood." He gently wiped away a tear that spilled from the corner of her eye. Just touching her that way sent a wildfire tearing through him. With a groan, he abandoned all caution and he reached out to pull her roughly against him, crushing her lips with his mouth. He felt her lips soften and grow warm with desire beneath his own.

He cradled her against him, her body soft where his was hard, hers yielding where his was demanding. His hands slipped down the arch of her back, sliding across the raw silk of her dress, his touch burning through the sheer fabric. He felt her tremble as his mouth hungrily kissed her lips, trailed along the line of her throat, found the warm hollow between her breasts, and returned to claim her lips again.

Mattie was afraid, lonely, hurt, hungry for love, and she needed him desperately. Her arms slipped around his neck as she returned his kisses with an urgency fed by her need.

He pushed her away from him, trying to control his racing emotions. "No," he said hoarsely. "No, Mattie. Not here. Not in Clive's study." He swept her off her feet, and holding her cradled in his arms against his hard chest, he carried her from the room. With determined steps, he went up the stairway and down the hall to his bedroom.

He kicked the door open with his foot and walked across to the bed, laying her gently on the blankets. He shed his clothing with fluid swiftness and knelt beside her to help with the fastenings of her dress. The yellow silk made a soft, pliant splash of color as it joined his rough jeans and heavy shirt on the floor.

"Why do I love you the way I do?" she asked as he folded her in his arms. "There is so little future for us."

"Hush, Mattie," he murmured as he held her close against him. "Don't speak. Don't think. Don't put more obstacles in our path than there already are. We love each other. We need each other. Just feel the love that is flowing between us right now. Let that be enough for tonight. Nothing else matters tonight. No one or nothing else exists in the whole world right now but just you and me. Only us—only our love—"

It was so easy for her to listen, because he was saying what she needed to hear. A sob of desire escaped her lips as she melted into his arms. She only knew that she could not survive much longer without knowing the overpowering, wonderful torture of him making love to her again.

He teasingly tormented and gently soothed her body with his hands and his lips, finding those secret places he had discovered in the small cabin during the raging storm and reclaiming them as his own. Her hands sought the hard muscles of his shoulders, her fingers trailed down across his back, touching, exploring, loving every part of him.

She clung to him in the darkened room, and the driving force of their need for each other took them into that timeless world of wonderful sensual fulfillment that left no room for the problems they had been discussing such a short time ago.

Mattie lay beside him, her head resting on his arm, the tangled covers partly covering them against the slight chill of the room. She lay still, letting the thoughts of their passionate lovemaking surround her and push away any other thoughts for as long as possible. He was quiet but she knew he wasn't sleeping.

"What are we going to do now, Morgan?" she asked softly.

"I don't know. What can we do?" he answered quietly. "Will you leave Allen?"

"How can we even talk about it right now? Clive just died. The flowers haven't even wilted yet on his grave. There are little Clive and Jonathan to consider. They don't deserve the scandal it would cause. And the ranch. Their ranch. We've got to think about this damned ranch." She turned her face and looked at him. "You know as well as I do that I can't leave Allen right now."

"Then I guess you pack up and go back to Salem. The sooner the better." His voice was harsh. "You go back to your husband and I'll go on with my own life. I need to plan a life of my own. I did a lot of thinking about what I wanted to do when I got back. I've been making some plans—"

"What plans?" She felt a wave of uneasy alarm. "You won't leave the ranch, will you? Where would you go? You won't leave?"

He shook his head. "This is good country to live in, Mattie. It's where I was raised. I like it here. But, like everything else, it is changing, growing. There's a lot of building going on, a big demand for lumber.'' He paused thoughtfully, and then added, ''I've been thinking some of a lumber mill. I've been looking at some land between Bend and Sisters. It's a good location—close to the highway and still within easy hauling distance of some heavy timber stands.''

''But what about the ranch?'' She waited anxiously for him to go on talking, wondering how his plans would affect the future of the ranch. Affect her.

''I guess I could go on living on the ranch and still go ahead with my own plans for the mill. The ranch was left to the two boys—it's up to us to take care of it for them.'' He reached out, smoothing her hair back from her face. ''I told you when we were talking earlier that the old man left the ranch to 'our' sons. I can't claim the boy openly, Mattie, but I know in my heart that he is mine, whether you will admit it or not. It's his future we're talking about. The old man found a way to tie me to the ranch after all,'' he said with a grin. ''He knew I wouldn't let you down. Or young Clive. And if I didn't know better, I'd swear he was trying to find a way to throw you and me together, too, with his planning.''

He raised up on one elbow and bent to kiss her gently on the forehead. ''I'll be here, Mattie. Guess I'll always be around when you need me. Now, why don't you slip back under the covers and go to sleep. I think you've had about all you can handle for a while. These last weeks have been rough on you, staying with the old man the way you did, and now this. Try not to worry anymore. I've got to go out to the corrals and check things for the night. See if you can't forget everything and just get some sleep.''

It wasn't until he had gone quietly out of the room, leaving her alone with her thoughts again, that she realized exactly what had been said between the two of them. The full impact of the meaning of the words caused her to sit up in the middle of the bed, jolted into consuming fury.

''He left it to our sons,'' Morgan had said. ''He couldn't leave it to Allen and me . . . so he left it to our sons.'' Morgan was only guessing, but he believed in his heart that young Clive was his son. But the old man! He must have pieced together bits of things he had heard or seen, or just plain guessed at, knowing a lot more about what went on and how people he loved felt inside than he had ever let on, until somehow he decided that young Clive must be Morgan's son, and that was why he wrote the will in the way he did. He wanted to protect the future of Morgan's son as well as that of Allen's, and he didn't trust Allen to do it. He had tied up the ranch in a trust for both of the boys, leaving Mattie as trustee. He knew damned well she couldn't live in Salem with Allen and have full control of the ranch without help—without Morgan's help. He had counted on Morgan not being able to walk away if she needed him. He had found a way to tie Morgan to the ranch. More than that, he had deliberately found a way to throw the two of them together. He was probably sitting back smiling to himself right now, up there wherever it is people go, feeling really proud of himself, knowing the ranch would go on just as he had intended, even if he wasn't here to run it himself.

Mattie's hands curled into tight, angry fists. "You conniving, meddling, interfering old fool! How dare you do this to me!" she cried out in rage to the empty room, feeling somehow that he heard. "How dare you play games with our lives this way! You just can't keep from meddling, can you?" From his grave, she knew, Clive was still trying to control things, trying to take care of his own, trying to make things right in his own way.

CHAPTER TWENTY-ONE

Mattie prepared for the trip back to Salem with lagging steps and a heavy heart. She couldn't shake the feeling that the ranch was her security, the place where she really belonged. The ranch was her home, not that monstrous house in the city where someone else took care of her babies, did the cooking, moved like a silent shadow through the rooms, keeping everything dusted and in order. At the ranch she could come and go as she pleased without worrying about how it looked to the people who were always watching, ready to gossip about her actions and criticize her dress. Here she felt sheltered and protected and yet at the same time free to be herself.

Morgan was at the ranch. She could look up from her work and see him riding out across the field or hear his sudden laughter floating in from where he talked with the men at the corral. She could turn and see him watching her from across the room and fantasize what it would be like to drop what she was doing and run across to where he stood, throwing herself into his waiting arms. She could almost feel him holding her close against him, feel the hardness of his body, the touch of his hands, his mouth roughly coming down against her eager lips. But fantasize about it was all that she could do. They had agreed that they would

avoid any circumstances that might take them once more beyond
the edge of control.

Mattie didn't know which was the worse torture—to be at the
ranch, where she could see him all of the time and know she
mustn't go to him with the abandon she felt in her heart, or to
leave and return to Salem, where she wouldn't be able to see him
at all.

The house was filled with memories of a past that was slipping
away from her, and she couldn't let it go. Each time she passed
the silent study she felt that if she went in and sat down and waited
Clive would come striding in, frowning over the nonsense that
had been going on, his boots leaving their tracks on the floor, his
thunderous voice echoing along the hall. Clive wouldn't allow
the ranch to fall apart while everyone went their separate ways. If
she left the ranch now and returned to Salem, nothing would ever
be the same when she returned.

Wes would be ramroding the ranch in his easygoing way,
sending off reports to her, which she would read and try to
understand. Morgan would be there, somewhere in the background,
making decisions, but she wouldn't be able to hold him there all
of the time, fitting him into the emptiness Clive had left. Morgan
was already missing for hours at a time, searching for the right
spot to build his lumber mill, beginning to build a dream of his
own that had nothing to do with the ranch—or with her. No.
When she left this time, nothing would ever be the same.

Allen had called several times during the last few days she was
at the ranch. He was irritable, impatient, demanding that she
wind up whatever she was doing and return to Salem. He needed
her. Things were happening—important things. She belonged at
his side, where he could depend on her to help him when he
needed her.

Somehow she had to pick up the scattered pieces of her life.
She had to return to Salem. She had to play the role of the wife
of the prominent young attorney general. She had to plan the
dinner parties, entertain his guests, join the other wives at bridge,
keep her appointments at the beauty salon, concentrate on all of
the senseless things that mattered so much in Allen's world. She
had to stop thinking of how much she wanted to answer the love

she saw blazing in Morgan's eyes whenever their eyes met across the room.

The boys were installed once more in the nursery under the watchful eye of their nurse. Jonathan settled down to his building blocks and games, happy to be back in the familiar surroundings he knew best. His laughing dark eyes and winning ways won the nurse quickly back under his spell. It was young Clive who rebelled, refusing to conform to the rules and the boundary lines of the nursery, bringing harsh reprimands down around his ears. The nurse shook her head crossly and blamed it all on the lack of discipline they had been allowed over the past few weeks.

"Really, sometimes I just don't know what to do with him, Mrs. Henderson," the nurse complained. "I don't believe taking him over to the ranch was the wise thing to do. Young children are so impressionable, you know. These are the forming years of their lives and it's most important how they are taught. Their surroundings, the people they see and listen to . . ."

Mattie refused to take her seriously. "He's so small. He's just a little boy. What could he possibly do that is so wrong?"

The nurse hesitated and then took a deep breath before she continued. "He's a stubborn and headstrong child. And his language! He said—well, I just can't repeat it, but it is no way for a three-year-old to talk. You certainly didn't allow him out around the barns over there, did you?"

Mattie turned away, trying to suppress a smile that tugged at her lips. He most certainly *had* been out around the barns. He had followed Wes and Morgan whenever and wherever he had the opportunity. She wondered what young Clive had overheard and repeated to shock his nurse so much.

"I wouldn't worry about it if I were you," she told the other woman. "He will forget quickly and go on to something new— and probably just as shocking." Mattie tried to sound reassuring. "He loved it at the ranch. He was starting to turn brown as a berry from being out-of-doors so much. He was happy. I wish we could have stayed longer," she added wistfully, "and gone under different circumstances."

"I know. It was very sad. And that is what bothers me. That

man—the one he calls his Uncle Morgan. Evidently he followed him around a great deal and, well, I don't really believe the man is a good influence on him. Clive looks up to him. I think that is who he is trying to copy."

Mattie caught her breath sharply and weighed her words with care before she answered. "Clive is a very active, healthy little boy with a little boy's imagination. He loves horses and cowboys and being out in the open. He could do much worse than his uncle when looking for a hero."

The nurse turned away, her lips drawn in a firm line, feeling her argument was losing the backing she had sought. "Well, I just wish he could be more like Jonathan. He never gives me any problems at all. He's such a good little boy."

"No two boys—or girls, for that matter—are the same," Mattie answered firmly. "Jonathan loves his toys. He wants to be around other people, wants to be loved and held. He is more openly affectionate. Clive is more reserved, restless, adventurous, wanting to seek things out on his own. If you don't feel you can handle them, let me know. But I won't have Clive stifled, made to fit into a mold of what you feel is the model little boy. Besides, it wouldn't work. He is too much like his grandfather, the man he was named for. To hold him close wouldn't be possible. He would only rebel all the more."

The nurse left the room and Mattie stood looking out of the window to the east, toward the range of mountains that separated the green, fertile Willamette Valley from the high desert country where the ranch lay. She had a faraway look in her eyes. Yes. Young Clive was so much like Morgan, even as small as he was. Restless, loving the out-of-doors, not afraid of anything as he sought out new adventures . . .

Her thoughts were interrupted by a light knock on the door and Mrs. Burton poked her head inside. "Excuse me, Mrs. Henderson. I felt you would want to know!" Her face was flushed, her eyes glowed with excitement, and her voice trembled as she talked. "It's the news, ma'am. Mr. Henderson just called, said I should tell you right away."

Mattie's eyes opened wide in surprise at the housekeeper's

outburst and her distraught display of emotion. "What is it?" she asked in alarm.

"It's the war, ma'am. It's over! They just heard. The war is over!" Tears of happiness were flowing openly now and she was laughing as she tried to talk. "The mister said the word is coming through right now, on the telegraph!"

"Thank God!" Mattie ran across the room, warmly hugging the other woman, her own eyes brimming with tears. It was finally over. "Does anyone else know? Have you told the others?" The reserve was gone and they were just two women weeping tears of joy over the news and what it meant.

"No, Mattie. I came up here first. I want to go and tell cook now. She needs to be told right away."

Mattie scarcely noticed that in the excitement the sedate housekeeper had slipped and called her by her first name. "Wait, let me come with you! We'll both go down and tell her." Mattie followed her flying footsteps down the carpeted stairway toward the kitchen.

The two women burst through the door with their news and before her very eyes Mattie watched the cook's starched stiffness crumple into something very human and vulnerable. Mattie felt helpless, not quite sure of what to say or to do.

"It's her sons, Mrs. Henderson," Mrs. Burton explained softly. "She is a widow, with only her two boys left. She was so afraid they wouldn't be coming back home. They're both over there."

Mattie looked back at the cook, who was helplessly trying to wipe away a flood of happy tears on her spotless white apron, and she felt as though she were intruding into something very private. "I didn't know," she whispered. "Stay with her. She needs you. She shouldn't be alone." And she turned and slipped out of the door, feeling deeply disturbed.

How little we know about people living close around us, she thought. She had always felt the cook was just a dour-faced, prudish old woman who turned out perfect dinners from the private domain of her kitchen, brooking no interference from any of them. But she had feelings, and she loved and she worried, and she cried her tears in private, hiding her fears and her breaking heart in a flurry of flour and rattling of pots and pans.

Mattie had the uncomfortable feeling that a few years ago she would have known without being told, would have understood. What was happening to her? How could she have changed so much? She turned and fled up the stairway toward the nursery, suddenly wanting to be near the boys.

The nurse took the news with an amazing calm, turning back to the lessons they had been working on when they were interrupted. "I'm a little confused," Mattie faltered. "I thought you would be as excited as the rest of us."

"Of course, Mrs. Henderson. The news is wonderful. I'm very happy. It just came too late." Her hand went unconsciously to the locket she always wore on a chain around her neck. "There are some who won't be coming home."

"I'm sorry," Mattie answered softly. "I didn't know. You lost someone, someone dear?"

The nurse nodded, so slightly it was barely noticeable. "We didn't marry before he left, like so many of them did. He thought it was better for me that way, in case—well, he just thought it would be better that way."

"Do you want me to stay with the boys for a while?" Mattie asked. "Would you like some time alone?"

The nurse stiffened her back. "No. I prefer to stay here, to keep busy. For me the war ended some months ago. I've done my grieving. I've found my peace and am able to accept things as they are, finally. Thank you, but I prefer to keep busy."

Mattie turned and left the nursery, going back down the stairs quite shaken and pale from the events of the past hour. What if Morgan hadn't returned from the war? What if his plane had gone down and there had been nothing left but a yellowed telegram. What if she hadn't had young Clive to hold in her arms when she knew she could never feel Morgan's body warm against her own. What if there had been nothing left of their love but a fading memory? Tears filled her eyes. How could she have possibly stood the loneliness, the emptiness, if she hadn't had young Clive as proof of their love, even though she couldn't have Morgan.

The news spread around the countryside like a raging wildfire. People were rushing out into the streets, laughing, crying, shouting back and forth to their neighbors. Reporters were out, moving from one group to another, taking notes, collecting stories. An impromptu band had collected and was marching in the street playing "Over There" and "Pack Up Your Troubles" with wild enthusiasm as young people danced along behind them, singing.

Newsboys were on every street corner hawking their last-minute street editions, filling the air with their cries. The telephone lines were jammed with calls, making it almost impossible to reach anyone by phone, as people tried to reach the other members of their families.

In the distance the sound of fireworks along the riverbank mingled with the noise of the city. The siren from the firehouse sounded at intervals, and the mills blew their whistles, echoing across the valley.

Everyone seemed caught up in the crazy, wild hysteria as they shouted back and forth to each other and pushed and shoved their way along the crowded sidewalks, stopping to hug each other, kissing friend and stranger alike, so anxious were they to share their joy. The sounds drifted up the hill to where Mattie stood at the window listening with tears glistening in her eyes.

"Excuse me, Mrs. Henderson. It's the mister on the phone again. He wants to talk with you."

Allen's voice was exuberant, carrying across the line to her from a background of noise and voices. "Great news, huh, baby? The whole town is turned upside down with the celebrating. You ought to see what it's like down here! People are going crazy! Listen, I'll be home to get you in about an hour. Be ready, will you? Wear something special. We got a party of our own going down here. Something—well, something that is going to surprise the hell out of you. Want you in on it."

"What are you talking about, Allen?"

"Wait until you get here. I'll explain it then. Hurry up, baby. Get dressed. I want you ready to leave as soon as I get there to pick you up."

"But where are we going, Allen?" she demanded. "I need to know so I'll know how to dress."

"Just wear something special, I told you." The noise in the

background made it hard to hear. "I can't talk any more right now. See you in about an hour."

Mattie put the receiver back on the hook, curiosity picking away at her. She glanced toward the clock and hurried up the stairs toward her dressing room. She pulled several dresses out of the closet, frowning at each selection. Wear something special, he had said. Damn it, what was he up to now?

She finally decided on a new dress she had never worn before. It was cut with a low V neckline and followed the lines of her figure, straight and narrow, to a hemline just below her knees. A sash tied just above the curve of her hip outlined the new lowered waistline that was in fashion. A matching cape of the same shimmering amber satin went with the dress. It had wide pleats at the neckline and then pulled in at the hemline in tight gathers, so that it flared out in the middle. It was a daring dress, cut to the very latest style, sent here from New York just for her.

As she slipped it over her head, her thoughts wandered back to another time, several years ago, when she had wanted to surprise Allen with a new dress—her only new dress, a dress bought from the racks in the general store in Bend. How proud she had been, walking down the sidewalk in the sunshine, seeing her own reflection in the windows of the stores on the way to his office. She remembered Allen's annoyance, the amused way Irene Bancroft had looked at her. It wasn't until now that she realized how poorly cut and out of style that dress had been—and yet she had been so proud of it. Now her closet was filled with dresses, all designed and made especially for her, and she wasn't particularly fond of any of them. How things had changed. How *she* had changed.

She slipped her slender feet into amber satin slippers with high heels and long pointed toes, dyed to match the dress, before turning in front of the mirror to check the seams up the back of her silk stockings and adjust the snaps on her garter belt. She straightened her dress and studied the image staring back at her. Her hair was cut short, parted on one side and waving down to form sharp little points near the line of her chin, showing just the tip of her ear. Small round dots of rouge highlighted her cheekbones and her mouth was a cupid's bow of red. Satisfied, she picked up the amber satin cloche, a close-fitting hat that pulled down on one side almost to her eye, and looked around for the beaded purse with the amber fringe.

There was a light tap on the door. "It's the mister again," Mrs. Burton announced, her flushed face beginning to show the strain of the hectic day. She paused to catch her breath from the climb up the stairs and then continued. "He said to tell you he hasn't been able to get away. He's sending the car for you. He wants you to come right away."

"Did he say where he was?" Mattie asked, frowning in irritation.

"No, ma'am, he didn't. I suppose the driver will have instructions." She glanced at Mattie's gown. "Will you be having dinner at home tonight?"

Mattie shrugged. "I don't know. No. Tell cook not to bother. The two of you take the evening off. After all, it is a very special day, isn't it? You must have friends you want to be with."

The car stopped in front of one of the newer clubs in town. Mattie leaned forward to watch the milling crowds of people who were pushing their way in and out of the double doors under the glittering lights. People blowing whistles, waving flags, calling back and forth, embracing each other as they met. The driver turned and gave her a one-sided grin.

"Look at that crazy mob, would you?" he said. "I think the whole world is a little nuts tonight. Partying, drinking, raising hell. It's sure not a good time to be driving."

She smiled in sympathy at him. "Is Mr. Henderson inside?"

"Yes, ma'am, he's in there. He said I was to deliver you here and see that you got inside without nobody bothering you. These people are crazy. Did you have anybody over there in the war?"

"Yes. My husband's brother."

"He going to make it back all right, you think?"

"He's home already. He was a flyer."

The driver tugged his eyebrows together thoughtfully. "Hey, is that the Henderson who was the flying ace? Got his plane shot down, didn't he? Wasn't he missing for a while? I remember reading it in the papers."

Mattie nodded. "Yes. But he's home now. He's safe."

"Well, you can be thankful for that, anyway," the driver continued. "There's such a bunch of them that weren't so lucky and won't be coming back. No wonder everyone is so crazy tonight—glad it's over before any more of them are lost." He came around and opened the door for her. "I'll walk you to the door. It's a regular riot out here tonight. Everyone means well, I guess, but some of them get a little carried away."

Mattie stood just inside the double doors looking about her, wondering where Allen was and how she would ever find him in this jungle of people. A band was playing with a lot more enthusiasm than skill but no one seemed to mind. Everyone was drinking, laughing, dancing, shouting back and forth, pushing and shoving against each other as they tried to make room for even more merrymakers arriving to join the celebration.

A man disentangled himself from a group nearby and grabbed Mattie in his arms. "Hey, pretty lady—shouldn't be alone on a night like this! Come on over and join our table!"

As Mattie tried to wriggle out of his enthusiastic embrace, a waiter appeared at her elbow, his black suit and white shirt beginning to lose some of its crispness. He frowned forbiddingly at the man attempting to lead Mattie toward his table. "Mrs. Henderson! I've been trying to watch for you." He was trying to remain composed and dignified, but the strain was showing plainly in his eyes. "Please come with me. I'll take you to where your husband is waiting."

Gratefully, she followed in the path he was trying to clear for her through the noisy crowd to a door marked PRIVATE, where he stopped and waited for her.

She gave him a puzzled glance. "He's in there?"

The waiter nodded and rapped sharply on the door before pushing it open. Allen sat behind a desk, leaning back comfortably in a deep, overstuffed swivel armchair, looking handsome in his dark suit and white shirt, his dark hair parted and smoothed back from his face. He was smiling, but there was a brilliant hardness in his eyes. Five or six other men were in the room, expensively dressed in evening clothes, standing near the desk or lounging in the comfortable chairs.

Allen came across to meet her, taking her by the arms and

kissing her affectionately on the cheek before turning to the
waiter. "Bring in another round, will you? Oh—and a martini for
my wife."

The waiter nodded and left, pulling the door shut behind him,
closing out most of the noise from the dance floor.

Allen led Mattie across to an empty chair before making
introductions. She remembered having met two or three of the
men before, at one place or another. The others she had never
seen before.

"What do you think of the place out there, Mattie?" Allen
wanted to know.

Mattie shrugged her shoulders and laughed at the memory of
the madhouse she had met when she arrived. "Total disaster!
That is the only way I know to describe it. Hysterical, chaotic
pandemonium—"

"No, not that," he answered, shaking his head with a frown.
"I mean, the supper club itself. What did you think of it?"

Mattie wasn't sure what he wanted from her. "There were so
many people it was almost impossible to tell, Allen. I suppose
under different circumstances, when it wasn't so crowded, it
would be a very attractive place. Tonight—well, really, I didn't
have a chance to look around. Survival was more on my mind
than checking out the decor. What more can I say?"

Allen glanced around the room at the other men. "I wanted
you to see it tonight, Mattie. I wanted you to be here with us, be
a part of it, when I signed the papers."

Mattie was confused. "What papers? I don't know what you
mean, Allen."

He had a cigarette in one hand as he waved in a vague gesture,
taking in the room they were sitting in and the building beyond.
"Papers for the supper club. I just bought it, Mattie. At least,
most of it. I own the controlling interest—or I will when we sign
the papers."

Mattie's eyes flew open, startled by his announcement, and
she looked toward the other men for confirmation, unable to
answer him.

The door opened, bringing in a wave of noise as the waiter
entered with a tray and set it down on the low table. Allen waited

until he had left and the room was quiet again before he went on speaking, savoring the moment to the fullest. He put a martini in Mattie's hand, holding his own glass out to her in a salute.

"A toast, Mattie." He touched the rim of her glass with his own. "Drink a toast with me, baby. To the success of our dinner club. To the success of the Willamette Heights Dinner Club."

"Dinner Club?" Mattie was stunned with the announcement. The whole day had been nothing but chaos—and now this. She felt as though she were moving in a nightmare and couldn't wake up. She suddenly didn't know or understand anyone around her, least of all Allen. A nightclub! Allen had bought a damned nightclub! If the talk of prohibition went into law, he'd be out of business before he got started. Allen was as crazy as that crowd of people milling outside! What in the hell was going on? She touched the glass to her lips, welcoming the cool, bracing bite of the alcohol as she tried to grasp the meaning of Allen's announcement.

One of the men stood up—middle-aged, balding, dressed in an expensive, well-cut gray suit, a diamond flashing blue lights from his little finger. "You have a brilliant young man for a husband, Mrs. Henderson. You should be proud of him. He's come a long way since I first met him in that little law office in Bend. You have that beautiful big home in the heights south of town, that ranch of his taking so much of his time but doing well, and now this place. On top of that, he's cutting quite a figure in politics, moving up through the ranks fast, like a man who knows where he's going. He's getting a lot of notice. Wouldn't be surprised if he wound up the next governor of the state! Wouldn't be surprised at all."

"The ranch?" Mattie wanted to know what he meant by the ranch taking so much time, but Allen interrupted her before she could say anything, his eyes flashing a warning at her.

"Not too many people know about me buying this club, Mattie. Got to keep it quiet," he said, changing the subject. "Nothing wrong with it, of course. What the hell. A lot of men in public office own other businesses. It's just that some narrow-minded folks frown on a man in my particular office mixing it with nightclubs. Doesn't make a lot of sense, does it? But we've got to keep it quiet anyway. It's none of their gawd-damned business—just better this way."

One of the men who had been sitting quietly, watching Mattie's confusion with amusement, stood up and walked toward the desk, holding out a pen. "We've stalled long enough, Allen. Let's get the papers signed. I'm missing out on one hell of a party while I'm sitting here. Got some . . . ladyfriends . . . waiting for me." He winked broadly. "Don't want to keep them waiting too long—not on a night like this. Know what I mean?"

The rest of the night was a blur for Mattie. After the other men left, she and Allen moved out to a table near the bandstand. The hilarity of the milling crowd was infectious and Allen was in a good mood. There were questions Mattie wanted to ask but there was no way to have a conversation between the two of them. People recognized Allen and came to their table to talk. Some moved on, but others pulled up chairs and stayed. Before long, it was just one large group, all intermixed with adjoining tables.

As Mattie's glass emptied, it was taken away and replaced with another icy drink. The cold, refreshing liquid tasted good to her in the stuffy warmth of the overcrowded room, and she would reach for it without thinking. Allen danced with her once, holding her close against him, but the floor was too jammed with milling couples for them to do more than stand in one spot and shuffle in time to the music. Others claimed her, unfamiliar arms guiding her, holding her too tight. Unfamiliar faces bending close, flirting, complimenting, leading her through the steps of new dances, until at last she began to relax, joining in the laughter and gaiety with a sparkling abandon, her eyes flashing with a new brilliance, her voice too loud as she reached for yet another drink.

Allen disliked dancing. He hardly ever used the cane any more, but his leg still bothered him, making him feel stiff and awkward on the dance floor. He hated anything that didn't show him to his best advantage, so he stayed at the table, the center of attention, as the men came up to talk to him and the women bent close and brushed suggestively against him as they claimed a kiss.

It was getting late. Mattie felt ill. The crowds began to close in on her and she needed a breath of fresh air. Her whole body felt odd, as though it didn't belong to her anymore. She was floating, drifting, her feet not quite touching the floor. She found a half-burned cigarette in her hand and didn't remember how it got there but had the dry tobacco taste in her mouth. She felt a rough hand on her arm, hurting her, and she impatiently tried to brush it away. She blinked her eyes, trying to see clearer through the haze that was closing in on her and focused on Allen looking down at her, his face dark and angry.

"Come on, Mattie, I'm taking you home." His voice was hard and critical.

She stumbled a little and closed her eyes for a moment, trying to make the blurred room stop spinning. "I don't want to go home, Allen. I'm having too much fun. I'm not ready to go home. I just need some air—"

"You're drunk." He was leading her roughly toward the shelter of the office near the back of the crowded floor.

Mattie started to giggle. "Am I? I've never been drunk before." Suddenly everything seemed funny and she wiped the tears of laughter from her eyes. "God, it's warm in here, Allen. Too much dancing. I need something cold to drink. I'm thirsty. Get me another drink." She looked up at Allen's dark face and began to giggle again. "You look funny when you're mad, Allen. I never noticed that before." She couldn't stop laughing.

"For Christ's sake, cut it out, Mattie." He tried to steady her faltering footsteps, but she kept trying to pull away from him. They were in the office and he shut the door firmly behind them. "Where's your coat? You left it in here, didn't you?"

She shrugged carelessly. "Don't know. Don't need a coat. I'm not ready to go home yet. I'm having fun." She swayed unsteadily and reached for the desk for support. "You know, Allen, I never really liked your friends before. Guess I was being stuffy, wasn't I?" She tipped her face up to him, suddenly serious. "Is that why you don't come home until late sometimes, Allen? Because I'm stuffy?" She spread out her arms and whirled around in a circle. "Not stuffy tonight, am I?" She burst out in merry laughter as she twirled, and then suddenly she stopped, covering her face with her hands. "Oh, my God! I think I'm going to be sick!"

Allen caught her by the arms as she started to fall. He reached for her coat, draped it across her shoulders, and half led, half carried her toward the outside exit and a waiting car. "You're drunk, Mattie. I'm taking you home." There was no tenderness in his voice or his touch.

Mattie remembered very little of the ride to the big white house south of town. The next thing she was aware of was Allen taking her coat from her shoulders and telling her to go into the bathroom and wash her face in cold water. How she had gotten home or up the stairs to their room was all a misty blur. Her head was throbbing to the beat of wild drums and her stomach was churning rebelliously, but she didn't want to give in.

"Not now!" she protested. "Not cold water!" She shivered at the thought. Through all of her laughter she felt a deep, empty loneliness inside. She wanted to be held, to be comforted. She wanted Morgan. She reached out her arms enticingly, her voice soft and sultry, her eyelids heavy. "Come here, Allen. Hold me." She wanted to feel Morgan's strong arms catching her, holding her close—feel the touch of his lips, the hardness of his body against her own, hear the soft laughter as he explored the curves of her body, bringing her senses to an awareness that made her want to cry out in ecstasy as he made love to her. Through the fog of alcohol, she tried to pretend it was Morgan as she wrapped her arms around Allen's neck, pressing herself against him.

"Do you love me, Allen?" she whispered suggestively. "Do you want me? Then hold me. Make love to me. Now."

Allen picked her up in his arms and carried her to the bed, laying her down against the pillows. As her heart cried out for Morgan, her hands caressed Allen until his need was as urgent as her own.

Their lovemaking carried a violence of passion they hadn't shared in a long, long time—maybe not ever before—and when their bodies were finally spent, Allen raised on one elbow and tenderly kissed her good night.

"You sure did get drunk tonight, Mattie." He chuckled softly.

"You're going to have one hell of a hangover in the morning. But tonight—oh, baby, tonight you were wonderful!!"

Mattie curled up into a soft ball, wishing the bed would stop spinning long enough for her to fall asleep. The pounding in her head made her think of thunder rolling through the mountains outside a small deserted cabin.

CHAPTER TWENTY-TWO

Mattie's heart was singing and her eyes sparkling with impish delight as she watched the winding road twisting out in front of them, her gloved hands firmly holding the steering wheel. Her large brimmed touring hat was pinned carefully in place, the ribbons fluttering gaily back over her shoulders in the light breeze from the open window. Two large suitcases were stowed in back, along with a picnic hamper filled with delicacies to nibble on when they stopped to rest. Her thoughts were racing eagerly ahead of the speeding car toward the ranch, already visualizing the familiar big, old ranch house, the rolling desert lands, the deep, rich mahogany-red cattle with their white faces grazing contentedly on the hillsides. Her two small sons were on the front seat beside her, playing with some toys she had brought along to make the trip go faster for them.

It had been so long since she had been there. Weeks had turned into months, the months stretching out endlessly until she could stand it no longer. She had finally decided that if Allen wouldn't take the time off to go with her, she would pack up the boys and make the journey by herself. There had been sharp words when she had gone to him with her decision, but Allen hadn't really put up much of an argument. He was too involved with so many things right now. The prohibition laws had put a new strain on his office and she knew he was walking a tightrope. The dinner club had been turned into a private club, for members only, referred to more casually as a speakeasy. So far Allen had been able to insure the patrons of a place to enjoy their favorite labels without being caught in a raid, but it was a dangerous game he played, publicly enforcing the laws prohibiting the sale of liquor and privately raking in the profits from illegal alcohol. Mattie suspected Allen was also playing the stock market heavily, and though she understood little about it, she knew he was riding a new, exhilarating crest of chance in his gamble for success.

Life in Salem for Mattie had turned into a constant round of entertaining—of parties, afternoon bridge games, martinis and cigarettes, going to bed in the early morning hours just before the sun came up, and sleeping until noon. She had learned to play the role Allen expected of her well, holding her position in the center of the clique of other wives, earning their respect as well as their envy, emerging unscathed by the petty jealousies and sniping because that was all that it was to her—a role to play, a game.

Now she had found a way to escape for two delicious weeks. She had kidnapped the two boys from the nursery and she felt as giddy as a young girl, rushing home from boarding school for the holidays.

The reports from the ranch had been sent monthly, carefully copied in Betty's precise handwriting, and she had read them patiently, assured that all was going well and a profit was being made. But the things that were important to her were not shown on paper. The figures showed how much was made from the sale of the cattle last fall, how many spring calves were counted, but there was no mention of how Morgan looked, riding easy in the saddle up across the ridge toward Willow Spring, the chiseled lines of his face turning brown in the summer sun. Once in a while Betty added a note or two about the mill that he was building—its progress, the problems—but it told her nothing of whether he still remembered their last embrace or lay awake at night, lonely, thinking of her.

From time to time Betty asked about Allen, wanting news from the city, curious about Allen's progress, but there was no mention of whether Morgan, in building his own life, had excluded her memory from his future. They had agreed once that too many other lives could be damaged or destroyed if she left Allen. But did the memories still haunt him as they did her? Or had he managed to forget her as he divided his time between the ranch and the lumber mill.

Mattie glanced sideways at the two boys on the car seat beside her. Young Clive was solemnly watching out of the window, not talking, but Jonathan, sitting between them, was keeping up a constant stream of chatter. Learning to talk seemed to be one of his favorite accomplishments and he was filled with endless questions.

"Will Aunt Betty be at the ranch, Mom?" he asked.

Mattie nodded her head. "She'll be there. She'll be watching for us, and I bet there will be warm cookies and fresh milk on the table, waiting for you."

"Will she remember who I am?" he asked worriedly.

Mattie looked down at his anxious face. "Of course she will, darling!" She reached across and patted his small hand where it rested on a chubby knee. "You boys are very special to Betty and Wes. They would never forget who you are."

"But I almost don't remember what she looks like—"

"You were very small, honey, the last time you were over there," she consoled. "You're a big boy now. You're three years old. It will be easier to remember this time."

"Do you think we'll have a good time?"

Mattie smiled at the doubt in his voice. "Of course we will. You will love it at the ranch. There are so many things to do."

He didn't look totally convinced. "If it's so much fun, how come Daddy didn't want to come with us?"

"Because Daddy has to work, Jonathan." Mattie slowed for a sharp curve, her full attention on the road ahead of them. They were getting close to Bend and they were beginning to meet other cars on the narrow highway. "You want to keep your eyes open, boys. Sometimes a deer will dart across the road in front of the car along this stretch. I want you to help me watch for them. The trees are so thick it's hard to see a deer until they're right in the road and I don't want to hit one of them."

Clive turned from the window. "Will Uncle Morgan be at the ranch, Mom?"

"I don't know. I suppose so. In the evenings at least. During the day he will be working at the lumber mill." Mattie's heart skipped a beat as she thought of Morgan, tall, rugged, with dust on his clothes and a twinkle in his eye.

"Who's Uncle Morgan?" Jonathan asked.

"Dad's brother, silly," Clive answered disgustedly. "Boy, you don't remember anything, do you? Uncle Morgan is big and strong and he isn't afraid of anything. He flies airplanes and he rides horses and—Mom, do you think Uncle Morgan will think I'm big enough to learn to ride a horse yet? I growed a whole bunch since he saw me."

"You're still pretty young, Clive," she answered gently. "There's a lot of time yet. We can go to the swimming hole. Do you remember me telling you how your father used to swim there when he was a little boy? I know what! I could teach you to swim this time, if the weather stays warm."

"Me, too, Mom?" Jonathan asked with a pleading look.

"Yes. You too," she answered, smiling down at him. "We can take a picnic and walk to the creek, and I'll teach both of you to swim. Don't you think that would be fun, Clive?"

"I suppose so," he answered without enthusiasm. "If Uncle Morgan is too busy. I'd rather go with him, though."

"Me, too, me, too," Jonathan sang out impatiently.

"Not you, Johnny. You're too young," Clive answered with all of the dignity of an older brother. "I'm just about big enough to go with him, don't you think, Mom?"

"Honey, we're just going to have to wait and see," Mattie answered, sidestepping the issue. "Your Uncle Morgan will be busy with his own work. Wes will be there, though. You remember Wes, don't you?"

Mattie slowed and pulled over to a gasoline station at the edge of Bend. Jonathan slipped off the seat and stood up, peering out of the window. "Are we there?" he asked anxiously.

"Not yet, sweetie. I have to buy some gasoline." She looked down at his tired face and smiled softly. "It won't be much further. Are you going to be able to stay awake?'' His eyes were heavy and he tried to hide a yawn.

"Well, hello there, Mrs. Henderson!'' a man called out, coming out from the garage clad in a pair of grease-stained overalls. "Good to see you around these parts again. You on your way to the ranch?''

"Yes. And real anxious to get there, too. It seems like it has been forever since we were there last. How is your family?''

"Doing real well, thank you, ma'am. Say, those two boys of yours are sure growing. Last time I saw that little one you was carrying him in your arms.'' He looked across at young Clive. "That one sure does get to look more like his grandfather every time I see him. You named him well. He's the spitting image of old Clive Henderson. Getting to be a good-sized boy. Going to be tall just like Clive, too.''

Young Clive drew himself up importantly on the car seat. "That's 'cause I'm four already. Pretty soon I'll be five.''

The station attendant went around the car carefully checking the air in all of the tires and raised the hood and inspected the oil, the water, the fan belt. "Everything looks in good shape,'' he called out to her. "Just let me get the dust off the windshield and the headlamps and we'll have you on your way again.'' He wiped his hands on the oily rag sticking out of his hip pocket. "You drive real careful now, Mrs. Henderson. Those roads can be dangerous,'' he cautioned.

Mattie nodded. "I've been telling the boys about the way the deer run across the road in this country. Especially in the evening. I had hoped they might get to see one.''

"Deer always been a problem along this highway,'' he drawled. "Folks are used to watching out for them. That's not what I meant. It's them blasted log trucks. You meet them on a curve and they think they own the whole road. They drive too blamed fast! You keep an eye out.''

"Log trucks?''

"That's right. You ain't been over here since they started hauling logs for the new mill, have you? They got some mighty big trucks and them boys are trying to make time during the good

weather so they wheel them right along. Just wait until you see
the size of the logs they are bringing in!''

A few miles out of town, Mattie turned east, away from the
mountains toward the high desert country where the big ranches
sprawled. The sun was already getting low in the sky, turning the
mountains into shades of dark greenish blue. Jonathan had slumped
back in the seat, unable to keep his heavy eyelids open any
longer, but Clive was sitting up straight, intently watching the
country spreading out in front of them as they turned off the
paving onto a dirt road.

The weariness began to leave Mattie's body from the hours
behind the steering wheel and she felt a new wave of anticipation
as they bounced along the rough road, leaving a cloud of dust
behind them. The evening sun was turning the sagebrush land
into shades of burnished reds and golds under a turquoise sky,
making odd-shaped bushes look like a silent Indian watching
them from a ridge or a weather-beaten silver log resemble a
coyote on the prowl.

She glanced over at Clive and smiled at the tired lines of his
serious little face. ''It won't be long now, son,'' she tried to
reassure him. ''The ranch is over the next ridge. We should be
able to see the house any time now.''

''You suppose Uncle Morgan will be there when we get
there?'' he asked.

She shook her head. ''I don't know, Clive. But Aunt Betty and
Uncle Wes will be there, waiting to see you.'' She turned her
head away, hoping he wouldn't guess at how much she was
wondering the same thing.

The sun dropped behind the mountains, changing the reds and
golds to blues and silver as Mattie pulled into the lane leading to
the ranch house. Betty and Wes had seen the dust in the distance
and both were standing on the porch, waiting for them. Jonathan
sat up, rubbing his eyes and yawning sleepily as he looked
around.

''Are we there yet, Mom?''

Wes opened the door and reached in to help the two small tired
boys from the car. ''Let's get these young men into the house
before they drop off to sleep standing on their feet,'' he drawled

as he swooped Jonathan up in his arms and took young Clive by the hand. "Would you look at how these two have grown up! Going to have the both of them out riding fence before you know it!"

"Bet you're starved, aren't you?" Betty took Mattie's arm, giving her an affectionate squeeze. "I've been keeping supper hot for you on the back of the stove."

Mattie took off her coat and watched the boys settled at the table, tall glasses of cold milk and warm plates of food in front of them. Restlessly, she opened the liquor cabinet and poured brandy into a small glass. She pretended not to see Betty's startled look when she lit a cigarette.

"The roads are in better condition now, but it still takes a long time." She straightened her tired shoulders and stretched wearily. "I stopped several times to let the boys out to run around. We brought a picnic lunch with us, but I didn't want to waste too much time along the way. I wanted to be sure to get here before dark."

"Don't you want something to eat?" Betty asked worriedly. "You ought to have something warm, Mattie. It'll be good for you."

"In a minute. I need to relax first. I'm really not hungry."

Betty frowned in disapproval as she took in Mattie's thin figure, the new lines of tension around her eyes, the thick, luxurious brown hair cut into a bob. Her lips drew into a tight line as she watched Mattie light another cigarette. "You chain-smoking those things? Doesn't look to me like you been eating right, either. You're too thin to cast a good shadow. You sure you want that other drink instead of some supper?"

"It's the style, don't you know?" Mattie tried to sound flippant with her answer as she ran her hands down along the length of her torso. "Thin is in. No bumps, no bulges. No curves. Did you know women are even wearing binders to make their breasts look flat? Flat-chested women are in vogue."

Betty glanced uneasily toward the table where Wes was helping the boys with their supper, wondering how much they had heard above their chatter. She had always considered this sort of thing as strictly woman talk, not discussed in front of the men or small boys. "Why don't you take them up to their room, Wes, while I finish cleaning up the dishes. I'll be up in a few minutes to see that they are tucked in properly."

"Isn't Uncle Morgan here?" Clive asked. "I wanted to see him."

"In the morning," Betty answered. "He's going to be at the mill late tonight. You will probably see him in the morning. Now, off to bed, both of you."

Hearing the authority in her voice, they slipped obediently off their chairs and followed Wes from the room toward the stairway.

Mattie sat down at the table, carelessly picking at the food Betty set in front of her. Feeling the hurt she knew she would see on Betty's face if she looked up, she tried to smile and close the unfamiliar distance that stood between them. "I'm sorry. The supper is fine. It was thoughtful of you to keep it warm for us. I guess I'm just not very hungry tonight. It's been a long day and I'm tired, that's all."

Betty went to the stove, checking on the fire and shutting down the damper. "Will you be all right here alone if Wes and I leave when he comes downstairs? We usually spend nights over at our own place unless we're needed here. We can stay if you want."

Mattie shook her head. "No. You go on home anytime you're ready. We'll be fine. I'm going up to bed soon, anyway."

"Well, I'll just check on the boys first—"

"No!" Mattie's voice was sharp, and then she added, much more softly, "No. I'll do it. I'll see that they are covered and ready for sleep. It will be a novelty for them to have their own mother there at bedtime." She tried to give a lighthearted laugh but somehow it sounded tense and brittle.

After Wes and Betty left, and the boys were sleeping soundly, Mattie took her drink in her hand and wandered through the empty rooms, listening to the silent echoes of the past. A thousand memories lurked in the corners, watching her, hidden by the dark shadows. When she tried to draw them close around her so she could feel their warmth, they slipped just out of her reach.

"I'm home, damn it! I belong here!" She cried the words out loud to the empty hallways. "Stop treating me like a stranger!"

She paused outside Clive's study. She started to push the door open and then stopped. She wasn't quite ready to see the changes she knew would be there. Someone else sat at the desk now, entering the figures in the ledger. The furniture more than likely would be rearranged after a bout of cleaning. Even the old dog would be gone from the hearth.

She wanted to push the door wide open and call out, "Hey! It's me. It's Mattie. Is it all right if I come in and sit for a while?"

In the stillness she could almost hear him roar with outraged disapproval if she were to walk in with a drink in her hand, a cigarette, and sit down in the chair by the fire, her skirts displaying a view of slender silk-clad legs.

The walls of the old house seemed to bend and nod to each other as they frowned and refused to recognize her. "Mattie? Mattie doesn't smoke, doesn't drink. Dress like that? Who are you? You don't belong here. Where's Mattie?"

"Go to hell!" she told them defiantly, her words echoing down the silent hallway. She turned on her heel and went up the darkened stairway toward her room.

Mattie was still awake, lying tense and unable to go to sleep, when she heard Morgan's stealthy step in the hallway. As she listened, she heard him pause outside the open doorway of the boys' bedroom for a few moments as though he might be standing there looking in on them, and then she heard his steps going on down the hallway and the soft closing of his bedroom door.

CHAPTER TWENTY-THREE

Early morning sunlight stole in the window and played across her pillow, touching her face. Mattie stirred in her sleep and luxuriously stretched her body out straight without opening her eyes, savoring that delicious moment of warm drowsiness that separated slumber from awareness of the day unfolding in front of her.

She lay listening to the sounds drifting up to her and smiled contentedly, knowing they were the sounds of coming home. The sound of a bull bellowing echoed far off in the distance, a man's voice, closer but still too far away to distinguish his words, the sharp beat of a horse's hoofs fading into the background of a hundred other sounds that made up the stillness of the Western ranch.

Mattie slowly opened her eyes and glanced toward the wind-up clock sitting on the dresser. It was early—far earlier than she had awakened to a morning for a long, long time, and yet she felt rested, relaxed, eager to be up. She let her thoughts drift back to the day before. The trip had been long, strenuous, and tiring, and yet it had been the easiest part of returning to the ranch. She had looked forward to it with happy anticipation, wanting to step from one world into the other as though passing through a door, expecting everything to be the same—and yet nothing ever is.

She had lain awake for hours the night before, restless and

unable to unwind, but when sleep finally came it had been dreamless and healing, restoring her energies and quieting the critical ghosts of the past who failed to recognize that she hadn't really changed so much.

Suddenly impatient, Mattie tossed the covers away and slipped from the bed, anxious to be up and moving about. On an impulse, she disregarded the casual tailored sharkskin sports dress in her suitcase and ran to the closet, digging back into the far corners until she came out triumphantly holding a pair of old jeans and a flannel shirt that had been discarded so long ago. With impish delight she realized that after all these years of wearing dresses and having two children, they still fit as easily as they had when she had first come to the ranch and become a Henderson.

The boys were still sleeping soundly, Jonathan curled into a warm ball, Clive with his arm tossed up across his pillow. She pulled the door softly closed behind her and hurried down the stairs, following the aroma of fresh bread drifting up from the kitchen.

Mattie stood silently in the doorway watching Betty working by the stove, slowly savoring the smells of bacon and maple syrup, seeing the plates on the table that told her the men had already eaten their breakfast and were gone, listening to the crackling of the wood fire in the stove.

"God, it's good to be home again!"

Betty turned, startled. "Well, good morning, Mattie. I didn't hear you. How long have you been standing there? Never expected a big-city girl like you to be up so early in the morning, especially after such a long drive yesterday."

"Mmmm, watch whom you are calling a big-city girl," Mattie threatened, with a lilt to her voice that had been missing the night before. She went on into the kitchen, picked up a mug from the rack, and went over to the stove to fill it with the hot, steaming brew in the large coffeepot. "You don't know how much I have missed this place—missed all of you. Missed being able to walk right into the kitchen and help myself to the coffee. Just to be able to feel the bustle going on, knowing there is a whole day spread out ahead of us with so much work that needs to be done, to be a part of it again, to be able to go to bed at night tired enough to fall asleep without any trouble.''

"Well, there isn't all that much bustling around in the kitchen since most of the cooking for the men is being done in the bunkhouse. It's just Wes and Morgan now, though I swear Wes can eat enough for two or three men. Don't know how he stays so wiry, the way he packs it away.''

Mattie tipped her nose, sniffing the air. "What have you got baking that smells so good?''

"I put a couple of apple pies in the oven while I was waiting for the bread to raise.'' Betty dusted the flour from her hands and reached up to smooth a stray strand of dark hair away from her face. "Thought the little ones might like warm pie in a bowl with milk and sugar for a treat. They aren't showing any signs of waking up yet, are they?''

Mattie shook her head, lifting a clean white towel to peek at the loaves of bread raising in the pans, almost ready for the oven. "You must have been up early.''

"I like to get the bread done before the kitchen gets too hot. This time of year it can get real uncomfortable in here if I need a hot fire during the middle of the day.'' She filled the big dishpan with hot water from the cistern on the side of the stove and began to wash the mixing bowls as she talked. "I still do the baking for the men in here—but that isn't so much. Just got to keep them in pies, and I bake bread every other day. It isn't like when you were here—back when you and I were doing all the cooking for the whole bunch of them. Men coming in off the range at all hours, tired and hungry, doing their washing up over on the stand against the wall just about the time we were trying to get enough water hot to do up the kettles. Seems like the less work we have to do, the more new things we get in here to make it easier. It's not hard to keep up with anymore. But, still and all, I'm not sure I'd get sentimental about it like you do. If I had the chance to sleep in as long as I wanted and had someone serve breakfast to me in the dining room, away from all the clutter, I'd probably find a way to get used to it.''

Mattie shook her head. "You wouldn't like it. Breakfast just doesn't taste the same. Most of the time I just have some juice and toast while I'm reading the paper. There's nothing wrong with the cooking—I don't mean that. She's an excellent cook, and I think sometimes she's a miracle worker when we have dinner guests without much notice. But I can't imagine what would happen if I dared to walk into her kitchen, pour my own cup of coffee, and sit down as though I expected her to visit with me.'' Mattie's lips curled up in an amused smile at the very thought. ''She'd probably resign right on the spot.''

She went over and sat at the table, casually lighting a cigarette. ''Come on, Betty. You can take time out to sit and talk to me for a little while, can't you?'' She added wistfully, ''Like we used to do. Remember? I'll help you later. If we both work together, we can catch up easy enough.''

Betty glanced up at the clock and then shrugged her shoulders. ''Don't see any reason why I can't. At least until the little ones wake up. They were too tired to eat much last night so they'll be wanting breakfast as soon as they come down the stairs.'' She filled her coffee cup and set it on the table, her eyes crinkling in warm affection. ''Wes has sure been looking forward to seeing them ever since we got your letter. He has a surprise or two to show them outside, near the barns.'' She slipped several thick bacon slices and a hotcake bathed in warm buttery syrup on a plate and set it in front of Mattie. ''While we're talking, how about you eating something. Maybe being thin is the style in the city, but to me you look just plain skinny.''

The smell of the maple syrup, the juicy crispness of the thick slices of bacon, the comfortable atmosphere of the warm kitchen were deliciously enticing and Mattie found herself eating with relish as they talked until, to her own surprise, she had eaten all of the breakfast in front of her. She pushed back the plate with a sigh. ''I haven't eaten so much in ages! And I enjoyed every single bite of it.'' She reached into her pocket and took out a slender silver cigarette case.

Betty watched her, frowning slightly. ''Can't get used to seeing you like that, Mattie. Guess living in a city is different, isn't it? How long you been smoking those things?''

Mattie shrugged her slender shoulders carelessly. ''I don't know. Awhile. Everyone does.''

"How's Allen? We've been wondering how that nightclub of his is doing, now that the prohibition laws have been passed. You haven't mentioned it in your letters. Is it still open?"

Mattie nodded. "Allen manages. It isn't that hard. Instead of being an open supper club, it's an after-hours private club now. Membership only. They check on everyone pretty close. Of course, it isn't any real problem anyway. Allen certainly isn't going to allow it to be raided."

Betty drew her brows into a puzzled frown. "I still don't understand. You can't buy liquor anymore. Guess we aren't even supposed to have what we got sitting out like we do. No one pays any attention, though. Morgan and Wes have a couple of drinks together in the evening, but that's about all. How do you manage?"

"I really don't know. Allen says the less I know about it the better, so I don't ask questions. I think it's coming across the border from Canada somehow, though I'm only guessing. It can be gotten easy enough, if you have the price and know the right people."

"And don't have to worry about the law," Betty added sarcastically.

"Let's talk about something else," Mattie said, wanting to change the subject. She didn't want to think about Salem or things better left alone.

"By something else you mean the lumber mill, don't you? I've been wondering how long it was going to take you to get around to asking."

Mattie looked down, studying her coffee cup, not wanting her interest to show too much. "Isn't it a natural thing for me to ask? I'm curious. Morgan wasn't here when we got in last night, and it looks as though he's gone already this morning. He's either working some hellish long hours at the mill—or he's avoiding me. Which is it, Betty?" she asked softly.

"Maybe it's a little of both," Betty answered tartly. "He's been working awful hard, Mattie. I worry about him. Getting that mill built wasn't that easy, especially starting it in the winter the way he did. Parts for the machinery didn't arrive on time—or they weren't the right ones when they got here—and, well, the whole thing has been a real struggle for him. He drives himself just like Clive used to. Sometimes I wonder what keeps the man going. He just doesn't know what it means to slow down and rest once in a while. It's not finished yet, but it's done enough so that he has been operating for the last couple of weeks."

"Is he having trouble getting logs?"

"No. At least, not so far. Up until now the loggers have been hauling up over the pass to that other mill or taking them north of here. Either way, it was too far for them to make much profit. He's got plenty of orders for lumber coming in, too. Once he gets the saws running full time, things should look better. He's running just one crew of about twenty men right now, but he figures in another couple of weeks he'll be putting on a night crew and keep them working round the clock."

Mattie's eyes opened wide in surprise. "A night crew? You mean run the mill all night, too?"

Betty nodded. "Pulling lumber off the green chain and loading out trucks can be done at night when he gets the rest of the electric lights put in. He's anxious to do as much as possible during the summer months, before winter sets in again. He's going to need a good stockpile of logs in the holding pond in case the weather turns extra bad and the loggers can't get into the woods till spring."

"Mom?"

Both women turned to see the two boys standing hesitantly in the doorway. At Mattie's smile as she held her arms out to them, they came on into the kitchen.

"I didn't know if we were supposed to come on downstairs by ourselves or not," Clive ventured. "Johnny doesn't know how to dress himself too good yet, so I helped him."

As Mattie caught them in a warm hug, she straightened the straps on the bib overalls she had bought for them to wear while they were here. "You did just fine, Clive," she reassured him. "I didn't hear you or I would have come to help. Are you hungry?"

Betty was already at the stove, stirring up the fire, moving the griddle over to the front part of the stove, and pouring out batter for small, round, dollar-sized cakes. "You boys got to eat a good breakfast if you're going to keep up today. Wes has been waiting for you since sunup.''

Mattie felt an almost forgotten warmth creep in around her as she watched her sons devouring the breakfast set in front of them. She was home. No telephones ringing impatiently, no sounds of cars in the street outside, no appointments, no schedules, no pressures. For the week or two that she was going to be here she could be herself, with no pretense, no critics watching, no newspapers.

Clive was eating quietly, his mind already racing ahead to the out-of-doors, but Jonathan was keeping up a stream of chatter, melting Betty with his liquid brown eyes, his dark curls, his winning smile, his constant questions.

They were nearly finished with their breakfast when Wes came stomping in the back door, his Western hat pushed to the back of his head, his eyes dancing as he spotted the boys. ''Well, men, is that breakfast or lunch you're tucking away? Betty never lets the rest of us sleep after the sun is up. How'd you manage to trick her into holding your plate for you?'' He pulled out a chair and sat down beside them, looking at the table with interest. ''I never had no apple pie for dessert, neither,'' he said, eyeing Jonathan's bowl. ''You look kind of full, pardner. Maybe I better help you out and eat it for you.''

Mattie and Betty laughed as Jonathan's eyes flew open and both hands reached out to save his portion of the hot apple pie as he looked up to Betty for help.

''Is Uncle Morgan outside?'' Clive asked anxiously.

''Shucks no, boy,'' Wes drawled. ''Like I told you—if you live on a ranch you got to get up with the sun. Morgan's been up and did his chores and left for the mill hours ago.'' He saw the way the boy's face fell in disappointment and he winked broadly at him. ''Of course, before he left, he left a message for you.''

''What did he say?''

''Oh, I can't just up and tell it to you. We got to talk it over, man to man, out at the barn. Of course, if you'd rather sit here dawdling over your food and talking to the women—''

The remaining food disappeared as if by magic and both boys slipped off their chairs, filled with impatience to be on their way.

Wes stood up, stretched his bandy legs, and pretended a sudden reluctance to go outside. Seeing their disappointed faces, he gave them an easy grin and led them toward the barn, both boys following closely on his heels.

Mattie was just finishing drying the mixing bowls on the soft, flour sack dish towels when the back door burst open and young Clive came in, his eyes glowing in excitement.

"He didn't forget me, Mom! He didn't forget!" he cried, dancing around Mattie, demanding her full attention. "I thought he didn't remember me, but he did! Come outside and see!" He was tugging at her, trying to draw her along with him toward the door.

Mattie dried her hands and followed, unable to resist the infectious joy on her son's face. Standing in the yard between the corrals and the house was a small black-and-white pony wearing a saddle. Wes was holding the reins, waiting for them. Jonathan was standing behind Wes, eyeing the pony with uncertain hesitation, not sharing his older brother's enthusiasm.

Mattie stood watching as Wes lifted Clive up into the saddle and saw how the quiet, reserved boy of the city came alive, with new color in his face, his eyes shining with pride as he took the reins in his small hands.

"Are you sure the pony is broken well enough for him?" Mattie asked worriedly. "He's so young. The boy doesn't have any fear . . ."

"It'll do," Wes said quietly. "Quit fussing, Mattie. He might get himself tossed a time or two, but it ain't going to hurt him none. It'll teach him to keep his eyes open, to watch what he's doing."

"It's a pretty little mare," she answered skeptically. "I haven't seen it before. We've never had any ponys here. Where did it come from?"

Wes looked uncomfortable. "No, don't reckon you've seen it before. It's new, but don't worry. She's a good little mare, gentle with kids. She'll be good for him to ride until he gets a little older, ready for something bigger."

"I didn't see any purchases of horses or ponies on the books," Mattie persisted.

"Well, we didn't exactly buy her. Morgan bought her himself. He got it from . . . from a friend of his who raises horses. Said he figured it was time the boy had a horse of his own. Time he learned how to take care of it and started in doing his own chores when he came over here to visit."

Mattie watched her son for a thoughtful moment, worry tugging at the back of her mind. It was hard to admit that he wasn't a baby anymore—that he was ready to take a few tumbles that she couldn't protect him from, even if it was only from the back of a small spotted pony. So Morgan had been thinking about them. But who was the friend who had encouraged him in the selection? And why did it seem to embarrass Wes when she persisted in her questions?

"Thought maybe I'd let him ride along with me out toward Willow Creek." It was then that Mattie saw that Wes had his own horse saddled, the reins tossed carelessly over a rail near the corral.

Mattie looked down at an insistent tug on her jeans. "Me, too, Mom. Me too!" Jonathan's face was a dark cloud, filled with envy. "Clive got a horse. I want one, too."

Mattie reached down to hug him close to her. "Of course you will have one, but not yet. Next year. You're too small, honey. Maybe later, after lunch, you and I can go out for a ride. You can sit up in the saddle with me."

Wes swooped the small boy up onto his shoulder. "Now, why would a man like Johnny here want to go riding with the women? He's going to ride up on old Stormy, holding onto the reins for me while I sit back and watch the scenery."

Mattie turned back toward the house, her mind busy. So Morgan had been looking forward to their visit after all. He had a pony ready for Clive. But why wasn't he here to teach the boy to ride?

As she came in the door, Betty was waiting, refilling their coffee mugs from the big blue granite pot. "You knew, didn't you?" Mattie asked. "About the pony for Clive. Why didn't you tell me?"

The other woman shrugged. "It was a surprise. Besides, Wes told me I should start minding my own business. He says I shouldn't interfere—that all of you will work things out in your own way, in time." She set the cups down with an impatient clatter. "Only I don't understand you, either."

Mattie raised her eyebrows. "What don't you understand about me? I'm afraid you lost me along the way somewhere. We were talking about Morgan and his giving a pony to Clive."

"We still are. You may think you have me fooled, but you haven't. Not one whit. We been too close all these years to not know something about the other's feelings, down deep inside. You can't hide from me the way you and Morgan feel about each other. It's always been that way between the two of you. That man's been on pins and needles ever since he knew you were bringing the boys over on a vacation, wanting everything to be just right for you, and when you get here, he takes himself off to the mill, not trusting himself to be here, to see you again, afraid he'll show how he feels. And you—well, if it were me, I wouldn't just give in and accept things the way they are. I'd have fought for what I wanted."

"Even at the expense of hurting others?" Mattie answered softly. "Ruining other lives? Life isn't that simple, Betty. There are always other people—other lives that intertwine with ours. There are promises that we have made that can't be broken that easily—not without hurting others. The price is too high to pay."

"You mean Allen."

Mattie nodded. "Yes. Allen, for one. His career is going so well. He is headed up the ladder, working for what he wants with his life. He loves me. He needs me at his side. It could ruin him right now if I were to leave. And there are the boys—think what it would do to them. No, Betty. Hurting others so much is too high a price to pay for happiness. Guilt would destroy it."

"Well, it just isn't fair!"

"Nor is it any of your business!" Mattie snapped sharply. "You should listen to Wes. I'm Allen's wife, Betty. And I will go on being a good wife to Allen and a good mother to my sons. I can't hurt them that way."

Betty reached out and laid her hand over Mattie's. "I'm sorry. I knew I was overstepping. You always thought no one guessed how you felt about each other, but the way the sparks flew across the room between the two of you, a blind man could have told what was going on. Guess loving you the way I do, and worrying over Morgan—seeing him drive himself the way he does, trying to forget—I just keep trying to figure out a happy ending. Only there doesn't seem to be one, does there? Guess that's why I'm so upset—and talk too much.''

"I'm sorry too. I didn't mean to snap at you the way I did. After all, you and I have been such close friends for so long. You're the only real friend I have. The only one I can sit down and talk to without having to pretend. Come on," she said with a sigh. "We've got work to do. Let's get to it." She picked up the dish towel, still lying where she had left it when Clive had called her outside.

CHAPTER TWENTY-FOUR

Mattie pulled the car up near a small building that sat away from the larger sheds and turned off the ignition. So this was the mill where Morgan spent his days and part of his nights. She slipped off the seat and stood on the wide running board, looking around at the busy scene sprawled out in front of her. A slight breeze ruffled her hair, bringing with it the noisy sounds and aromatic smells of pine logs being turned into freshly cut lumber.

Filled with curiosity, Mattie stepped down to the ground and sat on the running board, watching the activity going on around her. A large truck had just finished spilling its logs into the wide, shallow pond, and they sent up a spray of water as they hit the surface. A talley clerk handed the driver a sheet of paper showing the board footage scaled on the load. Mattie watched as the two men talked for a minute before the logger swung himself back up into the cab of the truck and began to drive away.

An enormous log was being pulled from the pond by sharp, iron mechanical jaws and she watched a conveyor belt carry it up a ramp to a huge, open-sided shed built on stilts. The earsplitting whine of the giant saw filled the air and the sawdust and chips flew as the steel teeth bit into the wood.

Under a long, narrow roof, there were men wearing heavy cords, flannel shirts, thick gloves, pulling long lengths of lumber off the green chain and stacking them to dry in the summer air.

Off to one side, a giant-sized wigwam built of sheet metal, standing at least three or four stories high, belched out flame from an opening in the top as it consumed the slash and bark trimmings that couldn't be used for lumber and had to be disposed of. Its sides glowed from the enormous heat that radiated out around it.

Mattie caught a brief glimpse of Morgan's broad shoulders as he walked from the green chain toward the shed that housed the saws. She felt her heart beat a little faster as he appeared again at the ladder, climbed up the dozen steps, and moved along the platform where the log was being fed into the saws by the conveyor belt. He was wearing heavy cork boots, pants with torn, ragged edges barely reaching the tops of his boots, and a plaid shirt with sleeves rolled several turns. He looked solid and rugged but moved with a sure, catlike grace along the plank walkways. This was the first glimpse she had had of him since coming back to the ranch. He was just a shadow or a sound, coming in late at night and leaving early in the morning before they were up—or not coming home at all.

From somewhere a shrill whistle split the air and the saws ground to a stop, leaving an unexpected quiet. The green chain slowed to a halt. The men stretched their tired backs and reached for their dinner pails. In groups of twos and threes they came out of the sheds and buildings laughing and talking together as they called it a day and headed toward their cars. Few of them noticed the young woman dressed in jeans sitting in the shadows on the running board of her car, away from the activity of the mill but watching everything with such an intent interest.

The mill was quiet now. A bird swooped down to sit on a log in the pond, busily looking for insects burrowed in the bark. The metal wigwam continued to burn, sending a warm glow out into the evening air. Once in a while a spark escaped and shot high up toward the sky, turning to cold ash before it fell again to the ground.

Morgan came from one of the sheds and walked with long, easy strides toward the small building where she had parked the car. He was carrying a clipboard in his hand, busy with his thoughts, and didn't see her standing there until she spoke.

"Hi," she said softly, and saw the startled look on his face turn to a warm caress as their eyes met before he had a chance to mask it behind a frown of casual indifference. She walked across to the porch, where he stood waiting. "Do you mind? I had to come over here—to see the mill. To see what you were doing." Her heart was beating faster, and she shoved her hands down into the pockets of the jeans, trying to saunter toward him with a deliberate casualness. "Wes said you might need a ride home. He thought one of the men took your car into Portland after parts. I wanted to see the mill, so I volunteered to come after you. Hope you don't mind."

His eyes were veiled now, hiding the warm caress she had seen when she caught him by surprise with her greeting. He turned away with a shrug. "All right. Come on into the office. I'll be finished in a few minutes. You can wait inside if you want." His words were noncommittal, giving her no clue as to whether he was glad to see her or if he wished she had stayed away.

Wordlessly, she followed him inside and watched him close the door behind them. He went across to the battered desk piled high with papers and she slowly looked around the small room—at the large, overstuffed chair with the faded upholstery, a table in the corner with an overflowing ashtray, the picture on the wall of Morgan's air squadron standing stiff and self-conscious in their uniforms, the cot against the wall where he must sleep when he spent all night at the mill. Nervously, she walked across to the window and stood looking out at the lumber mill, deserted in the late evening light, feeling the silence that invaded the office.

"You didn't need to come after me, Mattie," he said at last, looking up from the papers he had been working on. "I've got enough work to keep me busy here all evening. I've done it before. Worked late and slept on the cot instead of going home."

"Betty thought you needed a hot meal," she answered. "She's worried about you."

"There's a café in town." His voice had a sharp edge. "Putting this mill on its feet takes a lot of work. I can't go back out to the ranch every night until we're running full time. Betty understands."

Mattie turned away from the window, looking fully at him. "At least, not until after I leave. Isn't that what you mean?"

"Does it bother you that I'm not there?" He pushed the papers aside and got up from the desk, walking over to where she stood.

She looked up at him. Every nerve was taut with awareness of how tall he was, how broad his shoulders were, how masculine he was, as he stood looking down at her, close enough for her to smell leather and the aroma of freshly cut pine. "Yes. It bothers me, damn it!" she snapped. "I thought we would see you—I thought at least we could talk."

"Talk?" The corners of his mouth twitched in sarcastic bitterness. "What is there between us to talk about? I agreed to oversee the ranch for you. That was settled a long time ago. I was put in a position where I couldn't do much else, could I? You're getting the monthly reports, aren't you? Wes can answer any questions for you. We don't have much else to talk about, do we, Mattie? Everything else was said when you went back to Salem."

She took a half-step toward him, wanting to lash out in anger because he was refusing to understand, and yet she didn't know herself what she was trying to say. "I just thought we could talk about—oh, hell, I don't know! Anything. Talk about the pony you bought for Clive. He was disappointed that you weren't there to see him ride. Both boys were looking forward to seeing you. You are their uncle, for God's sake. It was a big adventure for them to come over to the ranch, and they expected you to be there—to act like you gave a damn if you saw them!"

She looked so vulnerable, standing there in the dim evening light with fire spitting from her eyes. He wanted to reach out, to touch her, to hold her in his arms. He wanted to forget about all of the long, hard hours he had worked, trying to get tired enough to sleep without seeing her face, hearing her voice in the shadows of his lonely room. He'd thought he'd almost succeeded. It filled him with a cold, raging anger to realize that just by walking into the mill yard she could start all of the old fires burning again, leaving him shaken, consumed with a need to hold her in his arms, to make love to her. He clenched his hands to keep from reaching out toward her. His jaw was set in a hard line, his eyes were cold as chips of ice, revealing the anger he felt inside.

"What is with you anyway, Mattie? What do you want from me?" His voice was hard, edged heavily with sarcasm. "You live with one man as his wife, and yet you still can't resist coming back here, trying to tempt me beyond the point of reason. You want me to play the role of the uncle—you expect me to look at my son and pretend I don't feel anything. He *is* my son. I am sure of it. I feel it inside, whether you will admit it or not. What are you after? What is it you expect of me? Talk?" He gave a bitter laugh. "You come over here to the mill in the evening, after the shift has gone home and the mill is deserted. You knew we would be alone—and you want talk?"

Mattie felt her face go scarlet at the unmasked insinuation. "All right!" she flung at him, her eyes snapping angrily. "It was a mistake to want to talk to you. It always has been, hasn't it? You have always twisted things around, refusing to understand. I should have known."

"Understand? Understand what, Mattie? What there is between us or what isn't there at all? Am I supposed to understand how you can let me hold you in my arms, let me make love to you, and then let you go as though nothing happened between us? I'm supposed to make love to you and then let you go back to your husband?" His eyes were hard, accusing. He wanted to hurt her as much as possible for all of the months he had spent trying to forget her. "Why did you come back, Mattie?"

Her eyes filled with tears that spilled over against her cheeks. She raised a hand to try to hide them from him, not wanting to let him see how deep his words had cut. "Maybe I came back because I just couldn't stay away any longer," she whispered.

Unable to look away, she tipped her head back and returned his angry frown with a look of challenging defiance, though she was trembling inside with uncertainty. He reached out and took her shoulders in his hands, holding her at arm's length with an unbelievable gentleness. As she stared at him, she saw the harsh, angry look fade and gradually turn to tenderness, shadowed with hurt. His eyes wandered slowly over her every feature as though rediscovering a precious memory.

"Mattie, Mattie, Mattie," he whispered hoarsely. "You shouldn't be here. It's no good."

"I know. I tried to stay away. I just wanted to see you, to talk to you."

"Oh, Mattie," he groaned, shaking his head. "What are we going to do?"

His fingers tightened on her shoulders and he pulled her roughly against him, cradling her in the shelter of his arms. With a sob, she buried her face against the hardness of his chest, feeling the roughness of the wool against her cheeks, and let the tears fall unnoticed on his shirt.

He tipped her face up so that he could look into her eyes. The anger and the bitterness were gone and his eyes were filled with desire for her, making her pulses throb in the hollow at the base of her throat, and he felt the quick rise and fall of her breasts through his clothing as she fought for breath.

He bent his head, seeking her mouth with his own. His kisses were hard and demanding, bruising her lips, and she responded with a hungry abandon, trembling at his touch.

Gradually, he turned to gentle tenderness as his lips began to caress her face, leaving a trail of small, nibbling kisses that set her whole body on fire. The tip of his tongue traced the lines of her ear and he nipped her earlobe with his teeth. She felt his hands sliding down the arch of her body to her hips, pressing her against him, and she felt the hardness of him that told her how much he wanted her.

He fumbled with the buttons of her shirt, sliding it off her slim white shoulders and exposing her round, firm breasts, the nipples hard and waiting for his touch.

His shirt fell unnoticed on the floor beside her own, as her fingers explored the hard lines of his chest, traced the thin white scar across his shoulder, and she felt him tremble as her hands wandered down the line of his thigh.

"Oh, Mattie," he groaned. "I love you so much."

"And I love you, too," she whispered as her hands crept up his back to his neck. And she clung to him with trembling anticipation as she felt him gently lift her in his arms and carry her toward the cot against the wall.

All of the long and lonely months of pretending, of trying to deny their love existed, vanished into the shadows, and she recklessly met his demands with an unleashed passion of her own. He slipped the jeans from her slender hips and her fingers found the buckle of his belt, unhooking it and releasing him to her touch. Slowly, they disrobed each other, touching, tasting, feeling, marveling at each new discovery, whispering endearments, until finally their bodies joined together to answer a love as old as time.

Morgan stood up and walked over to the desk, his body a copper tan from the last rays of the sunset coming in the window. He picked up a cigarette and lit it, slowly savoring the bite of the tobacco before he returned to sit down beside her on the cot. Without speaking, she reached out and took the cigarette from him, watching the lazy smoke curl upward in the dimly lit room as she slowly exhaled. The only sounds were of the wind whispering among the eaves, a board creaking somewhere, a bird calling to its mate as it swooped across the mill pond chasing insects. Without touching, without speaking, they felt and shared the warm, enveloping closeness that held them together.

Finally he turned to her, the old familiar teasing back in his eyes as he gently swatted her bare backside. "Come on, Mattie. Let's head out to the ranch. Betty's probably pacing the floor because her supper is getting cold, worrying over where we are. I want to get out there. I've got a couple of nephews waiting for me."

CHAPTER TWENTY-FIVE

Morgan, Wes, and Mattie had left the ranch house soon after sunrise, riding up to Willow Spring to check on the stock. It was one of those late spring days when the sky was robin's egg blue, with only a few feathery clouds lazily drifting overhead. The stream bubbled over the rocks and twisted its way through the gullies, still high from the winter runoff of snow in the mountains. The ground held enough moisture to feed the coarse range grass and keep the dust from filling the air. Mattie rode between the two men, her back straight, her face catching the warm breeze that riffled through her hair, her horse prancing restlessly at the slow pace.

The deep, rich red mahogany of the cattle glistened in the sun, their white faces as clean as though they had been scrubbed. The young calves cavorted about in their own version of the game of tag, pausing to look at the riders with curious interest. There was barely enough wind to turn the blades of the windmill at Willow Spring, but the pond was full and clear, and at least twenty or thirty white faces were near the edge of the water or standing contentedly under the shade of a lone scrub pine.

"We began moving most of them out toward the summer pasture last week," Wes explained. "They change off, but I keep two men out there at the line shack keeping an eye on stock. The coyotes are bad this year." He looked across at Mattie. "Well, what do you think?"

Mattie nodded approvingly. "I think everything looks great! You're doing a wonderful job, Wes. Clive couldn't have done better himself."

That was high praise, and Wes grinned his appreciation. "I've got to go on out to the line shack. I'll see the two of you back at the house this evening."

Morgan glanced up at the sun. They had been riding for several hours and the sun was past high noon. "Race you to the ridge, Mattie," he challenged, as he nudged his horse with his heel.

Wes looked after them for a long, thoughtful minute and shrugged his shoulders before riding on toward the summer pasture.

Morgan reined in his horse near the edge of the rim, letting it rest after the long run. Mattie reined up only seconds behind him, gasping for air as she laughed breathlessly.

"You can still beat me," she said, panting, "but it was a close race. One of these days, Black Diamond and I are going to fool you and come in first." She slipped from the saddle and went over to stand near a large rock, where she could be in the shade. She looked down across the valley toward the ranch house. Her hat had slipped from her head and hung by the strings at her back, letting the sun dance in her dark hair, bringing out reddish lights. A tan blushed her face, making it glow in the afternoon sunlight. She looked contented, happy, her slim figure relaxed as she stood looking down at the ranch sprawled below.

Morgan stepped down from the saddle and went over to stand beside her. "Don't know which time of day I like best," he said into the stillness. "In the afternoon like this, when everything is drowsy from the sun and so peaceful and quiet, or at the first crack of dawn, when everything is waking up, bursting with life."

She nodded, understanding. She sat down on a rock and pulled up a blade of grass, chewing thoughtfully on the end of it.

"Clive and I used to ride up here sometimes just to sit and talk. It was one of his favorite places."

They sat for a while in contented silence, not talking, just watching the shadows drift across the valley and listening to the sounds that drifted up toward them—the sound of a bull, bellowing his discontent, the quiet chirp of a bird in a bush nearby, the breeze whispering through the grasses.

"You'll be leaving soon?" Morgan asked at last.

She nodded, not wanting to talk about it. "Day after tomorrow." She looked across at him where he squatted on his heels, absently smoking a cigarette as he stared off into the distance. "What are you thinking about?"

It was a long moment before he answered. "Just looking down at the ranch house and thinking about how the old man must have felt. Thinking about how I'd like to sit up here and look down to see my kids playing in the yard, roughhousing, knowing life is good for them and they have no worries."

"Morgan, don't." Her eyes clouded and the happiness disappeared from her face.

"This past week has been pure heaven, Mattie, having you and the boys here, seeing you every day—but we shouldn't have let things get out of hand the way we did. Just makes the hell that's gonna follow that much worse. We should have kept to polite family conversations at the dinner table. I should have spent more time at the mill, the way I did when you first got here. I should have kept too busy to pay much attention to a couple of rowdy little nephews—not let it get to me the way it did when one of them looked at me like maybe I was ten foot tall, following me around trying to copy everything I do. Better yet, you should have stayed away. You shouldn't have come back, Mattie. I was just beginning to get my life organized again."

"I can't stay away, Morgan. Any more than I can stop breathing," she said softly. "If I can't come back to the ranch once in a while, I can't go on with the farce I'm living over there."

"We can't go on like this, either," he answered firmly, his

voice taking on a hard edge. "I'm not much good at back-door romances, sneaking around corners. I'll never love a woman the way I love you, Mattie, but I want a woman that's my own. I want a wife. I want to have kids that I can claim. I want a home. Maybe love isn't everything after all. Maybe the love we have is so special it has nothing to do with the cold, hard facts of everyday life."

Small alarms went off in the back of Mattie's mind. "I'm not sure I follow you. What do you mean?"

He shrugged his shoulders. "Just thinking out loud, I guess. Maybe when a man gets married, he should choose a woman for the way she keeps his house, the kind of children she would bear, the way she can work with him to build a future. Marriage is a long-term, working contract, and a man should plan it with his head and keep his heart out of it."

"What are you trying to tell me?" she asked cautiously.

He flipped the cigarette away impatiently and stood up. "Nothing. Just talking. Let's go back to the house."

Mattie followed him over to the waiting horses. As she swung up into the saddle, she took one last look out across the valley and saw a cloud of dust in the distance, inching its way up the ribbon of dirt road toward the house.

"Looks like we're going to have some company," she said, curiously watching the car. "Can't tell from this distance, but doesn't look like anyone I recognize. Are you expecting someone?"

Mattie was puzzled by the uneasy look on his face before he turned away, flicking the reins.

"Guess with all that has been going on, I forgot to mention it to you. That's Thad and Edith Randall, from a ranch over in the Wagon Wheel, Dry Lake area. There's a cattle auction in Bend they want to attend. They'll be staying at the ranch for a few days."

Mattie relaxed. "Good. It'll be nice to have some company. Have you known the couple long?"

He looked at her sharply, as though he were going to say something, and then changed his mind. "A year, maybe longer.

They're not a couple, Mattie. They're brother and sister. Come on. Let's get back to the house.''

The fun of the afternoon race was gone, and Mattie let Black Diamond pick his own pace. Morgan didn't take much of a lead, not acting as though he were in a big hurry to greet the new arrivals. Mattie was consumed with an uneasy curiosity by the time they reached the yard where Monty stood talking to the visitors.

A tall, slender woman, probably in her mid-twenties, dressed in a buckskin tailored riding costume, hand-tooled leather boots, with reddish-blond hair cut short, escaping into soft curls that were the only thing adding softness to an otherwise crisp, efficient figure, watched them approach.

As Morgan stepped from the saddle, the young woman walked over to meet him. ''So you were out riding! We stopped at the mill, but they said you had taken the day off to tend to business here at the ranch. I couldn't imagine why. There's nothing wrong, is there?'' She looped her hand possessively through Morgan's arm and then turned, as though it were an afterthought, to nod to Mattie. ''Mind your manners, darling, and introduce us.''

Mattie watched the back of Morgan's neck turn a dull brick red. ''Edith, this is Mattie Henderson. My sister-in-law. From Salem.''

Edith appraised her carefully. ''Oh, yes, you're married to Morgan's brother, Allen, aren't you? I heard that you were coming for a visit. How nice. Come and meet my kid brother, Thad. He's been standing over there admiring you ever since you rode in.''

Dinner was a stilted, uncomfortable affair, though Betty had done her best with a pot roast and all of the trimmings. Morgan sat at the head of the table and Edith automatically took the chair at the foot, as though it were her rightful place. With a shrug, Mattie sat at one side, next to Thad, a good-looking youth in his early twenties with devilish, roving eyes who kept up a stream of nonsensical chatter, flirting mischievously with her as he talked. Wes and Betty sat on the other side, eating quietly, neither of them showing any interest in adding to the conversation. Mattie had the distinct feeling that Betty was avoiding meeting her eyes when she glanced in that direction.

The food caught in Mattie's throat, tasting dry and flat, and her only thought was to survive until the dinner hour was over and she could escape to her room.

Edith paid a few polite compliments to Betty on the meal and then turned the rest of her conversation directly toward Morgan, discussing the cattle auction at length—the entries, who would be there—and speculated on the prices. Her voice was low, but it carried a preciseness that defied contradiction.

"Listen to Sis," Thad said, chuckling, to Mattie. "Let her get started on the subject of cattle, horse breeding, or stock ranches, and the rest of us might as well keep still."

"You live on a ranch?" Mattie asked, feeling as though she should make an attempt to say something to this friendly youth.

"Yeah. Sure. Born and raised there. Lost two older brothers during the war and with Dad all crippled up after a bronc busted him all to hell, Edith about runs the place. I got to admit she knows what she's doing, too."

Mattie raised her eyebrow in surprise. "But what about you?" she asked before she thought, and felt the color seep into her cheeks. "I mean, you must be a big help to your father, too."

He grinned at her, his eyes sparkling with mischief. "Not to hear Edith tell it. What I do best is raise hell in town on Saturday night. She doesn't hold out much hope for my future as a cattleman."

When the awkward meal finally ended, Mattie gave a quick glance toward Betty. "I'm going to check on the boys. I'll be right back to help with the dishes." She tried to slip hastily from the room, but Morgan caught her in the hallway, gripping her arm, making her stop.

"Mattie, wait. I've got to talk to you." His voice was firm, demanding.

She felt her upper lip quiver in rage as she turned on him. "Talk? What is there to talk about. It's all pretty obvious, I should think. I should have listened closer to you up on the ridge this afternoon. Is that what you were trying to tell me when you talked of a woman—a wife of your own? Your own children? Were you trying to tell me then?'' She pulled roughly away from him, fleeing to the study, closing the door behind her with a slam.

Morgan shoved the door open and came in, closing the door behind him and standing in the way, blocking her escape. "You are going to listen to me, Mattie."

She put her hands over her ears. "I don't want to hear anything you have to say. How could you! You let me throw myself at you. You let me make an ass of myself, throwing myself into your arms!'' She was trembling with rage, not able to think clearly. The words just came tumbling out of their own accord. "You let me follow you around this whole past week, mooning after you like a love-struck schoolgirl! You even encouraged me! Morgan, you made love to me,'' she cried out in anguish. "How could you!"

He took her roughly by the shoulders, his fingers painfully biting into her flesh, shaking her. "You listen to me. Edith has nothing to do with you and me—nothing to do with the way I feel about you, the way we feel about each other. What we have is between just the two of us. We both keep agreeing that it has to end, but when we are together neither of us has the strength to follow through. What we have between us is too strong. One way to forget you was to start seeing other women, I thought. I've got to build a life of my own. What do you think it does to me, knowing that when you leave here you go back into Allen's bed?''

"Well, at least I've been honest with you about it," she spat.

"Edith is a very independent woman. She comes on a little strong sometimes." He struggled to find the words that would penetrate her fury. "We're good friends. I've invited her and Thad to stay here at the ranch several times when they had business in Bend. She insinuated a lot more this evening than she had a right to. There is no understanding between us—no commitment.''

"Maybe not for you, but she certainly has made it plain that she considers you her property. Let go of me," she said through clenched teeth. "You're hurting me!"

His fingers bit deeper into the soft flesh of her arms, making her cry out in pain. "You're going to listen to me."

"Like hell I am," she flung back at him.

He pulled her roughly against him, bending his head until his mouth found her lips, kissing her savagely, bruising her, while she fought wildly to free herself from his hold. One arm slipped loose from his grasp and she drew back, slapping him as hard as she could, leaving the dull red imprint of her hand on his face. He let her go and his arms dropped to his side.

"All right, Mattie. If that is the way you want it."

There was a light knock on the door and Edith came into the room without waiting for an answer, looking at each of them with sharp appraisal. "I hope I'm not interrupting anything. A family argument?"

"What do you want, Edith?" Morgan asked without turning around, his voice still angry.

"The truck is here with the two bulls we brought from the ranch for the auction tomorrow. The men need you out at the barn, darling."

Without a word, Morgan turned on his heel and went out the door, his face set in a hard line, his back stiff and cold.

Edith raised her eyebrows as she looked after him. "Well, Mattie whatever you said to him, you sure put him in a foul mood!" She glanced back at Mattie's rumpled hair. "I felt something was wrong from the minute we got here this afternoon. Family squabbles can be a real pain, can't they? What were you fighting about?"

Mattie lifted her chin and smiled as sweetly as it was possible for her to at the moment. "Nothing important. A little misunderstanding. But, like you said, it was just a family squabble, and so we shouldn't allow it to bother our guests, should we? Now, if you will excuse me . . ."

Edith held up her hand. "Wait, Mattie. I think we need to talk."

"I'm sorry. I have work to do." Mattie brushed by her, walking with her head held high, out toward the kitchen, where Betty was already elbow deep in hot, soapy dishwater.

Mattie picked up the dish towel and started drying plates. "If you say one word! Just one word, and I'll . . ."

"Not me!" Betty shook her head solemnly. "Wes has been telling me for a long time to mind my own business, not to meddle. I know when to keep my mouth shut!"

CHAPTER TWENTY-SIX

It had been a long, restless evening and an even longer night for Mattie. She woke in the morning feeling exhausted, yet she couldn't stay in bed once the sun was up and the sounds of others moving about drifted up the stairs.

She had escaped to her room with a book the night before while the others were out at the barns. From her window she could see and hear the activity going on near the corrals. The men were all out there, helping to get the two bulls Edith wanted to take to the cattle show settled for the night.

Later they had all collected in the living room, but Mattie wanted no part in the discussions of plans for the following day. She knew Edith would be monopolizing the scene, controlling the conversations as well as Morgan's attentions, and she wasn't sure she was capable of handling the situation. She knew she had no right to feel as she did, but she couldn't seem to help herself.

Breakfast was an informal, disorganized gathering with the men eating at different times, hurrying on out toward the barns and corrals. Mattie helped Betty with the serving and the cleaning up afterward, knowing that Betty was as anxious as the rest of them to get the work done so they could prepare for the day in town. Edith was there, crisp and cool, too involved in conversations with her foreman and with Morgan to spare more than a casual nod and brief good morning to either Mattie or Betty.

As soon as possible, Mattie fled to the protective shelter of the study, closing the door securely behind her. One more day to somehow manage to live through, she thought to herself. She and the boys would be leaving early in the morning. She would be going back to Salem, back to Allen, back to the world where she belonged—back to the parties, the entertaining, the campaigning, and all of the rest of it that she hated.

By eleven o'clock, somehow, the chaos fell into order and the group was assembling in the living room before departure. The trucks had left several hours before and now the rest were ready to leave by car.

Mattie stood in the doorway looking around at the group of people collected there. Wes, wearing a new ten-gallon hat and a fresh shine on his boots for the occasion, was obviously looking forward to the day in town. Thad was lounging near the fireplace, laughing at something Wes had said. Thad looked so much younger than the other men, his hair curling almost boyishly across his forehead and without the muscles that develop with the hard work of a ranch.

Morgan was talking quietly with Tom Baldwin, the foreman from the Randall ranch. Tom had come in the evening before with the truck that brought their bulls. He was a soft-spoken, mild-mannered man in his mid-thirties, still bearing the traces of an eastern accent although he had lived in Oregon for the last five years and had been foreman at the Randalls for the last three of them.

There were several other men, men from neighboring spreads, and standing in the midst of the group was Edith, looking fresh and tailored. She wore hand-tooled leather boots and was dressed in a soft, pale green wool jacket over matching slacks. A Western-style hat topped her roguish red-blond curls. She was talking seriously with the men, her tones crisp and confident. As she looked up to see Mattie standing in the doorway, she shot her a calculating look and reached out to place her hand on Morgan's arm possessively.

Mattie felt a quick burst of anger and straightened her back defiantly as she walked into the room, going over to Morgan's side.

He glanced down at her, a smile touching the corners of his eyes. "I wondered where you were. Are you about ready to leave? The others are waiting."

"I have the bank drafts signed. You're going to need them, aren't you?"

Mattie felt the fire against her skin as their hands met. He took the drafts and tucked them into the inside pocket of his jacket. "Where's the boys?"

Before she could answer, the children appeared at Morgan's side, their faces full of anticipation of the day ahead of them.

Edith smiled down at them, the way adults do who aren't used to talking with small children. "You must be Clive, and you are Johnny. See, I already know your names."

"How'd you know that?" Johnny asked.

"Because your uncle told me all about you. Tell me, Clive, how do you like the pony?"

Clive raised his eyes, full of surprise. "How'd you know about my horse? Uncle Morgan gave him to me."

"I know. I helped pick it out. It came from my ranch. We raise horses. Lots of horses."

Clive looked at her with new respect and a little awe. Mattie saw the look and turned away, remembering Wes's hesitation about telling her where the pony came from.

"Do you have kids?" Johnny wanted to know. "Do you have kids there, too?"

"No." She glanced at Morgan. "Not yet, anyway." She turned back to the men, the boys forgotten, easily picking up the conversations on the adaptability of the white-faced Herefords to the Oregon range.

When they moved outdoors to break up into smaller groups for the trip into town, Edith went toward Morgan's car without waiting for the others to make any suggestions as to the seating arrangements. "Tom and I will ride with you, darling. I have a lot of things I need to talk to you about and it can be done on the way into town.''

Mattie watched as Edith confidently deposited herself between Morgan and Tom Baldwin. Thad rode with two of the other ranchers. Mattie handed Wes her car keys so that he could drive. She and Betty sat in back, letting Johnny and Clive sit in front with Wes.

It was a day of sawdust and heat, hot dogs, lemonade, and noise. Milling people and a few rowdy cowhands feeling the effects of too many friendly nips from hidden flasks completed the confusion. By midafternoon Clive's face was sunburned and his nose was red. Johnny's eyes were getting heavy from the excitement of the long day that had started much earlier than he was used to getting up.

Edith stayed in the sale barn, sitting between Tom Baldwin and Morgan, on the long, hard wooden benches. She discussed each entry with the two men, but she made her own decisions, did her own bidding.

Betty remained outside under the trees, where the other women collected, spreading out picnic lunches, watching the smaller children, eagerly catching up on their visiting. Mattie sat in the sale barn beside Wes for a while, listening intently to all of the tense drama going on around her, but when Jonathan began to sag tiredly against her, she stood up to take the boys back to the car.

''Please, Mom, I want to stay with Uncle Morgan,'' Clive protested. ''I ain't tired. Honest.''

Morgan took his eyes away from the auctioneer for a moment. ''Let him stay, Mattie. I'll keep an eye on him.''

Mattie caught the sharp look of irritation on Edith's face before she turned away. Clive slid into the spot between Morgan and Wes, resting his elbow on his uncle's knee while he solemnly watched the auctioneer. Mattie saw the way Morgan's hand dropped unconsciously to the small boy's shoulder. Tears stung the back of her eyes as she turned and hurried away, carrying the sleepy Jonathan to the car for a nap.

That evening Mattie sat out on the porch where she could catch

the cool, refreshing evening breeze before going up to her room.
The boys were in bed, the work was done, and she wanted some
time to be alone. The men were out at the barns, settling the new
bulls down for the night, and the house was quiet.

The screen door opened and someone came out, standing
quietly behind her. Without turning her head, Mattie knew who
the intruder was.

"I'd like to talk to you, Mattie." Edith's voice was crisp in
the soft evening air.

She sat down on the railing, swinging her expensive, leather-
clad foot casually as she leaned back against the post. "I take it
that Morgan never mentioned me to you before we met yesterday. You seemed surprised that I was so familiar with this
house."

"No. He didn't mention you." Mattie shrugged her shoulders
in an attempt at casualness. "But then, I'm sure he has a lot of
friends that he hasn't mentioned. After all, he has lived here most
of his life."

"I'm not just one of a lot of friends." Edith stopped swinging
her foot, leaning forward so she could study Mattie in the dim
evening light. "In fact, I'm not just a friend at all. It's more than
that."

"What are you trying to say?" Mattie kept her voice low,
hoping she sounded disinterested and a little bored.

"That I am in love with Morgan. He doesn't love me—not
yet—but he would if given a chance." She flicked a speck of
dust from her slacks. "I plan on marrying him. I usually get what
I want. I don't want any interference, Mattie."

Mattie looked up sharply. "Interference? What do you mean?
He makes his own decisions. I have no ties on Morgan."

"Just so long as you remember it," Edith answered deliberately.

The two women sat in silence for a while, listening to the sounds
of the night as they each weighed their thoughts carefully.

"Has he asked you to marry him yet?" Mattie asked at last.

"No. But he will. I'll be good for him, Mattie. We have the same
interests. We live the same kind of life. We talk the same
language. Stay out of it. Let him alone." Edith stood up, stretching her long, slender legs. "Thanks for listening to me, Mattie. I

think we understand each other, don't we?'' She turned and walked across the yard to meet Morgan, who was just coming in from the barn, leaving her words hanging in the air like a warning.

CHAPTER TWENTY-SEVEN

It was early, not much after sunrise, and Morgan could hear the sounds of others just beginning to wake up and move around. As he came out of his bedroom, he caught the smells of bacon and fresh bread drifting up the stairway. That meant that Betty was already in the kitchen. She usually always was the first one up. Even before Wes. Betty believed that no man was worth a grain of salt unless he started the day with a hearty breakfast and it was her duty to see that her menfolk had one. He knew that when he walked into the kitchen there would be platters of crisp bacon, light, fluffy biscuits, bowls of rich cream gravy, eggs, and a frown on Betty's face if he didn't eat.

He passed Mattie's bedroom door. She would be getting up soon and starting to pack for the long drive back to Salem, taking the two small boys with her. Already he felt the lonely emptiness that would be caused by her leaving.

As he started down the stairs, he heard the insistent ring of the telephone from the table in the hallway. He hurried his steps, taking the receiver from the hook, and answered. Behind him he heard Tom Baldwin coming down the stairs, stretching and yawning.

"Morgan? Abe." Morgan became instantly alert. It was the voice of Abe Donnelly, his foreman at the lumber mill. "Listen, you got to get down here to the mill gawd-damn fast! We got trouble.''

"What is it?'' Morgan's voice was tense, waiting.

"Must have been a spark from the logging equipment up where the boys were cutting yesterday. Must have been smoldering. We got a fire going back up in a canyon behind the mill—two maybe three, miles from here.''

Baldwin stopped at the foot of the stairway, listening, sensing something was wrong. "Got trouble, Morgan?''

"We haven't had a rain lately. The whole damned woods is as dry as a tinderbox and we got a fire started up in a canyon behind the mill.'' He was already moving swiftly toward the door, picking up his coat as he went.

"Wait. I'm coming with you.'' Baldwin was only a step behind him, sliding onto the car seat by the time Morgan had the motor running.

They didn't talk much at first. Morgan was concentrating on driving, trying to get as much speed as he could on the deeply rutted road. As they got closer toward the town, they began to see the reddish haze to the west, bright enough to outline the tops of the trees against the early morning sky.

The line of the horizon was a murky gray from the billowing clouds of smoke, and once in a while an open finger of flame would shoot up into the air, driven by the rising currents of the canyons.

"Looks like she's building up fast.'' Morgan swore under his breath.

"What can you do? How do you stop a fire like that?'' Tom watched the glow across the canyons grow brighter, feeling little twinges of fear and awe picking away at him inside.

"You ever fought fire in timber?'' Morgan asked.

Tom shook his head. "We've had a few grass fires. Nothing serious.''

"Grass fires can be bad. Forest fires are worse. It gets to burning in the tops of the trees and can travel with the wind. It's a nightmare.''

"Fill me in. What do I expect when we get there. What do we do?''

Morgan shrugged. "Hard to tell. Sometimes building a back-fire will stop it. Sometimes you have to dig trenches. Turning the ground over so it's got nothing to feed on will show it down— maybe. Sometimes all you can do is run like hell to get out of the way and pray the wind doesn't come up. They can travel pretty damned fast with a good wind behind them. A fire can jump a clearing and catch in the tops of trees on the other side and keep right on going, if the wind comes up."

By the time they reached the mill, men were arriving from all around the area—men who had seen the orange tint to the sky or men who had been roused from their sleep by a telephone call for help. They came with teams of horses hitched to wagons loaded down with plows, or driving cars, bringing shovels, axes—anything they could find that could be used to fight the fire.

Abe came running up to Morgan's car to meet them. "We shut the saws down. Got every man working on making a stand along the creek. We better plow a strip, start a backfire, do what we can to keep it away from the mill, keep it away from those houses."

"How far away you figure it is yet?" Morgan was watching the heavy smoke rolling down the canyon, bringing waves of heat with it, making his eyes burn.

"Maybe two miles. Some of the men were trying to stop it farther on up the ridge, closer to where it started, but the heat drove them back. The fire is burning up in the tops. She's moving pretty fast—everything is so gawd-damn dry."

Morgan watched the men unloading the plows, working with the axes, starting to pile up slash to build a fire line at the edge of the meadow along the bed of the creek.

"There's one thing that might work," he answered slowly. "There's an old burned-over area about a mile up the canyon between us and the fire. If we can reach it, we might be able to make a stand there and get it stopped."

Abe shook his head. "Too much of a chance to take. There's no road in there from this side. The other side has already been cut off. If the wind should shift, it could jump across and we'd be trapped. Hell of a way to die, Morgan."

As Morgan watched, the smoke thinned in places and he could see tall shards of hungry flame burst upward, hurling trailing balls of fire with an explosive force toward other trees, spreading the fire as much as a quarter of a mile away. If the wind didn't shift, his lumber mill stood right in its path. Beyond the mill was a group of houses at the outskirts of the town. He made his decision.

"You hold down the fort here, Abe. You know what to do. You've fought fire before. We got to get that thing slowed down. I'm going in. I'm not asking anyone to follow me. Any man that goes does it of his own choice." He went over to the truck and picked up a brush hook, leaving his coat across the fender. He saw the hesitation, the fear, on the faces of the other men as they watched.

"To hell with it." Baldwin walked over, picked up an ax. "I wasn't ever cut out to be a hero, but if you go, I'm going with you."

"If the mill goes, I lose my job, and maybe my house," another man said. One by one, Morgan saw a dozen men make their decisions, step out from the rest and fall in line. Abe began issuing sharp orders to the rest of them, and to a man they rolled up their sleeves and followed him to the edge of the meadow to begin the fire line.

Morgan, followed by the crew of fire fighters, crossed the meadow and picked up an overgrown trail that bordered the creekbed. The sides of the ravine were steep and heavy with underbrush, boxing them in as they followed the path back into the dark canyon. They were carrying saws, axes, brush hooks, shovels—whatever they could pack. The trail was rough, with overhanging branches catching at their clothing and scratching their arms. The heat poured down the ravine, billowing toward them, challenging them to keep moving, filling their lungs with the dry smoke, making their eyes smart with tears until it was hard to see the loose rocks underfoot. The men followed Morgan's broad back as he took the lead, coughing, cursing the smoke, and praying that the wind didn't come up.

After less than a half-mile, Morgan stopped and turned to look back at the single-file line of men behind him. "We're going to have to leave the creekbed here and work our way straight up toward the top of that ridge. It's the only way up there. There's no road or trail. Now's the time to turn back, any of you that want to. It's going to be one hell of a tough climb." He saw the hesitation, but they grumbled something about wasting time talking and wiped their faces on their shirt-sleeves before beginning the climb.

The side of the ravine was heavily timbered, with thick underbrush, loose rocks, old logs, and a spongy carpet of dried pine needles, making their struggle to reach the top not only strenuous but dangerous, and all of the time the smell of wood smoke grew stronger and the air heavier.

They broke out onto a flat, and several acres of old burned-over land spread out in front of them. The men fought to catch their breath as they stopped to rest and watch the flashes of fire easily visible now through the black, rolling clouds of smoke. The fire was in front of them, and the sounds were deafening.

"Holy Christ!" Tom swore in awe under his breath, his eyes glued in fascination to the inferno eating away at the growth of tall pine. "This must be what it is like looking into the gates of hell!" The flames were dancing high overhead in the tops of the trees. The ground underfoot was layered with past years of dry needles and old cones, giving it added fuel.

"Let's get at it!" Morgan tried to sound confident, knowing the other men depended on him to lead. "If the wind stays down, we can make it. Let's make a stand and backfire the burn."

They formed a line and worked with the shovels, the saws, axes, not talking, saving their breath for the job ahead of them. As they worked against time, their faces became grimy with dirt and sweat until it was hard to recognize one man from the other. They cut the brush and stacked it in piles, using the shovels to tear up the ground behind the line of limbs. They turned over the dry, waterless dirt to cover the needles and dead grasses.

Morgan had no time to think of anything else but to find a way to stop the forest fire, but somewhere in the far recesses of his mind he knew Mattie had put the kids in the car and was headed back toward Salem. She wouldn't be there when he got back to the ranch. Right now she was probably hoping she never laid eyes on him again. He should have said something to her about Edith Randall, but what was there to say? They were friends. Good friends. As far as he was concerned, that was as far as it went. He hadn't even kissed her, much less made love to her. Sure, Edith made it obvious she wanted it to go further. Hell, maybe it should. Maybe that was the way to forget Mattie. He wiped the sweat from his eyes and tried to ignore the ache across his shoulders as he cut away at the brush.

Morgan felt a change in the air before he saw what it was doing. He straightened up and looked upward to see the change. He could hear the crash of trees falling, hear the explosive sounds of new fires bursting out in the combustible under-growth, saw the way the smoke was thinning, giving way to raw flame.

"Gawd damn it, the wind is starting to come up!" The other men straightened their aching backs and looked over toward him, too tired to show the fear of what his warning meant. "Light the backfire!" he shouted. "It's now or never! We can't wait any longer. Get it burning!"

The men made torches and touched off the piles of limbs and watched the fire burn toward them, to where they had dug and clawed in the dirt. It smoldered helplessly in the loose ground as they worked to beat it out with their shovels. Needing fuel, it turned and worked its way backward, nibbling its way into the pile of slash they had built to lead it toward the main fireline.

He felt Baldwin's hand on his arm. "We got to get out of here, Morgan! It's jumped the canyon behind us. Moving in on the other side. We could get trapped. We got to get the hell out of here!"

Morgan turned his face upward, a sick feeling in the pit of his stomach. Baldwin was right. The backfire they had built was stopping it on this side, but the main fire had jumped the canyon and was working in from the other side. They had to get out of here. Only there was no place to run.

It was then that he saw how the sky had turned as black as night, the smoke mixing with giant storm clouds moving in from the east, and he felt the first few drops of water falling against his scorched cheeks. Above the roar of the fire, he heard the thunder, and the rain began to fall, light at first, then turning into hard, driving sheets of water.

The men sank to the ground, too tired to cheer, spreading out their arms to let their parched bodies soak up the moisture as the rivulets of water trailed across their soot-covered faces, leaving patterns in the dirt.

Morgan heard a shout and turned to see Abe leading a fresh crew of men up through the old burn, coming toward them.

The two groups of men intermingled, letting the heavy rain pour down on their heads unnoticed, shouting out their joy over the fire that was rapidly turning into a steaming, wet mass of smoldering coals.

"How's it look down below?" Morgan wanted to know.

"Got a good fire line established at the end of the meadow behind the mill. Some of the boys are staying there, watching. This rain saved our asses, and that's for sure! Never was so glad to see anything in my whole life. Ain't never going to curse the rain no more!" Abe slapped Morgan on the back. "These men are ready to stay up here, do the mop-up. We got to keep an eye on it, just in case. You guys head back down. The women got hot coffee, some food, dry clothes waiting."

Morgan and Baldwin were sitting on a ramp under the long shed at the mill, listening to the steady beat of the heavy rain against the roof, watching it run off into deepening puddles, filling the ruts in the road with mud. Most of the men had drunk the hot coffee, eaten the sandwiches, and gone off with their women to their homes, wanting nothing more than a hot bath and a chance to sleep. They were, dead on their feet, too tired to think.

Morgan reached out his hand toward Baldwin. "For an Easterner who'd never seen a forest fire before, you made a damned good showing out there. Thanks."

"Don't. I don't deserve it. I had to stay and fight. I was too damned scared to turn and run." Tom hunched his shoulders against the damp cold that was beginning to seep its way into his body.

"Just as well. For a while there was no place to run to. At one time we were pretty well cut off."

Baldwin stretched his tired muscles. "I don't even want to think about it. You about ready to leave for the ranch? The women are going to be on edge, wanting news."

"You go on," Morgan answered. "I'm going to stay here. I won't rest easy until I know it is all out. Sometimes the under-brush and stumps will lie there and smolder. Never know when it will flare up again."

"Nothing is going to happen in a downpour like this."

"Probably not. I just feel better staying close to town."

"What about Edith?"

"She'll understand."

"She'll still be worried." Tom scraped his toe in the mud forming at their feet. "You ought to think about what her feel-ings are, too, you know."

"You'll be going back. You can let her know everything is under control."

"Morgan, you ought to let her know yourself. It's you she's worried about, not me. She's a hell of a fine woman, Morgan. Most folks can't see past the hard exterior. She's so damned intelligent and sure of herself most of the time that she scares a lot of people away. They don't take time to know the real Edith that she keeps hidden away, out of sight. Underneath, she's gentle, soft, and she needs an awful lot of love. I wish you'd treat her more like a woman instead of like one of the men."

Morgan looked over at him, one eyebrow raised. "You trying to tell me you know her better than I do?"

"Maybe. Maybe I understand her better because I love her more than you do."

Morgan studied the muddy ground in front of him, watching the little dimples made by the large drops of water. "Does she know you feel this way about her?"

"No. Hell, Morgan, she doesn't pay any attention to me. I'm just there. I'd give it a damn good try if I thought I could win. Just warning you. But you've got nothing to worry about. She doesn't have eyes for anyone but you. I'm damn poor competition."

"You were a damn good man up there on the fire line."

"Thanks. It's no use, though."

Morgan reached out and slapped him on the shoulder. "Go on back to the ranch. Have a hot bath. Get some rest. You're so tired you don't know what you're saying." He stood up, looking up toward the mountains where they had spent the last twelve hours battling the fire. "Tell the women I'll be home after the mill shuts down tomorrow night. I'll give a call on the phone later. Get out of here, Baldwin. You look about ready to drop in your tracks."

Morgan went into the office and stood looking out of the window, watching Baldwin drive away. He watched the rain. It was coming down in sheets, driven by the wind. The parched ground was drinking up the moisture and turning into thick, clinging mud. The drainage ditches at the side of the road had filled with dirty swirls of water and was beginning to wash up over the roads. The mountain ridges behind the mill, barely visible through the curtain of rain, were full of tumbling, cascading waterfalls as the dry creekbeds swelled into boiling, racing streams.

He walked over to the desk and sat down, tiredly sorting through the papers that had been neglected during the day, but he was too tired to concentrate. He kept thinking of Mattie, leaving today with the two small boys. Thinking of Baldwin and his confession of hopelessness. Of Edith, sure of herself and used to getting what she had her mind made up to win. Edith made it plain she wanted marriage. He had told Mattie he wanted to marry. Edith would make a man a good wife—only he loved Mattie. He thought about Allen, who seemed to have everything in life he wanted and wasn't content. Morgan got up and went back outside. The cold, pelting rain revived him, taking away some of the tiredness, and he began to realize it had been a long time since he had eaten. Hunger was gnawing away at his insides, taking priority over his need for sleep.

He took a swing through the mill yard just to assure himself one more time that everything was all right and went over to his car. It was only a five-minute drive into town and the café where he usually ate.

He parked on the main street, near where Allen used to have his law office. There was a real estate sign in the window now. Some investment firm from Portland had moved in, breaking a small ranch at the end of town into smaller parcels, selling building lots. The small town was changing, growing.

Farther down the street, on the corner, was the remains of the small bar where he had spent a lot of memorable evenings. It was deserted now, put out of business by the prohibition laws and tight money. Suddenly he felt an urge to talk to Minnie, listen to the way she spread her own brand of gossip, sprinkled heavily with humor and not hurting anybody. She hadn't changed much— never seemed to age since the first time he could remember going into her bar. She was one of the few things in his life that always seemed to stay the same.

He left the car where it was and walked two streets over, to an area of small new homes built since the end of the war.

She opened the door at his knock and her round face beamed in welcome when she saw who was standing there, rain dripping off the brim of his hat.

"Holy tarnation, it's good to see you! I've wondered what happened to you. Ain't seen much of you since you started working on that mill of yours." She had him by the arm, pulling him inside. "Don't worry none about dripping water on the floor. Stand over there by the fire and dry out. I got just the thing to warm up the insides. Take off your coat and I'll pour a drink. You look like hell!"

"Thanks for the compliment." He grinned at her. "Guess I am a mess to come calling."

"From the looks of you, I'd say you just came in from working on the fire lines. Smell like it, too. This rain came just in time. If the wind had changed, we could have lost a lot of homes on this side of town."

A tea kettle started whistling on the stove, giving a warm, welcoming sound. He looked around him. She had the place fixed up really comfortable. There was a big braided rug on the floor, some photographs and picture postcards tacked on the wall, a collection of obsidian arrowheads from the desert country, matted and framed.

She was standing by the stove, her hands on her hips, watching him affectionately. "You had supper? I'm getting damned sick and tired of eating alone. You split some stove wood for me and I'll see what I can rustle up. Food always tastes better when there's a man's boots under the table across from me."

"Figured you'd be married again by now, Minnie. What happened?"

"Hell, Morgan, I been married five times already. If I can't find what I'm looking for after that many men, I ain't apt to ever find it." She gave him a broad wink. "Of course, that ain't sayin' I ain't still looking."

He went through the back door into the lean-to shed and found an ax. He could smell meat frying, fried potatoes with chopped onion and a bit of bacon for seasoning as he chopped. He came back into the kitchen with an armload of wood cut up into stove-size lengths and dumped them into the woodbox behind the stove. He rolled up his sleeves and washed in the basin of warm water she had set out for him. God, it felt good. He was beginning to unwind, relax, and feel almost drowsy as his tired body responded to the comfortable surroundings.

Minnie stood back and looked at the table. "How about it, Morgan? Think that's enough to tide you over until morning? I just baked those rolls fresh this afternoon. If you got any room after this is gone, there's some chocolate cake."

As they ate, she kept up a steady stream of talk. She loved to talk, and she probably knew more about the town and what went on in it than any other person alive. It was her town, her people. She had seen folks move in and settle down, seen babies born and watched them grow up and have kids of their own.

He leaned back and lit a cigarette. His clothes had dried, he was full, relaxed, and he was content to sit back and listen to the heavy rains beating a steady tattoo against the window as they visited.

"Seen Mattie back in town," she said, looking across at him. "She come over for a vacation?"

He nodded. "Brought her two boys over for a couple of weeks. She went home today."

"Noticed Allen didn't come with her. Everything going all right with them?"

"According to Allen, things couldn't be going better. That's why he didn't come with her. He's working double time right now, I guess. He's talking about running for governor, next election."

She mulled that one around thoughtfully. "Well, he might just make it. He always was a real smart one. Heard you had some other company, too. Still there, in fact."

It never ceased to amaze him the way she knew everything that was going on, though she seldom left the city limits herself. "Just some folks from over around Wagon Wheel staying at the ranch while they attend the cattle show."

She nodded. "Understand they must be real good friends. They've stayed there before, haven't they?"

"A time or two. I bought some horses from them."

"Yeah?" She raised an eyebrow and studied him. "She's a real sharp looker. Understand she's a damn shrewd businesswoman, too, when it comes to horses. Cows, too. I figure she must know a thing or two about judging men, considering who she has her eye on."

Morgan felt the color creep up around his shirt collar. "You listen to too much gossip, Minnie. Since you closed up the bar, you don't have enough to do to keep you busy. You ought to take up knitting or something—"

"Don't get coy with me, Morgan! I've known you since you started wearing long pants. You ought to get married and start a family. It ain't good for men to live alone. Pretty soon you're going to find yourself getting set in your ways, getting crotchety. Hell, if she don't manage to get her brand on you, maybe I'll marry you myself. All the men I married either died or wore out. Think I'll marry me a young one next time."

Morgan threw back his head and laughed. It felt good. Minnie was good medicine. He pushed back his chair and stood up. "Tell you what. If I decide to look for a wife, I'll damn sure put your name right at the top of the list. I got to be going. I've been fighting fire since sunup. I just realized how tired I am. Thanks for the supper and the conversation. It was just what I needed."

She walked to the door with him. "You remember what I said, Morgan. You get married. You ain't cut out to be a bachelor!"

CHAPTER TWENTY-EIGHT

Allen glanced at his watch. He was going to be late for the meeting at Cass Courtney's apartment. He had hesitated some about keeping the appointment at all, debating whether he should go to the speak for the evening and forget the whole thing or whether he should follow through on the challenge he saw in her eyes each time they had talked at the speak.

Curiosity finally made him decide to keep the appointment. She had said there were going to be some men holding a meeting at her apartment that he should meet. Her uncle would be there, from the East Coast, along with several of his associates. Without naming names, she had alluded that the men were powerful, men he should know if he wanted to get ahead.

Mattie would be home from her trip to the ranch sometime late tomorrow. It was about time. She had been gone for two weeks. He had talked to her earlier in the day on the telephone. She had said she would start out in the morning and drive straight through, getting there sometime before dinner. It would be good to have Mattie back home. Things always seemed to go smoother when she was around. Tomorrow she would be back home where she belonged. Maybe this trip would get it out of her system for a while and she would forget about that damned ranch—be content to let the ranch get along on its own. Wes was doing a good job,

Morgan was there—they sent reports for her to read so she didn't need to go there very often. He didn't want her at the ranch. He wanted her here, with him, where she belonged. He needed her.

He let his mind wander back to Cass Courtney. Cass was different from the other women he had been casually involved with over the years—she held a certain fascination. She was a real beauty, but there was something else—it was Class, spelled with a capital C. She was used to having money—lots of money. She had traveled. She spoke familiarly about the large cities in the eastern part of the country as well as Europe. She knew how to dress. Her clothes were conservative, almost plain, and yet they whispered of style and sophistication.

She was indifferent to the attention she drew when she sat in the speak slowly sipping her martini, casually listening to the older man who usually accompanied her, as though she were bored with what little the town had to offer for entertainment. She was restless, wanting something to add a little zest to her dull routine. The way her eyes had swept the club until they finally rested on Allen and she watched him, speculating, reminded him of a tigress on the prowl—quiet, stealthy, and dangerous. He wondered what she was doing this far west—what had brought her to the speak.

Their first conversations had been brief—hardly worth remembering. But the challenge was there in her eyes. While the other women giggled and flirted openly with him, she remained silent, letting him be the first to cross the line and make the approach.

Later she began coming to the speak alone, careless about convention, and he had been drawn to her, unable to resist the challenge to break her down and see what made her tick behind that cool exterior.

They had talked. She seemed interested in everything about him—his office, his ambitions, his career, his dreams for the future. He found himself talking openly, telling her his plans, talking about things he hadn't put into words even to himself, and yet with all of their conversations, he still knew very little about her. And now she had invited him to her apartment. She had invited him to meet her uncle and his associates. It was an invitation hard to refuse. He was curious.

A maid answered his knock at the door and took his hat and coat. He saw that there were five or six men there already, lounging comfortably in the deep overstuffed chairs, talking among themselves. He caught the aroma of expensive cigars floating on the air.

Cass glanced up and saw him standing in the vestibule looking around the luxurious apartment. She came across the room to meet him. She wore a floor-length, clinging gown that flattered her thin, boyish figure, accented her vibrant blue eyes, her ash-blond hair. She carried a cigarette in a long, slender holder in one hand and a glass in the other.

"Glad you could make it, darling." She stretched on tiptoe and kissed him lightly on the cheek. He caught the fragrance of her perfume as she brushed against him, a tantalizing whisper of roses covered with evening dew. "The others are here already. They came early. They wanted time to talk by themselves. Want a drink?"

He nodded and followed her across the expanse of deep-blue carpet to the bar against the far wall. None of the men looked up. He raised an eyebrow when she slid back the glass panel and revealed the rows of crystal bottles—the well-known, expensive labels. "Baby, someone forgot to tell you about prohibition," he said, admiration in his voice.

"It isn't hard to get the stuff, if you know the right people," she answered with a careless shrug of her shoulders as she poured him a drink. "And I do, Allen. All of the right people."

He lifted the glass, tested the aroma of the amber liquid, and slowly took a sip. "Top-grade stuff!" he said in appreciation. "Where did you get it?"

"None of your business," she laughed lightly at him. "Not until I'm sure you are here as a friend and not in your official capacity. Which are you tonight, Allen? A friend or a foe?"

"Who did you invite?" he countered. "The office or the man?"

"The man, darling. Definitely the man."

"What were you expecting, then? That I might have left a couple of men outside lurking in the hallway? You think maybe I'm here to raid the place?"

"If you are, you are going to spoil a lot of lovely plans I have for just the two of us later in the evening." Her voice was low, throaty, suggestive.

"Then I'll tell the boys outside to go away." He smiled at her and she smiled back, meeting his eyes squarely, without any coyness. "Who are these people?" His attention went back to the men seated behind them, intently talking in low, muffled tones. "Don't see anyone I know."

"Of course you don't. They are friends of mine—you haven't been invited into their circle yet. But you'll like them. They talk your language. You will like the air in here, too. Smell it? It reeks of money."

He took a slow sip of his drink. "How do I get an invitation into the magic circle?"

"Depends. Wait and see what happens. They are a careful bunch. They don't trust too easily. That's why they're where they are." She nodded toward the heavyset older man who seemed to be the center of the circle, the other men paying him respect with their close attention, the way they listened when he spoke. "That's my uncle, Martin Courtney. Your first require-ment is to be nice to me. I'm his favorite niece. Do you think you can handle that?"

"Then I'm already past the first gate. Being nice to you is one of the things I've had at the top of my list of things to do since the first evening I saw you at the speak." He twirled the ice in his glass, thoughtfully studying the men. "What are they doing here, Cass?"

"They're here to see Uncle Martin. He just got in from the East Coast last night. He likes to have someplace that's nice and private when he talks with the boys. Someplace they won't be disturbed or maybe have their conversations repeated and misunderstood."

Allen's brows went up in surprise. "Is he staying here with you?"

Her laughter was soft, melodious. "No, darling. Of course not. Uncle Martin has a suite of rooms at the hotel. He keeps them reserved the year round. But you know how it is. Hotels are so impersonal. Everyone watching who comes and goes." Her eyes rested fondly on the older man as she talked. "Besides, Uncle is a family man. Meeting here is more personal, more homelike. They feel comfortable talking together like this."

Allen looked at the thick carpets, the velvet drapes, the tables with ivory tops. "You got a nice place here, Cass. Must cost one hell of a lot of money to keep it up."

"And you have a dirty mind," she answered tartly. "He really is my uncle, you know. And he doesn't pay the rent. He spoils me in a lot of other ways. He likes to see me have what I want. I have enough money of my own to keep up the apartment, keep myself comfortable."

"What does this dear old uncle of yours do to make all of the nice green money we smell in the air?" Allen asked.

"Timber, among other things."

He looked up in surprise. Somehow he had thought she was going to say something else.

"That's right. Timber. Trees. Logs. And it takes hundreds and hundreds of acres of timber to keep his mills supplied. He needs contracts for hundreds and hundreds of acres of state-owned timberland to keep his sawmills running, turning out lumber. There's a building boom going on."

"Ah-ha." Allen nodded. "I see."

"What do you see, Allen?"

"Nothing. Everything. I think I am beginning to understand. Come on, Cass. It's time for you to introduce me to dear old Uncle Martin."

The older man didn't offer to get up out of his chair or to hold out his hand at the introduction. He drew deep on his cigar and studied Allen thoughtfully through the haze of smoke. "Been hearing a lot about you, Henderson. Like what I heard. Cass seems to think you have a lot of possibilities."

"I'm afraid I'm at a disadvantage," Allen answered, still standing and feeling annoyed at the way his proffered hand had been ignored.

Cass introduced the other men. They stood, reaching out a hand, making some small, casual comment. Allen recognized most of the names—names connected with mills—large mills—lumber men from both Oregon and Washington. The talk was

light, impersonal, as it is with people meeting for the first time.
Whatever it was they had been discussing so seriously only a few
minutes before was shelved when he joined the group.

One by one, the men made their excuses and left for other
appointments until only Martin Courtney was left.

"Sit down, Allen." A diamond flashed from his finger as he
waved a hand carelessly toward a chair nearby. "Cass tells me
you got a ranch over in the eastern part of the state. How many
head are you running?"

"Not as many as I would like," Allen answered, cautious
now, wondering at the direction of the conversation. "Don't
have the time to spend over there that I should."

The older man nodded. "Know what you mean. I raise Herefords myself. Purebred. Registered stock. Takes a lot of time. A
lot of money. Being the attorney general for the state doesn't
give you a lot of either one, does it?"

Allen was on guard now, choosing his words carefully. "I
manage."

"I'm sure you do, a smart young man like you. Understand
you intend to run for governor." There was nothing in the older
man's eyes or expression to give away his thoughts.

Allen nodded. "That's what I am planning. Going to give it a
damned good try, anyway." The caution flags were out in the
back of his mind. Cass must have done her homework well. He
was trying to remember what else he might have told her. He
didn't know Cass that well. Just a few evenings of talking in a
casual, rambling way over martinis at the speak, and yet she
seemed to have listened closer than he had thought. Not only
listened, but discussed him at length with Martin Courtney.

Courtney was watching him through half-closed sleepy eyes,
but Allen had the feeling that his mind was working like a
trip-hammer. "Well, glad to hear it. Like to see a man that's on
his toes, knows what's going on, anxious to get ahead. Only . . .
running for governor costs a hell of a lot of money. Takes more
money than running a ranch and breeding prize cattle. A man
running for governor needs to have a lot of understanding friends—
friends that can give him the kind of help he needs."

Allen didn't answer. He felt as though he had set down to a

game of chess and the men were lined up on the board. He waited for the other man to set out the rules, make the first move.

"Now, I never did run for any public office myself. I got too many other things to worry about. So it helps to know people who hold different offices. I like to give them a little help once in a while when they need it, just to keep my hand in things and know what is going on. You know what I mean?"

"I believe Cass mentioned you were in lumber," Allen hedged. "That would keep a man busy, all right."

Martin laughed. A deep, satisfied chuckle. "I see you know what I'm talking about. State land comes up for bid, a man has to know ahead of time about it. Even helps a little if he has some idea of what the others are bidding. When he gets a little help, he appreciates it. He shows his appreciation."

Suddenly, as though bored with the conversation, he raised himself out of the chair. "Give you a lift somewhere, Allen? I'm tired. Time I went back to my hotel."

"Thanks anyway." Allen shook his head. "I've got my car outside. I want to talk to Cass for a few minutes and then I'll be leaving, too. Got a full schedule tomorrow."

When the door closed behind Courtney, Cass turned to Allen, her arms winding suggestively around his neck. "He likes you, Allen," she said confidently. "He is going to want to see you again."

"How could you tell? I felt like he was brushing me off when he left."

"I told you. I'm his favorite niece. I can tell."

Allen took the glass from her hand and set it on the table, pulling her close against him as he nuzzled her hair. "What were the plans for later in the evening—the plans you mentioned when I first got here? To hell with dear old Uncle Martin and his boys. Tell me more about you." And his mouth came down on her lips, smothering her answer.

Without any coyness or pretense, she reached out and flipped the latch on the door and turned out the lights. Picking up a bottle of champagne and two glasses, she led the way to the bedroom.

The room was large, feminine, and at the same time inviting. A soft, low light silvered the pale blue carpet, outlined the large bed with the deep-blue velvet cover, the stacks of pillows. Cass filled the two glasses and set the bottle and glasses down on a small table within easy reach of the bed.

Slowly, dramatically, she loosened the fastenings on the long dress and let it slip down into a heap around her feet, where it lay shimmering like a pool of dark ink on the pale carpet. Allen caught his breath sharply when he saw she wore nothing under the dress, was standing before him nude, her body glowing softly in the silver light, her ash-blond hair slightly ruffled, her vibrant blue eyes heavy lidded and suggestive as she picked up her glass and watched him over the rim of it.

"Seduce me, Allen," she whispered. "Now."

"Are you awake?" Her voice was low, sultry, full of satisfaction.

"Yes. Why?"

"I just wondered. What are you thinking?"

"What an amazing woman you are."

"We go well together, don't we?" she answered smugly. "I like you, Allen. I like the way you make love. I like the way you look."

"How do I look?"

"Bold. Handsome. Totally unscrupulous."

"Do you like what you see?" he asked.

"I think so. I find you exciting, a challenge. I think I want to get to know you better, Allen Henderson." She stretched luxuriously against the pillows, reaching for the champagne glass and a cigarette.

"Do you always get what you want?"

"Most of the time. When I don't, I can be a real bitch. Remember that, Allen. Don't ever play games with me."

He thought of Mattie, laughing happily as she left for the brief vacation with the two little boys at the ranch. Mattie—proud, unsophisticated, still a country girl under all of the polish. "I'm married, Cass."

"I know."

"It doesn't bother you?"

"Not particularly." She ran her long nails suggestively across his shoulders and murmured drowsily, "Do you have to go home tonight, Allen?"

"No. Not for a while." He reached for her again, drawing her close to him on the rumpled covers of the bed, laughing at her quick, hungry response.

TWENTY-NINE

Mattie sat at the table in the breakfast room absently looking out of the window, her mind far away. In her hand was a letter from Betty that had come in the morning mail. Summer was reluctantly giving way to an early fall all through the lush Willamette Valley. It had been raining constantly for several weeks. She could hear the sound of water dripping from the eaves outside the window. The sky was gray and dismal-looking. The flower beds were losing their splashes of color as the blossoms hung their heads against the dampness and let their petals fall unnoticed into the mulch at their feet.

Clive was ready to start school for the first time when the new semester began in September. Jonathan had a cold and was fretting because he couldn't go to school when Clive did. To him being old enough to go to school was one of the most important things that would happen to him in his young life. He resented Clive being able to do something while he was left behind. Mattie had tried to explain to him that he would be going to school next year, but to Jonathan a year was a long, long time.

Mattie watched a large robin hopping along the ground under the shrubbery that bordered the lawn, picking at the bright red holly berries. Yes, she thought with a sigh, a year was a long, long time. It had been almost a year since she and the boys had returned from the vacation at the ranch, and it seemed forever.

She had kept her days crowded with engagements, trying to leave little time for daydreaming about what might be happening on the other side of the mountains, where the ranch sprawled in the high desert country. There were beauty shop appointments, afternoon bridge games, evenings of entertaining. The campaign for governor was in full swing now and she often went with Allen, sitting in the front row, listening to him give his speeches to different business groups. He wanted her at his side where the people could see her. A staunch family man. Respectable. A lovely wife who was the mother of his children. Stable. This is what the voters wanted, and this was the image he projected.

Mattie glanced down at the letter in her hand. Over the months Betty had written regularly. "I know you have told me to mind my own business," Betty had written soon after Mattie returned from the ranch on that last trip. "Wes had told me the same thing, and now Morgan should have told me, but he didn't. We had some hot words and I'm surprised that when I got through telling him what I thought he just didn't give me my walking papers. It just wasn't right that he didn't tell you about Edith Randall. Of course, her taking over like she was the mistress of the house didn't help any, either. That woman sure has a lot of nerve!"

It had been a shock to her, all right, Mattie remembered. She had been mad—but more mad at herself than at Morgan. What right did she have to make any claims on him or resent another woman obviously after his attention? Both of them knew there was no chance for the love that bound them together, and neither of them could let it die. It was so strong it consumed them, destroyed their reason, and yet they both knew it had to end. Morgan was right. They couldn't go on the way they were.

Later Betty had written that, even though there was no sign of Edith wearing an engagement ring, she had been back to the ranch for a few days and was as possessive as ever. It was supposedly another business trip and she brought that foreman, Tom Baldwin, with her as well as her young brother.

Mattie put the letter aside at the sound of Allen's steps on the stairway. He was late this morning. Even so, he couldn't have had more than a few hours' sleep. It had been well past midnight when he had come home. For months now, Allen had been staying away until the early morning hours several times a week, without any explanation other than that he was busy. He had work that kept him late, people he needed to meet with in the evening. The speak was taking up more of his time. The duties of his office were demanding, he had problems that he didn't want to talk about at home.

Mattie would hear him fumbling with the doorknob to the bedroom, swearing softly to himself as he stumbled against the furniture, smell the alcohol on his breath. On those nights she would lay staring into the dark, wondering where he had been, what he had been doing, and who was he doing it with this time. The dagger-sharp remarks from the other wives at bridge didn't matter because they were only random guesses, trying to annoy her to the point where she would flare up and make a reply without thinking, adding fuel to their vicious gossip.

Only yesterday Madge Anderson had smiled innocently across the card table at her and asked who the attractive blonde was that seemed to be taking command of the office work at the campaign headquarters. "I suppose it was only his duty to have dinner with her at the Willamette Heights Supper Club. I mean, after all, the work at the headquarters is all volunteer, and she does seem to put in a lot of hours there."

"I'm so glad Harvey is in farm machinery," Caroline had added to the conversation with a smug smile. "At least when he's kept out late with a business meeting, I know it is with other men."

"And Harvey is fiftyish and bald," Amanda quipped sharply. "Allen is in his thirties and rather handsome, to say the least. Just because the woman is an extremely attractive blonde and obviously rich has nothing to do with it. As a volunteer at the campaign headquarters she is putting in a lot of hard work. That is how elections are won, Madge."

There had been other women during the years they had been married. She knew it. Allen denied it, but a wife can tell. At least he was discreet about it, covering his tracks well. He was too concerned about his career and his public image to ever let his promiscuous evening affairs become open for gossip. The women were only taking guesses, looking for something to liven up the conversation. They thrived on scandal, true or imagined.

In one of her letters Betty had said that two huge, beautiful, registered Hereford bulls had arrived at the ranch for Allen. A whole envelope of papers came with them, giving their ancestry and a record of the prizes they had won. The papers said they came from a Martin Courtney of the Courtney Stock Ranch. Wes wanted to know what he was supposed to do with them and why Allen hadn't let him know ahead of time that they were coming.

When Mattie had questioned Allen about it, he had answered tersely that he had bought the bulls to improve the herd at the ranch. Mattie was surprised by his answer. It was the first time he had discussed the ranch since the reading of the will. When she had asked about the Courtney Stock Ranch and Martin Courtney, he had been sharp, saying only that he was a man with whom he was doing some business.

Mattie wasn't the only one worrying about the ranch, missing the time they spent there. Young Clive told her he was concerned about his black-and-white-spotted pony. Who was taking care of it for him? How would the pony understand why he hadn't come back? He fretted and worried and there was nothing Mattie could do to reassure him.

Allen came into the breakfast room, fastening his tie as he walked. He sat down across from her and spread out the morning papers while he waited for the cook to bring in his coffee. He glanced at the letter in her hand. "What was in the mail?"

She shrugged her shoulders. "Nothing much. A letter from Betty. Some bills. A couple of letters for you on the hall table."

"That's the reason for the daydreaming. A letter from Betty. You're getting lonesome for the ranch, aren't you? What does she have to say?"

Mattie looked up, surprised at his interest. "It's about time for the fall market. They're busy. You know what it's like this time of year over there."

"You thought about going over there for a week or so before winter sets in?"

Mattie laid the letter down and gave him her full attention.

"No. I haven't. There isn't much chance of you getting away now, when the campaigning is at the peak. The elections aren't very far away. How can you leave?"

"I can't. But that's no reason why you can't take the boys and have a little vacation before we settle down to the hard work just before elections. I'm going to be so busy with the campaign that I'm not going to have a free minute to call my own," he answered, giving her a sympathetic smile. "It's been rough on you, Mattie, and I know it. I appreciate what you've done. The voters love you. I love you. You've earned a week off at the ranch with the boys. It's good for them, too."

Mattie hesitated about the trip, her head telling her she should stay away while her heart was singing, already covering the miles ahead of her. Allen insisted that she go. When the car was packed, Allen helped the two boys up onto the high front seat and held the door open for Mattie. He held her a little closer than usual, kissing her good-bye. "Have a good vacation, baby. Have some fun. Get a good rest. Come back home to me smiling and ready to go into the last wind-up of the campaign. It's going to be a hell of a time, Mattie. I want you here at my side, rested, ready to take your bows."

Edith Randall had been at the ranch for several days when Mattie arrived.

"The place is more like a hotel than a ranch house," Betty grumbled to her as they sat over a cup of coffee after the breakfast rush. Wes had been up early, eating his breakfast with Morgan before he went outside to the corrals. Morgan left for the mill soon afterward, taking Tom Baldwin into town with him. Tom had some business to take care of at the county seat and Edith was going to meet him later. They would both be back at the ranch later to meet a buyer in the early afternoon.

"That woman is sure full of business," Betty complained, filling up her coffee cup as Edith's car left a trail of dust down the lane toward the highway. "Now that they have all left, let's sit down and catch our breath. We're long overdue for a good old-fashioned gossip." She tipped her head to one side, admiring the knit suit Mattie was wearing. "You sure do look city, Mattie.

You look real nice—even if you are too thin." She watched Mattie take a pack of cigarettes from her pocket. "You smoke too much, honey. You look so . . . tied up in knots. Guess it's about time you came back over here and relaxed a bit. You been keeping pretty busy?"

As they sipped their coffee, Mattie tried to describe the schedule she kept. She told what it was like to be continually in the public eye, open to criticism, especially now, with Allen campaigning for the office of governor. As Betty listened with wide-eyed interest, Mattie told about the speeches Allen made, the crowds that collected to hear him talk, the dinners, the entertaining they did in their home for people with well-known reputations. She made no mention of Allen's heavy drinking or the nights when he didn't come home. She talked about the campaign headquarters, the rallies, the women who volunteered to work at the headquarters, passing out folders, sending out mailers, answering the telephones, promoting him as their candidate. She made no mention of the rumors about a striking blonde she hadn't met but heard spent more time than necessary in the campaign promotions.

Betty shook her head. "It's hard to believe. Such a different life than we have over here. I don't know how you manage. And I have been sitting here complaining because I have those people traipsing in at all different hours. No mealtimes on schedule. Lord only knows what I would do if Wes and I had been lucky enough to have children."

CHAPTER THIRTY

The evening sun had disappeared down behind the line of the Coastal Range of mountains, sending long, dark shadows across the Willamette Valley by the time Allen was able to put the papers away in the safe and lock up the office for the night. It was one of those days when nothing went according to plan and he could feel the pressures closing in on him. He was tired. The nerves at the back of his neck were tied in knots. The last shipment of liquor from Canada had been stopped at the border and two men were in jail. The men could be trusted to keep their mouths shut, but still the element of chance was there, keeping him on edge. The local "dry" committee had been on his back for a week now, demanding more law enforcement against offenders of the prohibition laws. With the election coming up, he had to keep them happy, keep their trust in him from slipping. He had to do things such as giving that speech today to the Willamette Women's Club. God, what a farce that had been—fifty women, puffed up like so many pouter pigeons, declaring their rights as liberated females to take an active part in local government when they ought to be home taking care of the kids and making sure the old man's supper was on time. He had fawned and flattered, assuring them of their importance in his decisions as the future governor, telling them they were the real backbone of Western society. He had eaten their finger sandwiches and tiny decorated cakes as though he had enjoyed them, drank the tea, and thought in the back of his mind how there wasn't a one of them that would probably be worth a damn in bed.

If the feds had stopped the one shipment coming across the border, that meant they were on to something. He didn't want the trail leading to Salem—or to the speak. He turned the key in the lock and went out to where he had left the new Buick parked at the curb. One lousy bust by the feds that might point a trail toward his office and his chances of being governor would be blown all to hell. That meant more payoffs, more caution, tighter security. He had to watch his step. If that group from the women's club ever found out he owned the speak, they would rip him apart like a pack of hungry she-wolves. God, he wished Mattie was home. She would know how to handle them. But Mattie was at the ranch because he had insisted that she take a vacation.

He had insisted Mattie take a vacation because he wanted her out of town for a week or so. Cass was beginning to get pushy, and he needed more breathing room. He needed to put Cass back into her place without making her sore. He needed the backing of Martin Courtney right now. Courtney could make or break him. Cass was spoiled. She was used to getting whatever she wanted, and she had a dangerous way of making it happen. Right now she wanted to share the limelight with him. She wanted to stand at his side at the rallies, she wanted to appear at the dinners with him, she wanted *him*. He was walking a damned tightrope!

Cass was already there when Allen came into the softly lighted club. She was sitting at the small table not too far from the raised bandstand, a tall gin drink in front of her, toying with a cigarette. Even from across the room she stood apart from the others. She was dressed in blue, setting off her silver-blond hair, her vibrant blue eyes. Her skirts were short, showing off her long, slender legs, the narrow, pointed blue satin shoes with the spike heels. A band of silken fringe fell from her flat bustline almost to her waist, catching the reflections of the colored lights as it shimmered with the movements of her body.

He bent and kissed her on the cheek. "Sorry, baby. You been waiting long?"

She shrugged her slender shoulders carelessly. "It's all right. Not too long. You look beat. Things not going right for you today?"

He reached for the drink the waiter set down in front of him. "You know how it is." he answered vaguely. "This close before the elections, everyone gets antsy. God, this tastes good!" He felt his tight muscles begin to relax as the fiery liquor seared its way through his body. This was what he needed—a couple of good stiff drinks, Cass to help him get through the evening, and tomorrow or the next day Mattie would be home.

"Are you hungry, Allen? You want a steak?" Cass watched him from across the table, seeing the tight lines around his eyes, the hard line of his mouth.

"Sure. Why not. You ordered yet? I want another drink first. Got to unwind. God, what a day, Cass."

Something was on her mind. She only picked at her food before she pushed it away, and now she sat toying with the cigarette in the long, slender holder, only half listening to what he was saying.

"What is it, Cass? Something bothering you?" he asked at last. He didn't want to know. He had enough problems tonight. Couldn't she tell?

"Nothing. Bored, I guess. Restless." She flipped the ashes from her cigarette into the glass tray. "Is Mattie coming home tomorrow?"

He glanced sharply across at her. What was she worrying about now? "I guess so. Why?"

"I was sitting here thinking, while I was waiting for you. Allen, isn't our life ever going to be more than this?" She waved her hand vaguely out across the room, taking in the tables filled with people, the dancers doing the Charleston on the small floor, the laughter, the music that assaulted their ears, the glasses emptying and being refilled. He saw the lines of discontent on her face.

"This isn't New York, baby. This is the best I can do in this town." He reached across the table and laid his hand over hers.

"You belong in a better setting. Someplace where your style, your class will be shown off, like it deserves. Someday, Cass, I'll take you to all of those places. Chicago, New York—places where things are happening. You and me, Cass. We'll let this whole damned world know we're here, make them look at us, take their hats off to us!"

"That's not what I meant, Allen. It's fun, it's exciting—I love being a part of the campaign, I love the noise, the music, being with you. But when the evening is over and the lights go out, what do I have?" She pulled her hand away from his in irritation, the corners of her mouth turned down sulkily.

"What more do you want? It's all I've got to offer right now."

"You know what I want. When are you going to tell her, Allen? I'm tired of playing all of these silly games. I don't want to share you with a wife, always moving in shadows, not out in the open. I belong with you, and I want everyone to know it. I'm tired of sitting here at the speak waiting for you to show up when you can get around to it, making love in my apartment, knowing you won't still be in bed with me in the morning. I want to be at your side at the rallies, not just a part of the group. I want to be at your side where I can be seen and have the people watching know I belong there. I want to be with you when you're elected governor. I want to be the governor's lady, not his damned mistress. I'm tired of playing games, Allen. I won't play them any longer."

"Now look, Cass. I spend as much time with you as I can—"

"Sure." She looked down, drawing lines on the tablecloth with the edge of the fork. "Here at the speak, where the waiters know more than they should know or see but get paid enough to keep their mouths shut. At my apartment. No. I'm talking about the nights when I'm alone. The nights when your wife appears with you at dinners and things and I sit home with a damned book to keep me company. Do you know how many books I've read lately? And I don't even like to read!"

Christ, Allen thought to himself. A bad day like he had today, Mattie still out of town, and now Cass was on his back. And he had to keep her happy. If he didn't handle her right, she could ruin him. Allen lowered his voice, his eyes soft and pleading.

"You don't think it is easy for me, do you? You think I enjoy the way things are now? Going home to a place as cold as mine is? She doesn't understand. She frowns on everything I do to try to get ahead. If I didn't get out there and work my ass off, fight tooth and nail for everything I've got, I'd still be out there living on that ranch, spending my days in a one-room office with a pile of musty law books, wondering how the hell I'm going to pay the bills that keep mounting up on that piece of sagebrush land because my clients don't or can't pay me. You think it's been easy for me? You think I like looking forward to going home in the evening, tired, wanting nothing more than a cold drink and some encouragement and having a cold, unfeeling woman turn away when I reach for her?"

Cass leaned back in the chair, studying him thoughtfully. "Then why don't you leave her, Allen? Why do you stay with her?"

He shook his head. "I have to move carefully, Cass. I've worked so damned hard to get where I am now. It's been a fight every step of the way. Always in the public eye, always people watching, wanting to find fault—the opposition would love to dig up a scandal. They would tear me to pieces if they could. I've heard from my campaign workers that there are rumors going around about me now. My whole career could go down the drain. That's why we've got to be more careful, Cass. You can understand that, can't you? We've got to think about what people are saying."

"Does it mean so much to you? What people say?" she asked, watching him closely.

"Baby, you mean more to me than any of it! You mean more to me than the ranch, the family—even the governor's chair. Screw them! When the time is right, I'll walk out on all of it. It will be just you and me, then."

"When? If it's handled right, you won't need to lose the governor's spot. I don't want to run away. I don't want to hide. I want to be the governor's wife—the first lady."

"Got to pick the time just right. Don't push me!" He leaned back, his brown eyes moody, his face sullen. "Don't you start pushing me too, Cass. Everyone is pushing me, leaning on me.

We can't just jump into something like this. There is too much at stake. I've worked too hard. I won't take a risk now.''

He saw the shadow of doubt flicker in her eyes. ''Don't ever lie to me, Allen,'' she said softly. ''Don't play games. I'll ruin you if you do.''

''That sounds like a threat.''

''It is.'' The brittle challenge was back in her eyes. ''I've learned a lot at my uncle's knee. You better damned well believe it.''

He reached out and picked up her purse and handed it to her. ''Come on, let's get the hell out of here. It's too crowded. Too many people around. We're both on edge. Let's go back to the apartment. I want to be alone with you. I want to make love to you, Cass.'' He relaxed when he saw the doubt leave her eyes and a smile of anticipation take over. One place where Cass was never bored was in bed.

Allen lay staring into the warm darkness. He felt good. Just enough of a glow left from the liquor he had drunk during the evening to make him feel confident again—like there was nothing he couldn't do. Cass stirred in the bed beside him, turning her head slightly on the pillow, sighing contentedly in her sleep. It had been a good evening. After such a hell of a lousy day, things had turned out all right after all.

He put his arm up on the pillow under his head and stretched comfortably. Tomorrow night at this time he would be in the house on the other side of town. Tomorrow night Mattie would be back home and he would be holding her, telling her how much he had missed her. She would be all refreshed and glowing—like she always was when she came back from a stay at the ranch. He might even quit work early tomorrow—be home in time to have supper with all of them, so they could tell him the news from Bend. The boys liked to have a chance to talk, too. Clive would be full of stories about his pony. Maybe Johnny had learned to ride this time. Listening to Young Clive and Johnny talk excitedly about the ranch gave him a lot of good memories of when he had been a kid their age. Things he had forgotten after he had started to grow up.

He had to do something about Cass, though. She could be a real threat to his career. She could be dangerous. To a woman like Cass, giving her a little leeway let her think she could take over, wanting voice in everything until she castrated a man. He slid up on the pillow, reaching for a part of a glass of gin left on the bedside table, and lit a cigarette. Starting tomorrow he'd begin to ease away from her. Let her know the party was over. He'd stop coming over here so often. Cass was smart. She could figure it out without a big scene. The elections were coming up in three weeks. He had to walk easy until then. Had to move extra careful now. Once he was governor, dumping Cass wouldn't upset Martin Courtney. He wanted those contracts for the state-owned timber too much to let a woman sour the deal. The shoe had changed to the other foot. After the elections, Courtney would need him, not the other way around.

He took a slow drag on the cigarette. Maybe he could talk Cass into taking a trip, going back east where she belonged. He had to be careful how he handled her. She knew too many people, had too much money. He didn't want any last-minute upsets with the elections so close.

He watched the cigarette smoke curl upward in lazy circles. It was good knowing Mattie would be back soon. Things seemed to go smoother when she was there. There had been some rough years—she never did understand what it took to get where he was right now. A guy has to go out and mix with the public a lot. Mattie was a snob, when it came right down to it. She didn't like his friends, she was always bitching about how much he drank.

Well, he could handle Mattie. He always had. He had to do something about Cass, though. Cass was beginning to be in the way.

CHAPTER THIRTY-ONE

Mattie had made a firm resolution with herself during the long drive to the ranch that this time she would treat Morgan strictly on a brother-in-law/sister-in-law basis. She made certain that there was no chance for them to be alone in a room, no chance for any conversation that might get out of hand. There were times when she felt Morgan's eyes studying her from across the room and she would turn away, pretending that she didn't notice, but the pain it caused was there, deep inside, so strong at times that she almost failed in her resolves. Little things—the sight of his hands, so strong and firm as he reached for the bread plate at the table, the way he hunched his shoulders against the wind as he walked toward the barn, the little crinkle lines at the corner of his eyes that carried their own secret humor, the way he looked with young Clive tagging along at his side—so many little things hurt her so much and yet she carried her head high with an air of indifference. She didn't let herself cry until she was safely in her room at night. Time hadn't helped. She knew she could have stayed away from the ranch for a lifetime and she still would have loved him as much as ever.

Mattie went out of her way to meet Edith on a mutual ground, where they could at least tolerate each other and hope that maybe someday they might even find a way to be friends. Their lives were all becoming intertwined, a part of a pattern that affected all of them, and somehow they had to find a way to get along. If Edith should someday marry Morgan, she and Mattie would be seeing each other from time to time for the rest of their lives.

Though the thought of not seeing him every day was painful, Mattie was almost relieved when the week was nearly gone and it was time for her to return to Salem. At times the tension between them had been almost more than she could bear and she was smoking more, eating less, mixing a martini to quiet her restless nerves.

At first, Edith had been domineering and high-handed, as though she expected opposition, and she tried to establish her authority before it had a chance to be questioned. She was obviously puzzled over Mattie's attitude. Instead of questioning her right to stay here at the ranch when business brought them to Bend, Mattie went out of her way to encourage her, even asking her opinion at times about things concerning the stock.

For Morgan the week was a mixture of heaven and hell. The mill was in full production, running around the clock to try to fill the stacks of orders waiting on his desk. The loggers were fighting rain, mud, and bad roads to get the logs out of the woods and into the mill before the winter snows shut them down and they would be forced to sit around until spring without any money coming in.

Edith was pushing their friendship to the limits, impatient because it never seemed to go any further. Even friends were expecting him to marry her, teasing him about being shy when it came to proposing. It would be the smart thing to do, he knew. At times he almost decided to propose, but a quiet pixie with a boyish figure and a proud tilt to her chin got in his way and he couldn't go ahead with it.

During the past week Betty had chosen to take her stand in neutral territory, playing her role of hired housekeeper to the hilt, and her tight-lipped, impartial conversations, limited as they were, were irritating the hell out of him. Any other time she would be tossing her opinions out to all of them, asked for or not, trying to boss him around like she did Wes. The house was kept too clean, the meals too well planned, the routine too orderly, and it frustrated him.

This past week Mattie had been a woman he hardly knew. From the conversations he overheard, he knew that during the day she went riding out across the ranchland, sometimes alone, sometimes with Wes. She had been swimming with the boys, teaching them to dive from the old tree at the swimming hole. But in the evenings when he was home she dressed in the knit suits she brought from the city, she visited pleasantly and impersonally with Edith, she chain-smoked—and she ignored him. It had been his idea to fight the bond between them by building a life of his own that didn't include her, but he was getting pretty damned sick of the way everyone kept cramming the idea down his throat. Especially Mattie.

That young Clive had sure grown since he had last seen him. It did things to his ego the way the boy followed him around, trying to walk tall, not saying too much but imitating the things he did—even swearing sometimes. His face relaxed and the little lines at the corners of his eyes crinkled in amusement when he thought of some of the things that had happened during the past week. That Johnny was a good-looking little button too. Sharp as a tack. His favorite words were *Why?* or *How come?*

Morgan was sitting at the desk, his back to the window, listening to the sounds of the saws, the hum of machinery, trying to concentrate on the paperwork spread out in front of him. It had been a long, restless day for him, and it still wasn't much past midafternoon. Mattie had left today. She had been up early, trying to get the boys awake and organized, the car packed, wanting to be on the road in time to reach Salem before dark.

As he had watched the car grow smaller and disappear in the distance, he had felt a big emptiness eating away at him. The clouds overhead seemed darker, the scattered rain showers wetter, the wind a little colder. He had left the ranch soon after that and headed for the mill without going back into the house, without saying good-bye to Edith or any of the others. He wanted to be alone for a while, and then he wanted work—hard work that used the muscles and left the body too tired to think.

The phone on the desk rang insistently, breaking into his

reverie. It was Edith on the line—a different Edith, a more subdued Edith—or was it his imagination?

"Morgan, I have the car about packed, ready to leave. I'm going home. Tom will follow tomorrow with the truck."

Morgan drew his brows together in a puzzled frown. "Thought you had to meet with the Carlsons tomorrow. Something happen?"

"No." There was a long pause. "I just realized that I don't need to stay any longer. Tom can handle the meeting tomorrow perfectly well." Her voice was flat, without the usual crispness.

"Something wrong, Edith?"

"Morgan, I need to talk to you. Can you leave the mill and come home?"

"Is it important?"

There was another long pause on the other end of the line. "Yes." Her voice faded away, making it hard for him to hear. Then stronger, "Yes. It's important. Probably the most important decision I've made lately."

"You want to talk about it?"

"Yes. I've had all day to think about it. All week. It's been a hell of a week, hasn't it? I don't want to talk about it on the telephone—it's a party line. Come on back to the ranch so we can at least talk it out like two civilized adults."

"I'm not doing much good here anyway. I'll see you in a little while."

He hung up the phone and turned in the chair, staring out of the window without seeing the mill sprawling out in front of him.

Morgan reached the ranch house by late afternoon. As he drove home, he watched the dark clouds filled with wind billowing overhead, carrying the threat of a new storm. There had been scattered thunderstorms and rain for several days, making the air smell fresh and clean, keeping the creekbeds full, forming shallow ponds in the low hollows of the desert floor. He put the car in the shed and ran for the house just as the sky opened up, sending down a heavy downpour, drenching him. He came in the back way and left his coat on the peg near the door. He walked over to the cookstove and arched his shoulders against the warm heat seeping through his damp clothing.

Betty was in the kitchen, the ironing board set up near the window. There was a large basket of laundry, sprinkled and rolled, sitting on the floor beside her. She set the iron down on its pad and went over to the stove, pulling the coffeepot forward over the heat without saying a word.

He wanted to reach out and put his hand on her shoulder, the way he would have done a long time ago, before their lives all got so scrambled. He wanted to make some teasing remark about sneaking a piece of hot pie and listen to her sharp reply. He wanted to thank her for worrying about him, for caring enough to get so mad at him. You had to care a lot about someone to tear in on him the way she had done after Mattie left that last time. Things had been cool between them ever since then. It made him uncomfortable. Betty was like part of the family. He didn't like it when they couldn't talk.

She attacked the shirt lying across the ironing board, her back toward him. He couldn't see her face, but he could tell by her stiff back that she still wasn't ready to give up the role of impersonal housekeeper.

"Edith here?" he asked.

"In the study." She nodded her head, not saying any more than was necessary.

He shrugged his shoulders and walked from the room.

Edith turned from the window to face him as he came in the door, pushing it closed behind him. "I've been waiting for you. I saw you drive in."

He went across the room to the desk and poured bourbon into a glass, waiting for her to go on.

"I'm leaving this evening. I've been away from home too much. I need to get back."

He nodded. "I saw your suitcases in the hall."

"Is that all?" she asked. "You have nothing else to say? Damn it, Morgan. Can't you even pretend a little? Can't you pretend to feel just a little of what you felt when Mattie left this morning?"

He took a sip from the glass, waited to feel the liquor warm his cold body before he answered. "I'm sorry things aren't turning out the way you wanted. I mean it. Do you believe me?"

"Yes. I believe you." She took a hesitant step toward him, her eyes searching his face. "Morgan?" She stopped, picked up a cigarette, and waited while he lit it for her. She watched the smoke curl up in a thin line. "Did you see Tom in town?"

He bent, laying another log on the dying fire, watching the flame catch the dry bark and flare up. "Yes. I saw him. Why?"

"Did you talk to him?"

"No. There wasn't much chance. There were others around. He was in a hurry. Business, I suppose. He seemed in unusually good spirits." He straightened up and looked at her. "Was there a reason for his good nature?"

"I just wondered if the two of you had talked. Morgan, he asked me to marry him."

Morgan straightened up, surprise on his face, waiting for her to go on talking.

Her nervousness showed in the way her hand worked uneasily at a loose button on her jacket. "I told him that you and I were through—that anything, real or imagined, between us just wasn't there anymore, that I wanted him to get things together so I could leave right away, and he asked me to marry him. Morgan, do you think Tom is in love with me? I mean, does he really love *me*? Me, as a person—or is it the ranch, the money, the security he is after? You know him pretty well. What do you think?"

He looked at her and for the first time saw the hesitation, the self-doubt in her eyes, and heard her voice without its usual crisp self-assuredness. "How am I supposed to know the answer to a question like that? I think maybe he is. He seems to think he is in love with you. He has been for quite a while. Are you in love with him?"

"No. I like him. I respect him. He's a good man—a fair man. He would make a good husband, a good father. Morgan, I'm not sure I know what love is. I don't feel with him what I feel when you're near." She gave a small, hard laugh. "But is that love? Maybe it's just a strong sexual urge I feel for you. What's the difference between the two, Morgan. How am I supposed to know?" He saw her hand tremble as she stomped the cigarette out in the tray. "I haven't had much experience. I grew up on the ranch with three brothers. I know everything there is to know about breeding horses, running a ranch, raising cattle. I think I know most men better than they know themselves.'' Her voice caught in her throat. "I'm not sure that I know much about how to be a wife.''

He took a step toward her, feeling her hurt. "Edith, don't. Stop it. Just because nothing seemed to work out for the two of us, don't blame yourself. It wasn't your fault.''

"I loved you, Morgan. God, how I loved you. I thought I could love you enough to handle anything that got in our way. It wasn't enough, though, was it?''

"I don't know. Maybe we could still make it work. Maybe we should give it more time—just let things ride along like they are for a while and think it over.''

"No. It wouldn't ever work. I want to be loved. I want a man who thinks I'm all of the woman he could ever want. You want a woman to be a partner, not a lover. You want a woman to keep your house, have your children. I suppose that if I really loved you enough, I'd be willing to settle for that. I can't. I'm too selfish, too proud. I couldn't share your heart with another woman. That's the way it would be, wouldn't it? You're in love with her.''

He looked down at the glass in his hand, not knowing what to say. "What did you tell Tom? Did you give him an answer?''

"I believe Tom loves me in the way a woman wants to be loved. I told him I would marry him.'' Her voice was soft, almost a whisper.

He went over and put his hands on her shoulders, making her look up at him. "Will it work? Tom's too fine a man to sell short. Marriage is more than just playing house, Edith.''

"I know. But I also know that he wants *me*—I know that when he reaches for me in bed, it is *me* that he wants. He won't be pretending that I'm another woman when he makes love to me. That's what you would be doing, Morgan. No—don't deny it. This past week has been hell for all of us. The more the two of you tried to stay apart and ignore each other, the more evident it was that you're in love—the kind of love that I'm no match for. I can't compete.'' She gave a ragged sigh of resignation. "Tom knows how I feel. He wants me enough to settle for whatever I can give him, whatever is left.''

"Tom's a fine man.''

"I know. I'm going to try my best to be a good wife—the kind of wife he deserves. I'm really very fond of him. Who knows? We have so much in common. Maybe it is for the best after all. It could be a very good marriage, if we really work at it.''

She stood on tiptoe, kissing him on the mouth. "Good-bye, Morgan. I hope someday you will find happiness.'' She turned quickly and left the room before he could see the tears threatening in her eyes.

CHAPTER THIRTY-TWO

"I'm going to leave you, Allen. It's all over."

Mattie's words lay heavy on the air between them, carrying a deadly finality that left little room for argument.

Allen's face was a picture of explosive fury. He faced her across the room, refusing to believe what she had said. He had talked to her on the telephone earlier in the day, soon after she had arrived home from the ranch, and everything had been all right then. She had said she wanted to unpack and would see him at dinnertime. He had even quit work earlier than usual just to come home and see them before the boys went to bed. When he got here, the boys had already been fed and sent to their room for the evening. The housekeeper said Mattie wouldn't be eating—she was upstairs in her bedroom with a headache. He came up here ready to let her know how glad he was to see her back again. The damn headache was probably just from the long drive. A small brandy would help her relax and she would be all right.

When he came into the bedroom, she had been sitting in a chair near the window, with all of the lights down low, so the room was filled with shadows. Instead of coming into his arms, she had dark smudges under her eyes and she looked like she had been crying. The suitcases were still sitting in the middle of the floor and she hadn't even started to unpack. And now this!

Mattie had always been unreasonable, but what the hell was the matter with her now? He had too much on his mind to play games with her. She ought to know that. He had had a bad day, a bad week. He came home anxious to see her again, expecting a little sympathy and a night in bed with his wife, and this is what she had waiting for him. His first reaction was anger—hard, disbelieving anger.

"Where the hell do you think you're going to run off to? You've got no place to go. Without my name and my money, you've got nothing!"

"I'm going back to the ranch," she answered softly, without any emotion. "The ranch that you are letting people assume belongs to you. I'm taking the boys back to their ranch, where they can live and learn some of the principles Clive meant for them to know. Where they can start learning about a land that is going to be theirs when they grow up. You can't stop me, Allen."

"Why? For Christ's sake, tell me, why? Haven't I given you anything a woman could ask for? You, a squatter's daughter, going to be a governor's lady! Look around you—the house, the clothes, the car—everything! You've got everything. What in the hell's the matter with you, Mattie?"

"Maybe I'm damned tired of walking around with my eyes shut. Maybe that's what's the matter with me!" He saw the stubborn tilt of her chin, the way her eyes flashed, and knew she was beginning to get angry. "Maybe I want to get my pride back, Allen! Pride. Something your dirty money can't buy!"

"Pride? What the hell do you know about pride?" He flung the words across the room at her. "You sneaking off every chance you get, going back over to the ranch, tagging after Morgan? You think I don't know? Saying you need to go over there to work on the books? If Morgan wasn't there, would you be so all-fired anxious to make those trips to the ranch?" He came across the room toward her, walking slowly, watching her face, his brown eyes smoldering dangerously. "Is that it, Mattie? You think if you leave me, walk out on me, that Morgan will marry you? That's a laugh. He's always been able to have any woman he wanted. What kind of a man would he be to take his brother's leavings?'' he sneered, watching with satisfaction when he saw the barb cut deep.

"No, Allen. You're wrong. Morgan has nothing to do with my decision to leave,'' she answered quietly. "He has no idea that I am even considering it.''

"Then what is it? Something happen today? You sounded all right when I talked to you on the phone this afternoon.''

She nodded. Her anger was gone now. Only the hurt remained. "Yes. Something happened.'' She got up from the chair and went over to the table, picking up a cigarette. He saw the way her hands were trembling as she lit it. She looked tired, defeated, drained of emotion. "There was a reporter at the house today. He said he was writing a story on the candidates. A human interest sort of thing. A nonpolitical story for the *Daily News* on the candidates, their wives, their families, their homes—something to make the candidates look more real, he said.''

He was watching her closely, cautious, alert. "So what was wrong with that? People like to read that sort of stuff. About kids, especially. Kids and pets. Did he want pictures of the house?''

Mattie stubbed the cigarette out, shaking her head. "No. He asked me what my feelings were about a woman named Cass Courtney—a woman my husband's been seen in public with while I was out of town. He wanted to know how, as a wife, as a wife living in the public eye, I coped with knowing my husband had a mistress.''

"My God!'' Allen's face went white with shock. "The dirty bastard! I'll have his job for that! Since when did the *Daily News* turn into a scandal sheet? That punk won't be able to get a job selling pencils on the street corner when I get through with him!''

"Is it true, Allen?'' Her voice was low, expressionless. She had no more anger left. "There have been other women from time to time. I knew it. You didn't keep it hidden as well as you thought. But are you finally flaunting one of them in public? Is it true, Allen?''

"True? Hell, no, it isn't true. There's a woman who works at the campaign headquarters—I think her name is Cass something or other. You know how it is, Mattie. The whole group goes out to coffee sometimes, catches a show and has a drink in the evening. Maybe she was with a group that I stopped and had a drink with at the speak. How do I know? She was with one of the other guys and made it look like she was with me. Some bitch trying to get her name in the papers, get some publicity.''

"Oh, stop it, Allen. Don't say any more. I've heard it all before. Courtney. The name is familiar. Those two registered bulls at the ranch. They came from a Martin Courtney, didn't they? No. Don't say any more. I know the answer.''

He changed his tactics, just like she knew he would—just like he had always done before when lies and half-truths wouldn't gain what he was after. "Look, Mattie. Maybe I haven't been as careful as I should be. I forget how things look to other people. Then some damn young reporter out to make a name for himself picks up on it and turns it all around, into something it isn't, so it will make good copy. Mattie, I'm sorry. I wouldn't want to hurt you.''

She turned her head away, not wanting to look at him. She was filled with loathing. "It's no use, Allen. I've taken all that I can take. I've tried. Over and over and over, I've tried. So many times I've wanted to just walk out, but I stayed and tried to make it work. But it's no use anymore. I'm finished. I'm leaving you.''

"What about the boys, Mattie? Don't you give a damn what happens to them? Don't you see how much you will be hurting them if you leave now?''

She looked up. "Hurt the boys? How? I'm leaving to protect the boys.''

"You think if you walk out on me now it isn't going to ruin my campaign? Divorce isn't a word folks accept easily. Just before an election like this when folks are looking for scandal? The reporters will be all over us with their filth. It will be in every newspaper. You want that kind of muck touching the boys? You're angry as hell with me right now, but it won't be me you will be hurting, Mattie. It will be those two boys. Every day they go to school, every day they go out around other kids, they've got to put up with it. Kids can be cruel, baby! You better believe it. Is that what you want for the boys?''

He saw her falter, start to weaken, as his words hit home. "I didn't think much about the boys and how it would affect them. I was hurt, tired of all of the things that have gone on over the years that I pretended not to see." She shook her head. "No. This last was too much. They are young. They will forget. I can't take any more, Allen."

"Look, Mattie. Just wait until after the election. That's all I ask. Stand by me until then. Go out in public with me, let people see us together. Smile like you do and show them there isn't any trouble between us. Kill the rumors. Make it look like there isn't anything to the phony story the reporter dug up. Make it look like there isn't any trouble—just until after the election, honey. Think of the boys. Even if you hate me right now, think of the boys."

She didn't care about the damned election. She didn't care anymore what happened to Allen. Being the governor's lady was no incentive for him to hold out to her because she hated the title and everything that went with it. She hated every part of it. But the boys didn't deserve the scandal. The boys didn't deserve the newspaper stories that would follow. Once given the scent of a headline story, the other things that Allen was involved in might come to light under the prying of the reporters, making them less than proud of their father. She had to protect them. He had won and he knew it.

"All right, Allen. But only until after the election. Just until things quiet down. Then I'll leave quietly and no one will notice."

He looked down at her and saw the way her shoulders slumped in defeat, saw the hurt on her face, and knew that he loved her. Damn it, he had always loved her, from the first day he had walked into the dry goods store and seen her there, her eyes dancing with their own special fire. He had cheated on her—sure—but what man didn't? It didn't mean anything. He always wanted her there when he came home—waiting for him, smoothing things out, trusting him, making things right again for him. He loved her. He needed her.

He put his hand out, touched her chin gently, raised her face so she had to look at him. "Mattie—it will be all right from now on. Just stay by me and things will be different. I promise."

She looked at him and saw the raw hunger in his eyes. It made her draw back, feeling sick inside. "Don't, Allen. Don't touch me. Not now. Maybe tomorrow things will look different—but not tonight. We have both got to do this for the boys. But I can't pretend anymore. Not when we are alone. The thought of your hands touching me makes me ill. You disgust me."

She stood up, pulling her robe around her. "Now, I want to get some rest. It's been a bad day all the way around, hasn't it? Quite a homecoming. I'll move my things into the guest room. I'll be sleeping in there until after the election. Goodnight, Allen."

"Mattie! Wait. You can't. You promised." He took a half-step toward her.

"I promised to stand by you publicly—that's all I promised. And I will. But at home, in the bedroom, I've already left you, Allen. Just as sure as I am leaving the house after the election."

The next three weeks were a nightmare of exhausting activity for Mattie. Allen thrived on the tension, loving every moment of the campaigning—the dinners, the lectures, the rallies, the attention. He was able to get by with little sleep, riding on the crest of the excitement, a drink in his hand when his energy began to run low.

The name Cass Courtney wasn't spoken between them again. The argument was over. There was nothing left to discuss. She wondered a time or two, when he was away from the house in the evening and she had stayed at home, whether he might, perhaps, be with Cass. The thought didn't disturb her all that much. She found she just didn't care anymore.

She had made a promise to stay until the election was over and she would keep the promise. Then she and the boys would go to the ranch and live. Whatever problems arose through her being there would just have to take care of themselves when the time came. She couldn't think that far ahead right now.

When it seemed as though she couldn't keep going any longer at the hectic pace that was demanded, the day finally came that he had waited for—the day of the election.

Mattie had been at the campaign headquarters since the polls opened at eight o'clock that morning. She felt exhausted, mentally as well as physically, but she forced herself to continue smiling, talking with people, trying to show a bright confidence as she moved around the large room taking part in conversations with the different groups.

It had been a long day, a hard day, and now an even longer night stretched out in front of them as they sat at tables and listened to the last counts being tallied in from the outlying districts and put up on the giant-sized chalkboard on the wall.

For a while Allen had held the lead, then the totals swayed, evened out, and his opponent pulled ahead, staying in front for a time. There were empty glasses leaving their white rings on the furniture, smoke lying heavy in the air, tension building as the hour grew later.

Mattie watched Allen talking with a confident boisterousness, walking around the room with a swagger, holding his optimism up to the others like a banner they could follow. A new batch of votes came in and were added to the board. Allen had started to move ahead again. He pulled up even with his opponent. The final count was taken. It was decided. Allen would be the next governor of the state!

A cry of victory went up in the crowded room, reaching a pitch of hysteria. Reporters went crazy, flashbulbs were popping. A celebration was in full force and Allen was in the center of the crowd, drinking in their adulation.

Mattie watched from a sheltered place in a corner near the door. It was over. She was free. Allen stood in the center of the room, a cigarette in one hand, a campaign hat tipped at a rakish angle over one eye. She watched him laughing, soaking up the attention, enjoying the glory of the moment, knowing how much it meant to him.

Well, he made it, Mattie thought. He won. But who really knows just how dear the price of winning has been. With a sigh, she slipped unnoticed out of the door into the cool, refreshing night.

It seemed like hours later—the sun was already making a red streak against the horizon—when she heard Allen finally come home.

His tie was gone, his shirt was rumpled, his face showed the strain of the day with tired wrinkles around his eyes. He showed the effects of a night of drinking in his talk and in his walk, but he still wore that ridiculous white straw hat with HENDERSON printed in red on a grosgrain ribbon around the crown.

"You were so damned pleased about moving into the governor's mansion that you left without saying a word to anyone!" he accused. "Where did you go? How do you think it looked to the reporters? To the others? You weren't even there for the photographers to take our picture together."

"No one noticed when I left," she answered quietly. "There was too much confusion—too many people. The attention was all focused on you, Allen, not on me. It didn't matter to anyone. You're making too much of it." He had what he wanted. She had done her part, kept her promise. Now she was tired. She didn't want to argue. Not tonight. Not when he had been drinking.

"I told you, you've got to act the part. Where did you go, anyway?"

"I wanted to come back and check on the boys. I hadn't seen them all day."

He slumped down in a chair and began taking off his shoes. "Clive is nearly seven years old, for Christ's sake. Old enough to take care of himself without someone around to wipe his nose and do his thinking. He's old enough to look out for Johnny. You've got to stop fussing so much over them and let them learn how to take care of themselves. Your place is beside me, where everyone can see that everything is all right between us."

Mattie turned away. She was too tired to argue with him right now. Too tired to remind him that soon he would no longer tell her her place.

CHAPTER THIRTY-THREE

Mattie had been up before sunrise working on the last-minute details. Tomorrow Allen would be sworn in as the new governor of the state of Oregon. Tonight there was to be a private reception here in their home. It would be her last public appearance as his wife. Allen had carefully gone over the guest list that she had prepared, scratching names, adding others. Several senators, a judge or two, people in real estate and land development, owners of large timber holdings—it was an influential and powerful group of people. There would be close to one hundred in all, counting their wives—all brought together to mark the occasion of Allen winning the election and to congratulate themselves on the guaranteed success they expected during the next four years.

Mattie had been kept busy overseeing the preparations—settling the arguments among the staff, choosing floral arrangements, giving instructions to caterers—until at last, satisfied that all was as perfect as she could possibly make it, she escaped to the luxury of a long, warm bath before dressing for the evening.

When she heard Allen's footsteps in her bedroom, she came out of the dressing room wrapped in a velvet robe, her hair curling in wisps about her face from the steam of the tub, her hairbrush in her hand.

"You're not dressed yet." He was upset to see her still in her robe.

"I'm going to start now. There's plenty of time." She smiled to herself at his nervousness. Usually he always had control, was confident, sure of himself.

Allen had on the pants to his black tux, a stiff white shirt. "Here. Help me with these damned cuff links, will you?" Mattie took them from him and fastened them in place. "Everything in order downstairs? You sure those catering people know what the hell they are doing?"

"They should, for the prices they charge," she answered quietly.

"Forget the cost. I want everything to be right tonight."

"It will. Stop worrying." She began to brush her hair.

"You hear from Morgan yet? Is he going to be here?"

"We sent an invitation, but we haven't gotten an answer. I don't know if he'll make it. It's a long drive and I imagine he's putting in long hours trying to get the ranch ready for the fall market as well as running the mill."

"You'd think he would make time for something as important as this," Allen grumbled. "Suppose he has sense enough to get a tux? You did tell him on the invitation that it was black tie, didn't you?"

"If you're so worried about his appearance, why did you insist that we send him an invitation?" Mattie answered impatiently.

"Because I want him here. I want him to see that I've made it. I want him to see that I didn't need that damned ranch. Maybe he's content to smell like cow shit all of the time, but not me! I've come a long way, Mattie, and I want him to know it."

Mattie disappeared into her dressing room, coming back in a few minutes wearing a very special gown she had purchased just for the occasion. She stood in the doorway, waiting for him to look up, confident of the perfection of the dress and the way she looked. "How about me, Allen? Do I look all right or do you still smell the odor of the ranch on me, too?"

Allen sucked in his breath in astonishment at the vision in front of him and then let out a long, low whistle. "My God, Mattie, you look good! You've really done it this time, baby! Every man in the place is going to be after you before the evening is over."

Allen's uneasy nervousness was pushed into the background as he took Mattie's arm and they went down the stairway together to greet their guests. Everything looked perfect—the house, the buffet, the bar, the caterers in spotless white dinner jackets ready to serve the guests, and Mattie at his side looking lovelier than he had ever seen her before. With true showmanship he moved about from one small group of people to another, accepting their words of congratulations with a smile that enchanted the women, pleased the men. With a drink in his hand and Mattie at his side, lovely, gracious, smiling quietly as she said all of the right things at the right time, Allen was filled with confidence again.

It had been touch and go there for a while, he thought to himself as he looked around the room. Cass had threatened to cause trouble if he dropped her and Mattie wanted to walk out on him and call it quits. Cass kept hanging out at the campaign headquarters and leaving telephone messages for him at his office, refusing to believe that when something was over it was over all the way. He was tired of her. She bored him. At least Mattie had stayed. She wouldn't want to leave anymore once she saw what she would be giving up if she left. With Cass out of the way, he'd watch his step from now on and Mattie wouldn't leave. He was sure of it.

Mattie glanced around the large room with a feeling of accomplishment. Everything was picture perfect. The guests all seemed at ease, visiting comfortably. The men were impressive in their formal dress. The women were luxuriously clothed in satins and jewels, emblems of their husbands' success. The floral arrangements were beautiful, the house at its very best. The buffet was a delight to the eye, and the caterers were doing an excellent job. She was pleased with everything. And yet she still kept watching for Morgan's tall figure, his broad shoulders, the sound of his laugh, because she knew that for her the gathering wouldn't be complete until he had arrived.

As the evening wore on, Mattie became gradually conscious of a young woman standing alone near the bar—a woman with silver-blond hair and vibrant blue eyes. Each time Mattie glanced in her direction the woman would be sipping from a glass and watching her with a dark, brooding stare.

At last, out of concern, Mattie touched Allen's arm, pointing the woman out to him. "Who is she, Allen? She doesn't seem to be with anyone in particular. Do you know her?"

"Who? Where?"

"Over at the bar. The one just getting a fresh martini. She's quite striking to look at, but she seems . . . I don't know. Everyone else seems to be having a good time, but she seems so alone. Who is she?"

"How do I know?" Allen answered, but his voice was edged with a hard sharpness that puzzled Mattie. "Someone from the campaign headquarters, I suppose. Found a way to get an invitation. Damn it! Thought we had been so careful with those lists."

Mattie felt uncomfortable about the way the woman watched her and continued to drink. "Why don't you go over and talk to her, Allen. See if you can't get her to mix with the other people. She looks so unhappy."

As Allen started to walk away, Mattie heard a familiar low voice at her elbow, speaking her name. She turned to find Morgan standing beside her. She felt her breath quicken and her pulses start to race at the sight of his tall, broad figure clothed in a black tuxedo, his hard features softened in a smile as their eyes met.

"You are a vision tonight, Mattie." He complimented her with his words and with the look in his eyes. "By far, the loveliest woman in the room."

"I didn't see you come in," she said, faltering. He was so ruggedly handsome in the formal dress. "I've been watching for you."

"I went on upstairs by the back way," he explained. "I wanted to shower and dress before putting in an appearance." His eyes swept across the crowded room. "Where has Allen gone? I wanted a chance to congratulate him. This must be quite a night for him."

"He went over to the bar to talk to a guest. I don't see him right now, though." As she looked across the room for Allen, she noticed the woman with the silver-blond hair had left the bar and was nowhere in sight. Mattie dismissed her from her mind, her thoughts more on where Allen had disappeared to. "Allen might have gone into the library to talk with one of the men," she explained. "He'll be back in a few moments, I'm sure. He wanted to see you tonight. He was looking forward to your being here."

"I bet he was at that," Morgan chuckled.

"In the meantime, let me introduce you around. That group of men is in lumber, so maybe you know them already."

The introductions were completed and the men were asking about the mill when the housekeeper came up beside her, holding out an envelope. "Excuse me Mrs. Henderson. I have a message for the mister. I can't seem to locate him."

"I'll take it, thank you. I know you're busy. I'll see that he gets it."

The housekeeper smiled gratefully. "Thank you, ma'am. Does everything seem to be going to suit the mister?"

Mattie nodded reassuringly. "Everything is fine. You all have done wonderfully well." She knew how anxious the housekeeper was beneath her calm exterior. Turning back to Morgan, she placed a hand on his arm. "Excuse me for a bit, will you? This message might be important. I'll see if I can't find Allen."

Mattie stood at the library door, her hand on the brass-plated knob. She was about to enter, looking for Allen, when she heard angry voices from within. The voice of a woman, high pitched, a little hysterical, her words badly slurred as though from drinking. Mattie hesitated, listening, wondering whether she should go on in and interrupt.

"You can't do this to me, Allen. You won't get away with it! I won't let you. I tried to tell you—over and over I tried to tell you—but you wouldn't listen to me. I'm not like the others. I'm not just another woman you can use, someone to entertain you. I don't play cheap games, Allen. You can't make promises to me and not mean what you say. I'll ruin you if you walk out on me now."

Allen's voice then, lower, more controlled. "Shut up, damn it, Cass. Keep your voice down. What the hell are you doing here tonight anyway? This is by invitation only. You've got no business coming here."

The woman's laughter rippled out across the room, but it held no mirth. "Oh, that's right. Engraved invitations, going out to all of the right people. I ought to know. I helped address them. Remember, I work at the campaign headquarters. You invited people because they can help you or have already helped you. Helped you? That's a laugh, isn't it, Allen? Bought and paid for you is more like it. Bought and paid for your loyalty to their own stinking private enterprises with campaign contributions. Speaking of contributions, how do you account for the large sums you receive? Tell me how you do it, Allen. I'm curious. They aren't on the books anywhere, are they? I know. I've looked. How do you account for the car you're driving? That new, expensive Buick. What about the registered bulls my uncle sent over to your ranch? Do you have any idea how much those animals cost? Or maybe you don't care. After all, it isn't even your ranch, is it? The ranch you brag about doesn't even belong to you." The last remark was filled with contempt.

"You don't know what you're talking about." Allen was speaking very carefully, each word planned thoughtfully.

"Don't I? Oh, you're so wrong. I have proof!" Her voice was lower now, confident in what she was saying. "I have proof, Allen. Enough proof to ruin you. I can see that you never make it to the governor's office to sit behind that big desk you want so bad." A slyness crept into her words. "I could even send you to prison if I want."

Mattie stood frozen, her hand still on the doorknob, unable to move. She listened to Allen say, "You're drunk. Lousy goddamn drunk."

"Sure. Maybe I am. If I'm not, I've wasted a lot of good alcohol trying to get that way. I tried to drink enough so that I wouldn't feel anything when I watched you and her take your bows in front of all of those people tonight. She was right there beside you, wasn't she, smiling and greeting people as though she belonged there. I didn't want to feel anything as I saw the way you looked at her, as though you wanted her there beside you, as though everything was so great between the two of you. She was walking beside you where I was supposed to be. That was my place. You promised, remember?"

There was a catch in her voice as though tears were choking

her words. Mattie could almost feel her pain as she talked.

"You were going to leave her. You said you loved me. You said I was the only important thing in your life, that I meant more to you than the governor's office, than your family, than her, your frigid, uncaring wife, who . . ." The words were broken off as Mattie heard a sharp slap—a cry of pain.

"You leave Mattie out of this. Don't you even mention her name. You aren't fit to be in the same house where she is."

"Then it's true, isn't it?" The woman was whimpering now, tears in her voice. "I loved you, Allen. I knew what a bastard you were, and I still loved you. But you never meant a word you said to me. You never meant to leave her, did you? You were just using me—like you use everyone else. You use people, Allen. You use them and then brush them off when they aren't of any use to you anymore. You let me introduce you to men you wanted to meet, you used my place to entertain men who had the money but didn't quite rate an invitation to your home. When I think of the contributions I helped you to get!" She broke into laughter now—bitter, vengeful laughter that made Mattie turn cold.

"Well, I'm smarter than the other women you have told your lies to," the voice continued. "Smarter and with more connections. You overplayed your hand this time, Allen, when you tried to play games with a Courtney. I took the time and the effort to find the proof to enough things to ruin you if I want to. Maybe I should give them to Mattie, to your wife. I have them with me, you know. Right here in my handbag. All of the letters, the cancelled checks, photographs. You shouldn't have left me alone with so much time on my hands, Allen. I could take them to Mattie and see how long she will stay with you then." She paused. "How about it, Allen? You will be just like me then, won't you. Having someone you love look at you with loathing and walk out on you!"

"Give me those papers, you bitch. Give them to me or, by God, I'll take them!" Allen's voice was hard, angry, full of hate.

"Don't. Don't, Allen. Don't come near me—don't touch me! I warn you! I have a gun in my purse—I'll use it! Don't—oh, God, please don't!"

The sounds of scuffling and the raised voices were drawing attention. Several others had walked up behind Mattie, listening, wondering if they should go in and interfere.

The sound of a shot rang out, and then another—the thunder of it filled the closed room, leaving the strong smell of gunpowder on the air.

Mattie threw open the double doors and stepped inside, her heart pounding in her ears, her eyes filled with alarm. Allen was bent over almost double, grasping his middle, blood running across his white shirt, dripping from his hands. He looked toward her when she entered the room, his face white with disbelief and pain.

"Lies—it's lies, Mattie. Mattie, help me," he gasped before he fell to the floor and lay still.

Mattie stood in the doorway, spellbound, ashen, her mind refusing to work. The woman with the silver-blond hair was sobbing uncontrollably. "I didn't mean to—didn't mean to do it. I loved him."

A woman screamed. Mattie heard feet running, someone shouting to get a doctor, but she couldn't react. Mattie heard a woman screaming over and over, and finally she realized that it was her own voice, but she couldn't stop.

It wasn't until she felt strong arms holding her, shaking her, that the horrible screaming stopped. As she was drawn close, cradled against a hard, sheltering chest, she knew Morgan was there beside her. Morgan was holding her, protecting her, and she sunk into a peaceful, dark oblivion, where she was safe.

CHAPTER THIRTY-FOUR

The days that followed were a cold, vicious, and icy nightmare for all of them. Once Mattie woke to the unbelievable events surrounding the shooting, she faced reality with a remote, distant calm, meeting all of the demands made upon her. Her face was pale, but her chin was firm and her back straight. The old man would have been proud of her.

Morgan stayed in Salem, trying to run interference for her with the news reporters, who were having a field day, and the curious scandal seekers who found excuses to pay a call. But, even so, there were some that managed to slip through and confront the two small boys with questions, leaving them frightened and crying. That was the only time Mattie showed any deep emotion and she responded with a terrible fury, her eyes blazing with angry fire, as she drove them from the house.

Wes and Betty came to Salem at the first word of the disaster, and after the encounter with the reporters, Mattie determinedly packed the suitcases for the boys and insisted that Betty take them back to the protection of the ranch.

"But what about the funeral?" Betty questioned. "Shouldn't the boys be here for their father's funeral?"

"Allen is dead. Don't you understand?" Mattie answered coldly. "He's dead. He won't know if they're here or not. I don't want them hurt any more than they have been. They're too young. They don't understand. It isn't fair to them. I want them at the ranch. I want them away from all of this.''

"But what will people think?" Betty said, faltering.

"I don't give a damn what people think!" Mattie flared. "Not anymore. It has always been 'What will people say? What will people think?' The whole lot of them can go to hell as far as I am concerned. Most of those very people Allen called his friends have turned away anyway. They're afraid that as things Allen was involved in are uncovered, they too, might be exposed. I don't want the boys to hear the ugly whispers. No, Betty. Take them back to the safety of the ranch. The sooner, the better. I want them away from here.''

There was a funeral—a small, private service, with interment in the cemetery near the city Allen had worked so hard to call his home.

There was an inquest and a trial. Morgan stayed by Mattie's side continually during the long ordeal. He was unable to take away the pain she was going through, but he gave her his strength to draw on by a slight touch of the hand, a gentle arm to support her when he thought her courage might fail, a protective shoulder to shield her from the onslaught of photographers, reporters, phone calls, sly, hurting remarks.

Mattie appeared for the hearings in a simple black dress, severely cut, with no jewelry to break the harshness. She hated the jewelry that lay carelessly on her dressing table, knowing too well the price that had been paid for it. A close-fitting black cloche, pulled low over one eye, held a black veil that masked the tired lines of her face, the paleness from the curious onlookers. Through it all she kept a distant aloofness from the rest of them, carrying her head proudly erect, locking her emotions away where no one could touch them.

Even when Cass Courtney broke down on the witness stand, hysterically crying and repeating over and over that she hadn't meant to do it, telling an avidly attentive courtroom all of the sordid details of the relationship between herself and Allen—the plans, the promises, the nights they spent together as lovers— Mattie kept a silent, wooden reserve. Only Morgan knew what she must be going through. Her trembling hand reached out blindly for him, holding on to him, her nails biting into his flesh, until Cass's testimony was over.

At last the proceedings were brought to an end. They were able to go back to the house at the edge of town knowing that they could finally relax a little.

Mattie dropped her coat over the back of a chair and went into the front sitting room to stand in front of the fireplace. Though the temperature outside had warmed to some degree, she felt chilled all the way through, as though she would never be warm again. She lit a cigarette and slowly sipped the brandy Morgan placed in her hand. She was pale, near complete exhaustion, and yet she still went on fighting to keep control now that they were so near the finish. Soon she would be able to slip away. She could leave this house that she had always hated. She could begin the long, slow process of forgetting.

"What do you suppose will happen to her?" Mattie stared into the low flames creeping along the length of a log Morgan had added to the fire.

"It's pretty certain that whatever sentence she receives will be suspended," he answered quietly. "We won't know for sure until the final verdict. She has a battery of good lawyers and she has the backing of her uncle, who is a very influential and wealthy man. I doubt very much that she will go to prison. Does it bother you that she might go free?"

"Bother me?" Mattie considered the question for a long time before she answered. "I suppose I should be outraged, but no—it doesn't bother me. In a way, I feel very sorry for her. I wonder what she'll do now. Where she'll go. It's going to be very hard on her. I wonder if she'll be strong enough to pick up the broken pieces of her life and go on from here."

"What about you, Mattie? Are you going to be strong enough to pick up the broken pieces and go on? Have you given any thought about what you're going to do next?"

She tossed the cigarette into the fire and turned to look at him. The strain of the past weeks showed plainly on her face. "I didn't tell you. I had asked Allen for a divorce. I was going to leave him. I knew about Cass, about other things. I moved out of his bedroom. I agreed to stay in Salem until after the election and then I was going to leave. It was all over." A sob caught in her throat and she bit her lip to stop the tears. "It was all over. I didn't want it to end like this, though. Not like this."

He held out his arms and she fled into them, the last of her courage gone, leaving her defenseless and vulnerable. "Take me home, Morgan," she whispered. "Take me back to the ranch—to the only place I have ever called home. I need to be alone—someplace where all the open wounds can heal, where I can sort out the good from the bad, where I can start rebuilding something from the rubble. Take me home."

Gently, he kissed the tears from her eyes. "When do you want to leave?"

"Now. Right away!" She pulled loose from his arms. "I want to go as soon as possible. The boys are waiting for me. They need me. I shouldn't have left them for so long. I am so tired. I want to leave right now. I want to go back to the ranch."

EPILOGUE

The supper hour was over. The late evening sun balanced on the horizon before slipping down behind the high peaks of the Cascade mountain range. The air was still and warm, carrying a hint of the smell of sage. The high desert was burnished in dull golds with purple velvet shadows.

Mattie was in the study, sitting in the straight, high-backed chair, leaning comfortably back against the quilted chintz covering. There was a book lying open in her lap, but she was absently watching the fire flickering across the logs in the fireplace, daydreaming contentedly as she sipped the cold drink in her hand.

She had let her hair grow longer in the last few years, brushing it back in gentle waves, captured at the nape of her neck in a soft chignon. Her forest green wool knit skirt and matching long-sleeved knit top outlined the slender curves of her body, accented the high, firm breasts, the small waist. Her slim legs were crossed at the knee, displaying trim ankles.

Ten years, she thought. It had been ten years since disaster had altered the course of their lives. She had returned to the ranch and the walls of the old house had reached out to welcome her, to take her back and shelter her, to heal the hurt that had torn her apart.

She had taken the two small boys into her arms, trying to explain death, people leaving, lives changing in a way their young minds could understand. She had taught them how to cope with thoughtless remarks, cruel jokes, how to sort out for themselves all of the memories of the past so they could go on and face the future without bitterness. She had tried to explain to them the Allen that she had known. The Allen she told them about had been handsome, brilliant, full of a driving ambition to get ahead. And that he had brought about his own destruction by being too impatient, too anxious to take shortcuts, too eager to find the easy way to get to where he wanted to be. Maybe the things he had done were not right, legally or morally, but he had loved them, had wanted the best for them. She did the best she could to give the boys a father to remember without shame.

As the boys grew older and were able to understand, she told them the rest of the story. For several years now, Clive had known that Morgan was not only his stepfather, but his flesh-and-blood father, too.

Mattie glanced across to where Morgan sat at the desk, his head bent as he entered the rows of figures in the ledger, recording the stock records for the ranch. The bookkeeping for the large lumber mill at the foot of the mountains was done by a competent staff of clerks, but Morgan still took care of the records for the ranch himself. The light from the desk lamp glowed against his hair, emphasizing the brush marks of gray beginning to show at his temples. His face was leathery tan from all of the hours he spent out-of-doors, and his muscles were hard and lean.

As she watched, he stretched and leaned back with a satisfied smile and looked over at her, his eyes crinkling at the corners. "That does it for this evening, Mattie."

"The accountants brought the quarterly reports out today, didn't they?" she asked. "How are things looking?"

"A hell of a lot better than they did this time a year ago," he answered with satisfaction. "The market crash about finished a lot of businesses, but it looks as though the Henderson Mill and the ranch are going to make it."

"Jonathan has his heart set on going to the state college in Corvallis when he graduates. I know it's still a year or two away, but I hope he will be able to do it, Morgan. It means so much to him.''

"No reason why he can't. The way the old man had it set up, the profits kept pouring back into the ranch when things were booming during the war years. Now that the market has gone to hell and money is tight, the earnings are there for them when they need it.''

He stood up and stretched, walking over to the bar. He poured a measure of bourbon into a glass over some ice. "Funny, isn't it, how things turn out?'' he mused. "The only thing that was salvaged from Allen's estate, after the debts were paid off, were those two registered bulls Martin Courtney sent over here. I still can't get over the way Johnny took to the ranch like it was born right into him, using the calves from those bulls for his 4-H work, taking first place every year he entered at the fair. Wonder what the old man would think if he was here and could see the way Johnny has his nose in a book all of the time, studying animal husbandry, pasture rotation, experimenting with different feeds. He's going to make one hell of a rancher when he grows up, but he's going to do it all by the book.''

Mattie smiled softly, pride glowing in her eyes. "He wants to study business management at the same time when he goes to college. Agriculture and business management.''

A dull hum could be heard in the distance, rapidly growing louder until it was a roar, vibrating the house, blotting out her words, and then fading into the distance again. Morgan straightened his shoulders and his face turned into a look of thunderous rage as he raised his eyes upward. "God damn that Clive!'' he roared. "He makes me so damned mad sometimes, Mattie, I don't know what to do! I've told him time after time about buzzing the house with that plane! If he runs the horses through a fence, I'll . . .'' The veins stood out on his forehead and he smashed his fist down on the desk.

Mattie walked over to the window and watched as the Stearman finished the climb for altitude, tipped one wing into a "falling leaf'' pattern, straightened out, and came into a landing on the dirt strip not far from the house. Morgan had bought the plane three or four years ago and young Clive had inherited his love of flying. He handled the controls as naturally as though they were an extension of his own body.

Only moments later, Clive stood in the doorway to the study, grinning that one-sided, teasing smile at her. He was tall. Even though his seventeen-year-old frame had not filled out yet and he was thin, he nearly reached six feet.

"Clive, I want to talk to you." Morgan's voice was hard as he spoke, his eyes dangerously angry.

Clive came on into the room and Mattie turned her face up for his light kiss on her cheek. "Sure, Dad. Glad you got the time. I wanted to talk to you, too. I just flew over that stand of timber south of here—the one we were talking about at the mill today." He pulled out a straight chair and sat on it backwards, his arms folded across the top of it, his eyes glowing with enthusiasm. "Boy, you were right, Dad! Heavy timber. All virgin growth, ready for harvest! I'll bet it'll scale out as good or better than any stand we've cut into yet. If you want me to, I'll hike back in there tomorrow and check it out from the ground before we make a bid on it."

"Wait a minute, Clive. Don't change the subject."

Mattie sat back watching the two of them, smiling to herself as she saw the look of pride soften Morgan's features as he fought to keep stern. Clive had been working at the mill after school and during the summers since he was twelve. Morgan knew that, young as Clive still was, the figures he brought back to him on the stand of timber would be as accurate as any timber cruiser working for the mill.

"Clive, how long have you had your student pilot license?" Morgan asked.

The youth looked puzzled at the question. "About six months. You know that, Dad. Why?"

"How bad do you want to keep it?"

Clive glanced quickly over toward Mattie, hoping she would send him some signal to tip him off as to why the old man was so sore, but she lowered her eyes, suddenly interested in the book on her lap.

"I'd hate like hell to lose it, I guess."

Morgan's voice gathered force as he roared, "Then stop buzz-

ing the gawd-damned house! Don't you know how to come in for
a landing without tearing the roof off this place first?''

Clive tried to change the subject quickly, knowing he was in
trouble and that if he pushed the old man too far he could get
grounded, the worst form of punishment he could think of.
''Where's Johnny?''

''In his room, studying for exams.''

Uh-oh, Clive thought. Another dangerous subject. The old
man had issued an ultimatum about his grades, too. He stood up,
pushing the chair back into place. ''I'm going to take a quick
shower. I'm late already.''

''You're going out?'' Mattie asked, looking up with a frown.

He sent her a slow, easy grin, crinkling the corners of his eyes
with a hidden humor, a look she was all too familiar with.
''Won't be late, Mom. I promise.''

As the door shut behind him, Mattie walked over to stand
behind Morgan's chair and gently massaged the tight muscles
across the back of his neck. ''Relax, darling,'' she murmured as
she let her fingers trail across his shoulders and bent her head to
touch his face with her lips. ''He'll be home early. It's Friday
night. Even if he isn't, he'll still be at the mill as early as you
are, wide-eyed and ready for work.''

Morgan shrugged, knowing it was true. The boy played hard,
but he never lagged behind when it came to work.

''He's so much like you,'' Mattie said softly. ''Maybe that's
why the two of you clash so often. He's just like you were at that
age.''

Morgan felt himself relaxing, liking the feel of her soft touch
working away at his tense nerves. ''Maybe that *is* what keeps me
on edge, makes me get so damned mad at him sometimes.'' He
grinned. ''I remember the hell that Wes and I used to raise in
town, and the way the old man deliberately worked my ass off
the next day, when I was dying for sleep.''

''Daddy?''

The door pushed open and a little girl with soft brown eyes
peered around the corner at them.

''Come on in, Tish.'' His voice went soft, filled with warm
tenderness. ''Where you been, honey?''

The little girl came on into the room. She was seven years old, small boned and tiny, with long dark curls held back with a ribbon and hanging down her back. She was dressed in jeans, a baggy sweater, and sneakers. There was a smudge of dirt on her nose, but she didn't seem to notice. A large, shaggy dog followed close at her heels, her constant companion.

"Picking berries."

"You look as though you're ready for a bath and bed, Patricia," Mattie commented. "I don't know how one little girl can pick up so much dust in one day."

"I have a sticker in my finger. It hurts."

Morgan reached out his arms and lifted her gently onto his lap. "Where? Let's see if I can't fix it." The big, strong hands turned the small finger over and gently probed for the berry thorn, taking it out as she watched him trustingly with her large brown eyes, confident that he wouldn't hurt. He touched the tiny hand to his lips. "There. All well. Now scoot, Tish. Go get your bath, like your mother said."

When she left the room, her dog close at her heels, Morgan stood up and reached for Mattie. His arms closed around her, drawing her close against him, and she nestled contentedly against his chest. He felt the old, familiar hunger for her race through his body as he let his hands wander down the arch of her back, holding her against his thighs. He knew how quick her response would be to his touch.

There had been some bad years, but with her at his side, loving him as much as he loved her, his life was complete. These were the days to remember.

God, how he loved this woman.